THE LAND OF BLUE

JILL SYLVESTER

OLD TREE HOUSE
PUBLISHING

THE LAND OF BLUE

By Jill Sylvester

Old Tree House Publishing

Old Tree House Publishing
PO Box 462
Hanover, MA 02339

This is a work of fiction. Names, characters, businesses, places, events and incidents are either the products of the author's imagination or used in a fictitious manner. Any resemblance to actual persons, living or dead, or actual events is purely coincidental.

Editor: Rebecca McCarthy, www.thewrittencoach.com
Copyeditor: Jody Amato, jodyamato@gmail.com
Cover and Interior Layout: Yvonne Parks, PearCreative.ca
Author Photo: Tracy Colucci

Publisher's Cataloging-In-Publication Data
(Prepared by The Donohue Group, Inc.)

Names: Sylvester, Jill.
Title: The Land of Blue / Jill Sylvester.
Description: [Hanover, Massachusetts] : Old Tree House Publishing, [2017] | Interest age level: 12 and up. | Summary: Twelve-year-old Cassie Connor travels to the foggy, carnival style Land of Blue to search for her father who has mysteriously disappeared. Accompanied by three friends and a physical manifestation of the voice in her head, Cassie finds her efforts consistently and suspiciously thwarted. That is until Cassie falls through the Ripple and discovers an alternate, beautiful land, illuminating that things are not always what they seem.
Identifiers: LCCN 2017906782 | ISBN 978-0-9989775-0-8 (paperback) | ISBN 978-0-9989775-1-5 (Kindle) | ISBN 978-0-9989775-2-2 (ePub)
Subjects: LCSH: Preteen girls--Juvenile fiction. | Missing persons--Juvenile fiction. | Friendship--Juvenile fiction. | Families--Juvenile fiction. | Hallucinations and illusions--Juvenile fiction. | Imaginary places--Juvenile fiction. | CYAC: Preteen girls--Fiction. | Missing persons--Fiction. | Friendship--Fiction. | Families--Fiction. | Hallucinations and illusions--Fiction. | Imaginary places--Fiction. | LCGFT: Fantasy fiction.
Classification: LCC PZ7.1.S95 La 2017 (print) | LCC PZ7.1.S95 (ebook) | DDC [Fic]--dc23

DEDICATION

To my father—the likely reason I write in the first place—and my mother. I love and honor you both.

And to my family—Carl, Kyle, Michelle, and our bulldog Zack—you are my reason for being.

CHAPTER
ONE

Gray clouds filled the sky that August afternoon, and yet the heat still felt unbearable. Cassie Connor, in her worn-out denim shorts and second-hand red Fenway Park T-shirt, sat in the white plastic chair in the corner of her grandparents' porch, directly behind the overgrown shrubbery, so she wouldn't be seen. Waiting for the mail to arrive, the backs of her slim, pinkish-colored thighs stuck to the slats of the cheap chair.

Everything felt unbearable for Cassie these days. Her dad had left three weeks ago, and she didn't know where he'd gone, or why. The last time Cassie had seen him, he tucked her into bed, softly singing the lyrics to Queensryche's "Silent Lucidity." The song had been playing on the radio in Mom and Dad's old Ford Escape on the way back from supper at the China Dragon. Dad

1

had lowered the windows all the way down, the evening summer breeze lulling Cassie into slumber. As she lay in the back seat, her eyelids grew heavy. Just before falling asleep, she caught a glimpse of Mom's hand on the steering wheel and the green numbers on the dashboard clock glowing 11:45.

Cassie remembered her father, drowsy from the late night out, scooping her up from the seat, carrying her like a puppy into their first-floor apartment, as she watched half his face and the countless stars in the night sky. Whispering to Cassie as he walked up the three brick steps, the smell of cologne on his skin and beer on his breath, her father had told her a clear night sky meant it was going to be beautiful the next day.

But the next day wasn't beautiful at all.

When Cassie woke up Sunday morning in the second bedroom of their small apartment in Roslindale, a neighborhood of Boston, Dad was gone. Somewhere. And no one in her family would tell her where he went.

Frustration consumed Cassie as she slumped in the porch chair with her arms crossed over her chest, blowing her straight, sweaty, caramel-colored hair out of her face. She thought about the occasional letters sent home (well, not *home*, but to Cassie's grandparents' house in West Roxbury, a few miles away in a quiet neighborhood, where she and her mother now lived). Cassie couldn't figure out where the letters came from because her nervous, gum-chewing mother—who cried the entire day they moved in with her parents—always intercepted the mail before Cassie could see the return address. When mom wasn't home, Nana Helen, in her green polyester pants, high-tailed it to the porch, and snatched the mail from the postwoman's hands.

This infuriated Cassie. After all, she was twelve years old and starting sixth grade in a couple of days. She felt she had a right to know what had happened to her father.

Through the veil of thorny roses that had grown up and

over the porch trellis of her grandparents' house on Selwyn Street, Cassie watched four kids play kickball. A boy with jet-black hair approached one of the girls, who had a rather large, protruding forehead, and called her a praying mantis. When a car went by, he stepped up on the curb, his brand-new high tops half on and half off the concrete. Then a boy with red hair teased one of his own teammates—a shorter kid—calling him a wuss. Cassie observed and listened, biting her lip. She hoped the praying-mantis girl and the short kid would score home runs the next time they came up to the plate. *That'll put the mean kids in their place,* she thought.

Cassie thought it was strange that the short kid wasn't bothered at all by his teammate's taunts. He actually laughed along with the other kids while he waited for his turn. After a moment of consideration, Cassie decided the short kid's dad must come home for dinner every night from an important office job in downtown Boston. *It's easy to have fun, fit in, and play kickball when you don't have to worry about things,* she thought.

Cassie wanted to know if her dad left because he wanted to, or because he had to; maybe someone kidnapped him or something. Her mind raced. Her left leg bounced up and down, making a sweaty suction noise against the chair. She bit her thumbnail until there was nothing left to chew, and it started bleeding. Cassie tried to stop, taking it out of her mouth a couple times, but she just couldn't help it. Every time she bit her nails, a voice in her head—a cackling, yet soothing voice—encouraged her. *Go on, it's all right. It'll make you feel better.*

The voice instructed Cassie to do all kinds of things, especially when she worried about homework, or whether someone was upset with her, or about her family not being together. *Only land on the even-numbered steps if you want to get an "A." Step over the cracks in the sidewalk or the girls at school won't like you.* The voice even made her think about things that could happen, like, what if there was a fire in the house? *You had better straighten your bed every morning, just in case.*

Cassie followed the voice's instructions because if she didn't, then something really bad might happen, like the time she forgot to step over a crack on the sidewalk outside of school and Mr. Lovell, her favorite math teacher, got the flu. If Cassie messed up, say, stepping on an odd-numbered stair, she always went back and started at the beginning. She had no choice. She had been listening to the voice for a long time.

The birds chirped at the feeder, searching for food on the other end of the porch, while Cassie's lightly peeled forehead crinkled in deep thought. She tried to remember if she had stepped on a crack in the sidewalk by accident before her dad disappeared.

As she sat on the porch, biting her nails and jiggling her leg, the sound of the neighborhood kids' laughter reminded Cassie that she never really belonged. She knew the kids on the street wouldn't ask her to play, even though they appeared to be around her age. Perhaps it was because they couldn't completely see Cassie behind the overgrown shrubbery, but more likely it was because she felt stiff and didn't know what to say. Cassie didn't fit in with the kids who played kickball. Those types of kids liked peanut-butter-and-jelly sandwiches and playing outside for hours. Cassie preferred bologna-and-pickle subs, wondering about other people's lives when she was bored—and even when she wasn't—and listening to the grown-ups talk about all their problems (her mom called this "eavesdropping").

This exasperated her mother.

One rainy afternoon not long ago, Cassie's mother and her mother's friend Louise smoked cigarettes and talked about their absentee husbands at the kitchen table. Cassie poked her head out from behind the door, where she had been hiding and listening, and said they'd end up wrinkled old ladies if they didn't stop smoking. Mom threw her hands in the air, and asked the ceiling, "Why do I have to have the annoying kid?" Then she sent Cassie to her room.

Cassie knew almost everything she did bugged her mother.

4

Still, she felt it was a free country. She even said so, which caused her mother to huff and puff and smoke another cigarette because, "she couldn't *take it* anymore!"

Cassie spent a lot of time in her bedroom.

It was a good thing Mariana Papadopoulis was Cassie's best friend. The other kids at school didn't affect Mariana. She didn't care who was popular or who was the sportiest, whereas Cassie obsessed about those subjects, often thinking about what she lacked. Mariana couldn't have cared less, saying whatever she felt whenever she felt it.

"Are you worrying again because you're not one of the cool kids? Get over it already!" she'd say to Cassie. "Meanwhile, you're prettier than half the girls in school!"

Cassie compared herself negatively to the kids who wore nice clothes and came from families that had a lot more than she did. That's why Cassie always made sure she was nice to the unpopular kids. Mariana never judged her, though. She accepted Cassie despite her being a worrier, the same way Cassie accepted Mariana's "very strong personality," as Cassie's mother put it. And, Mariana preferred tuna, mayo, and tomato sandwiches, with a glass of milk, to boring peanut butter and jelly.

Another thing different between them though, besides Mariana's dark brown hair that frizzed out like a mad scientist whenever it was humid, were their families. Mariana came from a big Greek family, all of whom had big personalities. They hugged all the time, talked extremely loudly at family events, and couldn't be prouder of Mariana, even when she ate her tuna sandwich with her mouth wide open, still, at the age of twelve. Cassie's family, well, they were the opposite of that.

Ann Marie Connor, Cassie's pretty, auburn-haired mother, did not want to live in her parents' white house with the white picket fence on 59 Selwyn Street. This was mostly because Ann Marie had a "strained" relationship with her parents ever since they called Cassie's dad a "bum" (and not the kind in your underwear). That happened a few years ago on the very same porch, when Cassie was eight.

Cassie's mother had made her wait in the back seat of the chilly car, alone, while her mother shouted on the porch to Nana Helen, "How dare you call my husband names after the life we've lived with *your husband?*"

Nana said, "Watch your tone, missy. That's your father you're referring to."

Mom cried, "You, of all people, should understand what I'm going through!"

Nana Helen simply shook her head and muttered, "Go on home. We'll pray for ya in church."

Cassie remembered the leaves falling, green and orange, from the big tree in the side yard at Nana's house. Then, in her orange consignment sweater and faded jeans, her mom got back in the car, throwing her big yellow pocketbook into the empty passenger seat. Her fake silver bangle bracelets shook as she started the car. Cassie asked her if Nana Helen and Grandpa Jack called Dad a bum because he liked to drink most of the time.

"That means Grandpa Jack's a bum, too, right?"

Mom wiped away her tears and drove away, telling Cassie not to be "nosey" and not to get involved in grownup conversations.

The birds continued chirping at the feeder, pulling on Cassie's heartstrings because there wasn't any seed. She remembered her mother's voice on the phone one night in their old apartment, the night after Dad left.

"That's how desperate we are, okay?" she said, clutching the Dunkin' Donuts black coffee and wincing at the sound of the loud, rap music blasting forth from the neighbors' apartment next door. "We don't have anywhere else to go."

A volcano erupted in Cassie's stomach. She bit her nail, hard.

If Dad were home, Cassie's family would be going to China Dragon that night. That's what they did every Saturday night, for as long as she could remember. They always ordered the Number One on the menu, which consisted of chicken chow mein, pork fried rice, and egg rolls. Cassie drank unlimited refills of Shirley Temples. Dad ordered beers first and then Captain and Cokes, and her mom had two glasses of House Red. Her mother only got to drink two glasses of wine because she "had to drive."

China Dragon was also where Cassie's parents' friends went on Saturday nights. The ladies, with their flashy fingernails, called themselves the "babysitters." That meant they were their husbands' designated drivers. Those are the people in charge of driving everyone home safely. Alcoholic beverages make you tipsy. Mariana didn't even know what a designated driver was, and she had a sister in college! Cassie felt very grown-up when she told Mariana something she didn't know. Mariana always knew everything.

Cassie's heart beat faster as she remembered that last night at the restaurant. Jenny, the friendly Chinese waitress with the short, stubby ponytail, brought over another Captain and Coke for Cassie's father. This time, though, the manager came with her. He wasn't Chinese. He was bald and warned Cassie's dad to "keep it down." Cassie's father always talked more, telling funny stories, at the China Dragon. His friends called him the life of the party, which made Cassie feel special.

Saturday night was Cassie's favorite time of the week because she got to spend hours with her dad. She went out with her parents since they couldn't afford a sitter. Her parents laughed and had fun at the China Dragon. Dad paid more attention to Cassie, too. He'd put Cassie on his shoulders and tell his friends she was "his little China doll." Mom joked with the ladies and said she worried that Cassie was so fragile she might break.

Dad wasn't mean, like her mom was sometimes. One time when Cassie talked back, her mom wrung her hands and yelled,

"Why did I even become a mother?" Later, she apologized.

Dad never spoke like that to Cassie. He mostly sat quietly at home, staring off into space, or he slept. Cassie used to wonder what he thought about. She felt better when he smiled, even though it was through tired eyes as he lay on the couch. He smiled when Cassie brought home good grades, or when she learned the lyrics to the songs on the radio that he liked. Mom smiled more, too, when Dad joked and laughed, which was why China Dragon night was the best night of the whole week.

When the bald manager asked Ann Marie to tell Dad to lower his voice, Mom cleared her throat. She did that when she felt nervous. Dad scoffed, "Can't we have a little fun here?" The manager wiped his shiny head with a napkin. He said if Dad didn't quiet down, he'd have to call the cops.

That's when George and Jeannie—friends of Dad's from high school—stood up in the next booth and said, "C'mon Barry, Craig's a good customer. We'll talk to him. No need to call anybody."

The manager, in his sweaty white dress shirt said, "All right, make sure," walking away like he had just lost a poker game. Cassie felt relieved that Mom and Dad's friends took care of the situation. She didn't want to leave before they served the pineapples and fortune cookies.

As the heat streamed through the side of the porch, Cassie slid her bare foot across the floorboard. She knew her mother wouldn't take her to China Dragon without her father home. Dad was the fun one. Her mother didn't do much since that night. She didn't even see her friends anymore. She spent her time working the night shift at the Belgrade Avenue nursing home in order to pay the bills. During the day, her mom sat in the upstairs front bedroom overlooking Selwyn Street, in the rocking chair she brought from the apartment.

Her mother had never asked Cassie how she felt about Dad's disappearance. If anyone bothered to ask, Cassie would have said her dad was her favorite person in the universe. She thought of her mother as an iron pot in a cupboard. Cassie thought of her father as the warm butter in the pan before you made pancakes. Even though he didn't talk a lot, her dad often watched Cassie—like when she bit her nails—as if he understood. Cassie wondered if maybe he heard a voice inside his head, too.

The heat bore harshly on the back of Cassie's faded red T-shirt. Mom told Cassie that Dad left Sunday morning at breakfast. In her beige bathrobe, her long hair all over the place, her mother frantically rummaged through the kitchen cabinets searching for a cereal bowl, like she didn't know where they were kept, even though they lived in the apartment since Cassie was born.

Her mother took a deep breath and sat down at the wooden table with the one uneven leg. Through bloodshot blue eyes, her mother informed Cassie, with a trembling voice, that they had to move. They couldn't afford to keep their apartment. She mumbled parts of sentences. "Dad had to leave . . . I don't know for how long."

"Well, where did he have to go?" Cassie asked, in a tone higher than usual.

"S-somewhere," her mother responded, sipping her black coffee while staring at the black-and-white-checkered floor.

"I don't understand! We were just with him last night!" Cassie pushed back her chair and slammed her hands on the table.

"I told you," her mother said, her voice cross. "Somewhere. You are much too young for these things, and I won't be forced to have a conversation I don't want to have with my twelve year old!"

Cassie felt like a thermometer when the red part goes all the way up to the top. "That's not fair! Just because you don't like me half the time doesn't mean you get to keep information from me. He's *my* father!"

Cassie's mother knocked her Styrofoam cup of coffee over on purpose. "You listen to me young lady, this is for your own good! Stop asking questions and stop saying I don't like you! We're just

. . . like oil and water sometimes . . . " Her voice trailed off as she ran all ten fingers through her matted-down hair. "I don't need this aggravation."

Leaving the spilled coffee running over the edge of the unbalanced table, Cassie's mother got up with a start. She knocked over the wooden chair and headed into her bedroom, where ripped window shades hung in curtainless windows. Her mother wanted window treatments, like her girlfriends who lived in the suburbs, but she didn't have the money.

Cassie pulled her chair back in at the table with a heavy heart, swirling her soggy frosted flakes cereal with a tarnished spoon. She listened to the slow, plodding footsteps of their old landlord upstairs for a few minutes before pushing back her chair with her small hands, making a scraping sound against the linoleum floor.

When she stood up, her eyes blurred with tears, she noticed a white brochure on the floor that must have fallen from her mother's robe. The brochure's cover read: "(AA) Alcoholics Anonymous" in black lettering. Though her mother had told her not to ask questions, Cassie really wanted to ask her about the brochure.

Entering the doorway to her parents' bedroom, Cassie leaned against the beige wall as her mother picked up a tube of lipstick from the bureau. The pink tube stood next to all Dad's prescription bottles of pain medication. Cassie's mother drew the frosted pink lipstick on her lips as she stood in front of the faded mirror, using the weak sunlight that streamed through the sides of the shades.

"Everything will be all right," her mother said in a calm voice, never taking her eyes off the mirror. "It has to be, right honey?"

Cassie stood silently at the threshold, watching her mother in the dismal bedroom. Did her mother expect an answer? Cassie's jaw clenched tightly as she thought, *Does she even know I'm in the room?* She felt she wasn't a good daughter because she didn't say anything to make her mother feel better.

Cassie's only concern was her dad. Whenever he didn't go to

work and stayed in bed, Cassie worried that he had cancer. When his back hurt, Cassie got his pain medicine for him. When he preferred to be alone, Cassie worried that he was sad. She hoped it wasn't because of her or anything she did. Cassie didn't want to make her mother feel better. She only wanted to ask what that brochure was for and if it had anything to do with why Dad left. But even though her mother had been standing right in front of her, at the same time she really wasn't there.

The back of Cassie's neck dripped with sweat as she leaned forward in the porch chair. Irritably, she brushed her shoulder-length hair to one side. *What in the hell is taking the mail lady so long?* Grandpa Jack started sentences that way when he was aggravated. Cassie liked to say that in her mind because she wasn't supposed to say it out loud. Nana Helen said swears were for grown-ups.

"Rrrruff, rrrruff." Nana Helen's dirty, white, deranged-looking poodle, Bruce, stood atop the tweed living room couch, growling from behind one of the screened-in windows facing the porch. Cassie heard Nana yell from inside, "Shaddup you!" She didn't hear the heavy black work shoes as they stomped up the peeled, white, painted steps to the porch.

"Mail, Helen!" Maria, the mail carrier, called as she reached the porch. A feral cat followed, entering through the white picket fence. Cassie slowly unstuck her small frame from the plastic seat.

Nana Helen, built short and stocky like a bulldog, shoved open the front screen door with one hand. "I'll take that," she said, as she snagged the mail from Maria and then smiled briefly to avoid being considered rude. She glanced sideways at Cassie through her round glasses hanging from a string.

"It's a hot one, huh?" Maria asked as she wiped her forehead. She trudged back down the four wooden stairs, the stray cat on her heels as she opened the gate.

I wonder if the cat has a family, thought Cassie.

"Oh ya, it's a hot one all right," Nana replied, only caring about the mail in her chubby, tanned hands. Immediately, she handed the mail to Cassie's mother, who stood in the doorway chewing gum behind her pursed, cherry-red lips. Her mother always checked to see if a letter arrived, and made sure Cassie didn't gain any information if it did. Today there was no letter. Mom and Nana glanced at each other as if to say, "Whew. That was a close call. Mission accomplished."

Cassie's bottom lip quivered. Her brown eyes fought back tears, as she slammed her thin body back down in the lonely chair. *Tap each foot three times so you get another chance to find out information.* Cassie tapped each foot on the ground, toying with the idea of telling Artie, the Meals on Wheels delivery guy who would arrive that afternoon, that Nana Helen cheated the system. She wasn't terminally ill or in need. She was simply too lazy to cook.

"I can't tell her anything, Mother," Ann Marie said in a low voice as she wound her long locks into a ponytail on top of her head. "It's too much for her. It's too much for me," she whispered dramatically, like Cassie couldn't hear.

"You're doing the right thing, Ann Marie," Nana Helen replied. "She's only a kid."

Inside her head, Cassie yelled at the top of her lungs, *I'm twelve years old! I'm old enough! Why is everything a secret?!?*

Another day, wasted.

Cuts and scrapes in the wooden planks on the porch reminded Cassie of scraped knees.

Don't worry. I'll take care of you.

Bruce, Nana's partner in crime, trotted out on the open porch to join the fun, his beady black eyes on Cassie.

Even Bruce is against me, she thought.

When Nana Helen and her mother headed back indoors, Bruce scampered dutifully behind Nana.

No one cares about me. I'll never find out what happened to Dad. What if I don't see him again? Cassie banged her heel on the porch planks, wishing she were part of Mariana's family. Laurie Papadopoulis talked about "raising strong kids" and how "communication starts at home." She talked to Mariana, and her eldest daughter, Gina, about everything.

Just then, the blue Pinto with the rusty trunk skidded next to the curb in front of Nana and Grandpa's house, barely giving the neighborhood kids time to get out of the way. It was Artie, the Meals on Wheels guy, who didn't have the best driving skills, even though he was about forty years old.

Artie ran up the steps two at a time. With his thick, dark-brown hair and tall, skinny body, Cassie thought he was built like a Q-tip. He held a plastic bag in one hand with Styrofoam containers of packaged meals inside. Cassie clenched her fists on the arms of the chair and leaned forward.

"Hey Artie," she said slyly.

"Hey," he answered, as he briskly knocked on the frame of the front screen door. Sweat dripped from his face onto the plastic bag.

"She cheats the system, you know. She doesn't need her meals cooked any more than you need hair on your head." Cassie shook her head in disgust. "Pure laziness." A jolt of excitement exploded like a firecracker in her stomach.

But Artie dropped the bag inside the front door, shrugged his shoulders, and said, "It's none of my business, kid. I just deliver the meals."

The blood drained from Cassie's face as the firecracker fizzled. Nana Helen and Mom won again.

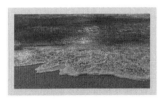

CHAPTER
TWO

The vacuum cleaner turned on inside the house. Cassie's mother cleaned when she was stressed.

She'll clean constantly here, Cassie thought.

Dust clung to all the furniture, because Nana never cleaned. Cassie found sprinkles on the kitchen floor from donuts they ate the previous week. This drove Mom crazy.

Cassie listened to the *vrrrrrmm* of the vacuum as her mother obsessively attacked every corner of the living room. The musty smell of the vacuum bag floated through the screen and onto the porch. Looking at the plastic green doormat that resembled Easter grass, Cassie thought about their old apartment. It wasn't even close to Mariana's fancy brick house, with the two-car garage, on West Roxbury Parkway, but Mom cleaned the apartment like it was a palace.

Her mother had shown Cassie how to use "elbow grease" as she scrubbed the shower whenever Dad stayed out late with his friends. Frantically cleaning the toilets, she'd say, in a singsong voice, "He'll be home soon. He's worked so hard all day." Cassie missed Dad those nights he stayed out late, but secretly loved the following morning because there was always a Charleston Chew candy bar in the freezer. Dad knew they tasted better that way.

Screeeeeech. Mrs. Newcomb, the ninety-year-old neighbor in her black fur winter hat, wheeled her metal grocery cart down Knoll Street. She did this every day coming back from the bus stop. She crossed onto Selwyn, her squinted eyes barely able to see above the cart's handle.

"Watch that ball!" she snapped at the kids in the street. Cassie didn't take time to notice the kids' reaction.

Holding her chin in her hands, Cassie followed the clouds moving behind Mrs. Newcomb's two-family house at 62 Selwyn Street, directly across from Nana's. It was late afternoon. Cassie knew the time of day by the shift of the sun's position behind the houses, even when it was cloudy. She watched the clouds to make the time go by faster as she waited for Mariana to get back from summer camp, for Dad to call, for life to be different.

Suddenly, Selwyn Street grew strangely quiet. Cassie heard the heat on the street, an electric rrrreeerrr sound hovering slightly above the pavement. The thickness of the air weighed on her chest, her breath rapid. Everything had somehow just . . . stopped. Cassie felt like an animal trapped in a net.

Click. The black gate latch of the white picket fence unhitched.

Press. Press. Press. Press. Methodical, quiet footsteps sounded against the brick slabs of the walkway, barely making a sound. They made their way up the four painted stairs.

Press. Press. They landed on the porch.

Cassie did a double take. A stout, elderly being with a kind, old face, wearing pencil lines for eyebrows grinned at Cassie under her short, dyed red hair that made her look like one of those fashionable grandmothers who had their hair done at a salon. The old being paused on the top of the porch and reached a thick arm into the pocket of the black cloak that covered her dense body. Retrieving a handful of seed, she spread the contents on the ledge of the empty bird feeder on the opposite side of the porch that no one in Cassie's family bothered to fill.

This thoughtful stranger was only slightly taller than Cassie, who stood at four feet seven inches the last time she checked. Wearing black-soled shoes that stuck out from under the long cloak, the being strode toward Cassie like a hostess in a restaurant. Then, as if she had known Cassie all her life, the stranger with the dark, brown M&M-colored eyes, spoke.

"Rather hot, isn't it?" she asked lovingly, like one of those nice grandmothers you see on TV. "Seems downright impossible to escape."

Cassie rubbed her eyes in disbelief. The kickball bounced in the street. When she finally removed her closed fists from her face, she opened her eyes to see the cloaked figure still standing in front of her. Gazing at Cassie in admiration, the old creature acted as if she knew something Cassie didn't.

"I'm sorry, do I know you?" Cassie asked, shaking her head side to side like a wet dog.

The woman grinned, her black mischievous eyes forming into slivery shapes. "You don't recognize me, do you Cassie? Well, that makes sense. After all, it's only been auditory up to this point. I'm Agatha."

"Agatha?" Cassie asked, tilting her head.

"Yes, my nominal identification for the voice in your head."

Cassie's stomach flipped. Unsticking herself from the chair, she stood up and gripped the porch railing.

"Wait," Cassie steadied herself. "You mean, you're the one who talks to me in my mind? Telling me to do things so something bad won't happen?"

Bruce appeared in the window. The dirty white fur ball bared his teeth and let out a low, drawn-out growl from behind the sheer curtain. Agatha waved him away, and he left. Just like that. Bruce never obeyed anyone easily. It occurred to Cassie this lady had special powers. She was definitely not from Boston.

"You mean watching out for you all these years? The counting of stairs to ensure accuracy, the repetition of thoughts to be sure things are as they should be? Keeping your life under control, that's the perspective I prefer. My dear girl, what would you have done without me?"

In a trance, Cassie turned and looked past the bird feeder into Emil and Barbara Heimer's first-floor window of their triple-decker, their refrigerator covered in shiny magnets and postcards.

Agatha clasped her hands behind her back. "I've watched you blossom into a fine apprentice, listening and following my orders all these years. Yes, yes, fine indeed. That's why I felt it was time to come to you in form." Agatha leaned in, as if she had a secret. "That only happens if you're special, you know. Most hear the voice but don't know we're really there. When the student is ready, the teacher appears." Agatha raised one penciled eyebrow, cupping a hand to the side of her mouth. "Besides, things aren't going well, are they?"

Cassie's stomach plunged like an elevator. *How did Agatha know that? But, if she's the voice who's been speaking to me all these years, she must know everything.*

Agatha must have read Cassie's thoughts, because the corners of Agatha's mouth turned upward.

"It's time to take matters into your own hands, Cassie Connor, and I am precisely the one to help you." Her black cloak grazed Cassie's feet as Agatha rested her arms on the wooden railing. "I'm going to take you to your father."

Cassie gripped the railing so hard her knuckles turned white. Agatha placed a gentle hand on her wrist, her nails thick and merlot red, her eyes searching deep inside Cassie, to a place Cassie didn't even know existed.

"The question is, are you with me?"

Cassie froze.

"They think you're too young," Agatha whispered. She jerked her head toward the inside of the house, clearly indicating Cassie's family members. "I, on the other hand, am on your side. You are old enough, and have a right to know the truth."

A current flowed through Cassie's body, allowing her rigid stance to soften.

"In a bit of an unconventional manner, but an accurate one just the same, you'll need to trust me, Cassie, the way you always have. See here now, come closer."

Cassie bit the nail of her ring finger. There wasn't anyone else willing to give her information about her father. She moved shoulder-to-shoulder with the dark cloak. The birds chirped at the feeder as Agatha rubbed her wide, wrinkled palms together, slowly at first and then briskly as a smoky gray mist rose from her hands. When she opened them, the mist evaporated, revealing a scene beneath. Cassie's mouth dropped open as a movie began to play right there in Agatha's palms.

First, she saw a small room with gray, tiled walls. Then, a steel bed with sheets the color of chickpeas. There was a door in the back of the room, and on the other side, another gray wall.

After a few moments, she saw him.

In the front of the room, near a door that led into a corridor, a man with light brown hair, straight like her own, sat on a metal chair.

Dad!

His brown eyes opened, yet barely blinked.

Cassie's heart hammered in her chest as she blurted, "Why is my dad alone? Where is he?"

Agatha took Cassie's hands in her own. "Your father is in great turmoil. I assure you we are trying to take care of him. I've come not only to show you where he is, but also to ask for your help. You actually called me, in a sense, from a thought frequency of despair and sadness, but we'll have time for that later. The first course of action is to find the right place to Zipper."

"Zipper?" Cassie asked.

"Why, that's how we get to the Land of Blue, of course," Agatha said, striding over to peek through the screen windows. "Once we've located our area for departure, we will leave in three days—your dimension's time—in order to perfect your Vibration for the journey." Opening the front door, she cocked her head to one side. "I always thought kickball was a bit boring, myself. Shall we?"

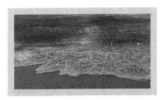

CHAPTER
THREE

Cassie's stomach fluttered as she followed Agatha inside her grandparent's house. She wanted to ask questions, but Agatha seemed so busy, checking behind coats that dangled on the front hallway rack, and assessing the space behind the living room couch. She muttered, "No, not there." Cassie stayed close behind, like a shadow.

Her mom was dusting furniture in the dining room, adjacent to the living room, when she noticed Cassie and paused. She put her hands on her hips and asked, "What are you looking for?"

Cassie stopped in her tracks.

Ann Marie swept her hair, falling from her ponytail, away from her tired eyes. "Hellloooo . . . ? What are you looking for?"

Cassie's heart raced as fast as the horses at the old dog track in Revere, until she figured it out: Mom doesn't see her. Mom can't see Agatha.

Her shoulders relaxed. Cassie answered smugly, "Just thought I'd pick up what the vacuum left behind."

Mom raised an eyebrow. She squinted and went back to dusting the chunky legs of the dining room table.

Cassie followed Agatha back into the front hallway, turning left as they headed toward the kitchen. A few feet in front of them, Grandpa Jack abruptly opened the basement door. He had just mown the lawn, and carried a can of Narragansett beer in his sunburned hand. He rubbed the back of his flaky scalp, which Cassie thought looked like the whitish-gray color of a matchstick.

"Oh, drat, we can't Zipper there," Agatha said, as Grandpa trudged down the basement stairs. "Chuck occupies the cellar."

"Chuck?" Cassie asked, rubbing absently at her arms.

"Your grandfather's Entity—an energetic guide on a Vibrational match. Let's just say, like attracts like." Agatha pointed down to a two-foot, oddly cute, gray creature with bulging eyes, wearing a black shirt, pants and black soled-shoes that made him look like a blackjack dealer, who stood in front of Grandpa.

The creature's skinny arm protruded out of his pickle-shaped body and he beckoned, "Let's go, let's go!"

Grandpa followed him, obliviously, down the creaky stairs.

"Chuck's a lower Entity," Agatha explained, as she strode into the kitchen. Nana Helen never looked up from the kitchen table as she played solitaire. "First time out from the Land of Blue—amateur job—more like babysitting."

"Grandpa is an easy job?" Cassie asked in bewilderment.

"There's not much to do, is all," Agatha remarked, as she glided into the pantry, just off the kitchen and pulled the string hanging from the cloudy light fixture.

Cassie counted the three boxes of Oreos and two packages of Saltines on the pantry shelf. She didn't think anything about

Grandpa Jack was easy. He had bloodshot blue eyes that looked monstrous under his black-rimmed, Coke-bottle glasses when he didn't have his contacts in, and he liked things just so.

For example, for $1.50 a week, Cassie made his lunch every night for work the next day. (Grandpa Jack drove a trolley car for the MBTA, where he had worked all his life. His route was the Green Line, which left Park Street downtown and went all the way to the outskirts of Jamaica Plain.) Anyway, Grandpa insisted on bringing a brown-bag lunch. When he drank beers with Emil Heimer at the chain link fence between their houses after they mowed their lawns on Saturday afternoons, Grandpa said, "For Christ's sake, you'd have to be a millionaire to buy lunch in the city."

Grandpa's lunch contained the following: a salami sandwich on rye with German mustard (not Dijon), a bag of Cape Cod potato chips, a pickle wrapped in waxed paper that could not, under any circumstances, leak out onto the sandwich, and a sixteen-ounce can of Schwepps ginger ale. The German mustard was a big deal. It could be spread on only one slice of the bread. If it squirted onto the crust or the waxed paper underneath, Grandpa made Cassie start over.

Even though Cassie kind of understood the need for Grandpa Jack to have things a certain way (she liked things lined up straight on her bureau herself) her stomach ached every time she thought about making Grandpa's lunch. He was really tough when things didn't go his way, and a buck fifty didn't seem like enough.

Sometimes, when Cassie felt annoyed, she'd think, *One time, I'm going to smear a quarter cup of Dijon on both sides of the rye, just to think about Grandpa's red face when he sits down to eat on the steps of City Hall Plaza.*

Cassie's Grandpa Jack was particular about lots of things. Every morning, he made sure the orange juice was shaken just right before he poured it into his little juice glass with the clear fruit designs. If Cassie, her mother, or Nana Helen poured it, he'd ask with his scrunched red bulbous nose, "Are you sure you shook that carton? I didn't see you shake it. Shake it now, just to be sure."

Nana Helen got so aggravated. Cassie heard her swear under her breath as she stomped in the pantry, pretending to get napkins.

When Grandpa asked Cassie to shake the orange juice carton, she bit the inside of her mouth. Her mother, though, would simply shake the carton like he asked, with a blank look on her face like she was a kid lost in a department store. She never said one unkind word. But Cassie knew, in a way that you don't know how you know, but you just know, that her mother was bothered.

Cassie glared at her mother every time she didn't have the guts to stand up to Grandpa Jack. She wondered if maybe her mother kept quiet so they wouldn't get thrown out on the street. Then they'd be homeless.

Agatha led the way back to the front hallway, where the olive green carpeted stairs led to the second floor. Behind Agatha, Cassie skipped the third, fifth, seventh, ninth, and eleventh stairs.

Agatha's black eyes shined with validation. "Such good work, listening to my voice, keeping things in perfect order and balance. Extra treats for you when we arrive at the Land of Blue."

Cassie thrust her shoulders back as she landed on the upper stair, breathless, in the second-floor hallway.

"Agatha," Cassie asked, resting against the wood-paneled wall. "Do you go to any kids who aren't worried?"

Agatha stopped. "Why? You don't have those kinds of thoughts, do you?"

Cassie had to think about that. Not really.

"Right then. On to other introductions. That, my dear," Agatha said, pointing and indicating Mom's bedroom, "is Dot."

Cassie peeked inside the tiny bedroom that overlooked Selwyn Street. Perched on the back of Mom's brown rocking chair, next to Nana's Singer sewing machine, was a sleek, black, bird-like creature. The creature swung back and forth, filing its clawed nails with one of mom's nails files. Noticing Cassie's surprised face, the creature yawned and returned to filing its nails.

"Dot is your mother's Entity," Agatha said, as she tapped Cassie's head three times. "Definitely not the right place for us to depart."

Across from the staircase was Grandpa's bedroom. Agatha looked over at Cassie after she eyed Grandpa's meticulous room. "Also not a good place to Zipper."

Cassie twisted her toes together. She despised Grandpa's room, the neatness of it—even though the rest of the house was messy—but most of all, the smell. Grandpa Jack's room stunk like mothballs. Cassie scratched the top of her left foot with the side of her right. Why did old people smell like mothballs? And why did Nana and Grandpa have different bedrooms? Cassie was seven when she asked her grandmother that question. Nana Helen answered, "If it ain't broke, kid, don't fix it."

They passed the tiny green-and-yellow-striped bathroom down the hall and across from Nana's spacious bedroom, and finally arrived at Cassie's room at the end of the hallway. Cassie's room used to be her mother's when her mom was growing up. There was one window that offered a view of the tarred piazza at the back of the house, facing Knoll Street, and another window that faced the Heimer's triple-decker. Agatha entered the room, ignoring both windows and searched under Cassie's twin bed as she blew dust bunnies out of the way.

"Too small," she sighed, as her eyes darted about. She stood and spotted the black metal doorknob of the closet door.

"Hmmm, what have we here?" she whispered, as she opened the wooden door wide, and stood back to assess its contents. With a brush of her hand—the kind of hands that likely made good spaghetti and meatballs—Agatha whisked aside the one beaded dress that hung in plastic wrap. That was the dress Nana Helen wore to weddings.

Agatha pressed her soft shoes inside the deep closet. "I believe this will do just fine." She spun her stout body, her black cloak swirling about. "Yesss, this will do just fine."

Cassie carefully selected an elastic band from a neat stack atop her wooden bureau, and asked, "What do I have to do to get ready to zip? Is that what you called it?" She pulled her hair up in a ponytail, not noticing the tiny burst of light that appeared in the upper corner of her bedroom, above the old bureau. It glowed like a firefly.

"It's Zipper, dear. And in order to Zipper, we need to prepare for where we are going. Trust me, you are very close to being ready. Verrry close." Agatha came out of the closet and caught the small yellow burst of light out of the corner of her keen eyes. Amused, she retrieved a small, clunky black device from the pocket of her cloak.

"Your energy, dictated by your emotions," she continued, "must be on a frequency in alignment with the Land of Blue." Agatha pushed a button, and began to move the device around Cassie's body. "Though you maintain a decent frequency for sure, the Energy Vibration Meter on my trusty Surveyor indicates we have a little way to go. Now, don't worry—we can take care of this, but it will require some homework on your part. Simply focus your thoughts, over the next three days, on the image I showed you of your father."

Cassie's heart sank into her stomach as she recalled her father in the isolated room. Worry crashed over her like a wave.

"It's not easy, I understand," Agatha said, her eyes on the Surveyor. "However, you must hyperfocus on helping your father, and what you may have to do to save him."

Cassie watched as a black arrow moved on the Surveyor. The screen displayed a dull color chart, ranging from a dusty blue, the color of sidewalk chalk at the top, to a gray color at the bottom, similar to how the sky looks right before a storm. Three quarters from the top of the screen, above the dusty blue color, was a solid black line. Above the line was empty space. Agatha beamed. The arrow, as she measured Cassie, landed at the very bottom, in the gray range.

"Look how quickly you adjusted to a slightly lower Vibration to match your father's own. Wonderful! Such a sensitive and compassionate child you are. You'll do fine, if . . . " she warned, " . . . if you stay focused on the image."

Cassie nodded, solemnly promising to complete her task.

"Now," Agatha explained, "all we need are three days, dusk, a simple chant, your will, and my skills, of course, and we'll be off!" She lowered her voice and tilted her head toward Cassie's family downstairs, "By way of Zippering, they won't even notice you're gone."

Cassie wiggled her toes while Agatha put the Surveyor back into her pocket. She wanted Mariana to come along. Mariana was the strong one; she helped Cassie whenever she felt nervous.

"Would it be okay if my best friend came, too?" Cassie asked as she bit her thumbnail. Tapping a finger to her lips, Agatha said, "Understandable. I should have expected that. Hmmm. Let me tune in." She closed her eyes for a few moments, muttering to herself, "A bold girl, this Mariana, which may present a problem long-term. Although she's detached from others' misfortunes, and therefore wouldn't need adjusting energetically, if my predictions are accurate."

Cassie gnawed at the skin around her fingernail as Agatha opened her eyes and returned to the closet.

"Room for another, room for another . . . " Agatha continued to speak softly to herself as she measured the closet's dimensions. She turned to face Cassie and said, "I always say, the more the merrier in the Land of Blue!"

Clasping her hands together under her chin, Cassie stepped into Agatha's space. Even though the image of her father would be hard to think about, Cassie didn't want to disappoint this special being. After all, she made specific accommodations.

"And by the way," Agatha said as she closed the closet door, "I am your Entity. Here to serve." She bowed and added, "And you to me."

Cassie stared, her lips parted.

With her back turned, Agatha strode like a mother duck to the bedroom door. "Three days, to the minute, I will return for you and your friend. So long, as it's never good-bye."

And just like that, Agatha was gone.

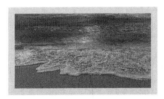

CHAPTER
FOUR

Close to dusk on the third day (which was also, coincidentally, the second day of sixth grade), Cassie sat cross-legged on her bed waiting for Mariana. She checked the digital alarm clock every few seconds.

The dream Cassie had the night before kept appearing in her mind. Agatha stood beneath a dark sky, mixing ingredients in a large pot. She tasted the mixture to be sure it was just right. When Cassie awoke, she felt Agatha was far away, in a strange and dark place.

She bit all her fingernails off in school, wondering if Agatha would be back at dusk as promised. She never even went to Mariana's house to welcome her back from summer camp, even though they talked on the phone prior to the first day of school. The Papadopoulis' treated Cassie so nicely, and since Agatha told her to concentrate on the image of her father, she didn't want Mrs. Papadopoulis to try to make her feel better.

While she waited for Mariana to walk the six blocks to her grandparents' house, Cassie thought about her new math teacher. Mrs. Burke had long, shiny dark hair and a pretty smile that made her eyes small. She kept a picture of her family on her desk—her dark-haired husband, two children, and a shiny, golden-haired dog (who didn't look a thing like Bruce.) Cassie admired the picture of Mrs. Burke's happy family every time she sharpened her pencil (at least seven times a day.)

Cassie noticed new details in the white frame each time, such as the Xaverian Brothers High School jacket the athletic son wore. Cassie once heard Mrs. Burke say that her kids' names were Kyle and Michelle. Cassie guessed Michelle was eight years old and had a fun personality. The smiles on everyone's faces in the picture made Cassie's throat burn, even though she was happy for Mrs. Burke's perfect life.

Moving to the edge of her bed, Cassie chewed the skin around her nails and imagined Mrs. Burke's fun family times—picnics in the Arboretum, movie nights on Fridays, and vacation trips to Disney World, when Grandpa Jack hollered from the kitchen, "Hey! My lunch isn't made! Whaddya doing?"

Cassie plodded downstairs, trudging over the odd-numbered steps. The tin foil, waxed paper, and brown bag were lined up perfectly on the table when she entered the kitchen. Robotically, Cassie opened the fridge and reached for the jar of pickles, the can of Schwepps, the package of salami, bread, and the container of German mustard. She barely blinked as she proceeded to make Grandpa's sandwich, carefully spreading the mustard over the rye. She wrapped the sandwich neatly in the waxed paper and tin foil and placed the pickle in a separate piece of wax paper so it wouldn't make a mess. Finally, Cassie placed the wrapped sandwich in the brown bag with the soda, Cape Cod chips, and a folded napkin.

"Are ya done yet?" Grandpa snapped, as he walked in, heavy-footed in his black work shoes. He reached up to the cupboard above the kitchen sink and snatched a small juice glass with his freckled hand.

"Yeah," Cassie answered, bright lights shining through the window as Emil pulled into his driveway, coming home from work.

Grandpa Jack placed the glass on the table and said, "Do me a favor, and pour me a nice glass of OJ before I head out for the night." Then he turned to the sink and washed his raw, cracked hands.

Cassie took the orange juice carton out of the refrigerator and shook it with two hands, for fifteen seconds, just to his liking.

Grandpa Jack dried his hands on the starched dishtowel.

"By golly, now that's the way it should be done," he said, nodding. "Your grandmother ought to take notes."

Cassie pulled on her lip as Grandpa gulped down the OJ.

He smacked his lips in satisfaction. "Ahhhh."

Bzzzz. The doorbell rang.

"I'll get it!" Grandpa barked, as he abruptly placed the empty juice glass in the sink. "I'm going out."

"Hi, Mr. Riley," Mariana said, as she ducked under Grandpa Jack's arm. A chilly gust entered the house from the shifting September air.

"Hello," Grandpa grumbled, as he grabbed his eggshell-blue parka from the coat rack.

Slam!

Mariana rolled her eyes and wiggled her body in disgust. "I don't know how you live with that. I know he's your grandfather, but seriously." Mariana never held back in telling a person how she felt. Her opinion of Grandpa Jack was that he was consistently in a bad mood, which was basically the truth. She tossed a Tupperware container on the cream-covered bench in the front hallway.

"My mom sent over baklava, thought your mom might enjoy it with your dad being gone. We've missed seeing you at the house."

Then, she whispered curiously, "Where is she? Where's Agatha?"

Cassie tightened her stomach. She had told Mariana pieces about Agatha (". . . I met this person, she called herself an Entity . . .") over the first two days of school. This presented a challenge because Peggy McCarthy, the towheaded blonde girl who joined them at lunch every day, listened while they tried to talk in hushed tones.

"You're going to be that old lady someday who takes in a hundred stray cats," Mariana said whenever Cassie added another misfit to their lunch table.

"Anyway," Cassie continued, "she's kind of like a creature from some other place."

"Are you sure she wasn't a ghost?" Mariana asked as she ate her tuna sandwich.

"No, she was fleshier than a ghost. She's my Entity, like, my own guide! She knows me better than you do! And she showed me—in her hands—where my dad is. I don't know how she did it, but she did. You have to come with us, to help me bring my dad home."

Mariana had eaten her tuna sandwich with her eyes like slits, listening to every word Cassie spoke. She had gulped down her milk and declared, "You aren't going anywhere without me."

Cassie led Mariana upstairs and silently prayed that Agatha would be there. She heard Nana enter the house through the back piazza, back from walking Bruce, and made sure to land only on the even stairs as she pulled Mariana behind her.

"You still do that?" Mariana asked as her long, thick hair swayed side to side.

"It's a habit. You know I can't stop," Cassie said, as she lunged over the eleventh stair. "You do stuff, too."

"Like what?" Mariana asked doubtfully, stepping into the upstairs hallway.

"Like eat with your mouth open, and you're in middle school."

"That's not a habit."

"It's a bad habit," Cassie informed her, glancing sideways at Mariana. Tugging on the waist of her navy-blue jersey, Cassie stopped outside her bedroom door. Please let her show up, she thought.

"Is she in there?" Mariana asked, her face close to Cassie's.

Cassie opened the creaky door and checked inside. Nothing. She opened the door wider and glanced around her entire room. Finally, she examined the closet. Mariana stood next to her bed with raised eyebrows.

"Agatha?" Cassie asked sheepishly. *Nothing good ever lasts!*

Oompf! A loud noise came from the hallway, sounding like two people accidentally colliding into each other outside Nana's bedroom.

"My, it's busy in this house," Agatha complained, entering the bedroom. She brushed off her cloak and closed the door.

Cassie spun around, her heart leaping into her throat.

Mariana's eyes popped open like a Slinky bursting out of its container. "Whoa! This is Agatha?" She blinked. "I want one of those!"

Cassie raised her chin. Mariana extended a finger, barely touching Agatha's long black cloak, when she jumped backward about a foot. Mariana looked as though she'd been pricked by the needles of a porcupine.

"Be careful what you wish for, my dear," Agatha cautioned. "If you're going to be coming with us, you need to respect one's personal space."

"W-where are we going, exactly?" Mariana stuttered.

"Show her, Agatha," Cassie said, her heart racing as she thought of her father in the empty room. "Show her with your hands, the way you showed me."

"As your Entity, Cassie, that is meant for you and me alone." Agatha turned to Mariana. "My only requirement is that you follow your friend, who'll receive instructions from me. Make no mistake," she said with a twinkle in her eye, "I'm pleased you'll be accompanying us to the Land of Blue." Instantly, out of her hands she made a red flower appear, inserting it in Mariana's hair.

"Wow!" Mariana exclaimed. She whispered in Cassie's ear, "This is going to be way cooler than what we learn in sixth grade."

Cassie's heart soared. She couldn't recall a time when Mariana had viewed her as the leader. Although Cassie didn't fully understand where they were going, or just how they were going to help her dad, she felt excited and confident that in time, she would.

Agatha accessed the Energy Vibration Meter on the Surveyor. Mariana held her lean arms tight to her body as Cassie instructed, while Agatha measured the energy space around Mariana's athletic frame. "Yes. I was right, of course. Bold and self-possessed, yet magnificently detached, certainly able to sustain an initial trip, with my approval. Perfectly planned, if I do say so myself."

The arrow landed slightly above the black line, in the clear space at the top of the dreary blue color sequence. Agatha pushed the button to the start position, clearing the screen.

"How come there's blah colors under that black line but empty space on the other side?" Mariana asked, leaning over Agatha's shoulder.

"Anything on the other side is of no importance to the Land of Blue," Agatha answered sweetly.

Cassie was wedging her right foot inside her red canvas sneaker when she caught sight of the yellow glow of light in her peripheral vision, high up in the corner of her bedroom. It shined brightly despite its small size, and dripped, as from a faucet. Cassie turned her head to see the yellow light descend in mid-air, evaporating before it reached the hardwood floor. She blinked.

As if to prove to her that what she saw was real, the watercolor yellow circle shone forth again. This time pulsing, as it tried to form itself into a larger circle, similar to one on an artist's palette. Cassie almost felt sorry for the little circle, making quite an effort to be noticed. Then, like it was too much effort, it dripped . . . and dripped . . . until it disappeared.

Agatha caught sight of this as the arrow shook erratically on the Meter near Cassie's energy space. "Never mind distractions. Merely brain tricks, I tell you, when you need it least. Come now, we'll try to keep the noise down as best we can. It's always the loudest the first time out. Plenty of room. Plenty . . . of . . . room," she said with a satisfied smile.

Cassie stole a glance of the corner again, her curious nature getting the better of her.

Agatha's tone was stern. "Stay focused. Where I come from, we require good listeners. On that note, why don't you put on your father's shrunken sweatshirt from your bottom drawer, it gets a bit chilly on Blue."

Cassie blinked to release the moment and took out the navy blue Knights of Columbus sweatshirt out of her bottom drawer. She pulled it over her head and turned to join Agatha, and Mariana, who held a stiff posture while she watched the old creature. Agatha tossed aside Nana's dress and ushered the girls into the closet. She took a deep breath and finally decided they were ready.

"Mariana dear, join hands with Cassie," Agatha said, glancing down at the Surveyor. Mariana rubbed her sweaty palms on her jeans and locked hands with Cassie, whose eyes were fixated on her Entity. Agatha whispered under her breath, but Cassie couldn't make out the words. Suddenly, trails of wispy smoke emerged from the floorboards beneath their feet. Agatha's arms stretched, tentacle-like, until wrapped snugly around the girls.

"Consider me your navigation system," Agatha instructed, looking into Cassie's uncertain eyes. "Now concentrate on your father's heartbreaking absence."

Cassie felt prepared. The image of her dad played repeatedly in her mind during the last three days. Curls of smoke entered Cassie's nostrils. She scrunched her face like a crumpled newspaper, recalling the movie she watched in Agatha's hands. Her heart ached as she pictured her father in that room, upset about something she didn't understand.

Agatha began to chant in a smooth voice:

"Darkness threatens those we love,
Hopes for this one yet remain
Choice and selection
Once an election
Now we enter Blue Domain."

Dust from the closet floor swirled about the soles of Cassie's sneakers. Rising to her ankles, the feathery sensation tickled like a light breeze, and then a forceful wind as it climbed about her legs, stomach, and shoulders. Cassie felt dizzy and stepped back with her right foot. The picture in her mind of her father broke into little pieces, scattering into the howling wind.

Mariana clutched Cassie's hands. "It's like we're in the middle of a tornado!" Cassie dropped her head down. In the distance, she heard Nana's voice calling faintly from downstairs, "What's going on up there?"

Agatha yelled out, but in Cassie's voice, "We're just fine, Nana Helen!"

Cassie's eyes widened.

The wind rumbled, shaking the closet door.

"Do you like roller coasters?" Agatha asked the girls, raising her voice above the noise.

"Heck yeah!" Mariana answered.

Cassie's eyes remained glued to the floor until Agatha swooped in on her like a hawk. "Trust me, dear. It's always hardest the first time. All you need to do is focus your will and hold on tight. I'll take care of the rest." Bending to Cassie's ear, she whispered soothingly as the wind roared. "Just do as you're told and the noise will quiet."

Cassie's shoulders relaxed a bit.

Just then, her father's voice cried out somewhere in the distance, "Help me! Someone help me!" Cassie's heart pounded painfully in her chest. She tightened her fists, determination swelling inside her body like a tsunami.

Agatha leaned in closer. "Good girl. You know, you're the only one who can save him." Cassie's legs suddenly lifted off the floor, Mariana's pink tennis sneakers hovering next to her red ones. A fluttery feeling burst in Cassie's stomach as the tornado-like energy carried them up, up, up, swirling and spinning them faster and faster. Cassie's legs weakened, her hands loosening from Mariana's tight grip.

And they were gone.

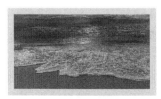

CHAPTER
FIVE

Where am I? Cassie's eyelids crinkled as she opened and closed them, seeing nothing but pitch black, her surroundings eerily quiet. Her arms pressed snugly against her sides, Cassie felt as though she was buried under snow from the neck down on a cold winter's night. Icy air burned her insides.

"Just a minute," Agatha's voice spoke with authority. "These things can happen."

Vroomp.

Like a crumb being sucked up by a vacuum cleaner, Cassie's body jerked backward, thrust into a different space. There were people everywhere. Dark-skinned, attractive women hurried by, dressed in flowered garb of bright yellow, pink, and purple, their silky-haired children in tow. Dark-haired men chatted as they shuffled, crowded together like a deck of cards. Voices on intercoms announced departures and arrivals. Green and white signs pointed to Gates A, B, and C, and there was lots of . . . *Oomph!* luggage. *Ouch!*

The well-dressed strangers looked back distractedly at Cassie as they hurried to their destination. *Am I in an airport in another country?* She darted her eyes back and forth. Cassie's cheeks flushed as children laughed and pointed. Unable to move, she had a weird feeling she was only half dressed.

"A-Agatha?" Cassie whispered, meekly.

"Yes, dear, I know. Whenever you're worried, Agatha is there. Oh, I'm going to cause quite a fuss making my presence known here."

Cassie felt someone yank her shoulders, whisking her away, out of the bustling airport, back into darkness. For a moment, nothing happened. Then a burst of small sparkly stars appeared in the distance, forming an outline of one person, then two people. Their arms and legs materialized first, followed by their shoulders and faces, all out of the stars.

"Look at me!" Mariana exclaimed, running toward Cassie. "I'm energy!"

Agatha emerged behind Mariana, her forehead wrinkled with concern. "Are you all right, dear?" Cassie nodded, warmth rising in her chest at the sight of familiar faces.

"I think we're in space!" Mariana said, spreading her sparkling arms wide. "What happened? You let go of my hand!"

"Now, now, it was merely a hiccup of sorts. They'll have a lot of fun with that one, in that part of the world," Agatha winked. "However, on a more serious note, we must be careful not to encounter any detours again, as the Land of Blue is counting on our timely arrival. Stay close, and let's not let anything distract us from the journey ahead." Agatha's voice was gentle, but firm.

Cassie's shoulders drooped. *I don't know why I let go. I'm such a baby.*

Mariana waved her hands up to the sky, watching the energy

sway with them. She delighted in her effervescence.

I wish I was more like Mariana, she thought.

Agatha patted Cassie on the head and proceeded to extend her arms around the girls. Reaching for Mariana's hand, Cassie vowed silently to do better this time. Agatha began to chant:

> "Darkness threatens those we love,
> Hopes for this one yet remain
> Choice and selection
> One's own election
> Now we enter Blue Domain."

Cassie clenched her jaw so hard she thought her teeth might break. Instantly they lifted off the ground, did a backflip, and spiraled out of the void at breakneck speed.

Moments later, Cassie's sneakers touched ground. Light moisture hung in the air. Two bright silver moons shined in the night sky as clouds rolled slowly across, providing only slivers of light with which to see. Cassie's glittering arms, torso, and legs arose in the night. Mariana's outline arrived next, materializing from nothingness. Patting herself down, Agatha's shimmery silhouette fleshed out to solid form. Cassie and Mariana patted themselves too, the three of them eventually looking exactly like they did back in Cassie's bedroom.

Mammoth rocks lined the left side of the pebbled path on which they arrived, illuminated by the silvery moonlight. A cliff on the right side of the path overlooked a large, dark body of water, stretching out as far as Cassie could see.

"We landed on a mountain!" Cassie shouted, placing her hand on one of the slabs of majestic silvery stone. Ahead, toward the end of the path, Cassie saw the contour of another mountain across the way, dazzling under the twin moonlight. The tops of palm trees between the two mountains swayed in the welcoming breeze. Cassie thought it was the most mysterious place she'd ever seen.

"Yeah, but where?" Mariana asked, straining her eyes in the dark. "It looks like we're in Hawaii, except the last time my family and I vacationed there, we didn't teleport."

"We don't teleport on the Land of Blue, dear, we Zipper," Agatha said as she observed the landscape from the cliff, "and to answer your question, we're in Option's Port." Agatha's stiff red hair lifted slightly in the wind coming off the water. "Hopefully, we won't be here long," she said as she scanned the horizon. Her voice trailed off, as if talking to herself.

Mariana knelt down and felt the rocky road beneath her feet, selecting a few pebbles to put in the pocket of her dark pink sweatshirt. "Souvenirs for back home," she said. "I'm imagining we landed on the moon, only there's two of them!"

"Agatha," Cassie said, fidgeting with her hands as she joined her Entity on the cliff. "Is this where my dad is? In Option's Port?"

"No, though he has traveled these parts before. We'll reach your father in good time. The Land of Blue is far more exciting than Option's Port. This is simply a choice point prior to getting there." Agatha quickly put a finger to her ear. "See, I am tuning in to the frequency of the wind, checking on the transportation I've arranged to take us to our destination. By my calculations, *The Enticer* will be arriving in a pulse or two, Land of Blue time."

Cassie pressed up and down on her tiptoes. "Where is the Land of Blue? Is it far from here?" *Am I annoying her the way I annoy my mother?* Cassie wondered. She searched Agatha's face for signs of agitation as she bit her bottom lip. *Bite harder to make sure you're not.*

A smile spread across Agatha's face.

"The Land of Blue is there," she said, and pointed past the vast expanse of water. Cassie squinted, wishing she had listened to her mother and eaten more carrots.

"I don't see anything."

"Not to worry," Agatha chuckled, "you'll be there soon."

Agatha's words slowed in tone and texture, like slush being poured into a paper cup. "Unless, of course, you can't endure the long and strenuous path ahead. Are you weak?"

Cassie scuffed the path with her sneaker. *Mom says I'm fragile. Will I make it?*

"What are we talking about?" Mariana asked, stepping between Cassie and Agatha.

"Make sure your laces are tied tight," Agatha said. "It's rocky terrain on the few miles down to the shore."

Cassie bent down to tie her red sneakers. She tied them so tight they choked the top of her foot. Even though Cassie considered herself to be in decent shape—she ran the mile last year in eight minutes—she had never hiked a mountain.

Agatha sauntered ahead, like a tour guide.

"What if we get hurt on the way down? I don't want to miss our ride." Cassie retied her sneakers, just to be sure. *What if I disappoint Agatha?*

"Would you stop worrying? They're not going to leave without us," Mariana said as she lightly tugged on the pom-poms on the back of her ankle socks. "They're coming just for you, aren't they?"

CHAPTER
SIX

Cassie's feet began to burn and hurt as they walked farther and farther, for what seemed like hours, down the curvaceous mountain. Sand and rocks crunched beneath her shoes. The hooting sounds of owls and hawks pierced her ears as they flew overhead. With the aid of the moonlight, Cassie tried with all her might to keep her eyes on the rocky, twisting road.

"This is a hike of all hikes, huh?" Mariana asked, her strong legs leaping over the stony obstacles. "I'm glad my dad and I went to Blue Hills last week for our monthly date. 'Cause otherwise I don't think I'd be ready for this!"

Cassie's stomach hardened. She tried to lunge forward like a daddy longlegs, but stumbled on a jagged rock sticking out of the ground. Mariana walked ahead, oblivious. Thoroughly inflamed,

Cassie reached down and grabbed a rock the size of a tennis ball and flung it at Mariana's heels.

"What was that for?" Mariana asked, jumping out of the way.

Cassie dug her fists into her sides, her face red. "I'm so happy you and your dad go on monthly dates!"

Mariana's nose crinkled in confusion. "It's not my fault my dad's home with us." Walking forward, Cassie tripped on more stones, the air muggy and sticky against her skin.

"Ugh! These stupid rocks! I can barely see anything! I need a drink, did anyone bring stupid water?"

"I didn't, but look on the bright side—we're getting closer to the base!" Mariana pointed down to a small stream visible between the two mountains. "If that's natural spring water you can drink it right from the stream! Why don't we pick up the pace? Just watch your footing. My dad said good hikers watch their footing." Realizing she just mentioned her dad again, Mariana froze in her tracks. She turned slowly to view Cassie's expression.

Cassie, her eyes filled with tears, covered her face with her hands.

Mariana threw her hands in the air. "I was only trying to help!"

Cassie plunked herself down on the dusty, rock-laden road. *I always mess things up. I'm a lousy friend.*

"C'mon," Mariana said, walking back to Cassie. "Let's just forget everything and start over. My mom calls it a rewind moment."

Agatha marched back toward the girls.

"Go easy on your friend," Agatha's voice cut through the humid atmosphere. "Some of us can lose our sense of adventure at the same time we long to start the journey. Let's use Option's Port for the rest stop it is, and take a few moments."

"Rest stop?" Mariana asked in disbelief. "We've been walking for miles!"

Cassie blew on some pebbles through her crisscrossed legs. Her eyes blurred and her stomach growled. Raking a fistful of pebbles with her hand and flinging them off the cliff, she considered going home.

Only the fragile go home.

Cassie pulled her knees up to her chest as the last pebble fall short of the cliff's edge. *Agatha said I'm the only one who can save my dad. I can't go home. He needs me.*

Digging her heels inside her sneakers, Cassie set her feet on the ground and pulled herself up to standing. "Let's go."

Agatha nodded in approval. Cassie locked arms with Mariana, and continued to follow her Entity down the descending path. As they drew closer to the bottom of the mountain's base, the backs of Cassie's thighs felt tight. She was sure she noticed glowing yellow eyes watching her from behind crevices in the jagged stone, but when she blinked and looked back, there was no one there.

Shuddering, she whisked her attention toward the water glad *The Enticer* was on its way.

At last, a set of stone stairs came into view, leading down to a small strip of beach. A narrow stream flowed over rocks and boulders at the base of the opposing mountain. Cassie felt more at ease as she followed the trail out to the larger body of water. A small, rickety wooden dock was stationed at the shoreline.

"Someone else is here!" Mariana pointed to a hut on the sand, glowing beautifully from a fire burning inside. Smoke rose through an opening at the top, reminding Cassie of a teepee, its straw exterior like sheaths of gold. Cassie's insides raced as she wondered about the hut's owner. Mariana quickened her gait down the stony ledges.

Always create order when you know not what lies ahead.

Cassie breathed in the sweet, tropical air as she remembered to lunge over the odd-numbered stairs. Tall, dark-green palm trees were scattered on the small strip of beach around the hut. As the wind blew their arched, feather-shaped fronds, they appeared to dance. Cassie stepped onto the squishy, moist sand. The door of the hut opened, dragging across the sandy floor.

A black-haired, olive-skinned woman, wearing a white peasant dress, appeared behind the doorway. Shaped like a gorgeous vase of pottery, she wore a long thick braid that hung over her shoulder. A fuchsia-colored flower was tucked behind her ear.

"Hello travelers," she spoke, her voice as soothing as running bath water. "May I interest your companions, Agatha, in a cup of Kamalu?"

Agatha slid in front of Cassie and Mariana, as they strained their necks to see the beautiful stranger. "Your timing is impeccable, Tufa. However, *The Enticer* will be arriving. And since there'll be plenty to drink when we get to the Land of Blue, unfortunately, we'll need to . . ."

"Come now," the relaxed, middle-aged woman said. Cassie noticed a dimple on the side of her pretty face. "Surely, there is time for a quick cup. After all, your travelers may be in need." She held a jug on her hip snugly, as if it were a child.

Agatha glanced down her rounded nose at Cassie, whose throat was rather parched.

"I'm dying of thirst. Will you come with me?" Cassie asked.

Agatha rubbed the back of her neck.

"That's a lovely idea," Tufa said, watching Agatha closely.

Agatha recoiled at the offer. "The fragrances in there are too much for sensitive ones like myself. Perhaps you could take a drink from the stream as Mariana suggested."

The sound of a ship's horn rang mightily in the distance. Agatha's impatient countenance gave way to a smile.

"Ah, right on time, as I assumed. Cassie, I've had a change of heart. You may go, without me, for a quick cup. But none of your fancy concoctions, Tufa," Agatha warned, wagging a finger. "We're on a schedule, understood?"

Tufa nodded, with a twinkle in her eye. "Understood."

Agatha gently touched Cassie's elbow, giving her permission. *You must be quick, so as not to disrupt the schedule.*

"C'mon, Mariana," Cassie said, holding out her hand. When Mariana didn't take it, Cassie turned to look for her and saw that Mariana had moved a few yards away from them on the sand. She squatted on her heels, examining something Cassie couldn't see.

"Check it out!" Mariana said. She held up a shiny piece of green sea glass between her thumb and forefinger and showed it to Cassie.

"That's so pretty!" Cassie cried as she stepped closer.

Suddenly, Mariana flinched and shrieked, "Yikes!" The dazzling piece wriggled out of her grasp. A tiny crab-like creature revealed itself from underneath the colorful glass. Its legs flailed in the sand.

The glass lay in a scooped indentation on the creature's back, until it made a pucker sound, and the jewel separated from owner. At once, the creature stopped moving. Cassie stepped gingerly across the sand and crouched to pick up the luminous glass.

"Ahhh, you've found Wisdom Glass," Tufa said, joining them on the beach. Her white peasant dress rippled in the warm breeze. "A true treasure. Similar to sea glass on your frequency, only better." Her dark eyes sparkled in the light of the moons. "Perhaps you'd like a closer look."

Cassie and Mariana squinted as they brought the Wisdom Glass near their faces. A tiny message appeared, scrawled on the shiny surface, white and powdery like it had been scratched by a fingernail: "We always have a choice."

"Duh," Mariana said, curling her mouth. She turned her attention to the unmoving creature. "After I held it, the jewel popped out. Then it died."

Cassie scooped the creature out of the sand and held it in her hands. "Why? That's so sad." Her voice quivered as she caressed the helpless creature. *I should have told Mariana to leave it alone. It's my fault for wanting a drink.* Cassie dug into her palm with her fingernail.

"Things die, Cass," Mariana said, as she placed an arm around Cassie's shoulder. "My Ya-Ya calls it the circle of life."

"Your friend is right," the exotic woman agreed, standing barefoot over the girls in the sand. "There is no despair in a life that has fulfilled its purpose. This creature's sole task is to pass wisdom to another. This message may not mean anything to you now, but it has completed its mission. Now, it may rest."

Mariana stared at Tufa for a moment, and then stood beside Cassie, who continued to kneel, holding the lifeless creature with a pained expression on her face. Eventually, Cassie decided to dig a little hole in the wet sand with her fingers. She placed the creature inside, and covered it with her hand. Mariana slid more sand on top with her tennis sneaker. Cassie prayed silently that the creature didn't feel any pain.

Agatha startled Cassie by placing a hand on her shoulder. "There, there. I'm not a fan of Wisdom Glass either. Take as much time as you need to mourn. It is so difficult when we see something, or someone, in pain. We just want to save them from their suffering. It's awful. Dreadful, actually."

"I assure you . . . " Tufa began.

"I dare say," Agatha interrupted, turning her attention to the outstretched sea. "Cassie won't be able to join you now, my old friend, for as you can see, *The Enticer* is approaching." Cassie and Mariana spun around. In the distance, a large floodlight scanned the dark water, back and forth.

"It's a ship!" Mariana said, excitedly.

Cassie jumped to her feet.

"Something of the sort," Agatha said with a grin. "An impressive vehicle, at any rate. And it'll be docking in a pulse, so come now, help me retrieve the ladder that will bring you aboard. Thank you for the offer of a cup of Kamalu, Tufa. In the many eons we've known one another, you've been the thoughtful one."

Tufa cleared her throat as the floodlight moved closer to the shore. She shifted her gaze toward the mountain above the stream. Cassie looked at the mountain too, but didn't see anything up there.

Suddenly, Cassie began to cough spasmodically. "Agatha, may I please have just one drink? I'll be very quick, I promise."

Agatha assessed the waves lapping the shore. "I suppose Mariana can help with the rope ladder. But remember, Tufa, we're now on the Land of Blue's time."

"I remember," Tufa laughed, the way a nice mother finds humor in her child's antics, even though Agatha appeared much older than the svelte, beautiful woman. Cassie noticed Tufa nod in the direction of the high mountain, like she was communicating with someone.

Agatha gave Tufa a stern look and continued down to the dock. Waves splashed up and over the wooden boards of the small dock as *The Enticer* neared.

"I wanna stay out here and find more Wisdom Glass!" Mariana said as she scanned the ground. "Don't worry, Cassie, I won't pick them up!"

Cassie entered the tiny hut, noticing the large hole in the roof revealing the midnight sky overhead. A welcoming fire danced under an iron kettle of bubbling liquid. Tiny jars lined shelves on the wall, while the fragrance of lilac wafted through the air.

I wonder why Agatha doesn't like it in here.

Cassie eyed a tiny brown jar, remembering how Nana Helen had complained about that lady at the four o'clock Mass who wore the lace napkin on her head. Nana said she "reeked of perfume." Cassie thought the lady smelled nice.

It's so peaceful here, she thought. A cozy-looking straw bed with a fluffy white comforter and pillow lay tucked in the corner, a few feet from the fire. Cassie felt relaxed in a way she hadn't felt in, well, ever.

"I'm Cassie," she said, scratching her arm.

"I know," Tufa replied, as she ladled bubbly liquid into a small bowl shaped like half a coconut. "I've been awaiting your arrival. I brewed Ylang Ylang, Lavender, and Chamomile to make a cup of Kamalu. Would you like some?"

Cassie thought the bed belonged in the Goldilocks story. *If only I could rest my head for a few minutes.*

"Go on if you like, and rest. There's always enough time, if you allow there to be."

Cassie rubbed her elbow as she noticed Tufa's slightly calloused heels, wondering how she knew her name. Instantly, a feeling of familiarity rippled through Cassie, causing her to shudder, though she was certain she had never seen this woman before in her entire twelve years of life.

With her gentle hands, Tufa handed Cassie the cup. The sweet, calming liquid ran smoothly down Cassie's arid throat as she slurped the Kamalu until it was almost gone. Cassie left a small amount at the bottom, because she didn't want to appear greedy.

Don't take too long, now.

Cassie drew her eyebrows together, squeezing the cup between her hands. "I can't rest," she said, "I'm leaving soon for the Land of Blue."

"Yes. Tell me, what is the reason for your journey?" Tufa crossed her legs in the wooden chair next to the kettle, her eyes reflecting the firelight.

"My father's there. I'm going to save him," Cassie replied as she lifted her chin.

"Ah, yes, I understand the importance of your mission," Tufa said gently. "A father and daughter's relationship builds a foundation for life, does it not? Have you considered, though, the purpose of Option's Port?"

Cassie watched Tufa as though she were a piece of pottery being spun on a wheel. Outside, the ship's horn blared in the night. Cassie gasped and blinked.

"I can't miss my ride. What if I stayed talking to you and the ship left without me?"

With a shaky hand, Cassie placed the nearly finished bowl on a small wooden table by the door, trying not to spill any. Tufa observed her frantic movements from the chair, and swirled her toes rhythmically on the sandy floor. She raised her eyes to Cassie and said directly, "But what if it didn't?"

Cassie met Tufa's gaze. Oddly, Cassie felt like she wanted to stay inside the hut. There was something so familiar about Tufa. Her curiosity grew stronger. "I feel I know you somehow," she said. "Have we ever met?"

Tufa stirred the bubbling Kamalu. "If you believe so, then it is so. If you believe not, then no. Such is the essence of truth."

Cassie rubbed her forehead.

"Do not try so hard to comprehend," Tufa laughed. "All we need to know is revealed in its right time."

Cassie wanted to ask what was inside the multiple jars on the shelves. *Don't wear out your welcome.*

Cassie reached for the bamboo door. "Thank you," she mumbled.

Tufa bowed her head to Cassie, and stood to select one of the small jars. She chose a green one and brought it down from the shelf.

Cassie gripped a handful of straw that lay across the door and asked, "Could you come with us? Agatha said the more the merrier in the Land of Blue."

Tufa carefully poured oil onto her fingers. "I am needed elsewhere. The Land of Blue is not where I belong. However, should you elect to journey onward, know you may always visit me here . . ." She touched the center of Cassie's forehead with her fingertips, the oil soft and fragrant on her skin. " . . . A mere thought away."

A pang of sadness vibrated through Cassie's heart. She ran her finger across the straw on the door, and breathed the scent of lemon.

The ship's horn rang a third time. Cassie winced as she remembered one Saturday afternoon when Grandpa blasted the car horn from the driveway when she and her mother were running late for church.

Tufa placed a soft hand on Cassie's back, and Cassie felt a mild current of electricity run through her body. "Option's Port serves as the place where one may stop to consider what feels right, and to decide what action they will take."

"I'm sorry," Cassie said, pulling at her earlobe. "Agatha didn't want me to stay long. My dad needs me."

Tufa smiled, her white teeth revealing another aspect of her beauty, as she gestured toward the door.

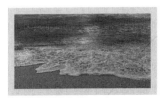

CHAPTER
SEVEN

The palm trees swung wildly on the beach under the midnight sky as Cassie emerged from the hut. She couldn't believe her eyes. A large midnight-blue vessel, like a pirate ship, sailed toward the dock. Several large masts with navy-blue sails whipped frenetically in the wind. Forceful waves crashed around its bilge, and painted black lettering across the hull spelled out: *The Enticer*. Shiny, handsome, winged, black horse-beasts, with massive heads three times the size of regular horses, ploughed through the water with their gigantic, muscled chests as they pulled into port and began to rotate *The Enticer* back around in the direction from which it came.

Erratic movement on the quarterdeck of the ship pulled Cassie's attention upward. Adorable little trolls, with rubbery, navy-blue skin, and round, uneven eyes waved hyperactively to get

Agatha's attention. Flapping their wide mouths and flashing toothy grins, they jumped up and down like they were on a trampoline and began to give direction signals over the railing with their skinny arms to the winged horse-beasts, sending them this way and that. The massive creatures whinnied in confusion, which caused the mischievous little trolls to laugh so hard they fell down and rolled across the deck.

"Oip! Oip! Oip!" the blue trolls yelled, trampling over one another.

The troll who appeared to be in charge mumbled a lower-toned, "Oip, oip" under his breath as he waddled like a penguin from the captain's quarters across the deck. Huffing and puffing at his naughty crew, the head troll glanced down repeatedly at Agatha, as if he was afraid he'd be blamed for their behavior. Agatha gave a crisp nod from the dock to the diminutive captain and surreptitiously winked at the troublesome trolls.

"Would you look at all of them?" Mariana squealed, gesturing Cassie to the end of the dock as dozens of rubbery blue trolls popped up like popcorn over the railing of the ship. "They're hilarious!"

"It's like we're famous!" Cassie said, standing next to Mariana as the trolls threw pieces of candy overboard. "I feel like I'm at a parade!" She reached out to try to catch some of the flying candy.

"The Mooshkoos have been eagerly awaiting your arrival," Agatha said. "Any friend of mine is a friend of theirs."

"Mooshkoos!" Mariana shouted. "Hey, you always wanted a pet, Cassie. Maybe we can take one home!"

"Come help me tie the rope ladder," Agatha instructed. She stroked the coat of one of the exhausted horse-beasts that snorted on the wet dock. "The Constantines need a break."

Agatha signaled up to the Mooshkoos with her hand the way a catcher signals a pitcher during a baseball game. The Mooshkoos obediently tossed down a flimsy rope ladder. Agatha showed Cassie and Mariana how to tie each end of the rope to two stakes in the wooden boards of the dock. The Mooshkoos chanted, "Oip! Oip! Oip!" while the girls worked, their funny eyes swirling like kaleidoscopes.

"Yikes," Mariana flinched. "They look like my little cousin, Christos, when Brigham's runs out of Cookie Dough."

"They're experiencing an adrenalin rush in anticipation of returning to Blue," Agatha explained, standing over the girls. "It takes a lot out of the Mooshkoos to leave the environment they know and love so well." She rechecked the girls' work to make sure the rope was tight, and said, "Good enough. As they say in your dimension, 'let's prepare for departure.'"

"Isn't there anyone getting off the ship?" Mariana asked, craning her neck toward the passengers huddled in small groups on the foredeck.

Agatha never bothered to look up. "Actually, most prefer to remain on the Land of Blue. As you'll soon find out, it's a very pleasurable place."

Cassie and Mariana glanced at each other warily.

"Don't fret," Agatha said, clearing her throat. "After we've taken care of business, you'll Zipper home. You have my word."

While Agatha entered information on the Surveyor, Cassie counted the twenty-seven passengers she could see on the ship. *Wouldn't everyone want to go home, to the people that love them?* she wondered.

A woman with somber green eyes and a gaunt face, wearing a dark-green hoodie, stood at the stern of the ship, next to a group of men drinking cans of soda. Cassie wondered if the lady was hoping to find a family member, too, or if she planned to stay on the Land of Blue permanently. Her heart pounded in her chest, like it was trying to get out.

Did Dad want to stay for good? No. He wouldn't have left me on purpose.

Cassie bit her lip hard. A group of messy-haired teenage boys laughed and teased each other on the main deck. They shared pieces of candy out of their jacket pockets, and asked each other for more. Cassie did that to Mariana when they bought Swedish fish. One was never enough for Cassie.

No matter how much fun it is on the Land of Blue, I know Dad wants to come home, she thought.

The Constantines neighed loudly, their high-pitched notes skimming across the deep water.

"All right then," Agatha said, clapping her hands together. "Shall we?"

"Hey Aggie!" a male voice called in the dank air. "Wait up!"

Agatha lowered her head in the direction of the opposite mountain. An oily, rail-thin creature with slicked-back hair scaled the grassy, rock-laden path at the mountain's base. He wore ripped blue jeans and a black-and-white-striped shirt, which reminded Cassie of a jailbird costume her dad's friend, Frankie, wore last year to the Knights of Columbus Halloween party. Behind him walked a slim, jet-haired boy, who appeared to be Cassie and Mariana's age. He tripped on his way down the rocky path. The creature rolled his beady eyes with impatience.

Agatha put her hands on her hips and said, "Well, I'll be darned. If it isn't Sal Hawke. How many hundreds of pulses has it been since I've seen you?"

"Hey, don't remind me, eh?" Sal said in a hoarse voice as he leaped with one hand onto the dock. "I got a job and a half ahead of me with this one. It must be payback." Sal playfully slapped the timid boy on the back as he walked the plank on the dock. His long, claw-like fingernails grazed the boy's skin. "Heh, heh, just kidding, kid. You're going to do fine." Sal wheezed laughter.

The boy sort of laughed while he cracked his knuckles.

Sal shimmied up the rope with ease and shouted, "Weeeoooo! What a rush!"

Agatha chuckled. "They always come home."

Cassie, dreamy eyed, gaped in the direction from where the boy and Sal descended.

Agatha snapped her fingers in front of Cassie's face and whipped around sharply toward the hut as Tufa headed toward the water's edge. "I hope you didn't affect my traveler, Tufa, with any of your soporific concoctions."

"A gentle reminder, Agatha, Option's Port belongs to neither me nor you," Tufa replied, wisps of her dark hair blowing in the breeze. "Once you leave these parts, however, you may do as you please."

Agatha turned on her heels. Her black cloak whirled behind her portly frame. "Come now," she said as she put an arm around the handsome, tentative boy. "Let's make acquaintances since we'll be traveling companions."

Mariana extended her hand and said, "Hi, I'm Mariana."

The tanned boy shook her hand and said, "Hi, I'm TJ."

Mariana critiqued the nervous boy under her breath to Cassie, "That is one weak handshake."

He looks like a lost puppy, Cassie thought, extending her hand. "Hi, I'm Cassie. Are you going to find someone on the Land of Blue?"

"Yeah, my older brother. Sal, my Entity, is taking me there." TJ gestured toward the chiding figure almost at the top of the ladder.

Cassie's heart beat rapidly. "My dad's there, too. My Entity, Agatha, is bringing me."

"Well, it's nice to meet you both," TJ said, stuffing his hands in his pocket. "Sal's a little rough, but it'll be okay. I'm not used to hiking mountains or anything, but I made it, right?"

Sal scaled the side of the ship, while TJ tracked his movements in alarm, pinching the rough skin on the back of his upper arms. Cassie sighed. She didn't want to be next to climb the flimsy ladder dangling over the dark water. Cassie's rule was that she didn't go in water when she couldn't see the bottom.

Sal wheezed right before the top. He reminded Cassie of

the old guy at her mom's nursing home job who smoked like fifty packs of cigarettes a week and wore an oxygen tank. "Don't be such a fuddy duddy, boy!" Sal fist-bumped the Mooshkoos who were waiting for him as he reached the top rung of the ladder.

"Oip!" the Mooshkoos cheered, welcoming Sal onto the bustling deck.

Mariana checked in with TJ and Cassie and then threw her shoulders back and stepped up to the ladder, blowing hair out of her face. "I don't know why they don't just make a ramp."

Like an Olympic gymnast about to begin her routine, Mariana inhaled. Her long arms gripped the sides of the braided rope as she stepped onto the first rung and then the second. Her toned legs adeptly pushed up and balanced from rung to rung. Halfway up, she cupped a hand beside her mouth and shouted down to Cassie and TJ, "It's easier if you don't look down!"

The rope ladder swayed from the breeze at first only slightly, but then in longer and longer arcs, until eventually Mariana swung through the air, left and right.

"Ahhhhh!" she hollered.

Cassie stood dumbfounded. She couldn't tell if Mariana was frightened or having the time of her life.

After the ladder straightened out from the subsiding breeze, Mariana took another deep breath, nimbly finishing the climb. She raised an arm in the air at the top like a pro golfer.

"Oip! Oip! Oip!" the Mooshkoos cheered in unison as they helped Mariana over the side. They fussed over her as they welcomed her aboard, taming her flyaway hair and smoothing her rumpled pink sweatshirt.

Mariana leaned over the side of the ship with both hands and yelled, "Did you see that? That was *not* as easy as it looked!"

Cassie puffed air out of her cheeks like a deflated balloon.

"Even the girl beat ya!" Sal jeered. "Let's gooooo! I want to have me some Escape. Heck, I may even have two." He thrust out his scrawny chest as he breathed the moist night air deeply through his beak-like nose. "Ah, it's good to be back!"

TJ pushed the hair out of his eyes as he tentatively placed both feet on the bottom rung of the ladder. The rope wobbled and TJ's knuckles blanched as his legs straightened in fear. He took a moment, bending his thighs slightly, then clambered up the rungs. The ladder wobbled again, whisking TJ to the left.

"Whoahhh," he cried, his eyes as wide as donuts as the ladder hurled him toward *The Enticer's* hull.

Cassie was afraid his eyes would stay stuck like that forever.

"Have you ever done Tai Kwon Do?" Mariana asked, straining her voice from the deck. "Just use your core!"

Cassie picked at the skin on her arm as she watched TJ dangle from the twisted rope ladder. She bet TJ, like herself, had never done Tai Kwon Do in his life.

"Like this?" TJ asked, his face red as he tightened his stomach muscles.

"Nice!" Mariana said, giving TJ a thumbs-up.

His face scarlet, TJ squeezed every muscle in his lean frame as he inched and grunted his way back to face the center of *The Enticer.* Breathless, he climbed the remaining rope.

"Somebody wants to see their brother, eh?" Sal slapped TJ on the back and helped him over the side.

One Mooshkoo in a bandana jumped on TJ's back in celebration while another Mooshkoo in overalls combed his dark hair back into place.

Cassie counted the twenty-six ladder rungs, by twos, with her finger as she stood in line to go next at the end of the dock. Agatha squeezed Cassie's shoulder. "Take your time. This is to see if you have what it takes."

Cassie twitched her toes in her sneakers as she studied the woven pattern in the bottom rung.

Do I have what it takes? she wondered.

58

"We haven't got all night!" Sal demanded.

Cassie grasped the rope ladder tightly with both hands. She held it steady and raised her foot past the first rung. She pressed it down onto the second rung, and pulled her body up.

It is more crucial than ever that things are in order.

Cassie's entire body clenched as she tried to find stability on the flimsy rope. She stepped up onto the fourth rung, then the sixth.

It has to be done perfectly, or your dad won't come back.

The decrepit rope shook.

Did we tie the rope tight enough? What if I fall? She wondered.

Cassie's heart beat like a snare drum. She looked down and yelped at the sight of the black water below. The Constantines stomped their hoofs, the size of cinderblocks, creating agitated waves.

"I told you not to look down!" Mariana said, grabbing her head with both hands.

"Shut up," Cassie said, under her breath. The skin on the top of her palms burned against the knotted rope. *Everything's easier for you, Mariana. I could climb faster if I didn't have to stay on the even-numbered ropes. You don't understand.*

Cassie clutched the rope and stopped climbing for a moment. She closed her eyes and felt the heat of tears rushing up through her body, toward her face.

Do it the way you need to, in perfect order. If you step on an odd-numbered rung, you could lose your chance to bring your father home. Where would that leave you?

Cassie clenched her jaw and climbed again. She grunted over the odd-numbered rungs. When she reached the fourteenth, her arms shook visibly, causing the rope to spin her like a top.

"Ugh! Just step on each one! It doesn't matter if it's odd or even!" Mariana pleaded.

The navy-blue Mooshkoos sprung up and down like coils, enjoying the drama as they watched Cassie climb.

I told you, you don't understand. Cassie gritted her teeth. *It always matters.*

Then, without warning, she heard another voice.

But what if it didn't?

Cassie froze. *Who was that?*

Cassie squeezed her eyes shut as she tried to drown out the noise from the stampede of the Constantines, the chatter of the Mooshkoos, and the murmuring conversations from the passengers on *The Enticer* as they waited impatiently to depart.

I have to do it the way Agatha tells me, she thought.

Waves crashed against the ship.

Why can't things be easier for me?

She stretched her right leg up to the sixteenth rung and accidentally skimmed the fifteenth with a graze of her sneaker. "You stupid hand-me-down!" she growled viciously toward her shoe.

Then she panicked. Cassie knew she had to keep going, but her sneaker touched an odd rung. Everything was messed up now.

"Come on!" passengers yelled down from the main deck.

Cassie scolded herself, the way Mom scolded her when she had to go to the bathroom every time they went somewhere. *What if I don't get to Dad in time? What will happen to him?*

"You've got this!" Mariana shouted.

"Yeah! If I can do it, you can!" TJ said as his hands gripped the side of the ship.

You are proving yourself greatly. What if we didn't count that one? After all, this isn't a regular set of stairs.

Agatha's voice poured over Cassie like thick maple syrup over pancakes.

Yes! It doesn't have to count.

"Oip!!" A Mooshkoo pointed excitedly to a dark bottle he held in his rubbery hands.

"Oip Oip!" Another Mooshkoo, wearing a bonnet, chirped as he pointed to another Mooshkoo wearing a sports cap, who handed out neon, frozen, pink-colored drinks resembling pink-slush lemonade. A tray was fastened around his waist from a pair of suspenders, making him look like a hot-dog vendor from Fenway Park. The cute Mooshkoo held up a drink in Cassie's direction, beckoning her to come aboard.

"See! They're waiting for you!" Mariana screeched. "I'm not having one of those awesome-looking slushes they're handing out—*for free*—until you get up here!"

They're waiting for me. My father is waiting for me.

A surge of energy rushed through Cassie's veins. She willed herself to step up and over every other rung as she reached the twenty-fourth, then the twenty-sixth rung, where a swarm of Mooshkoos advanced like bees to help her onto the ship. Cassie climbed over, and as soon as her feet touched the solid floor of the ship, the Mooshkoos gave her cheers and hugs like it was her birthday. Cassie almost felt the tears rush back up toward her face.

I didn't think I'd make it.

"I don't get you," Mariana said as she moved out of the way of a few Mooshkoos play-wrestling each other in celebration, because now they could officially set sail. "You sure do make things harder for yourself."

Cassie leaned against the railing, where a large man wearing a leather jacket, jeans, and workboots and a chubby, blond-haired woman with a small child on her lap sat on a bench a few feet away, twitching their shoulders and biting their nails as they waited to set sail.

Behind her, in the stern of the ship, a group of unshaven, burly guys in jeans and white T-shirts hooted as they played cards at a small table with two Mooshkoos. The rough-looking guys eyed their opponents closely, anticipating the others' moves. Cassie noticed the red deck of cards in the middle of the table and pulled at her lip. Her dad and his buddies used to play poker with a red deck, at the apartment until late into the night.

Dad wants to come home. No matter how fun it is here.

Cassie thought she could make things *more* fun at home. Her dad liked to play Yahtzee, so she would make sure they played every night. That's all there was to it. She leaned back into the railing.

A Mooshkoo in a jumpsuit and straw hat shuffled over with three ambulance-red drinks for Cassie, Mariana, and TJ. He handed them the slushy drinks in large mugs. He saluted them, extending a finger out from the tip of his nose like Pinocchio's and cheeped, "Oip!"

"Uh, oip," TJ repeated, and returned the salute.

"The drinks are called oip?" Mariana asked, wrinkling her nose.

"The drinks are called 'bahd'," Sal interjected, sliding in and messing up the hat on top of the Mooshkoo's head.

"Bot?" TJ asked, straining to hear above the noise of all the activity on deck.

"No. 'Bahd.' B-A-D. It's a popular drink on the Land of Blue." Sal grabbed a dark brown bottle from the Mooshkoo's tray and showed the label to the kids. The white label read: "Bad, pronounced 'Bahd'.'"

Sal took a swig. "Ahhh, now that's good Bad. Haven't had me some of this since I was a young'un. Us Entities, we gravitate toward a good drink of Escape."

"What's the difference?" TJ asked, leaning against the railing next to Cassie.

"Bad you drink for the taste. That's why kids like it. They go for what tastes good. Escape, well, that's an acquired taste, and a bit of a means to an end."

"Oip," a Mooshkoo nodded in agreement. Sal high-fived the Mooshkoo's small hand.

"How could you tell what that meant? Every word they say is oip," Mariana scoffed as she threw her hands in the air.

"Mooshkoo language isn't that hard, actually," Sal said, elbowing the Mooshkoo's skinny arm before he plopped down on the metal bench seating that ran under the masts in the center of the ship. He slapped the seat for the kids to sit down. "It's all in the tone. Check it out."

Cassie and TJ crowded around Sal on the bench.

The Mooshkoo smiled, yellow teeth like corn niblets protruding out of his mouth. On command, it pointed to the bottle of Bad, like he was giving them a test. "Oooooooip."

"See?" Sal nodded coolly. "You got it?"

"Yeah, I kind of get it now." TJ nodded his head up and down like Sal.

"Okaaayyy," Mariana said, wiping off a section of the bench before she sat down.

"Just go with it." Sal rolled his eyes.

"I kind of get it," Cassie said, sitting on her hands. "His tone meant that Bad is awesome."

Sal flicked Cassie on the arm. "You're going to do great, kid!"

Across from them, a small child, sitting with his parents on the bench under the railing, wailed. "Me want some! Me want Bad!"

Cassie and TJ both got up and offered the boy some of their Bad as the Mooshkoo in the bonnet scurried over with two Bads for the little boy in order to prevent a full-blown tantrum. She handed the parents two dark bottles of Escape for their troubles. The parents gulped them down in relief.

Cassie, TJ, and Mariana slurped their Bads as they stood next to each other by the railing, looking out and down at Agatha, who still stood on the dock. She untied the rope from the stakes, causing the ladder to fall away from the dock and flap against the side of the ship.

"How's she going to get up here?" TJ asked, puzzled.

Suddenly, Agatha extended both arms up toward the ship, and to the kids' surprise, they kept going. Her arms stretched out about forty feet, like a pair of antennas, until her hands latched onto the railing. She raised herself up and over the side of the ship, onto the deck, as nimbly as if she were hopping over a post-and-rail fence. A Mooshkoo sporting a pair of fisherman's work boots high-fived Agatha and fastidiously rolled up the ladder, stowing it neatly in a nearby container.

"I'm getting too old for these things," Agatha said devilishly as she patted down her windblown red hair.

Cassie, Mariana, and TJ stood dumbfounded, not even feeling the puck that slapped against their heels as two masked Mooshkoos played an intense game of knee hockey.

Agatha patted Cassie on the head like a beloved pet and whispered, "Well done."

Cassie's cheeks flushed as she drank her glowing red Bad.

Mariana lightly elbowed TJ before slurping from her generous mug of Bad and asked, "Can Sal do that?"

"I've taught Sal Hawke everything he knows," Agatha said, leaning into Cassie, Mariana, and TJ as Sal bent down and played knee hockey with the Mooshkoos. "He only climbed the rope because he's rusty. Here, have some Blobs," Agatha tossed them brightly colored candy pieces out of her cloak pocket.

Mariana popped one in her mouth, her face gradually turning lime green.

"Whoa," TJ said, starting to laugh. He tried a mustard-yellow Blob, rolling it around and around in his mouth.

"You're yellow!" Cassie exclaimed. "I want to try!" She stuffed a Blob in her mouth, noticing the texture was somewhere between a hard candy and a jelly bean. She felt a rush of cold air rise to her cheeks, like walking outside on a winter's day, when Mariana burst out laughing.

"You're purple!" TJ cried, clutching his stomach in laughter. "Let's see what other colors we can turn!"

"Ain't it fun?" Agatha squealed, leaving them to enjoy. "And there's a lot more where that came from."

"Oip!" the Mooshkoo in charge called from high atop one of the masts.

TJ and Mariana noticed the standing passengers rushing to

find seating and scrambled to empty chairs and unoccupied bench seats on the main deck. Bads in hand, they found a section of seating for three under the masts and plunked down on the hard bench.

Cassie remained standing for a few moments, looking over at the mountain and sipping from the mug of Bad that was way bigger than the Slush-Puppy size her mother allowed her from the 7-11 back in Boston. Something caught Cassie's eye back on shore. She realized it was Tufa standing down at the water's edge, waving up at her. Cassie's stomach knotted as she waved back.

Cassie and Tufa's connection severed as Agatha, in a booming voice, shouted at the Constantines, "Let's get this show on the road!" The mammoth beasts flapped their shiny wings and thrust their tree-trunk-sized legs through the choppy waters. *The Enticer* began to lift slightly, moving away from Option's Port.

Agatha cupped the sides of her mouth and called sweetly over the railing to Tufa, "Take care, my noble friend! I'm sorry there wasn't more time!"

Cassie gripped the railing with one hand as they drifted away, holding her mug of Bad in the other.

"Take care yourself, my old friend," Tufa answered graciously. "When it comes to fate, there is always time." She called to Cassie, her peaceful voice echoing across the tumultuous water. "Remember, child: we always have a choice."

Agatha locked eyes with Tufa as the passengers and creatures cheered at the rise of *The Enticer* off the water. Cassie quickly scrambled to join TJ and Mariana under the masts.

Agatha jerked her arm, causing a lightning bolt to erupt over the night. "Onward! The Land of Blue awaits!"

CHAPTER
EIGHT

"This is kinda creepy," Mariana said to Cassie, pulling her hands inside the sleeves of her sweatshirt to get warm. "I can't see those moons anymore and there isn't even a star in the sky."

They had traveled for what felt like hours during the late night on the open sea under a chilly, dark canopy. The restless Mooshkoos alternated between cleaning the deck floors, littered with empty cans, Escape bottles and Blob wrappers, and sitting down to drink what was left of their mugs of Bad. It amounted to more sitting than doing. Previously the ship bustled with activity, but now most of the passengers were settled down in the bow, nodding off in their seats, because *The Enticer* had run out of Bad and Blobs. The small child who had consumed two entire Bads by himself lay passed out in his mother's arms.

Cassie stood from where they were sitting and crossed the few feet over to the railing, to see if they were at all close to land. All she could see were dark, scaly sea monsters swimming alongside *The Enticer*, just below the murky surface. *Mariana's right, everything is creepy.*

Cassie's thoughts drifted to the warmth of Tufa's hut, when an abrupt, loud *whack* snapped her out of it. She turned to see a bearded man in a red-and-white flannel shirt slap his hand on the card table set up near the back of the ship and stand up to claim his winnings. A muscularly built, scruffy-faced Entity next to the bearded guy raised his hands in victory. Three Mooshkoos surrounded the winner, like dogs waiting to be fed. The bearded man grabbed a dark bottle of Escape for himself, hidden in a cooler under the table, and handed additional bottles to the Mooshkoos in celebration.

As they chanted songs together next to a fluorescent light rigged to the side of the table, Cassie wondered how they didn't notice the spooky creatures that were now raising their slimy heads over the railing.

They must be used to it, she thought. Sitting down on the bench under the railing, occasionally glancing skittishly behind her, Cassie didn't think she could ever get used to the slimy, slithering monsters.

"Don't mind the Trespassers, kid," the muscular Entity said, jumping up to sit on the rail behind the card table. "They're just looking for attention."

TJ, who finished learning how to tie a rope knot from Sal on the quarterdeck, brought it down to show Cassie, resting his forearms on the railing as he noticed the Trespassers for the first time. "Has your dad been away long?" he asked, plopping down on the seat next to her, trying to distract himself from the invasive creatures.

"It feels like it," Cassie said, keeping her eyes on a dented plank in the deck as the sails whipped in the wind, making snapping noises. She felt queasy as the Constantines thrust through the water with their tree-trunk legs and skimmed the surface with their wings. The bobbing motion created forceful waves that churned the ship forward.

"My family and I talked about it at home, Cassie," Mariana said from the bench under the masts, as she put her hands on her knees. "Not behind your back or anything, just when we were having dinner one night. Anyway, I was saying that maybe your dad needed a break from the stresses of life. Maybe he secretly wanted to travel the world. It's not that strange. My uncle backpacked through Europe after he graduated college."

"Did he have kids?" Cassie shot back.

The sea monsters slithered up over the side of the boat and leered at Cassie. Then they slid back down into the secretive water.

"Well, no," Mariana conceded, tilting her head.

"Well, you can't compare them," Cassie replied smugly.

TJ lazily clapped his hands together, his brow furrowed. "My brother, Eric, left without letting me know either. One day we were playing video games in our den and then the next . . . "

TJ ran his hand through his hair. "I don't think my parents even noticed."

Cassie tucked her hair behind her ear while she listened to TJ.

"Eric pretty much took care of me, making supper and stuff. It's hard not having him around," TJ said, rubbing his forehead.

A stone's throw away, a handful of Mooshkoos spotted one single Blob under the card table, and began to wrestle for it. Mariana, TJ, and Cassie turned their attention to watch the Mooshkoo in a do-rag win the match, knock over the card table, and pop the Blob into his wide mouth. He chewed obnoxiously until his face turned purple.

"Oip! Oip!" Three Mooshkoos banged on the table in protest until the Mooshkoo in charge slid down one of the masts like a firefighter on a fire pole.

Waddling over with a huff and a puff, he pointed at the other passengers on the bow, chirping, "Oip, oip, oip, oip," in a scolding manner.

"That must mean, 'shut up'," Mariana said. "Anyway, why does your teenage brother have to take care of you? Where are your parents?"

"Oh, they're never home," TJ responded, as the Mooshkoos shamefully waddled by and returned to their duties. "They own a liquor store and work twenty-four seven. Eric and I fend for ourselves."

Mariana wrinkled her nose. "Don't your parents have to check what you want for dinner and remind you to do your homework?"

"No, they don't do that," TJ said, scratching his arm.

"But that's awful! You must feel so alone every day after school since no one's there. That must be the worst feeling in the world!" Mariana cried, shimmying to the edge of the bench.

Cassie covered her eyes with her hand. *I feel so bad for TJ. He probably won't be friends with us now.*

Mariana winced as she stood up and shuffled over to sit down next to Cassie. "I did it again, didn't I?" She swatted at a Trespasser nearing her shoulder and said, "Shoo!"

"It's all right," TJ said, as he pretended to tie his already-laced black high top sneaker. "I don't have the kind of family that does pizza-and-movie nights."

"Neither does Cassie!" Mariana reached across Cassie and nudged TJ's arm. "You know what? If you went to Franklin Park Middle, I could totally see the three of us hanging out. We don't fit in with the popular kids either. Right, Cass?"

Cassie's face grew hot.

Mariana continued rambling, "She cares what other people think way more than I do, but my point is that it gives us something in common. Hey! Maybe *not* being popular is the new popular!"

TJ laughed as a trickle of pink Bad dribbled down his chin.

"Well, I'm glad we have stuff in common, and that I got to meet both of you."

Cassie relaxed her shoulders and extended her legs out from the bench.

Three Mooshkoos rushed past, jumping over her feet. They headed in the direction of a little girl with high pigtails and a quivering bottom lip, who dropped her pacifier two yards away on the main deck. Her mother tried desperately to clean off the pacifier that had fallen in a sludge of Escape.

When they reached the screaming child, the Mooshkoo in dreadlocks banged a bongo drum while another Mooshkoo strummed a ukulele he retrieved from a stowaway container. The third Mooshkoo, dressed in a blond wig and boa wrap, sauntered down from the quarterdeck, singing a silly "oipy" song.

The girl's mother mouthed "Thank you," since the performance delighted the previously red-eyed child. The dreadlocked Mooshkoo called out, "Oip!" and Sal, on cue, threw him a bottle of Escape from the quarterdeck. The Mooshkoo sweetly handed the saggy-skinned mother the bottle so she could relax.

Meanwhile, on the railing behind the card table, the bearded Entity spit sunflower seeds into the water for the Trespassers. One scaly Trespasser, long and slimy like a bass fish and an alligator all in one, leaped out of the sea. It caught the seeds in its wide mouth as water splashed over Cassie, Mariana, and TJ.

Immediately, an adorable Mooshkoo, with only one ear, waddled to the stowaway container under the masts and pulled out three waterproof ponchos.

They take care of everyone here! Cassie thought.

As she put on her poncho, Trespassers kept peeking their frightening heads up over the railing. Awful thoughts crossed Cassie's mind as one creature darted behind her ear and hissed, *What if your dad doesn't want to go home with you?*

TJ inched to the edge of his seat as he tried to avoid the

Trespassers slithering in his direction.

"This is definitely not your family whale-watching trip," Mariana commented as she observed a group of men and women who appeared to have just blown in with the wind. They landed on the quarterdeck, surrounding Sal as he drank from a flask. *The Enticer* rose and fell vigorously on the chaotic waves.

"For the nausea!" Sal toasted the flask as he held on to the newcomers. The group laughed as the turbulent seas jolted *The Enticer* forward, and Sal took his leave. He tottered over to the edge of the deck and plunked his rail thin frame down next to TJ.

"Maybe we should get some of that," TJ said, nodding his head toward Sal's flask.

Sal shook his head. "You don't want none of this at your age. Burn your throat like striking a match. Stick to the Bad. They'll be plenty of time for Escape. It's good ya got me to tell ya everything you need to know, eh?"

Sal whistled and a Mooshkoo immediately waddled over, providing one of the few Blobs left—in a business-envelope yellow— to ease TJ's symptoms.

"Who are those people? They weren't on the ship when we got here," TJ said as he raised his head, his skin envelope-yellow.

"Second timers. Zippered directly. No need to bother with Option's Port after the first time on Blue. Don't worry, kid. Won't be much longer. We've already entered Blue territory." Sal slapped him on the back before getting up to rejoin the others on the upper deck.

Cassie stared up at the raging masts as Mariana stood and made her way over to the card table, using the railing to steady herself, to ask one of the Mooshkoos for a glass of water. Suddenly, Cassie heard in her mind, *I hope I don't throw up in front of them. They seem nice. I hope I see Eric right away. Will he be happy to see me?*

Cassie leveled her gaze and turned to TJ, sitting a few feet away on the bench. He locked eyes with her and then quickly looked away, as if he knew.

"Sorry, I . . . I didn't mean to share," he said, listening to a group of passengers who heard they were in Blue territory and began singing at the bow of the ship.

"It's okay," Cassie said, sitting on her hands. Her heart hurt for TJ. She thought about what his home must be like, not having his parents around. Even with her father gone, Cassie had her mother and grandparents there, making sure she ate three meals a day. She gnawed at her fingernail.

TJ must be lonelier than me. I hope he has a dog to keep him company while his parents are working. Her worry thoughts returned to her father. *Who is taking care of him while he's on the Land of Blue?*

Cassie glanced back at TJ. If she picked up his thoughts, did he pick up hers?

She bit the side of her lip. "Um, did you get one of mine?" she asked.

"I think so," TJ said, absently picking up a few Blob wrappers on the deck floor.

Trespassers, now in packs as if expecting food, glared at Cassie and TJ.

"Lighten up!" Sal ordered as he returned and sat back down beside TJ. "You gotta learn how to enjoy the ride! Hey," he said, dramatically changing his tone to one of concern. "Lots of fun to be had on the Land of Blue. What's your fancy?"

TJ shrugged. "I like video games. And fried dough. Eric used to make it homemade, right from the stove."

"It's a wonder you're so thin, eh?" Sal said, elbowing TJ in the ribs. "Plenty of Stimulators on Blue, and lots of fried dough, but on Blue we call it Yum. Just wait 'til you see the food in the Pits and the Blobs in the Zebbies! I told ya, the Land of Blue knows what everyone likes, even before they know it themselves!"

"That does sound good," TJ said, scratching his head. "Maybe that's why Eric hasn't come home. Maybe it's all the fun on the Land of Blue, and the fried—I mean, the Yum."

"Oh, we'll get you lots of Yum and you can play tons of Stimulators, don't you worry. I know this ain't easy for ya, but you heeded the call of an Entity, and for that you'll be rewarded. Consider me your savior, kid." Sal ruffled TJ's hair.

TJ managed a smile, though Cassie thought he still looked queasy. The choppy, chaotic waves made it hard to enjoy the ride, and now the dark skies began to clap with thunder.

"We may need to ask the Mooshkoos for barf bags instead of ponchos," Mariana said, coming back over empty handed.

Cassie felt so squeamish, she couldn't lift her head. The combination of the rough seas and the annoying Trespassers was relentless.

Agatha, who had been conversing with the Mooshkoo in charge in the Captain's Quarters, strode down the shellacked wooden steps toward Cassie, a determined look on her face.

She extended her antenna-like arm out over the railing of the ship. "Enough!"

Instantly, the creatures sunk back into the sea. Cassie relaxed her shoulders while TJ's neck fell back in relief.

"It can become difficult in these parts of Blue," Agatha explained, gathering her cloak and positioning herself between Cassie and TJ, causing Mariana to have to stand up and go back to the other seating under the masts. "Perhaps I should have warned you about the intrusiveness of the Trespassers, and also of the outside thoughts you may have been able to pick up."

Cassie and TJ glanced at one another apprehensively.

"Yes, I should have known, with your sensitivities. How skilled you both are. Sal filled me in over a tall mug of Escape." Agatha winked at TJ. "It's the Mind Mail communication system on Blue. Though you have to be within range to hear someone's thoughts," Agatha used her hands to measure approximately three feet on either side of Cassie. "And you have to share the same frequency to be heard. At any rate, the Trespassers are done for the night. You should feel better now."

They did.

Agatha patted both their knees and stood up, striding over to another section of passengers who weren't feeling well, while Mariana returned to the bench and sat between Cassie and TJ.

"She's good," TJ said, allowing the droplets of water sprayed up from the steady movement of the ship to fall on his forehead like rain.

Cassie grinned and straightened her spine as the sails rippled overhead, under the night sky. She welcomed the quiet in her mind as she began to close her eyes. She could hear Mariana and TJ debate which Bad flavor they preferred—grape or orange—though as Cassie's eyelids grew heavy, their voices seemed more and more distant.

As *The Enticer* lulled on the waves, Cassie's mind wandered back to Tufa's hut and the delicious taste of Kamalu. Dreamily longing for another cup, Cassie felt the presence of something on her left side, in the space between her and Mariana. She groggily put her hand in the air, like shooing away a fly in slow motion. *Was there something there?* Through her nearly-closed eyes, she saw nothing except a blurry image of the back of Mariana's bushy brown hair as she chatted with TJ.

Cassie waved her arm again in the open space. *A ripple. There was a ripple.* A strange thought occurred to Cassie, that if she wanted to, she could have put her hand through it and reach through to the other side—to another world that vibrated right next to the one she was in. *If she wanted to.*

Her eyelids fluttered. She saw Agatha watching her from a few feet away.

Stay focused. Don't allow for distractions.

The Constantines startled Cassie as they raised their gigantic heads high above the side of the ship and flapped their wings.

The Enticer suddenly lurched forward and flew across the

water at rocket speed. The launch pulled Cassie out of her relaxing trance and made her dizzy with fear. The ripple was gone.

"What just happened?" TJ shouted, as high-speed winds whipped against his face. He gripped the bench underneath. "I feel like I can't breathe anymore."

Mariana clutched the railing behind her with one hand and yelled back, "Same here!"

"Here, put these on," Agatha said calmly as she sauntered over and handed each of them small masks, resembling oxygen masks on an airplane. "These will help you adjust to the change in Vibration."

Agatha distributed additional masks to dozens of Mooshkoos who rushed to her side to receive the paraphernalia.

Cassie, Mariana, and TJ cupped the masks to their faces as *The Enticer* powered forward like lightning. The Mooshkoos scurried about the deck, hanging on to the railing and to one another as they handed out masks to the other passengers. Inhaling, Cassie felt the dizzy sensation subside.

Mariana perked up, yelling through her mask, "Well, those came in handy!"

His head down, TJ noticed a yellow half-bitten Blob on one of the planks. A little boy sitting across from them had apparently dropped the Blob when the ship shifted into high-speed. The boy fought back tears. Reaching over with one arm, as he steadied himself with the other hand on the bench, TJ returned the Blob to the little boy, who looked as if TJ had just rescued his dog.

The ship slowed and came to a stop.

The chatter of the passengers increased as they all began to take off their masks.

Cassie relaxed her grip on the bench. "That was nice of you, to help that boy," she said to TJ.

"I'd have wanted someone to do that for me," TJ shrugged.

Mariana uncrossed her legs and asked, "You're, like, one of the nicest boys ever. The boys in our school would totally bully you, huh Cassie?"

TJ's face turned maroon. "I'm not that nice."

Cassie quickly whispered, "Don't mind her. My mom says she doesn't have a filter."

As the Mooshkoos retrieved everyone's masks and stuffed them in the stowaway containers around the ship, Agatha hoisted herself up on one of the unoccupied folding chairs in the middle of the deck, cupping her hands to her mouth, and instructed, "Hang on everyone! This is where the real fun begins! We descend to the Land of Blue!"

Not a moment later and *bam!*, the sea dropped, almost right out from under them, causing Cassie to wonder what would have happened to Christopher Columbus had the Earth not been round. *The Enticer* nose-dived like an airplane, yet remained on top of the slanted sea like it was hooked on a train track that ran underneath the surface of the water.

"Yeee haaaa!" Sal hollered from the upper deck as his greasy hair flew straight back off his face.

"Aaaaaaaaaaa!" the Mooshkoos screamed in unison, making the same sound kids make when they're on a roller coaster having the time of their lives.

Mariana and Cassie clasped hands, their eyes squeezed shut, as they continued to fall. They were headed somewhere deep.

Then, without warning, they leveled off.

The ship slowed to a cruising rate, and Cassie opened her eyes. Unable to move just yet, she stared at a damp plank. Mariana slowly let go of Cassie's hand, carefully unfolding one finger at a time. They both lifted their heads and checked on TJ, who gradually let go of the tight grip he had on the seat.

The air was different. Raw, like on a foggy night.

They each sat up fully, discovering the sky had changed to a dusky, rolling cloud-cover like splotches of gray-blue tie-dye in the evening sky. Cassie felt they were all a long way from home.

"Ah! Blue!" Agatha said, breathing in the musty, basement-like air and stretching her arms wide. Cassie realized Agatha hadn't needed a mask.

Like kids with mosquito bites, dozens of Mooshkoos fidgeted on the main deck.

"Oip! Oip! Oip!" a Mooshkoo wearing a cowboy hat and boots said, as he trampled over the others to the side of the ship and pointed to a large, open pier.

Another navy-blue Mooshkoo, his eyes red and wild at the sight of the pier, clambered over a Mooshkoo in front of him sporting a navy-blue Land of Blue sweatshirt, eager to get to the front of the line that now formed at the bow of *The Enticer*.

"Land of Blue! Ho!" Sal belted out as he stood recklessly atop the railing of the bow, holding a bottle of Escape in each hand.

"Easy boys, we're just about there," Agatha called to the Mooshkoos and other Entities on board who were scrambling to the railing. She bent over and said with a wink to the mother of the boy who dropped the Blob during the wild ride, "Boys will be boys."

The mother nodded in understanding and chugged a large swill of Escape.

"Geesh, does it ever get bright around these parts?" Mariana asked curiously as she assessed the murky blue sky. "I'd just like to see one star!"

"Don't cha know night time is the right time?" Sal said, dancing across the railing behind them. He let out a loud burp, lost his balance, and dropped one of the bottles of Escape. It crashed into several large pieces of brown glass on the deck. "Party time!" he said, jumping down and blowing rings of smoke out of his mouth that morphed into shapes of video games and fried dough. "I promised, right?" he said, elbowing TJ in the ribs.

Sal didn't seem concerned with the mess, because a Mooshkoo-in-Training—according to the badge pinned to his chest—waddled over with a whisk broom and dustpan to clean the deck while another group of Mooshkoos teased him from their places in line.

TJ gently poked Cassie in the arm and pointed to Sal making shapes out of smoke, "He's pretty cool, huh?"

I wonder if he'd get lung cancer from that, Cassie thought.

The Constantines slowed to a paddle. Cassie briskly rubbed her hands together in the chilly air as they approached land. She stood and saw one-story shops and little brick buildings lined up tightly against each other. Street lanterns speckled the cobblestone streets. Buildings were strung with little blue fluorescent lights. Hordes of people bustled in and out of the many shops and stores in the town square, past the pier, food and drink in hand.

In the distance, behind the cobblestone streets stood a mammoth gray wall that ran as far to the left and right as Cassie could see. Made of stone, it reminded her of the Great Wall of China. The entire atmosphere was gray, just how it looks on a rainy, foggy evening.

The Trespassers swam alongside the boat as it pulled into port. Glaring up at Cassie, their slimy, film-covered eyes darted this way and that as they skittishly stayed on the lookout for Agatha. *Be careful what you wish for,* they hissed inside her mind as she stepped into line with Mariana and TJ. Agatha, sensing the Trespassers presence behind her as she organized the bottlenecked line, shooed them away.

Dozens of happy-faced Mooshkoos on the pier awaited *The Enticer's* arrival as they worked together finishing their chores. They mopped, put faucets on wooden barrels, and sampled the contents to be sure the drinks tasted just right, and screwed light bulbs into the street lamps on the welcoming dock.

Passengers on board grew impatient as they pushed and shoved to get to the front of the line to disembark. Cassie tried to ignore them, stepping out of the way every time she felt a push against her back. She stood on her tiptoes to get another look at the Land of Blue as they inched toward the pier. Dimly lit side streets led away from the busy town on both sides to somewhere she couldn't see.

"All you can drink and eat!" someone yelled from the noisy town square. Covered tarps and vendor carts draped in blue lights filled the streets with candy, pizza, fried foods, and sweet treats.

It's like a carnival! Cassie thought.

Bump!

"*The Enticer* has arrived!" boomed a voice from the pier.

"Finally!" yelled a woman from the back of the line. "I'm ready for a drink!"

"Me too," Mariana said to Cassie and TJ. "The air is so smoggy here."

The crowd gathered on the pier to greet the new passengers quieted. One of the street lamps shone down on the dock, creating a spotlight. On cue, they parted. Two gray-blue monkeys, one big and one small in stature, wearing bandanas around their heads, swaggered onto the dock. They flanked a blond elf with pork-chop-shaped sideburns and two enormous buckteeth. Cassie thought his buckteeth made him look like a chipmunk.

The elf marched his little black-shoed feet over to a high-backed chair positioned at the end of the pier, near *The Enticer's* exit ramp. He scrambled into the chair and signaled to Agatha with a nod of his fairly large head. Agatha was tallying the number of people in line, but stopped when she received the signal. She whistled with two fingers in her mouth and a do-ragged Mooshkoo immediately appeared by her side.

"Kurt has arrived," Agatha announced to the impatient passengers in line. "Now we're ready." The Mooshkoo at her side opened the door to the exit ramp and everyone—Mooshkoos, passengers, and Entities—Cassie, TJ, and Mariana in the middle of the line—barreled into Blue.

CHAPTER
NINE

"Look, TJ! There's the Yum you wanted!" Mariana shouted, pointing from the new line formed in front of Kurt's platform area on the well-lit pier before Cassie could ask Agatha why Kurt was important.

Mariana stood on her toes and pulled the drawstring of her sweatshirt tighter around the collar, reading the neon signs that read "Sweet Yum and Frozen Bad Here!" hanging outside many of the buildings. Cassie, TJ, and Mariana watched outrageously dressed vendors sporting towering, jester-styled hats, just beyond the fancy, black iron Welcoming Gate. Entities, with their black shoes, and odd, yet endearing faces, sauntered back and forth on the pier as signs flashed behind them: Join Us in the Zebbies and the Pits.

The scene reminded Cassie of the city festival she'd gone to one summer with her parents. The main difference was that the air here was so foggy and dense. It reminded Cassie of the gray clumps of dust when you empty the vacuum cleaner.

"Cassie already has her dad's nice navy-blue sweatshirt on, would you like one Mariana, so you fit in?" Agatha asked, as a vendor wheeled by a rolling coat hanger with dozens of Land of Blue sweatshirts.

"Hmm, I'm more of a pink girl. Thanks, though," Mariana replied, coughing as she pulled her pink sweatshirt a little tighter.

"I know TJ here will want one of those," Sal remarked, as the vendor stopped. He yanked a few pewter coins out of his pocket and handed them to the vendor who accepted the payment, and saluted Sal as he extended his finger from the end of his nose.

"That's cool," TJ said as he checked out the white Land-of-Blue lettering and pulled the sweatshirt over his head. He coughed as well, adding, "The air is heavy here, huh?"

"What's the holdup?" The scruffy-looking card player in the white T-shirt bellowed from the back of the line that swerved along the pier. "I gotta get me some Escape!"

"Easy, fella," Sal said coolly, as he looked over his shoulder. "Once you pass Kurt's inspection, you'll be in."

Agatha huddled Cassie, TJ, and Mariana in line and said, "And once you pass through, you're free to roam about the Midst, where you can enjoy as much Yum, Blobs, and Bad as you prefer."

TJ eyed a sign that read: Beef Blobs. "I might start with those!" he said in a raspy voice. "Then I can have Yum for dessert!" He smacked his lips at the sight of all the food and drink offered in the busy square.

"Beef Blobs? I don't know about that," Mariana said, curling her nose, "although you'd get your protein. Personally, I'm going for the Frozen Bad."

"I'm going to have Frozen Bad too!" TJ said, high-fiving Mariana in line.

"Agatha," Cassie said, breathing into her hands for warmth. "Does my dad know I'm here yet?"

Agatha strained her neck above the crowds toward Kurt's platform as she answered, "We're going to see your father, dear, but first, as any good caretaker never fails to neglect, you must eat. Without proper nutrition, well, I don't know if you'd be up to all the help I'm going to require from you."

I wonder what I have to do? Cassie thought.

"Excuse me, everyone, make way, make way," Kurt said irritably as he marched his little black shoes over to Agatha. Up close, Cassie read the gold Energy Inspector badge pinned to his black buttoned-down shirt that was open to reveal a leopard-skin T-shirt underneath. He whispered in Agatha's ear.

Cassie scraped her lip with her bottom teeth as she waited.

Kurt pitter-pattered back to the platform, his dirty blond mullet flowing over his shirt. Agatha squeezed Cassie's shoulders and said, "You must understand I have work to do. I need to count on you so I have time to tend to my other duties as well. I'm sure with your understanding nature, though, you will."

"Oip, oip, oip, oip," the do-ragged Mooshkoo waddled over and grumbled to Agatha. He pointed to a few difficult passengers in the back of the line who were demanding extra Escapes while they waited.

"I definitely understand that oip," Mariana said, observing the Mooshkoos. "They're complaining."

"Whaddya know, you're catching on," Sal remarked, picking his teeth with a toothpick.

Agatha bent down to the level of the disgruntled Mooshkoo. "Let them know that their impatient Vibrations only assist them in passing inspection more quickly."

Sal chuckled as he stood beside the line. "Some people just don't get it, eh, Aggie?"

The little Mooshkoo chirped "Oip! oip! oip!" and scurried

back to the frustrated passengers.

Cassie gnawed on her finger while she asked Agatha, "What is your job exactly?" But before her Entity could respond, a young, tired woman in a stained shirt, holding the hand of a weary-eyed, pig-tailed girl, stepped out of the line. She asked Agatha where they might be able to freshen up before they reached inspection. She seemed self-conscious about her appearance as she fidgeted with the hem of her shirt.

"Oh, come as you are!" Agatha said, as she embraced the tired mother in a hug. "The Land of Blue accepts all creatures, in any condition. There's no judgment here!"

Some other women in line, with their hair strewn about and puffy bags under their eyes, sighed in relief. The line inched forward toward the platform where Kurt and his bodyguards inspected each passenger.

"Uh oh," Sal said as he strained his neck toward the front of the line.

The crowd murmured and moved aside as the pair of muscular gray monkeys, who Agatha referred to later as Big and Small, trudged down from the inspection platform back up the ramp and onto *The Enticer*, gripping the arms of a bloated man with a ponytail. Cassie didn't know anything about him, but she knew he was a passenger on the ship with them because she recalled seeing him onboard.

"I'm sorry!" the guy cried. "I was only asking questions to educate myself. I didn't say I was going to make a different ch—"

"Hey! Keep your mouth shut," Big ordered, squeezing his arm harder as they forced him to the bow of the ship, where they instructed him to sit so everyone could watch. Then they tied him up with rope stashed under the benches.

The crowd stared in fascination as the man hung his head. Big and Small, in their black bandanas, left the man alone and headed back toward Kurt, pausing when they reached Agatha.

"How off was he?" Agatha asked, out of the side of her mouth.

"The arrow landed under the black line, but only two color notches from the top. Too close for Kurt's liking," Small said in a husky voice.

"Well, I'm sure he'll enjoy his trip back home. The Mooshkoos on board will make sure of it," Agatha said, clasping her hands as she eyed the whimpering man above them.

Big and Small laughed and saluted Agatha before rejoining Kurt on the platform.

The crowd fell back into a straight line. Cassie could hear them all trying to guess what the ousted man had done to fail inspection.

"I heard someone say he joined that group, you know the one," muttered one woman.

"My brother was with them for a while, but it wasn't for me," whispered another.

A man from the front of the line yelled to the ousted guy, as he passed inspection and headed through the Welcoming Gate. "Hey Joey, have fun by yourself! I almost got ousted because of you!"

"What happened?" Cassie asked.

"Tsk, tsk," Agatha said, as she listened to passengers ridiculing the man tied up with rope. "That, my dear, is what happens when your individual energy threatens to affect the Vibration on Blue."

"But what if he was here to see someone?" Cassie asked, pulling at her lip as passengers in line chastised him for further delaying the line.

"Well, that's a shame."

"I wouldn't want to be him," TJ said, raising his chin toward the sole passenger aboard *The Enticer*. "And I definitely wouldn't want to mess with them." Big and Small flexed their biceps while Kurt continued to measure each newcomer's Vibration.

A hunchbacked Entity, with dirt on his face and an uneven scar on his chin, eyed Sal from the Welcoming Road. He sauntered through the gate, cutting through the crowd—with no consequence from Kurt—and tapped a thick, wormy finger on Sal's bony shoulder.

"Roger!" Sal cried and opened his arms wide.

"Good to see ya back, Sal. It's been too many pulses."

Sal and Roger slapped one another on the back and Roger gestured toward the front of the line. Sal impulsively followed and twitched his shoulder, like he forgot something. Reaching back a long arm, he sunk his fingers into the back of TJ's neck. "It's all who you know, kid. C'mon."

TJ shrugged, calling back to Cassie and Mariana, "I guess I'll see you later!"

"Lucky!" Mariana yelled.

A few moments later, Kurt declared, "This one's good! And, of course, that's fifty Lures for the legendary Sal Hawke!"

The rambunctious crowd on the pier, who had been downing tankards of Escape and eating sandwiches dripping with velvety cheese, ceased what they were doing and roared in applause.

TJ passed inspection, Cassie thought.

"You'll catch up with your handsome new friend in the Midst," Agatha said without looking up, as she busily entered data into her Surveyor.

After a dozen newcomers were cleared, Cassie approached the platform. Big and Small loomed over each of Kurt's shoulders as he scanned everyone with a Surveyor just like Agatha's. Cassie's heart beat faster each time Kurt slanted his eyebrows, waiting for the arrow to land somewhere in the range of gloomy blue colors underneath the black line, ensuring each person's Vibrational frequency stayed low.

The same color scheme on Agatha's Surveyor was displayed on Kurt's, with a dusty blue color at the top to an almost fully gray hue at the bottom of the glass screen.

A trio of unkempt men in business suits in front of Cassie and Mariana quickly passed inspection as the arrow on the Meter landed three quarters of the way down on a silvery blue-gray the hue of steel. The last guy in the group swayed in front of the platform while he waited to go next. He was staring sadly at a picture in his wallet when Big, in his sleeveless gray T-shirt, motioned with his chin. The man continued to glance down at the picture, unaware.

"Fella!" Kurt hollered.

The man, in tan dress pants that landed a few inches above his dress shoes, lifted his head.

Kurt flicked his head in the direction of the man's friends. "Your colleagues are waiting."

"Let's go, Patrick, let's have some fun," one of the men called as Small released the Welcoming Gate. "Billy's in school anyway, won't even know where ya are. C'mon, you don't want to end up like that other guy."

The man clutched the wallet-sized picture.

Is he looking at a picture of his son? Cassie wondered.

The man staggered to the platform. He wore an uncertain look on his face as he swayed side-to-side, apparently still seasick from the ride.

The indecisive black arrow at first landed on the gray color at the bottom of the screen, then swung up to the solid black line, and then plunged down in the middle of the blue color range, as it wavered back and forth. The man gripped the photo in his tremoring hands two feet in front of Cassie.

"Put the picture away," one of his colleagues hollered from outside the gate, as he caught sight of someone barbarically eating a huge drumstick inside the town square. "I'm starved, for crying out loud."

I don't know if I should be here, Cassie heard the man say in his mind. She leaned in closer. *My kid's having a hard time in school. Maybe I should go home.*

Kurt narrowed his eyes, as if the man was under a giant microscope. The arrow hovered under the black line for a few seconds, while Big flared his nostrils.

The man's friends hollered a third time and he shoved the

picture in his pants pocket. The arrow promptly nosedived toward the gray color at the bottom of the meter.

"Pass!" Kurt flashed a hint of a satisfied smile as his voice rang out on the pier.

The thick-browed Small pushed open the heavy iron gate, allowing the group of men access to the cobblestone Welcoming Road. Entities who surrounded the gate greeted them like it was Disney World.

"Good Dusk!"

"The power of numbers!"

"So glad you joined us!"

Kurt's voice vibrated through the chilly air. "Next!"

Cassie cautiously stepped up to the inspection area.

"Do you want me to go first?" Mariana asked, putting a hand on her shoulder.

Cassie nodded.

Kurt turned to Agatha, one eyebrow raised. Upon Agatha's approval, Big motioned to Mariana to approach the platform. She held her toned arms by her sides, and the large monkey scanned the space around her body. Agatha clasped her hands knowingly around her waist as the arrow landed slightly above the black line, in the empty space, on top of the display board.

"What's going on here?" Kurt asked, jumping down from his canvas chair.

"I take responsibility for her, " Agatha said. "She's with my Potential, kind of a package deal, if you will." She took Cassie's hand. "We've got ourselves a special one here, Kurt. One for whom I was willing to make an exception."

"All right. Understood. But is there any Potential in this one?" Kurt asked, his brow furrowed. "I've got a few Entities I could recommend."

"Definitely not what we're looking for. Trust me," Agatha said, closing her eyes.

Cassie rose up on her toes. She felt secretly happy Mariana wasn't getting an Entity. Mariana had her family.

"Pass," Kurt said gruffly.

Mariana clapped the tips of her fingers high above her head as she skipped over to the Welcoming Gate.

"A special one, huh?" Kurt remarked toward Cassie, as he stroked his chin. "Let's see."

Cassie stepped up to the platform and stood in place, facing the swarms of people and Entities laughing and drinking outside the Welcoming Gate as Kurt measured her energy space.

Beads of sweat formed on Cassie's forehead.

"Good!" Kurt declared, hooking his Surveyor back on his belt loop and handing Cassie a tin badge with the word "Potential." "Welcome to the Land of Blue!"

Cassie clutched the badge as if she won first prize at the science fair, and hurried over to join Mariana.

Standing on the rung of his chair, Kurt added, "And one hundred Lures for our beloved Agatha!" The crowd cheered, as he emptied a handful of pewter coins into the pocket of her cloak. Agatha bowed her head and saluted the crowd as she crossed the platform to Cassie, with no need for inspection.

Cassie pinned the badge to her dad's old sweatshirt.

"Well done, girl," Agatha said, as she clasped Cassie's hands.

Cassie felt a lightness in her chest. She never saw where the arrow landed, but it must have been right where they wanted it to be.

"Make no mistake," Agatha sighed, straightening Cassie's Potential badge, "I'd love for you to be with us longer, and move to a higher status than Potential, but alas, it's only temporary." Small released the latch and opened the Welcoming Gate. "Unless," Agatha continued in a sing-song voice, "you have so much fun you change your mi-ind!"

Cassie paused at the entrance. "I'm here to get my dad and then we're going home, right?"

"Of course!" Agatha said, not looking at Cassie while she straightened the arms of her cloak. "One must keep their sense of humor about them during times of duress. Come, let's enter the beloved Midst, the heart and soul of the Land of Blue!"

CHAPTER
TEN

Cassie felt her pulse rise as they passed through the Welcoming
Gate. Rock music blared throughout the boisterous square.
Sporting towering, jester-style hats and colorful beads draped
from their ears, wiry-thin vendors hovered a few inches above
the cobblestoned Welcoming Road, straining their voices to be
heard above the crowd, "You know you want some!" Vendor after
vendor greeted them with balloon animals, sticky, sugary treats,
and necklaces in bold colors. Cassie and Mariana tasted the sweet,
fragrant products displayed at various cart stations lined in rows
along the Welcoming Road, captivated by each hovering vendor.

Along the gray cobblestones, Entities and their charges danced,
sang, and drank tall mugs of Escape under the dusky, evening sky.
Cassie noticed the man, who'd had the picture of his son, standing

off to the right, happily clanking mugs of foamy Escape with an Entity with uneven ears as they congregated near a vendor cart of gooey cheese sandwiches. A dimly lit road was visible a few yards behind the flashy vendor cart, but there were too many people in the way for Cassie to see where it led. She felt relieved that the guy didn't look sad anymore, even though she wondered why he didn't go home. She couldn't stand when people were sad, because somehow that made Cassie feel sad too.

The yeasty, heavenly aroma of Yum wafted over to Cassie, causing her stomach to growl.

But no one could be sad here. Look at this place! she thought.

Directly in the middle of the cobblestone road, prior to turning into the town square, a large metallic-blue framed screen, the size of a movie-theatre screen, perched atop an overflowing black fountain of Escape. The words "Energy Vibration Meter" pulsed in black at the very top. A large, black arrow pointed to a gray-blue color, like an elephant's skin, far below the black line. It resembled the Surveyor screen, only much, much, bigger.

Cassie stared up at it in fascination.

"That's the Meter for the entire land," Agatha explained, waving to a Mooshkoo cleaning the streets with a push broom. "It constantly assesses the sum total of everyone's energy so we maintain order. Simply put, the arrow needs to point below the black line at all times. The lower the better. Now! Are you ready to indulge?"

"Where do we start?" Mariana asked, reaching to touch some bubbles floating by from one of the vendors. "This seems like a blast!"

Agatha took each of the girls' hands as they rounded the corner, turning left into the area known as the Midst. A line of elves high-fived them as they entered, making Cassie and Mariana feel like football players at the start of a game. A tall man perched on a unicycle, hovering a few inches above the ground, rode past, juggling for Cassie and Mariana. Mariana giggled and he called out, "My Bads are the best! Make sure you visit my station, cause you don't want to miss 'em!"

"That's so cool! Everything is, like, higher here," Mariana said as the man adeptly pedaled by, floating above the cobblestones.

"And therefore more enjoyable," Agatha responded, draping an additional necklace around Cassie's neck. Agatha acknowledged the skilled vendor in the rainbow suspenders, who saluted her in return.

Cassie cleared her throat from the heavy, suppressed air that entered her lungs. *Was Dad here? I bet he tried Bad in every flavor!*

"Good Dusk, Whitney," Agatha said to a woman with bloodshot eyes who wore a "Permanent by Association" badge. The woman immediately perked up and beamed radiantly at Cassie and Mariana, tidying her two girls who had chocolate smeared all over their faces. A duck-like Entity, wearing a bonnet and black shoes, had been following quietly behind the mother and her children.

"Good Dusk, Agatha," the Entity saluted.

"Good Dusk to you too, Shirley," Agatha said, taking a moment to tousle one of the girl's already messy, strawberry-blond hair. "On your way back to the Settling?"

The broad-billed, muddy-colored duck gave a thumbs-up as she continued behind the woman and her children, who didn't seem to notice her presence.

Mariana coughed. "It feels like there's smog, except you can't see any, like you can from the smoke stacks on the expressway in Boston. And why does everyone keep saying 'Good Dusk'?"

Agatha chuckled. "That's our frequency here, as the land only exists under dark skies."

Just then an Entity with swirling, red and white eyes joined their conversation, while a group of women drank from fancy glasses filled with Escape and had their toes painted in an area of turf behind the pier. "Good Duuusk. I'd be haaaappy to answer any other questions you may have," the Entity purred like a cat. "Actually, I'm searching for something I lost. A lovely little creature who has gone and run about the Midst, and now she's missing, much to my chagrin."

"Oh!" Cassie said, taken in by his rotating, peppermint-candy–colored eyes. "That's awful!"

"Yes, it's making me so sad," the Entity said as he teared up. "Maybe you could help me find my companion."

Mariana wrinkled her nose as if the Entity spoke in a foreign language, but Cassie felt sorry for him.

"Sly," Agatha said, lifting her chin. "They're with me." While she spoke, she waved to various vendors and Entities who greeted her by name. "And we have business to take care of this Dusk. But your efforts won't go unnoticed."

"Thanks. I learned from the best." He bowed and then landed his bulging eyes on a group of teenagers ordering Bad from a vendor performing magic tricks on the side of the road.

Agatha gave Sly a proud smile before slipping him a pewter token piece from her cloak.

"Off to get another Bad!" Sly said, sauntering across the cobblestones toward the teens.

"What else would we spend our hard-earned Lures on?" Agatha asked cheerfully.

Mariana waved to the vendor on the unicycle as they approached his station. "Good Dusk!"

"And Good Dusk to you! Do try the Bad drinks in my section, won't you? It would hurt my feelings if you went anywhere else." The entertaining vendor twisted his face into a frown atop his glittery red unicycle.

Nearby, other colorful and comical vendors shouted, "Over here for the stickiest, drippiest, sugariest hula-hoop-sized Yum!"

"Try my forty-five-fingered Bad!"

"Hey, over here! I've got the biggest Gulps and Blobs in every neon color!"

"Ugh!" Mariana said, clutching the side of her head with her hands, "I don't know which one to try first! This is crazy!"

"Let's go to him," Cassie said, pulling Mariana over to the tall, thin vendor atop the unicycle, who turned his frown into a wide smile.

"Tell me," he said, juggling humongous tankards in the air, "was it my sad face?"

"For her it was," Mariana said, draping her arm around Cassie. "These better be the best Bad drinks ever!"

The playful vendor added another tankard to his juggling act and said, "You'll see. And I'll even make 'em forty-seven-finger size to beat my competition. I'm Robin, by the way."

"Nice to meet you," Cassie said. "What's a forty-seven-finger drink anyway?"

"Yeah, what's that?" Mariana asked as the funny vendor, draped in colorful beads, tossed the tankards to an elf standing by his station and proceeded to pour the largest drinks the two of them had ever seen.

When Robin was finished, he stacked two fingers up and up until they reached the top of the frosty glass. "That's just about forty-seven fingers, by my calculations."

"Wow," Mariana said, barely above a whisper. "That looks good. Enormous, but good. My mother would kill me."

"I'm thirsty just looking at it," Cassie said.

The Tylenol-pink-colored drink filled the glasses, as Robin raised the pitcher higher and lower in a teasing manner. The drink splashed out and over the top of the glasses. "Enjoy!" Robin said, dropping a few pasty-blue marshmallows on top and handing the glasses to the girls.

"We will!" Mariana said, holding her Bad with two hands. "Wait! How do we pay? I don't have any money. Cassie, do you?"

"No," Cassie answered, as she hesitated to take her first sip.

"Girls, girls," Robin said, laying his unicycle down on the cobblestones as Agatha watched in amusement. "You're Potentials! You don't pay for anything when it's your first time! Ah, I remember my Potential days," he said, putting one hand over his chest, "brought here by my Entity. Will's still around, though he's got new Potentials now. He doesn't need to work with me anymore." Robin proudly tapped the "Working For Permanency" badge on his black T-shirt under the light of the street lamp. "And once I prove myself, I'll become a Permanent!"

Mariana sipped her drink and asked, "Is that like the athletes, nerds, and mean girls in middle school?"

Robin laughed. "I know what cha mean, kid. I was half-troublemaker, half-class clown, myself. But to answer your excellent question, there are four levels on Blue. They are—quiz me now girls, and put my education to the test—" he cleared his throat ceremoniously. "Potentials, which are you," he pointed playfully at Cassie's badge on her sweatshirt. "'Working for Permanency,' which is me," he said, pressing his thumb to his chest. "'Permanent by Association,' which are the families of the Permanents, and finally 'Permanents', who are the lifers. And then, of course, there are the Entities, who make it all happen. Do I know my stuff or what?"

"So the Permanents get to live here and drink Bad every day?" Mariana's eyes bugged out of her head.

"Yessirreee, which is why I do what I do. And . . . ," he beckoned with his finger for them to come closer, " . . . there are unlimited refills!"

"What?" Mariana exclaimed, slapping her thigh. "This place rocks! My mother never lets me have more than two sugary sweets a week! No wonder your dad is here, Cassie!"

Cassie shot her a look.

"You know what I meant, right? I mean, if you live here you get to eat and drink this stuff every day! It's like when my sister worked at Friendly's and got to sample the ice cream. She loved that job! Except she gained like ten pounds and she was really bummed out."

"I guess you're right." Cassie laughed between sips of frozen Bad.

Agatha reached up and handed Robin, who was back on his

unicycle, three pewter tokens from her cloak. "Verrrry well done. You can be sure I'll mention it to the Dusk Ruler during Vibration Meetings."

"Thank you," Robin saluted. "See you two later. I've got work to do." He pedaled over to a young couple trying to decide between mustard-yellow or ambulance-red Bad.

"Look!" Mariana pointed across the road to a large shark-blue, tarp-covered tent. "There's an arcade! I love video games! My parents don't let me play them, though, because they're too distracting. And don't even tell me they're free, too."

Agatha snickered. "Yes, dear, the Stimulators are free, which means both of you may enjoy being distracted for as long as you'd like. Some parents can be such fuddy-duddies."

Cassie finished her drink as she took in the zig-zag of beaming lights under the tent at the end of the Midst, where a pulsating blood-red sign on top of the blue tarp flashed Welcome to the Cove.

Agatha glanced down at her Surveyor. "Girls, I need to take care of a few things. Why don't you head to the Cove without me and enjoy all the Midst has to offer young Potentials like yourselves?"

You're leaving us? What if we get lost? Cassie panicked.

"Don't worry, dear, you'll be fine. Besides, there are plenty of Entities willing to help Potentials who lose their way. Just don't cross the Welcoming Road to the area known as the Settling. That area is only for those who earn special status on Blue. Are we clear?"

Cassie felt a pang of jealousy burn inside her chest.

"Sure," Mariana answered, half-listening as she slurped the rest of her forty-seven-fingered Frozen Bad. She seemed more interested in the red, yellow and green lights bouncing off the sides of the Cove.

Cassie's legs felt shaky as Agatha began to address other individuals in the Midst, disappearing into the crowd. Cassie remembered the time she had a stomachache one morning before kindergarten and didn't tell her mother because she didn't want to mess up her mom's plans to get a haircut. Cassie had stood helplessly on the rounded cement curb outside the Morris School where her mom dropped her off and watched until her mom's brown car was no bigger than a freckle. As she balanced her feet on the curb, Cassie desperately wished she had asked her mother to stay home. She mostly wished her mom had *known* to keep her home, without Cassie having to say anything at all.

Are we all right here without an adult? Cassie wondered, stepping up on her tiptoes to try to find Agatha in the crowd.

Tap three times on each hand to stay safe.

Cassie drummed the first three fingers of her left hand on her left thigh. 1-2-3. 1-2-3. 1-2-3. She did the same with her right hand on her right thigh.

"C'mon!" Mariana grabbed her hand, pulling her toward the Cove. "It'll be just like when my mom drops us off at the mall!"

Short, stout Entities and pipe-thin, bow-legged Entities strode a few steps behind their Potentials as Cassie and Mariana made their way across the crowded road. Raucous laughter and loud conversation filled the air as creatures ate Blobs and drank mugs of Bad and pints of Escape in the foggy Midst.

"Good Dusk," an Entity said, stepping into their space, as the girls were halfway across the cobblestones. "Potentials? Are you in need of an Entity?"

"No," Mariana winced as though a spider dangled in front of her face.

"Thank you, but I have one already," Cassie said proudly.

"Carry on then," the Entity responded, with his nose in the air.

"They're pushy, huh?" Mariana asked as they wedged between droves of Entities, Potentials, and Permanents. At the Cove's entrance, they spotted Sal and TJ in a far corner, laughing in front of the bright lights of a large Stimulator machine.

"Finally, a place that resembles daytime!" Mariana said, jumping beside TJ. "Did you taste one of those humongous Bads? They're amazing!"

"Hey," TJ said. "Not yet. Check this out—this is awesome—watch!" TJ hit the *Now!* button on the black machine. He vanished, only to reappear inside the Stimulator, visible through the hazy glass screen.

Cassie and Mariana's jaws dropped as TJ navigated his way through a red-and-blue maze, dodging evil men in white suits who tried to capture him and lock him in a little room in the corner. The word "victim" intermittently flashed on the screen.

"Hurry up and get out of there!" Mariana hollered. "That guy has a sword, or is that a needle?"

The *pshoo! pshoo!* sounds of the Stimulator went berserk as TJ narrowly dodged the little demons waiting for him behind spiny bushes.

Bowbowbowbowbow. The game ended when TJ was captured by a slimy troll who dragged him over to a man in a white coat.

"Awww! I almost had it, huh Sal?" TJ asked, reappearing in the Cove next to Cassie and Mariana, his hair soaked as if he had run a marathon.

"That's crazy!" Cassie exclaimed as the characters vibrated on the screen, recharging for the next player. "Weren't you scared?"

"That's half the fun, right?" Sal elbowed TJ.

"Look at this," TJ showed them, slapping the *Now!* button again. "I don't even need tokens! I can play all night!"

TJ flipped his hair back as he started another game; only the back of his Land of Blue sweatshirt faced Cassie and Mariana.

Maybe I should remind him about Eric, Cassie thought.

"I want to play!" Mariana took hold of the controller at the open game next to TJ. She pressed the *Now!* button, and instantly neon red, blue, and green colors flashed all over the fingerprinted glass screen, milliseconds apart. Mariana appeared as though she'd been hit with a stun gun. Her eyes goggled, entranced by the frenetic screen.

Before she could change her mind, Mariana waved at TJ and

Cassie from inside the Stimulator. She patted a troll quickly on his flat head, and a bell rang. Cassie's mouth dropped open, half-horrified, half-intrigued, as Mariana bolted like lightning around a dark cemetery, away from a group of trolls, only visible by their yellow eyes, whose job was to eat her for dinner. The trolls chugged bottles of Bad as they stalked their prey.

"Aaaahhhh!!" Mariana yelled from inside the screen. Luckily she made it out of the cemetery and into the protective arms of a roly-poly police officer in the middle of a busy street. From behind a cluster of tombstones, the trolls drooled in disappointment.

"Yes!" Mariana yelled as she reappeared back in the Cove beside Cassie, TJ, and Sal. "That was intense! I actually feel a little nauseous. How do boys play those games all day?"

A gray-snouted Entity, with dark rings like an opossum around his eyes, stood guard at a Stimulator near the entrance of the Cove. The Entity loomed behind a high school kid with tons of freckles who held a bottle of Bad in his right hand. A line of boys formed a queue behind the freckled kid, eager to play. The red-haired teen waited to throw the bottle at the Stimulator screen, which featured nothing but a large, empty window pane. Suddenly, a monster popped up in the window and stuck his tongue out at the teenager. *Smash!* The glass bottle just missed the target.

The snouted Entity jeered, "Aw, c'mon kid, you were so close! You got to get this one in order to move up to the next level." Cassie couldn't tell if the boy heard him or not, as he neither reacted nor responded.

The line of teenagers multiplied, making a U-shape around the game. Cassie imagined the boys in Mrs. Burke's class who would have loved to play Stimulators for as long as they wanted.

Just then, thoughts not her own raced in and out of Cassie's mind.

I want a turn!

More, Mommy! I want more Bad, Mommy!

Hey, let's not go back yet, let's head to The Pits!

Cassie slowly turned and looked behind her at the hordes of adults and children traipsing past in the nonstop Midst. Like trying to catch bubbles in the air, Cassie attempted in vain to connect each thought to its rightful owner.

"Yum! Bad! Blobs in every color!" shouted the vendors. They seemed tireless, as they performed magic tricks to entertain Potentials, such as making rainbow-colored Blobs appear from their noses and ears.

Robin's audience roared in applause as he made a tire-sized Yum appear magically out of his bare hands.

"Let's go," TJ said, motioning with his head toward a five-year-old standing next to his cigarette-smoking father as they waited to play the Stimulator. "I'm ready for one of those Bads."

That was nice of him, Cassie thought as TJ fixed the collar of his sweatshirt and left the Cove with Cassie and Mariana and headed toward Robin's station. Sal, gliding behind TJ, stopped to strike up a conversation with another Entity who was thrilled to see him back on Blue.

TJ ordered a forty-five-fingered Bad from Robin, tasted it, and exclaimed, "You're right, this is good stuff!"

"Glad you like it, my friend! You know it's good when it keeps ya coming back for more!" Robin announced from his unicycle.

"Look." TJ observed a line on the other end of the Midst toward the Welcoming Road that was so long, it swerved like a snake. "If that's a ride, I bet Eric'll be there. Let's go!"

TJ, Cassie, and Mariana ran to check out the line, where a pot-bellied guy standing at the end looked like he hadn't slept in days.

"What's the line for?" TJ asked breathlessly.

"Oh, this here's a chance to earn Lures! All you gotta do is be willing to give it away!" The unshaven guy grasped a large brown bottle of Escape in his sausage-sized fingers. "They pick Permanents who they think are ready to become an Entity. Whoever gets chosen gets sixty-six Lures. Sixty-six Lures," he repeated dramatically, "is enough for three whole days' worth of Escape! Hey, I'm Chris, by the way."

"What's a Lure?" Cassie asked.

"Here, I'll show ya," The man reached into his pocket, no easy feat as his large belly protruded over his silver belt buckle. He retrieved a pewter triangular coin—the same one Agatha had given to Robin, and what everyone used to pay for their wares. "A Lure is good for one Escape and one meal. And I eat and drink a lot of 'em." He patted his large stomach.

"Well you got some competition cause I think I'd make a great Entity," a woman wearing a faded brown, felt hat countered, her hands on her hips. "Plus, I could use a little transformation, even if it did make one ear larger than the other. Amy's the name. I've got half my cousins living in the Settling. Kurt and the boys are pleased with my networking ability."

"Well, this one thinks he'd make a great Entity too," a middle-aged woman scoffed, referring to her husband, who gulped down a bottle of Bad without coming up for air. "Meanwhile, he can't even remember the last thirty-second Glimmer, and who forgets that?" she said under her breath. "How's he going to keep tabs on someone else?"

"Can it, Billie." The woman's pudgy, pink-faced husband said as the line moved forward.

"What's the thirty-second Glimmer?" Cassie asked, placing her empty Bad into a trash can next to the line.

"You haven't experienced the thirty-second Glimmer yet?" Amy asked, surprised, until she saw Cassie's status badge. "Ohhh, I see, you must be a brand-new Potential. Well, you will."

"When?" TJ asked, cracking his knuckles.

"Yeah, when?" Mariana chimed in. "Is it awesome, like everything else around here?"

"Oh, no, it's the Land of Blue's least favorite time. It's when they sky changes color and everyone runs for their lives," Amy explained in a hushed tone as she leaned in closer. "I don't want to cause a panic for the others, because no one wants the fun to stop, but we all know we're due."

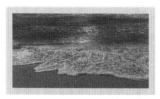

CHAPTER
ELEVEN

Cassie swallowed hard, lightly coughing as she inhaled the smoggy night air. "What do you mean, the fun stops?"

"The Land of Blue only operates at dusk," Amy explained, gesturing toward the foggy evening sky. "When the Glimmer hits, light appears overhead briefly, and that means everyone has to go indoors. If anyone were to stay out, the Vibration of the whole land would change. So you can bet five Lures that Kurt and his boys make sure everyone heads inside. I told you I'd make a great Entity. I've been here a long time." She pressed her faded Permanent badge against her black leather vest.

"What would happen if the thirty-second Glimmer came right now? My Entity isn't here," Cassie asked, biting her nails.

"Mine isn't either," TJ said, searching over people's heads to find Sal, who was speaking privately with Roger in an alley.

"Muahaha!" An Entity with a hump on his shoulder burst forth from the trash barrel, ketchup smeared all over his face from half-eaten sandwiches in the garbage. He belched and bellowed as he pounded his chest, "Now I can have me some more!"

TJ laughed, "Makes sense to me."

"That's disgusting," Mariana said, curling her nose.

"There you are!" Sal said, squeezing the back of TJ's neck. "Come on, let's do some damage on the track. You ain't seen nothin' 'til you've seen this."

TJ, Mariana, and Cassie said good-bye to the people in the Give-It-Away line and followed Sal over to a race-car track by Welcoming Road. Three small, flashy cars were lined up at the fence like go-carts.

"Want to give it a go?" Sal asked TJ, raising his eyebrows up and down.

"Sure!" TJ said. "Eric and I love go-carts!"

A beefy-armed teenager, responsible for allowing each person access inside the track, sat in a chair at the entrance to the fence, a "Working for Permanency" badge pinned to his Land of Blue sweatshirt.

"Hey, Presley," Sal said, with a nod. The teenager saluted Sal and gestured TJ inside the track. Sal turned to TJ and said, "You're all set. Pick a car, any car."

Cassie and Mariana exchanged glances.

Jumping inside a yellow, spray-painted car, TJ gripped the wheel and looked admiringly around the interior. A minute later, he stuck his head out of the small driver's side window and said to Sal, "I just need a helmet!"

"Never mind the accessories," Sal replied from the fence. "That's the thrill of it!"

TJ bore an uncertain look on his face and settled into the black leather seat.

"That boy's gotta toughen up," Sal muttered under his breath. Cassie bit her lip as TJ immediately took off at an aggressive speed.

"Okay, we're *not* going on that," Mariana declared as TJ whizzed by on the oval track. On a giant screen, the speed of his car clocked over one hundred miles an hour.

Sal taunted TJ mercilessly as he sped by and veered off the road. "Seriously? Hasn't anyone taught you to drive yet?"

We're only twelve, Cassie thought.

"Ah, we're only twelve," Mariana said, putting one hand on her hip.

Cassie wished she had the courage to say it out loud.

Sal picked his teeth with a toothpick as he replied, "I learned by then, motormouth."

Rounding the track a second time, TJ almost crashed into the plastic bushes serving as a buffer in the corner. Sal rubbed his hand over his face.

"You'd think Sal was training him for NASCAR," Mariana whispered to Cassie.

Cassie couldn't take her eyes off TJ. *Please don't let him get badly hurt.*

TJ zipped around the track a third time, without a crash.

"I did it!" TJ exclaimed, jamming the car in park and staggering out the window. He held a hand to a large bump protruding from his forehead.

"Well, whaddya think?" Sal slapped TJ on the back.

"I gotta say," TJ said, tripping over his feet, "once I got over the rush, it was fun!"

"No other way, my boy. If there's no rush, what's the point? Right, Presley?" Sal punched the oafy teenager, who had nodded off in his chair, in the arm.

"Huh? I hope the kid had a great time. That'll be three Lures," Presley said through half-closed eyelids.

Sal stepped within an inch of Presley's face. "Hey, do you need more training or shall we delay your Permanent status? This here's my Potential. No charge for him—until he advances to Permanent." He pointed a finger at Presley's chest. "Remember that."

The plump teenager immediately straightened up in his chair. "Oh, yeah, I forgot. Half asleep, is all. Any time for you, kid."

"That's cause Potentials are like VIPs, right?" Mariana asked, leaning in between Sal and TJ.

"Yeah, right," Sal said, draping a long arm around TJ as he guided him to a nearby vendor distributing Bads at a rapid pace. "Let's get you another Bad, kid, take the edge off."

Cassie glanced past the brick building on the corner of the Midst, at the edge of the Welcoming Road, as she shuffled behind Sal, TJ, and Mariana. Through a gap in the crowd, she noticed a sign at the beginning of the dimly lit road on the other side of the Midst that read: "Welcome to the Settling." Squinting, the road appeared laden with cracks and badly in need of repair. Just past the sign, a street lamp flickered over Big as he sat sprawled in a seat on a small platform, similar to the one on the pier.

A mother trudged down the poorly paved road, holding the hands of a young boy and girl as they stepped lazily over the jagged cracks in the cement. When they reached the platform, Big scanned his Surveyor around the entire family and waved them through. The little girl, who looked about seven years old, kept turning back toward the noisy Midst.

I wonder where their dad is, Cassie thought.

Standing in place as TJ and Mariana ordered their Bads, Cassie watched the mother and her children head down the mysterious road until they were out of sight.

"Don't you worry about nobody but yourself," Sal said, startling Cassie as he whispered in her ear. "Her dad's just having a nice Escape after a hard day's work." He winked, adding, "You gotta love Mind Mail."

"What's down that road?" TJ asked Sal as he returned, clutching a mug of Bad.

"Nothing that concerns either of you right now. You just concentrate on enjoying that drink," Sal grazed TJ's chin slightly with his fist, keeping his sharp nails inside his hand.

"Okay," TJ complied, slurping the enormous highlighter-yellow Bad.

Sal, distracted by the cars on the track, raced over to the fence to join a group of Entities cheering for the tobacco-sauce-red car.

"Maybe you'll find your dad down there," TJ said, nodding toward the Settling.

"Where?" Mariana asked, rejoining them with a veiny grape-colored Bad.

Cassie muscles tightened. "Agatha said we couldn't go down that road."

"Hey, Ernie! Good Dusk, Jane!" Sal yelled, greeting two Entities who stopped to talk with him at the track as they came in from the Welcoming Road. "There's nothing like the Midst, eh? It's truly . . . "

"The most excessively enthusiastic and pleasurable place!" boomed a male voice from behind Cassie, Mariana, and TJ.

Cassie whirled around to see a man dressed in a black pirate's hat with a long, dirty, white feather sticking out of its side. He stood almost six-and-a-half-feet tall, with long dark hair like a horse's mane, and a black beard hanging two inches past his chin. A long black trench coat covered his skyscraper-like frame.

"There's something for everyone's uncontrollable and insatiable desires in the Land of Blue!" the man bellowed with his chin to the sky. He opened one side of his trench coat and revealed an array of colored Blobs—from ambulance-red to hospital-white—that ran down to the heels of his high black boots.

"Girls, may I be the one to introduce Captain Byron Pantaleone, or Captain BP for short." Agatha's cackling voice rang out behind them.

She's back! Cassie thought as she spun around to see her Entity.

Agatha bowed dramatically to the tall, flamboyantly dressed man and said to the kids, "Go on and have a look if you desire."

Cassie, Mariana, and TJ flocked to Captain BP like kids to an ice-cream truck in July.

"On sale, for free!" Captain BP threw his head back and let out a hearty, deep laugh.

"Seriously? We can have as much as we want?" TJ asked, his eyes bugging out, unsure where to begin.

"Never more serious, my boy!" Captain BP bellowed like an actor in a grand theatre. "Go on! Ponder, ruminate, muse all day! How I empathize with the habitual indecisiveness!"

TJ reached for several chewy Blobs and a packet of colored crystals, some of which he shoved into the pocket of his faded blue jeans. When he sprinkled some crystals in his mouth, his nose got longer for a moment and then returned to normal.

"Oooooh, that's fun," Mariana squealed. "Let's see what those chocolate-looking Blobs can do." She selected three brown Blobs: milk, milk with caramel, and dark chocolate covered in radioactive-red squishy fish. "My mom says chocolate has antioxidants in it," Mariana said as she bit into the bar with caramel. "Ooh, that's good!" She rose off the ground, hovered in the air for a few seconds, and landed back on her feet.

Cassie quickly bit into a chocolate-covered Blob that tasted like marshmallows, and her feet lifted off the ground. "Wow! I could eat these all day!"

"Oh, you delight me you do, with your insatiable cravings!" Captain BP remarked, as he clutched his chest. "You joyous children make me feel like the most important person in the Land!"

Agatha raised one penciled eyebrow. "Rather irrational and loquacious, aren't we?"

"If there was a most important person, of course," BP

said, humbly.

Agatha shook her head. "Now, though you may take what you like, don't forget to save room for a meal at The Pits."

Cassie reached out her hand for a few more Blobs.

"The crazy colors get 'em every time," Captain BP nudged Agatha with his elbow. "Who can resist Blobs in every color? Only the pathologically boring, that's who!"

"Speaking of boring, "Agatha said as she smoothed her coarse red hair. "I ran into Tufa on Option's Port. Good thing I got things moving or we'd still be there."

"Tufa!" Captain BP snapped. "Well, it's been many a Zipper since I've seen Tufa." He stroked the end of his beard. "Probably handed out some abnormal herbal concoction. Can't hold a candle to BP's Blobs."

"I should think not," Agatha said. "Go on, kids, grab a few more Blobs so you may enjoy them after supper."

"But dear Agatha, there are no intensely concerned and hovering mothers here to tell them what to do! Let me have a little fun with them, will you? They're so impressionable at this age—savoring every Blob down to the last drop—unlike the grown-ups who have already outgrown Blobbery fun," Captain BP pleaded. The feather flickered on the large-brimmed hat that covered most of his face. "I've worked with generations on this sort of thing. I dare say, take advantage of not having to follow the rules, young ones! You're on the Land of Blue, where there is pleasure galore! Devour it while you have the chance!" Captain BP spoke like the fastest auctioneer on TV Cassie had ever seen.

Cassie, TJ, and Mariana stared up at BP in fascination, rooted in place before Agatha led them away. "Eats too much of his own stash," she said in a hushed tone. "C'mon, let's have a proper meal."

Captain BP lunged forward to approach a group of teenagers gathered around Sal at the track as he took in Lures to be placed on the red car.

"I'll meet you at the Pits!" Sal yelled to TJ as he stepped up on a few rungs of the chain link fence.

Agatha waved and guided Cassie, Mariana, and TJ back through the packed road. After all the Blobs they had consumed, Cassie, Mariana, and TJ began talking very fast as Agatha listened in amusement.

"My tongue is buzzing!" TJ said as his tongue swelled to four times its regular size before returning to normal.

"Mine is too!" Cassie said.

"I feel weird," Mariana said as her tongue rolled out of her mouth like a red carpet.

Streams of harsh light poured out from the opening and closing doors of the many Pits as customers staggered onto the pavement. The Pits and Zebbies lined up against one another along the cobblestones, in the center of the Midst, with an occasional alley in between. Flashing signs above their thresholds read: "All you can eat! All you can drink! Kids eat free!"

"Whoa, kids eat free?" TJ asked, stepping aside so a family could pass by.

"Every adult who frequents the Pits earns one Lure, good for two pints of Escape. Their children are allowed to eat for free. We take care of our people." Agatha's shoulders thrust back as she educated them on the Blue economic system.

"So the more you go, the more you get to spend," Mariana reasoned, tripping on an uneven cobblestone.

"Yes, dear, that's correct."

"Now that's genius," Mariana said, lightly tapping her forehead. "People must be eating and drinking all the time!"

"Who's hungry?" Agatha asked, clapping her palms together. She stopped in front of a brick building with an ashtray container out front. Two concrete steps led to a heavy, old, wooden door.

Mariana raised her hand. "Me! It smells really good around here, and I need some real food!" She sniffed the aromas of sweet

Yum and hearty sausage corndogs coming off the many vendor carts.

"Me too," TJ chimed in as a group of teenagers tossed a ball in the plastic grass area across the cobblestone road.

Do they know Eric? How big is the Land of Blue? Cassie heard TJ wonder as he stood in front of the Pits.

Cassie's stomach dropped. She wanted desperately to ask Agatha when they were going to find her father, but since Mariana and TJ were hungry, she didn't want to upset everyone's plans.

TJ hustled up the concrete steps and held open the heavy, wooden door with the thick brass doorknob as Agatha led them inside. Mariana held her nose as they walked by the ashtray container. The wooden door reminded Cassie of a pirate's cove, as Agatha led them down two steps to an underground tavern. The bright light of florescent lamps on the stone walls lit up the otherwise dark, musty room.

"Good Dusk, Jimmy," Agatha waved to the shaggy-haired man working behind the counter as he saluted and served his customers tankards of Escape.

A blond-haired guy, wearing dark-rimmed glasses and a "Working for Permanency" badge, made a beeline over to the table Agatha selected. "Good Dusk, Agatha. Are you ready to order?"

"Philip here has just started working on Blue," Agatha said, clearing a few leftover crumbs off the table before she sat down and crossed her legs on one side of the wooden bench. "Let them know how you like it, Philip."

"It's a marvelous job, and perfect system, yes it is." Philip answered in a robotic tone as he laid a tablecloth over the table and straightened it to perfection.

"Excellent, just what we like to hear. We'll take the heartiest meals the Pits has on the menu. My companions are on their first trip," Agatha said, clasping her hands atop the dolphin-blue tablecloth as Cassie settled in next to her on the bench.

"Well then, The Works for you all," Philip bowed and hurried behind the counter to fill their order.

Like a sudden gust of wind, Sal entered the tavern and slid next to TJ on the opposite side of the table. "Had to take care of some business. Now let's eat, cause you haven't eaten 'til you've eaten at the Pits." Sal reached past Mariana, grabbing a laminated postcard on the end of the table that listed the Blue specials for the day.

Quicker than Cassie had ever been served at the China Dragon, Philip whipped large pints of blinding-yellow Bad, along with plates of greasy stick fries, across the table. Next, bowls of ketchup and neon-orange grilled cheese sandwiches glistening with butter dropped in front of their faces.

"I haven't eaten this good in months!" TJ said, grabbing a sandwich and a handful of dripping fries. "I could definitely hang out here permanently."

Sal exchanged glances with Agatha.

"Is that fake ketchup?" Mariana asked, picking up a few fries and reaching across Sal's face to a bowl of what looked like red paint. She dipped the fries and stuffed them in her mouth, sighing as she chewed, savoring the salty deliciousness. "Mmmm . . . my mother would have a fit if she knew I was eating fake food."

"This one's a trip, eh?" Sal snickered.

Cassie helped herself to a cheese sandwich as hip-hop music began blaring from the tavern's speakers. Cassie didn't want to be the one to break up the fun, but she really needed to ask Agatha when they were going to see her father. Staring at the blurry stucco lines on the concrete wall behind TJ's head, Cassie remembered her mother getting frustrated whenever Cassie had to use the restroom at the China Dragon. Her mother would complain, "You just went! Can't you just wait until I'm done with my wine?"

Cassie pulled at a loose thread on the tablecloth as she thought, *I've come all this way, isn't it time yet?*

No one understands your needs better than I do, young lady. I brought you here, didn't I? Good Duskiness. I certainly understand your mother's frustration. You wouldn't want to lose my support, for where would you be then?

Cassie's face flushed. She pulled on a section of her blue jeans as her heart beat the way it did when she gave the wrong answer in class. Slowly lifting her head, Cassie listened as Agatha conversed with Philip, who had come over to ask if anyone wanted seconds.

"Here," Agatha said, handing Philip a few shiny Lures. "You're doing such a fine job. Maybe you'll be nominated for Permanency status at one of our upcoming Vibration Meetings. I, for one, will put in a good word."

"Thanks! I'm really ecstatic to get my own place in the Settling," Philip said in a complete monotone as he cleared the dishes.

"I'll throw one in for the try-hard," Sal said, tossing a Lure toward the end of the table. "I remember those days."

Cassie, not wanting to ask anything else for fear of being reprimanded, examined the shiny Lure resting upon the tablecloth.

"Hey, there's writing on that," TJ noticed. "What does it say?"

"Let me see," Mariana leaned over and grabbed the pewter piece, bringing it up close to her face. "It says, 'For A Job Well Done'."

Cassie twitched her toes in her sneakers as her curiosity grew, but she didn't dare say a word.

"Why does it say that?" TJ asked, as Mariana placed the Lure back down on the table.

"Because we all work hard to earn Lures," Agatha replied. Glancing sideways at Cassie, she added, "And it's nice to be appreciated." Cassie pinched the skin at the bottom of her thumb.

After Agatha took care of the bill and they rose to leave, Jimmy called to them from the counter. "Don't go, the fun's just getting started!"

Several patrons at the counter chimed in, "Stick around!"

Cassie remembered the fun times her dad and his friends had at the China Dragon.

"Whaddya have in mind?" Sal asked, twitching his shoulder.

"Perhaps we'll return for a late-night snack," Agatha said, linking arms with Sal as she addressed the patrons. As they exited back up the steps and out to the Midst, she whispered to him, "What would you do without me to keep you on track? Remember, my comrade, this is a business trip."

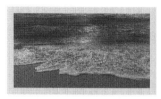

CHAPTER
TWELVE

U pon leaving the Pits, clusters of teenagers hung out in the dark listening to rock music as they leaned against corners of the brick buildings scattered down the road next to the alleyways. Cassie wondered if Eric was among them.

Mariana grabbed Cassie's arm, pulling her out of the way of a stampede of rowdy, staggering individuals leaving one of the other Pits. "You were really quiet in the restaurant," she said to Cassie, once they were safe. "Did you like the food? I didn't, it was so heavy!" Mariana rubbed her stomach. "I might have indigestion, like those people in the commercials."

Cassie shrugged as they walked ahead of the others. "It's better than my Nana's cooking. Anyway, can I ask you something?"

"Of course, I'm your best friend, remember? Who else would

Zipper with you to come here? Well, maybe most of the kids in our class because it is nonstop fun," Mariana laughed.

"No, seriously," Cassie paused, and then asked, "do you think I'm annoying?" Her voice rose about two octaves from her usual tone.

Mariana put a finger to her chin. "Annoying. Annoying. Hmm . . . " she replied.

"Mariana!" Cassie said, stomping her foot against a protruding cobblestone, while a group of energetic Potentials burst forth from one of the Zebbies. "You're not making me feel good."

"Well, my mother says it's not another person's job to make someone feel good," Mariana retorted. "And no, I don't think you're annoying. I was trying to think of the right term—oh yeah, I got it—nervous wreck. That's what my Ya-Ya calls people who bite their fingernails. I'm sorry, but nobody bites their fingernails like you."

Cassie sighed. "I know. I know. But I don't drive you crazy?"

Mariana linked her arm with Cassie's. "Stop worrying so much! I probably drive you crazy. Listen. We're going to find your father and he's going to be so happy to see you. Then you can get out of your grandpa's house, even though it's a nicer place than where you used to live. You know what I mean."

Cassie stopped and an Entity bumped into her from behind. "Oh, excuse me," Cassie apologized.

"Look," Mariana continued, "I'm sorry, but at least you know you get the truth from me. My parents tell me it's an admirable quality."

Cassie managed a smile. "That's true. I wish I was more like you, Mari. You don't care what anyone else thinks."

TJ caught up to Cassie and Mariana, hitting his chest like he needed to burp, while Sal and Agatha conversed a few steps behind.

"Does anyone have a bedtime in this place?" Mariana asked, looking around at the brightly lit buildings and up at the thick, foggy sky. "It's been dark since we got here, yet the streets are always lit up like Lansdowne Street near Kenmore Square!"

"When one feels tired, they may sleep," Agatha answered, waving and returning salutes to various Entities and their Potentials in the activity-filled street.

"Where?" TJ asked. "There aren't any houses."

Agatha started to answer, but caught sight of a weary elf sweeping the front steps of one of the Zebbies. Agatha stopped, a stern look on her face until the elf, noticing her, immediately perked up and began sweeping to the beat of the music. Agatha saluted and turned back to TJ.

"Creatures may sleep in the generous, affordable housing offered to Permanents in the Settling, or in my personal headquarters if they're of Potential status. That's known as Strays and it's just outside the other end of the Midst, near the Cove. We're headed there now so you'll know where it is, in case it happens."

"In case what happens?" Mariana stopped and asked as a man shuffled past smoking a cigarette and simultaneously eating what appeared to be a Danish pastry. "The thirty-second Glimmer?"

I wish I had asked that, Cassie thought.

"Ah, you've heard. Yes, everyone has to be indoors when the sky changes color," Agatha explained, before whistling to a Working for Permanency to neaten his cart while he played toss-the-empty-Bad with a Potential on the nearby grass. "You won't experience a full Glimmer though, as all Potentials must be Zippered back from whence they came during the awful disruption."

"Are we getting close to a thirty-second Glimmer?" Cassie fretted, biting her lip.

"I'm afraid so. I will give you plenty of notice, though," Agatha said, patting the trusted pocket of her cloak. "The Surveyor lets me know when it's time."

"Eric'll be with us then, right? And Cassie's dad will be with her, too?" TJ asked, hanging back a few steps.

"Oh, I'm sure," Agatha answered, smoothing down her red hair.

Cassie couldn't help but ask, "What if someone stayed outside during the thirty seconds?"

Agatha chuckled, "Good Duskiness, no one would elect to do that. It would affect the entire Vibration." She bent over and said stealthily, "And if the Vibration changes, all the fun changes, too." She stood up straight, beheld the lively scene, and said, "Everyone enjoys complete pleasure on the Land of Blue. Why would they want to break the rules?"

"You'd have to be stupid to mess up your chances to eat and drink as much Bad as you wanted," TJ said.

"Let's just go to that place you own," Mariana said, checking out the rolling gray sky.

"Strays, dear."

"Yeah, there."

"Sal, are you coming with us?" TJ asked, straining his neck to search for Eric as they approached the Cove.

"I'll be there, or at the Pits, enjoying another nice, cold glass of Escape until the Glimmer!" Sal answered, stopping to high-five a Mooshkoo who hopped out of a Zebbies store next to a family of five.

Two freckle-faced boys and a strawberry-haired girl plunged their hands into brown-paper bags and pulled out handfuls of neon-colored Blobs, which they gobbled as they jumped down the three concrete steps to the street.

"Keryn has more than I do!" the fair-skinned boy whined. He kicked, jumped, and flailed his arms, eventually throwing himself on the ground.

"You get up right now or there won't be any more candy!" the mother scolded, to no avail. Cassie noticed she wore a Potential badge on her pink-checkered blouse.

The Mooshkoo turned to Agatha from the steps, begging for help. His bottom teeth bit his upper lip like a bulldog as he threw his rubbery blue arms up in the air.

"Excuse me, dear," Agatha said to Cassie. She confidently strode over to the mother and father, who argued loudly in front of the Zebbies about how to subdue their son. Calmly, Agatha leaned over to the frantic Mooshkoo and whispered in his ear. The Mooshkoo clapped his hands in excitement, "Oip, oip, oip, oip." Then it shot like a bullet back into the Zebbies.

"Clearly, that meant, 'Good idea!'" Mariana said, from the road.

The Mooshkoo returned with an overflowing brown bag of Blobs. The boy ceased his tantrum, rose to his feet, and grabbed the bag. He happily gobbled every piece he could stuff in his freckled face.

"Thank you!" sighed the mom in relief, petting the Mooshkoo, who blushed under his rubbery blue skin. "You saved the day!"

"Give the people what they want!" Agatha said, popping a Blob into her mouth. She chuckled as the delighted crowd watched her face turn pink. "Now," she lowered her voice to speak to the parents of the appeased boy, "please consider the Settling when the time comes."

The parents shook her hand. "We're already applying for Permanency status!"

"That's what we like to hear, huh Aggie?" Sal asked as he wedged his hands into the back pocket of his black jeans and rose up on his toes.

"If it wasn't for me, that plan wouldn't have been carried out effectively," Agatha remarked to Sal. Then to the others, "Carry on, and enjoy our magnificent land!"

Meanwhile, the Mooshkoo who saved the day looked upset that he hadn't been offered any Blobs in compensation. The inside of his round eyes made circular motions like a kaleidoscope as steam began to rise from its ears. Agatha's face grew angry, like parents whose children embarrass them in public. She whistled loudly and immediately and Big and Small appeared. They grabbed the agitated Mooshkoo by the arms and carried him down an alley, located between two brick Zebbies.

"Where are they taking him?" Cassie asked Agatha, grabbing

at the sleeve of her sweatshirt.

"Oh, dear," Agatha said, wringing her hands together. Without even thinking about it, Cassie started to wring her hands too. "I want to be sure we make it, as it's getting later than I anticipated."

"Make it?" Cassie asked, forgetting all about the upset Mooshkoo.

"It's getting near time. Come with me," Agatha instructed.

Cassie, TJ, and Mariana followed Agatha and Sal around the corner to a tidy, grassy square of property just outside the Midst. A neatly painted blue sign, labeled "Strays," poked out of the manicured grass next to a fancy, small brick walkway that swerved up to a charming garden cottage. Agatha prodded a brick back in its place that had come undone at the foot of the four stone steps before leading them inside the gray, antique Victorian, wooden front door. Cassie liked the gray rose-and-vine design inlaid in the piece of wood running horizontally across the middle of the door. She ran her finger over one of the leaves in the vine until Agatha sighed impatiently. Cassie put her finger in her mouth and stepped inside the well-kept front foyer, where a vase of red and yellow flowers that reminded her of McDonald's rested neatly upon a small table next to the front desk, across from the front door.

"This is pretty fancy," TJ said, noticing the ornate, copper chandelier hanging from the ceiling. Two gray-and-white paisley wainscoted hallways ran perpendicular off the foyer, toward the guest suites.

"Hey! My neighbor, Mrs. Pappas—whom my parents don't care for because they said she's manipulative—she has fake flowers like that at her house too!" Mariana said, pointing at the flowers as she stood next to a gold-painted coffee table where a stack of papers containing information on how to apply for Working for Permanency status sat on top of the glass.

"You always got something to say, huh?" Sal commented, shutting the front door.

"Good Dusk," Agatha greeted the Mooshkoo, dressed in a white apron and gray head scarf, dusting behind the desk. Agatha slid a few pink Blobs, retrieved from her cloak, across the glossy, polished counter.

"Oip!" A happy expression formed on the Mooshkoos' sweet face as she gobbled the Blob and immediately whisked around to stare into a large pewter-framed mirror, positioned in the middle of ten key slots to each of the rooms, to watch her face turn pill-pink.

"You're welcome, pet. These are my guests, who need to be kept safe during the next Glimmer," Agatha said, pressing her stiff red hair to her head, checking her appearance in the mirror behind the front desk. "Please see to it that the Potential suites are prepared."

The fastidious Mooshkoo saluted Agatha and reached under the counter to select an array of white throw blankets and white pillows, Stimulator game discs, and two unopened corrugated boxes labeled: "Colorful Blobs for Kids." She shoved her supplies under her rubbery arm and took off down the gray-carpeted hall beside the front desk as Agatha moved to a far corner of the foyer, under a hand-painted picture of *The Enticer* docked at the pier, titled "*The Enticer at Dusk*," to speak with Sal.

"Did you see all those games that Mooshkoo had? I hope we get to play them while we're waiting," TJ said, leaning his elbows on the front desk. A picture frame leaning against one of the white columns running from the ceiling to the floor listed upcoming entertainment in the Midst. "Maybe they even have a pool," he added, referring to the other gray-and-white wainscoted hallway across from the leather couch.

"I wonder what the rooms look like, cause this is a three-star foyer," Mariana said, checking out the copper lantern lights hung outside the door of each suite and the blue-and gray handstitched throw pillows on the sofa.

Agatha straightened a silver-framed oil painting of the stone wall running behind the Land titled, The Great Wall of Blue and said, "Sal, while their suite is being prepared, take TJ and Mariana back to the Cove." Then, turning to Cassie, who stood at the front desk touching one of the stiff red petals in the flower vase, "I believe there is someone you are waiting to see?"

Cassie stopped, gripping the petal between her fingers so hard it wrinkled as Agatha waited beside the front door. She immediately wanted to tell Agatha she was sorry for being a pest at the restaurant.

Agatha grinned, while Sal hopped over an armchair covered in blue-and-gray paisley fabric, and grabbed the gold handle on the front door.

"Can we try to find that Captain BP guy? His Blobs were the best. C'mon, Mariana," TJ said, snagging a pamphlet that advertised an upcoming "All-You-Can-Eat Blobs" contest.

Mariana placed her hands on Cassie's shoulders when they were halfway to the door. "Don't worry, okay? I'll see you when you get back . . . with your dad. Hey, since we're not going to be here for much longer, do you want me to bring back Blobs for you?"

Cassie smiled and nodded, "Thanks."

"Wait," TJ paused at the threshold, pinching the back of his arm through his sweatshirt, as Sal opened the front door. "Shouldn't I go with Cassie? What if Eric's in the same place as her dad?"

"No, kid," Sal said, shaking his head. "You got a better chance finding Eric in the Cove. That's where he was last sighted, according to the Surveyor, right Agatha?"

"You saw Eric at the Cove?" TJ asked Sal, who leaned down to snatch a Blue Goings-On pamphlet from a magazine rack on the floor by the door.

"I'll fill you in once they're gone," Sal said, squeezing the back of TJ's neck and stuffing the pamphlet in his back pocket. As an afterthought, he beckoned to Mariana. "Hey you, let's go."

Mariana whispered in Cassie's ear. "As many times as Sal puts his hand on that kid, he's actually pretty nice to him, too. I think he might be growing on me."

"Yeah, he's just looking out for TJ," Cassie agreed.

"Good luck," TJ said, tapping Cassie on the arm before he followed Sal outside.

"You too," Cassie replied, her stomach doing flips as she joined Agatha at the threshold of the door.

"You guys are going to be so happy having your families back together, even if it means we won't be coming back to the Land of Blue," Mariana said, stepping down onto the stone steps.

Sal glanced up at Agatha from the Beacon Hill bricked walkway.

"I'll introduce you to Eric when we find him," TJ said to Mariana. "He kinda looks like me, only he's a lot bigger, because, you know, he's in tenth grade."

Cassie walked down the steps, into the dusky night alongside Agatha as TJ and Mariana ran back into the Midst, TJ immediately taken in by the bouncing, frenetic lights of the Stimulators under the Cove's tent.

"Go!" he cheered on a pudgy Potential who disappeared into a Stimulator screen.

Mariana looked back at Cassie before entering the tent in the corner of the Midst and yelled, "Boys and their video games, huh?"

Agatha pushed Cassie's Potential badge firmly against her sweatshirt on the walkway, the way loving grandmothers snugly button winter coats before their grandkids go outside in the snow. Cassie bit her lip as she watched Mariana grab the controls of another Stimulator, her brown tresses whipping back and forth.

"Shall we, madam?" Agatha asked, linking her arm with Cassie's, the bricks returning to cobblestones.

Cassie's heart picked up speed as they turned left out of Stray's onto another road that led away from the noise and frenzy of the Midst. The few street lamps flickering along the dark, windy cobblestone road teased that they might extinguish at any moment.

Cassie thought, *This is kinda like the Settling Road on the other side of the Midst.*

"Is my father in the Settling?" Cassie asked, her voice cracking. She didn't want Agatha to think she was nosey.

"Good Dusk, Agatha," a few elves saluted with one hand as Agatha and Cassie passed by. They carried clear, empty vials in large, plastic containers on their shoulders as they briskly marched their little feet down the road.

Everyone knows Agatha. She's the most popular person in the Land, Cassie thought.

"To answer your question, your father is currently being cared for in a facility located in the farthest part of the Land of Blue—where Kurt's elves are returning from now—known as the Fix-It."

"What's that?" Cassie asked, noticing the elves picking up speed as they raised themselves above the ground and hovered over the cobblestones toward the Fix-It.

"It's where we put those who need assistance and where we restore order. Your father had been staying in the Settling comfortably until he began ignoring a bit of the rules. That's why we're hoping you can help."

Cassie felt the blood rush to her ears. "Did my dad do something wrong?"

Agatha lightly touched Cassie's arm. "It's all right, dear. We just need your help in keeping the Vibration on Blue intact. We're trying to get your father well—you know those awful backaches he gets—and regretfully, he hasn't complied. Therefore, we're counting on you to get him to take his medicine. We simply want to release him back into the Midst, into happiness and pleasure, and of course, to send him home."

Cassie scuffed along the uneven cobblestones under the inconsistent lighting of the street lamps, imagining her father being tied up by Big and Small for not obeying the rules. Her stomach was in knots as elves on bicycles with giant containers labeled "Have To Haves," in pink-Pepto-Bismal lettering, whizzed by in midair, pedaling furiously in the direction of the Fix-It.

"But my dad always takes his medicine," Cassie blinked. "I get it for him on his bureau when he's too tired to get out of bed." Cassie liked taking care of her father on the nights her Mom had to work. He always said, "You're a good girl," whenever Cassie brought him his medicine.

"I know you'd do anything to make your dad feel better. That's why we're counting on you." Agatha's dark eyes reflected the low light of a street lamp up ahead as she took Cassie's hand and squeezed it tight.

Why isn't he doing what he needs to feel better? Cassie wondered, picking at the skin on her forehead with her other hand. The street lamps cast tall, spooky shadows on the gloomy road. Cassie never remembered a time her dad didn't take medicine for his pain. She had to be sure her dad took whatever Agatha said he needed to feel better. Then he could come home.

"Ahh, that's the spirit," Agatha's voice purred like a stray kitten looking for a bowl of cold milk. "Now, tell me how things are going with your father's side of the family."

Cassie tilted her head. "My dad really doesn't talk about his family. My grandparents died when I was a baby. I have a bunch of uncles who live in Boston, but my dad doesn't speak to them. I heard my mom on the phone one day telling her friend they had a 'falling out,' whatever that means."

"A 'falling out,' you say? Oh, dear. Verrrrryyy difficult— sometimes downright impossible—to repair," Agatha said, releasing Cassie's hand. "Unfortunately, these things happen frequently in families."

"They do?" Cassie asked, her eyebrows squishing together as wind whipped through the scraggly trees lining both sides of the road.

Agatha made a "tsk, tsk" sound before waving to a group of elves returning to the Midst on their bicycles, container-free. "It's tragic no one's explained these things to you before."

"No one tells me anything," Cassie tucked her hair behind her ear.

Agatha mumbled, "A falling out. Difficult to break the cycle."

"What does that mean, 'difficult to break the cycle'?" Cassie asked, her eyelid twitching.

"Fortunately, I mean unfortunately, it means that what comes before us usually ends up happening to us," Agatha explained, with her hands clasped behind her back as she strode along the road like a lawyer in a courtroom.

A man and a woman in hooded sweatshirts and sweatpants each held a vial in their hands as they shuffled silently along the cobblestones, occasionally stepping into the shallow line of trees that lined the road leading back toward the Midst.

"Thank Duskiness for those Have to Haves!" Agatha called to the couple up ahead.

The woman replied, "You can say that again. I wasn't feeling too good."

Cassie recoiled when the woman neared; the woman's face was so thin, and her eyes so large they practically bulged out of their sockets. After they passed by, Cassie saw two three-foot-tall Entities behind the young couple, carrying on their own conversation.

"Agatha," Cassie asked her Entity. "How come some people don't seem to notice their Entities?"

"Not everyone is as lucky as you, or TJ, to meet us in form," Agatha said, as if paying a compliment. "Most of you merely hear us, often mistaking us for your own thoughts. Imagine that."

A small road, akin to a driveway, branching off to the right of the cobblestones, came into view. At the end of the short, paved road Cassie saw a jetty revealed by a dimly lit street lamp. The jetty led to a clearing, which was hard for Cassie to see from the road leading to the Fix-It. She stopped to see tree branches creaking in the night as an Entity trudged down the road, looking like an elephant seal traversing on sand. He headed toward the end of the jetty, where Cassie saw wisps of shadowy light—like smoke from a blown-out candle—float from the top of his flat head into the dusky sky.

Where is he going? she wondered, when Agatha's voice rang out in the night.

"Another one needs you, Raymond," Agatha called from the tip of the road.

Raymond acknowledged Agatha with a salute from his long, gas-mask-like snout. When he reached the end of the jetty, he careened on his black-soled shoes for a moment. Then, raising his snout to the sky, like a plane waiting for takeoff, he lifted off the rocks. Swirling and spinning, Raymond rose into the sky until he was out of sight.

"Where did he go?" Cassie asked, not noticing the group of elves pitter-pattering back to the Midst hands-free, as Agatha continued walking in the direction of the Fix-It.

"He left to aid yet another child in your dimension."

"Why?"

"When a child sends out a Vibration of fear, worry, or despair, we adhere to them, like magnets." Agatha touched the tip of Cassie's nose.

"How did Raymond know a kid was worried?"

"His field buzzed."

"Did your field buzz for me?" Cassie asked, checking the back of Agatha's head to see if there was any smoke floating from her red hair. There wasn't.

"Of course," Agatha said as the road began to brighten. "And good thing, because you needed me."

CHAPTER
THIRTEEN

Their destination was an old, rectangular brick building with barely any windows, and massive light fixtures mounted upon the roof. Harsh light from the many bulbs and aluminum reflectors flooded the road under the dusky sky, reminding Cassie of Fenway Park at night. Weeds lined the long concrete walkway out front, where a large Energy Vibration Meter was stationed on a lonely patch of brown grass. The arrow pointed steadily toward the same range of elephant-skin gray. A sign reading, "The Fix-It Facility" hung over the front entrance.

A blacktop courtyard at the base of the Fix-It, surrounded by a chain link fence, contained a basketball hoop and a few uncomfortable-looking metal chairs cast in shadow under the glare of the intense lighting. The massive stone wall Cassie had seen from *The Enticer* loomed behind the building, appearing as if it was guarding something. A crumbly cement lane next to the courtyard led down and around to the back of the building, near the intimidating wall.

Quickening her gait, Cassie left Agatha and ran past the lane, the courtyard, and up the concrete walk, breathlessly reaching the main entrance. An opening, similar to a mail slot, lay just above the metal doorknob. Cassie knocked on the cold steel door. After a moment, the slat opened, falling at her eye level.

"Are you here for refills?" a hefty, strawberry-haired lady asked through the slat. Her chubby cheeks took up most of the horizontal opening.

"Refills?" Cassie asked, pressing her thumbs together atop the second concrete stair.

The woman eyed her suspiciously and snapped, "Visiting hours are over."

"Over?" Cassie cried. "But we just got here, and my dad is here, and I know he's been waiting for me, his name is—"

"Sorry, sunshine, those are the rules." The lady with the abundant blue eye shadow cracked her bubble gum, giving her fleshy cheeks a workout.

Agatha reached Cassie's side. "Good Dusk, Nurse Moody."

"Good Dusk, Agatha. I'm only doing my job."

Cassie thought she saw the gum-cracking nurse wink at Agatha through the slot.

"I do appreciate you following the rules. Tell me, Nurse Moody, has Craig Connor taken his Have to Haves yet?" Agatha asked, and bent over to secure a latch on a smaller steel door to the right of the main entrance that looked like a door for pets, labeled Pick-Ups.

"No, Agatha, I'm afraid not." Nurse Moody shook her head sadly. "He's still trying to do it his way. And let me tell ya, cupcake," she said, making eye contact with Cassie, "he's in severe pain."

"Well, w-when are the next visiting hours?" Cassie stammered.

"I have to get him to take his medicine. You have to let me in!"

"Next visiting hours, hmm," Nurse Moody mused, tapping her chin. "Not until after the next thirty-second Glimmer."

Fear shot up from Cassie's toes to her throat. "But you said I can't stay during the Glimmer!" she said, turning to Agatha, who stood on the concrete stairs. "That means I'll have to leave without him! Can't you talk to the person in charge? You know everyone!"

"I appreciate that. However, Dr. Fox, who manages the Fix-It, is a very busy man. He and I report to the Dusk Ruler, who is counting on us to attend to our assigned duties. I wouldn't want to upset the order of things. You know how it goes when one does that," Agatha said, raising an eyebrow.

Nurse Moody blew a giant electric-pink bubble through the slat.

Agatha continued while Cassie pinched the skin on her cheek. "We must follow the rules and wait for the next visiting hours. I am deeply regretful we did not make it in time, what with all of the festivities taking our attention. You have enjoyed yourself though, while you've been here, haven't you?" Agatha's voice held a hint of disappointment.

Cassie pinched her skin harder. She didn't want Agatha to feel she was unappreciative, but this news made her heart sink. She muttered, "I had a lot of fun."

The sound of a metal door banging shut could be heard in the near distance. A shadow moved near the empty chairs in the courtyard. Stepping into the glaring light, a man appeared—a seeming Entity from the waist down as he waddled by like a troll in his beige work pants and black work shoes, yet regular looking from the waist up, wearing a Land of Blue sweatshirt and sporting a thick, curly head of brown hair. He bounced a navy-blue basketball twice before taking a shot. *Swoosh.*

"Who's that?" Cassie asked, as the man picked up a push broom and began sweeping the courtyard.

Nurse Moody yawned through the slat. "Oh, that's Carlos. He's in charge of cleanup."

Agatha thought for a moment and called down the small hill toward the courtyard. "Carlos, would you mind entertaining my Potential for a moment or two while I speak privately to Nurse Moody?"

"Shur!" Carlos replied, setting the broom against the fence. "I was just taking a break un momentito anyway. Send her down, Agatha. She's in good manos."

Agatha spoke inaudibly with Nurse Moody through the slat and then motioned, with a wave of her hand, for Cassie to go. Cassie tentatively scuffed down the stairs to the concrete path that led to the courtyard.

"Hola, mi nombre es Carlos," said the stocky, tanned creature as he kicked a few pebbles away on the court with his black shoe and waddled over to unlock the fence.

Cassie stepped off the concrete path, walked over a stretch of grass, and entered the tarred courtyard.

"Chu look just like your papa," he said, picking up a blue basketball and tucking it under one of his muscular, construction-worker-type arms.

Cassie's eyes widened, "You know my dad?"

"Sí," Carlos answered and began to dribble the ball, crisscrossing it between his thick, troll-like legs.

"Are you his Entity?" Cassie asked, eyeing Carlos's oddly shaped lower body.

"No, no," Carlos chuckled, his liquid brown eyes shining under the glare of the lights as he set the ball on the ground. "I'm just the janitor. I take out the basura y stuff like that." He pointed to a garbage bag leaning against one of the metal chairs. "But I see chur papá cada día when I make my rounds. Dass where I found this," Carlos pulled a photograph out of his pocket and handed it to Cassie.

Cassie took the smooth square with trembling hands. It was a picture of her when she was four years old, sitting atop a pony at the Bubbling Brook Farm. She had a petrified look on her face, which apparently was a theme because every time Nana Helen took out a photo album she'd say, "For Pete's sake, there you are again looking like a scaredy cat!" In this picture, Cassie's dad stood beside her, his eyes at half-mast like he had been up all night, as he held his daughter upright in her ballerina-pink rain slicker.

Cassie stared at the old photo, fighting back tears.

"I so sorry visiting horas are terminado," Carlos said. "But I bet Agatha bring chu back for the next sheeft."

But what if she doesn't? What if she gets sick of me? Cassie thought, gripping the picture.

"No seas negativo!" Carlos said, tugging on the tip of the light-blue T-shirt peeking out from under his navy-blue sweatshirt.

Did he hear my thoughts too? Cassie wondered.

"Sí. Mind Mail," Carlos chuckled, "which I sure chu know about by now when chur standing in someone's espacio personal. It's bueno y malo."

Cassie stared at Carlos, listening.

"El punto es, keep those thoughts positivo, chica. Chu'll be back," Carlos gently took the picture out of Cassie's hands. "I gotta make chur this gets back to him." He tucked the faded memory back into the pocket of his work pants.

"Do you know why my dad isn't taking what he needs to feel better?"

"No, chica, I don't. Dr. Fox and his gente don't tell me mucho."

Cassie scuffed the blacktop with her sneaker.

"But," Carlos added, causing Cassie to lift her gaze. "I can tell chu they don't like when patientes don't toma their Have to Haves. Upsets da systema. Dass the problema, chica. Trying to do things on his own, your papa. Takes real courage to do dat. Doc says he knows best, dat your papa needs his Have to Haves, and dat there's no other way to get better. But chu no hear dat from me. The doc don't like when Cogs break the rules." Carlos shook his curly head of hair.

"Is that what my dad is? A Cog?"

"Sí, and there's a whole lot of dem in the Fix-It. That's why it's un edificio grande." Cassie scanned the length of the long building, the few windows containing bars across the glass, reminding her of the Nashua Street jail. Cassie looked over at Carlos. For a moment, she thought he looked sad. Then he changed his tone. "Hey! Did chu know if you have the same frecuencia as someone else chu can use Mind Mail también? When you're not even in their space! But chu'll figure that out later. Pero ahora," he said, glancing up the walkway, "chu want to know how to use it when chu're home, across dimensions?"

"What do you mean?" Cassie asked, feeling her pulse rise.

"Mira me," Carlos spread his calloused hands out in front of him. "Picture writing down chur thoughts on a piece of papel en putting it in an envelope, like you do in chur dimension. Only de envelope's in chur mind, see? Then chu imagine sending it from chur cabeza to mine. Since I see chur papá cada día, I could keep chu posted if chu sent me Mind Mail from home. But that'd be up to chu." Carlos picked up the ball and took a shot, bouncing it off the rim.

"I can send you my thoughts on purpose?" Cassie asked, a puzzled look on her face.

"Sí! Go on, try it now." Carlos waddled about ten feet away from Cassie. "Picture the envelope with my name on the outside of it, big letters—chu know, CARLOS IS THE BEST—just keeding. Then, pictur it leefing your mind, floating out of your cabeza, traveling across the espacio between us, and appearing right before my eyes. Chu see it?"

Cassie closed her eyes, her forehead wrinkled like a ridged potato chip. "I think so."

"Bueno," Carlos said, glancing up the walkway again. "Now

chu jus need to do dat at home. Chu send me a note, and I'll send chu one back. And if I send chu one and chur busy, jus return it unopened." Carlos bounced the basketball to Cassie.

"I get to decide whether I want to read it or not?" Cassie asked, catching the ball.

"Shur, chica. It's up to chu whether or not chu open chur mail, right?" Cassie thought about all the junk mail Nana Helen threw out in the kitchen Rubbermaid trash bin. "Ees always up to you, chica. Hey, would chu mind taking this bag of basura down the lane there to the dumpster? Cuz I gotta do something before Agatha comes back for you. Can chu handle it?"

"Okay," Cassie said, setting the ball on the ground.

"Thanks. I be right back." Carlos bowleggedly headed over to the end of the brick building at the back of the courtyard, fishing a key out of his pocket in order to gain access through a blue door.

Cassie picked up the tied bag of trash, trudged out and around the courtyard, and ventured slowly down the dark, broken-cement lane. She stepped over the granola-like pieces of pavement the same way she stepped over the cracks in the sidewalks at home. She had to be sure nothing bad happened to her dad.

Cassie felt like she was doing something wrong, as she sensed something watching her from behind the wall. At the end of the lane, the dumpster sat, looking like a hungry, green monster with its mouth wide open. Empty bottles and cans lay on the ground beside the dumpster, along with torn paper wrappers, syringes, and other sludgy brown pieces of used food wrappers.

Cassie took a deep breath and held it as she quickly tossed the garbage into the open pit, and turned to run back up the walkway. But just as she was about to take off in a sprint, she noticed something on the ground by her feet. She bent down to pick up a pair of gold-rimmed glasses. She reached back toward the dumpster to toss them in, but stopped. She suddenly felt as if her body was being commanded by an outside force. Slowly she placed the golden rims on the end of her nose, and viewed her surroundings. To Cassie's surprise, all of the trash now appeared to be jeweled treasure, just like the Wisdom Glass on Option's Port.

Cassie curiously removed the glasses. Piles of empty mugs and loads of dark bottles of Escape bulged from the belly of the dumpster. Again, Cassie placed the glasses on the end of her nose. Thousands of jewels shone before her in colors of magenta, fuchsia, and emerald. Her lips slightly parted, she looked behind her to be sure no one was there and then reached out a shaky hand and selected a ruby-red piece, smooth between her trembling fingers.

A pebble fell from the stone wall. Quickly, she flung the red jewel back in the dumpster and stuffed the glasses in the pocket of her jeans.

I'll ask Agatha about the glasses. She'll explain things to me, like she always does.

Running back up the crumbly lane, the glasses jingled in her pocket. Carlos simultaneously emerged from the blue door and entered the courtyard. "Gracias, chica. That dumpster gets filled up rápido round here."

"Y-yeah," Cassie stammered, patting down her pants to quiet the glasses.

Agatha opened the gate to the courtyard. "We have an issue."

"What happened?" Cassie asked, going over to meet her at the gate.

"Well," Agatha sighed. "Without your father in compliance, I'm going to be in quite a bit of trouble for bringing you here."

"Oh no," Cassie said, biting her nail. "I don't want you to get in trouble."

"Well, there may be a solution yet." Agatha tapped a finger to her lips. "If you sign this form instructing your father to take his Have to Haves so he can see you, and of course, to manage his pain the way he always has before—"

"They help him, I know they do!" Cassie cried.

Carlos turned away, picking up Blob wrappers that drifted in from a light wind coming from behind the building.

"Yes, dear, I know. He must keep taking his Have to Haves. However, if you sign this document telling your father the only way he can see you is to take them, the doctor will allow you first visitor status after the Glimmer. I assure you the line can get rather long, as there are many who come to visit their loved ones who are here to heal."

"But when will that be?" Cassie's voice cracked.

"S'cuse me, but I need to get going," Carlos said. "Nice meeting chu, chica. Hope we can talk again."

"Gracias, Carlos," Agatha saluted.

Carlos grabbed the broom on his way back to the building, stopping to look up at the sky as a few more wrappers blew in from the suddenly warmer, incoming air.

"Bye Carlos," Cassie said, waving offhandedly as she turned back to her Entity. "Of course I'll do anything, but I don't want to wait. I've come all this way!"

Agatha appeared irritated as she rested her hand atop the fence, her red hair lifting stiffly in the breeze. "There are rules I must follow to maintain the high status I've attained on Blue. That status, may I gently remind you, allows me to help you get what you came here for."

Cassie felt a sharp pang of guilt spread throughout her body like an ink spill. *What if Agatha gives up on me because I'm so annoying?*

"You're either with me or you're not." Agatha rapped her thick fingernails on the metal fence. "Now, what's it going to be?"

Cassie took the pen and paper Agatha retrieved from her cloak. "I'll do whatever you need me to. I know you'll bring me back to Blue." She read the prepared note:

Craig Connor,

Your daughter is pleading with you to take the Have to Haves you desperately need to get well. Once you do this, we can get you back where you belong. Please heed her request.

Signed,

_____

Cassie held the paper against the chain link fence and signed her name. Her penmanship was shaky at the thought of spending even one more day away without her father.

"That's a good girl," Agatha said, taking the paper from Cassie. "Of course I'll bring you back, my Potential. It's always easier to return to Blue once you know the ropes."

"Do we get to stop at Option's Port?" Cassie asked, clutching the top of the fence, never taking her eyes off the signed piece of paper.

Will Dad take the Have to Haves right away? Will they get to him in time? she wondered.

"No interruption from Option's Port," Agatha grinned. "You already proved you have what it takes to be in the Land of Blue. Our bond is even stronger now, Cassie. That means we can get back next time much more quickly."

Cassie sighed, relaxing her grip on the fence, her allegiance to Agatha solid.

Agatha shuddered at the rolling gray sky overhead and glanced quickly at her Surveyor.

"It's almost time for the Glimmer. Such a frightening time."

"What happens now?" Cassie asked, noticing a few strangers hurrying down the concrete path from the Fix-It as they headed back to the Midst entrance, holding vial containers in their hands. "It happened so soon. I don't want to leave!"

"Of course, Blue is such a special place here and we, er, I, want you to stay longer too." Agatha said, patting Cassie's arm. "But I must get you back. You're not strong enough yet to handle the Glimmer."

But I want to be! And I also want to be able to go to the Settling and earn special status.

Agatha stroked Cassie's cheek, her calloused finger rough on Cassie's skin. "In time. Come, let's gather your friends. It's time to Zipper back. Remember, it's always quicker on the return."

Agatha locked arms with Cassie and ushered her out of the courtyard and swiftly back down the cobblestones in the direction of the Midst. The lightening sky brought with it a breeze so warm Cassie considered taking off her sweatshirt. By the time they neared the end of the road and Cassie could see the Strays' cottage on the grassy corner across from the Midst, the Entities, their Potentials, and Permanents frantically ran for cover. They trampled one another to get inside the many Pits and Zebbies, desperate to escape the gradually changing sky. Cassie felt a lump in her throat when they finally reached Strays.

"Hurry dear," Agatha said, shooing Cassie inside the front door of the welcoming cottage, as if a tornado was fast approaching. "We must stay indoors until it's time to Zipper."

Where are Mariana and TJ?

Shutting the door tightly behind them, Agatha said, "Don't worry about the others, Sal has done this more times than you've bitten off your fingernails."

Cassie's cheeks flushed like hot coils on a stove.

Bang! The front door opened, hitting the wainscoted wall behind it and leaving a mark. Agatha chuckled as Sal escorted Mariana inside.

"That was crazy! Everyone was screaming, trying to get inside somewhere, and yet the air felt better than it usually does, huh TJ?" Mariana asked, but TJ wasn't there.

Cassie rushed to the door to find TJ headed back into the chaotic Midst, walking toward a tall, dark-haired, dark-skinned teenager who was trying to get inside an overcrowded Zebbies.

"Eric!" cried TJ. "It's me!"

"Kid, let's go, get in here!" Sal yelled to him from the front door as the sky began to lighten.

TJ dodged one pushcart after another as vendors rushed to store their wares in alleyways before heading indoors. TJ continued to call, "Eric!"

But the noise from the Midst made it impossible for Eric to hear TJ's voice.

"Get inside, kid! Who do you belong to?" Kurt and Big grabbed TJ by the arm as they continued to corral customers in the street.

"But I see him! He can Zipper back with us now!" TJ said, pointing to a group of boys shoving and pushing to get into one of the Zebbies.

Sal, out of breath, flew over and grabbed TJ by the scruff of the neck. "Sorry, Kurt, Big. He's with me. Won't happen again."

"Let's hope not. Wouldn't want to bring that up at the meeting. Now get indoors!" Kurt commanded.

Big, under Kurt's direction, inspected alleyways and trash cans, making certain there wasn't a poor soul left in the square.

Cassie strained her neck to look over Mariana's shoulder at Strays.

"You're gonna get me in trouble, boy!" Sal said, dragging TJ to safety with his claw-like nails. "Eric'll be fine. We'll put him up in the Settling and take good care of him. You'll get him when you come back. Your energy isn't ready to be here during a Glimmer, but don't worry, I have faith in you."

In the Strays' foyer, TJ plopped down on the couch, dejected he had missed the chance to see his brother, but also proud Sal had complimented him. He rubbed the red mark on his neck as

Sal slammed the front door. A square frame of a smiling group of former Potentials-turned-Permanents on the wall beside the door turned lopsided.

Cassie pulled at her bottom lip while she surveyed TJ's forlorn face.

"Come now, all of you, while Sal and I make arrangements for both yours and Cassie's return," Agatha said, snagging a key to room number nine from behind the front desk.

She led Cassie, TJ, and Mariana down the hall adjacent to the front desk and opened the white-painted door, revealing a cozy room containing three midnight-blue beanbags draped with white throw blankets and white pillows, cartons of Blobs, a make-your-own-Bad machine in the corner atop a fancy bookshelf, and three flashing Stimulators ready to be played. "Enjoy the Potential suite for our most special newcomers while we plan for your return accommodations."

"Woah!" TJ exclaimed, stepping inside the spacious, white-carpeted, gray-walled, brightly lit room.

"I've never seen anything like this," Cassie said, checking out the ornate fancy mirror hanging on the wall, as voices yelled in the street, audible through a large set of shutters. She examined the freckles splattered across her nose, not liking them very much.

"I should think not," Agatha said proudly. Turning to the Mooshkoo who had entered to prop up the beanbag chairs and pour mugs of Bad from the do-it-yourself machine, she said in a hushed tone while she adjusted one of the lanterns on the wall, "Please close the shutters. We don't want to alarm the children."

"Gosh, you'd think the sky was falling," Mariana said, as frantic screams of the last few stragglers could be heard outside.

Immediately the Mooshkoo went about the suite like a whirling dervish, closing every slat in the shutters within a matter of seconds.

"This is like the Four Seasons if kids were in charge," Mariana commented, selecting a few chocolate-covered Blobs out of a pretty, Enticer-shaped bowl and nestling down in one of the comfy beanbags.

"At least Eric will have special status if he's staying in the Settling," Cassie said to TJ as she ripped open one of the cartons of Blobs. "My dad used to be there, too, before they brought him to the Fix-It to get him better. It's a good thing we have Entities to bring us back, cause I don't know about you, but next time I'm not leaving without my dad. No matter what." Cassie shoved a fistful of Blobs in her mouth and plunked down in another beanbag, her face glowing macaroni-orange.

TJ dropped into the last beanbag, chomping on a handful of Blobs. "Me too. I guess we're in this together, then." His mouth went round and round, his face the color of a kaleidoscope wheel.

"That's the spirit!" Agatha said, triumphantly. "Perhaps, as a reward," she added, running her finger along the ledge of the bookshelf, "you can even stay a little longer next time."

"And who wouldn't want that?" Sal asked as he entered the suite.

TJ smiled up at Sal like a junior-varsity player looking up to the varsity captain, and turned to Mariana and Cassie. "Both of you will be back, right?"

"If Cassie goes, I go. Besides, I plan to go head-to-head with you on that shark-infested waters Stimulator. I was getting pretty good at swimming away, don't you think?" Mariana asked, chewing on another chocolate-covered Blob, her ears enlarging out of her head so big they looked like they'd explode. "I don't know how you played ten games in a row, though. My head hurts."

TJ laughed, "Are you kidding? I could play Stimulators for days. Sal, can we play now?"

"Well," Sal began, eyeing the flashing Stimulator games like a hot-fudge sundae.

"Once the Glimmer passes and you have returned," Agatha interrupted. Sal and TJ deflated like two balloons. Agatha chuckled and said, "Oh, how proud it makes me when you enjoy our Land the way we do! Now, we'll just be a flash, and we'll come back to take you all home before the Glimmer erupts." Agatha shuddered and left the Potential Suite with Sal trailing behind her black cloak.

After the door closed, TJ said quietly, measuring with his hands, "I was this close. Eric was right there. I wish I could have made it into Zebbies."

"Maybe they just didn't want you to get hurt," Cassie said, eating another Blob.

"You guys don't understand," TJ said, running his hand through his hair. "Eric is more like a parent to me than my own parents. They're always busy, in the store. They don't ask me if I have homework or what I get for grades. It just . . . " his voice trailed off. "Eric is the only one who really cares about what happens to me."

Cassie's heart hurt. She leaned forward and said, "Well, I care what happens to you. And that means you have to be here when I get back. Remember, we're in this together."

"I'll be here too," Mariana declared, inching forward in her beanbag chair as her ears returned to their normal size. She put both hands behind her head and said, "Besides, Cassie needs me. I'm her voice of reason."

"It's true," Cassie said, pulling at her earlobe.

TJ looked at the blank screen of the Stimulator as the room quieted, resting his head in one hand and with one finger of his other hand he traced the fleurs-de-lis design in the carpet. Mariana closed her eyes and rubbed her forehead. Cassie sunk deeper in the beanbag and stared at a stack of books on the bookshelf, whose titles she couldn't read, while biting her fingernails. They all waited for Agatha and Sal to return.

The noise outside gradually lowered until they could barely hear a whisper. Suddenly, Big and Small yelled to Kurt from across the street. "I think we're good, Boss!" causing Cassie to snap out of her trance.

She remembered the Mind Mail tip Carlos taught her, and said to TJ, "Maybe I can teach you something I learned about keeping in touch when we're home."

TJ lifted his chin.

"Can I do it too?" Mariana asked, perking up. "Or do I have to have a tough home life to do it?"

Cassie and TJ made eye contact.

"I did it again, didn't I?" Mariana said, sitting up and reaching for the box of Blobs. She fished out a red one and chomped it.

TJ shared a knowing glance with Cassie, his mouth clamped tight. Cassie realized her feelings weren't as hurt this time because she didn't feel alone.

Just as Cassie opened her mouth to tell them about Carlos, she felt a gentle tug in her mind, as if someone wanted to pull her away from the conversation. She closed her eyes and immediately the image of an envelope flashed into her mind.

> To: Cassie
> From: Carlos

With her eyes still closed, she opened the envelope. The piece of lined paper, like the ones in her notebooks at home, read:

> TEST!

Cassie squeezed her eyes tight to prevent her from squealing, and quickly visualized her own piece of paper. On it, she scrawled the words:

> Got it!

She stuffed it in an envelope in her mind's eye and addressed it to Carlos at the Fix-It. Finally, she sent it up and out of her own head and down into the top of Carlos's thick, brown, curly hair.

She opened her eyes. TJ and Mariana were popping Blobs

into their mouths and watching each other change color. Everything had become eerily quiet outside, the way it felt after a carnival leaves town.

Just then, the hue of the room began to brighten around the shutter frame, akin to the sun rising in the early morning sky.

Is the Glimmer doing that? Cassie wondered.

She wanted to peek through the slats, wondering how just a Glimmer of light could be as bright as the sun. Suddenly, the door of the Potential Suite burst open and Agatha and Sal surged forth. Agatha extended her arms all the way around Mariana and Cassie, while Sal seized TJ by the shoulders and pulled him into the corner. Then, with a rather forceful *ZIP!* they were gone.

CHAPTER
FOURTEEN

Mrs. Burke wrote with black marker on the whiteboard at the front of the classroom. "Three-and-twenty-six hundredths times ten to the fourth power equals . . . ," Mrs. Burke's mouth was moving, but Cassie couldn't hear a word she said.

I wish I could have a forty-five, maybe even a forty-nine-fingered mug of Bad right now, she thought.

The leaves outside the classroom window, on the second floor of the old brick school building, mixed red and orange like Fruity Pebbles cereal. Cassie kicked the rung of her chair as a few reddish-green leaves fell softly to the ground. Mrs. Burke's voice sounded far away that late October afternoon while Cassie, for the tenth time, thought about the Mind Mail she received from Carlos the previous week.

Slowly coming out of sleep, right before she was fully awake that Tuesday morning, an envelope dropped into Cassie's mind. She opened it carefully in that dreamy sleep state, so as not to miss a word.

Good Dawn Cassie,

Doc at the Fix-It is pleezed. Chur papa's been taking his Have to Haves—lots of them! Only ting is, chur padre's been talking 'bout going back to the Settling, but chu didn't hear dat from me. Wasn't he s'posed to go home wit chu? I think it would be muy bueno if you could make arrangements with Agatha to come pronto. Keep up chur studies.

Carlos

Cassie rubbed her eyes as the sun rose in the light gray sky, brightening her stark room and making it harder to keep her eyes closed. The envelope faded.

Why would Dad want to go to back to the Settling? If he's taking his Have to Haves, he'll feel better and want to come home, right? Oh! Maybe he needs to get something he left there. Yeah, that's probably it.

Back in the classroom, Cassie rubbed her face with her whole hand as she stared at the whiteboard. How could Carlos tell her to study at a time like this?

"Okay, everyone, I'm going to hand back the scientific notation tests," Mrs. Burke announced, holding a stack of paper in her arms. "When the bell rings, you may be dismissed."

Cassie's stomach dropped. She hadn't done well on the last quiz, even though she was usually an A and B student. She hated every minute of expanded and scientific notation. She drummed the first three fingers of her right hand on her right leg three times, and then drummed the first three fingers of her left hand *1-2-3, 1-2-3, 1-2-3* on her other thigh.

Whap! Mrs. Burke dropped the test papers on each student's desk, the clicking sound of her fancy boots marking her way through the quiet classroom. Tracy DeNapoli beamed as she received her paper, promptly gathering her backpack and water bottle from under the table in order to leave when the bell rang. Tommy Shaw groaned, flinging his head back when he checked his grade, while the room erupted in whispered bursts of "Yes!" and fist-pumps.

Cassie slumped in her seat and bounced her leg up and down. Mrs. Burke returned everyone's test except Cassie's. The classroom noise grew as all twenty-four students whispered to one another about their test grades, waiting for the bell to ring. When it did, they grabbed their folders and backpacks, and filed out the door. The room now empty, Mrs. Burke approached Cassie and gently placed her test on the desk. At the top of the paper, circled in red pen, Cassie saw: "67".

That's practically an F! Cassie gulped, her heart hammering through her chest, blood rising to her cheeks.

"I know you don't enjoy the material, Cassie, but I also know you are more than capable. I can't help noticing that you seem somewhere else lately. Is everything all right?" Mrs. Burke made Cassie want to cry, with her glossy black hair and her nice smell, like baby powder and roses. She pictured Mrs. Burke's kids burying their faces in her long, soft hair whenever they were sad, and wished she could do that too.

But she's not your mother.

Cassie felt stuck, like she couldn't move. She bit her nail to remind herself she was there.

"Let's take a walk, okay?" said Mrs. Burke, her voice sweet and soothing, like tea with sugar.

Cassie followed her favorite teacher downstairs, past the girls' bathroom, and to an office by the exit sign that led to the black-tarred recess area.

Leaves scattered on the chilly court.

I wonder when I'll see Carlos again.

"Cassie?" asked a voice coming from the left. Cassie turned to see a middle-aged woman in a moss-green blouse standing in the doorway of the office. She had her hands on both thighs, as though she had called Cassie's name a few times.

Cassie recognized the brown-haired lady. She visited Cassie's classroom every week to take Todd Anderson out to talk. The last time he left the classroom, Lisa Kurker whispered, "He has to talk about his feelings because his parents don't live together anymore." Lisa knew everybody's business.

"Hi, I'm Mrs. Beals," the coffee-eyed woman said, reaching out her hand. Cassie shook it, noticing one thick, silver bracelet wrapped around her wrist. Mrs. Beals motioned to a chair with a tan padded cushion on the other side of her metal desk. One other padded metal chair sat in a corner next to a window. "Please have a seat."

"I'll leave you two to talk," Mrs. Burke said, gently shutting the door. Cassie liked the way Mrs. Burke's eyes squinted whenever she smiled.

Mrs. Beals sat down behind her desk and picked up a squishy mound of delicately beaded, pastel-colored foam. She began kneading it in her hands, pulling off a piece and handing it to Cassie across the desk.

"I've heard you're a very smart girl," she said, her voice kind, like the woman who handed out the weekly bulletin at Mass. "This year, though, your grades haven't been where your teachers think they should be. I'm wondering if you have any idea why that might be?"

Cassie plucked at the foam in her hands. "I don't know. I don't like math much."

Mrs. Beals molded her piece of foam into the shape of a

flower. "How about English or Social Studies? According to your other teachers, your grades have been slipping there too." Cassie stared at the braided area rug on the floor and thought, *As soon as I go back to Blue, I'm having two Yums.*

"Do you like animals?" Mrs. Beals asked, forming the pastel foam into a cat. Cassie raised her head.

"Tell me, only if you want to, if you could be any animal, what would you be and why?" Mrs. Beals' tone reminded Cassie of Mrs. Papadopoulis when she asked the girls whether they wanted one or two black-bean brownies.

Cassie rotated her ankles. "I guess I'd be a horse, a white horse. 'Cause they're powerful."

"Great. Is there an animal you wouldn't want to be?" Mrs. Beals squished the cat back into a ball.

Cassie stared at the bare wall between Mrs. Beals' desk and her bookshelf filled with puzzles, books, and board games.

"A crocodile."

"Why?"

"They look scary when they sneak out of the water." Cassie tied her shoelaces.

"Crocodiles do look scary when they come out of the water," Mrs. Beals agreed. "Do you think about them often?"

As she knotted her sneakers, Cassie saw Mrs. Beals' sturdy brown shoes under the desk. She recalled the nightmare she had had the previous weekend, where a crocodile threatened to eat her, like Captain Hook in *Peter Pan*. Agatha had appeared, with a grin like the Cheshire cat, telling Cassie they would be going to Blue *very soon.* Cassie woke up drenched in sweat, the clock flashing 2:00 a.m.

"Well, in case you do think of them often, would you like me to show you a simple breathing technique that might make you feel better?" Mrs. Beals asked, wheeling her rollaway chair out from behind her desk.

"Sure," Cassie glanced at the tan clock hanging on the far

149

wall. Nana Helen would be there in five minutes to pick Cassie up from school.

"Breathe in deeply through your nose and squeeze all of your muscles really tight, from your head to your toes, even your face, really tight, like this." Mrs. Beals mushed her face up like mashed potatoes. "Then let it out, repeating the exercise three times. It's called squeeze and release, a technique for whenever you feel stressed, or whenever those crocodile thoughts enter your mind. Do you think you can try that?"

"Sure," Cassie said, while Mrs. Beals wrote something on a pad of yellow lined paper.

"Great. Would you like to talk again next week?"

Cassie counted the games and puzzles on the three-level bookshelf. She didn't think it was as bad as Lisa Kurker made it sound. *Maybe it'll even get me out of classes.*

"Okay," she shrugged.

The classes you're failing.

Cassie bit her lip as thoughts of her poor grades reentered her mind. The black hand of the wall clock rigidly lurched forward to 3:00.

"You can go. I'll see you next week," Mrs. Beals said, wheeling back behind her desk and making a notation in her leather calendar book for the following Tuesday.

"Okay. Thank you."

"Oh, and Cassie," Mrs. Beals added, as Cassie's hand touched the doorknob.

"Yeah?"

"I don't like crocodiles either."

Cassie quickly made eye contact with Mrs. Beals and left the office, her heavy backpack falling off one shoulder. Artwork of painted, splattering leaves made by the fifth graders, hung outside the music room, blurred together as Cassie walked and then ran to meet Nana Helen in the auditorium.

After Grandpa Jack's all-time favorite supper, hot dogs and canned baked beans, Cassie swiftly skipped each odd-numbered stair as she headed to her bedroom to focus on her math and science homework. She paused in the upstairs hallway, pressing her ear to Mom's closed bedroom door, because she thought she heard her mother crying. Her mother hadn't joined them at supper, answering, "No thanks, I'm not hungry!" when Nana called from the bottom of the stairs.

The floor creaked as Mom swayed in her rocking chair, listening to that sad old song she played over and over. The lyrics of "We May Never Pass This Way Again," drifted out of the peanut-shell-shaped keyhole. Cassie swallowed hard as she crouched down, closing one eye to take a peek.

Only Mom's periwinkle-blue workpants were visible at first as she rocked back and forth. Shifting her gaze upward, Cassie saw Dot, Mom's Entity, yawn from the top of the chair. Cassie held her breath as she watched them go back and forth, Mom moving her hand up to wipe her nose. She crouched down even lower to see if her mother was crying or had a cold. Her thighs burned as she witnessed her mother's red, raw eyes filling with tears. Dot patted her mom on the shoulder, filing her orange claws at the same time, although Mom didn't notice.

Remember, not everyone is as special as you are. Tap three times on each thigh to make sure it stays that way.

Doing what she was told, Cassie's thighs weakened and gave way. She bumped her knee against the lightweight door, causing it to swing open and hit the old radiator inside the tiny room. Mom's red-rimmed eyes narrowed. "You're eavesdropping again, you nosy little ughh! I'm getting ready for work, and now I'm going to be late! Haven't I told you again and again not to be rude?"

Cassie gritted her teeth. *Why do you always push me away, making me feel worse? Aren't you supposed to be the grown-up?* Dot waved to Cassie from the wildly moving empty chair.

"I, I thought you were crying," Cassie put a thumbnail to her mouth. Her angry feelings gave way to the guilty ones.

"You won't see me crying, young lady. I'll be damned if this whole thing gets me down." Mom swiped her nose and grabbed her keys off the Singer sewing-machine table. Storming past Cassie, she trudged down the musty stairway, her high ponytail swaying behind her as she left for work.

Don't fret, dear. The hour is almost near. Trust in my voice, the only one who's with you when you're sad and afraid.

Cassie felt warm inside. Plodding down the hall, she heaved her backpack onto the crocheted afghan lying in a heap on top of her vanilla-colored sheets. Mom used to be a stickler for those kinds of things when they lived in the apartment, but had been too tired coming in from work early that morning to notice the unmade bed. Cassie didn't think making a bed was important anyway, when you were just going to sleep in it again the next night. Lying on her stomach, she attempted to concentrate on her science homework that was spread out over the lumps in her bed.

"Allll-right!" Grandpa's voice yelled from downstairs. "I'm going up the line!"

The door slammed shut.

"You do that," she heard Nana Helen grumble as her grandmother threw the trash out onto the back piazza.

Then Nana and Barbara Heimer, who was watering her mums outside, struck up a conversation—right underneath Cassie's window while she tried to study—about celebrities on *Dancing with the Stars*.

Through the sheer white curtains, Cassie saw Grandpa stiffly march down Knoll Street toward Clancy's Bar. After he passed the Bevilaqua's house, his shadow faded. That's when a tiny burst of yellow light caught Cassie's eye in the upper corner of her bedroom, above her dresser with the doily on top, the same place she had observed it the first time. Curiously, she turned to examine it.

The splash of yellow light formed itself into a shape. *It's like it's trying to get my attention,* she thought. Just like the first time, it dissolved and melted down toward the dresser, but didn't leave any sort of mark or stain as evidence of its existence. Cassie stared at the now-empty space for a few moments, the cream wallpaper with its geometric patterns blurring into one another. Cassie waited a moment. *Figures,* she thought.

Reaching over to turn on the desk lamp across from her bed, she leafed through her agenda: read chapter six in earth science, do fifteen rounding problems in math, complete map in social studies. *Yuck. Yuck. Yuck.*

Cassie listened to the muffled voices of Nana Helen, Barbara, and now Emil Heimer, who arrived home from work at 7:30 like he always did. Cassie became aware that she was in the house without either of her parents. Exploding like a bottle of ink, her heart pounded in her chest.

I caused Mom more stress by annoying her earlier. I wish I didn't spy. I wish she was home. Cassie pulled her entire pinky nail off in one bite as tears slid down her cheeks. That one had just grown back, too.

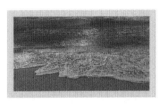

CHAPTER
FIFTEEN

Cassie couldn't focus on rounding 3.421 and 61.96 to the nearest hundredth and tenth as Nana slammed the back piazza door closed, coming inside for the night. Cassie ripped the corner page of her workbook, tempted to tear the whole sheet in half. *Why do I need to know this anyway? It's so stupid!* She pushed the workbook, and the rest of her binders, off the bed and onto the cold, hardwood floor. Giving up, she crawled into bed early, without brushing her teeth.

Tugging the red crocheted afghan with the cream color in each square over her head, Cassie closed her eyes and began her Mind Mail:

Carlos,

Agatha will tell me about the Settling. She's
the only one who tells me everything. Does
my dad know I'm coming back for him?
It's hard to do my homework because I
just want to get back to Blue.

Cassie

She folded the letter in her mind's eye, stuffed it in the
envelope, and sent it up and out of her forehead, visualizing it
drifting down into the top of Carlos's head.

Focused on a spot on the white stucco ceiling, she identified
a horse's face swirled in the paint texture. Light from the third floor
of the Heimer's triple-decker shined directly into Cassie's bedroom.
Barbara and Emil were night owls, staying up late to enjoy the
Tonight Show. Since it was early, Cassie knew the lights wouldn't
be shutting off anytime soon. Wrestling with sleep, she pulled the
covers tighter over her head.

*You won't be able to sleep, or do well in school for that matter,
until you've seen your father. Grades, shmades. Only I understand what
you're going through. No one else in that awful house does. I'll take
care of you.*

Agatha's protection comforted Cassie as she relaxed her legs
against the stiff sheets. She knew Agatha would explain about the
Settling when she was ready. Cassie tapped her thigh three times on
each side just in case. She felt Carlos meant well, reminding her to
study, but Agatha's voice had been with her a lot longer.

Cassie's thoughts drifted to the conversation she had that
afternoon with Mrs. Beals. Peeking out from under the covers, the
scratchy, wool afghan slightly coming up over the sheets, she dared
herself to find a crocodile shape in the ceiling. The horse had gone,
like shapes of clouds that inevitably pass you by. *I knew the horse*

wouldn't stay, she thought, forcing herself to find the scaly crocodile as punishment, with its long, windy body and big, sharp teeth. She began to tremble, throwing the covers off and dashing downstairs, stretching over every odd-numbered step with her cold, bare feet.

Cassie heard the familiar *vrump* sound coming from the living room as Nana plopped into her lime-and-banana-yellow-plaid armchair, preparing to knit and enjoy "her boys." Nana Helen called the Boston Bruins and Boston Red Sox players her boys. Tonight, the Red Sox playoffs were on. Bruce sat by Nana's callused heels, exposed in her washed-too-many-times, rose-pink slippers. He snarled at Cassie when she crossed the oak threshold into the living room.

"Stop that, you bad boy!" Nana hollered, slapping the mangy-haired poodle on the top of his bony head. After, Nana seemed to think better of it because she leaned down and lovingly scratched him under his dirty white chin. "I'm sorry, Brucie. Bad boys are my favorite."

Cassie leaned against the left side of the threshold. Nana could be so hot and cold.

"If ya don't want to sleep, why don't cha sit down, for Pete's sake?" Nana barked over her large owl-rimmed glasses as she picked up her knitting needles. She had been working on a baby blanket for some Bingo lady's new grandchild. Nana gestured to the empty sofa under the porch windows.

I wouldn't sit on that if you paid me a hundred dollars, Cassie thought. She had vowed never to sit on that thing when she and her mother moved in. That was Grandpa's couch and every afternoon after work, he sat there reading *The Boston Globe,* solving the crossword puzzle, and picking his nose at the same time. Then, he wiped it on the couch. Cassie saw it with her own eyes, and every time, she fought the urge to throw up. She didn't get how someone who liked things so tidy could be so gross.

Brrrring. The phone rang. It was 9:30.

"Get the phone, will ya? It's probably your mom checking in. You bum!" Nana hollered at the TV when one of her boys struck out at home plate.

"Hello?" Cassie answered reluctantly.

"Hi, honey," Mom said, her voice gentler than it had been earlier that afternoon. "Listen, I was thinking. Why don't you and I go for ice cream sundaes this weekend, just you and me."

Guilt.

Cassie held the receiver for a moment, staring at her pale face in the fingerprinted mirror in the front hallway while the TV blared in the background. "Sure," she replied.

"Okay, I gotta go, Gertrude had another accident." Mom sounded exhausted.

"Bye." *I'm sorry you have to work late at night, Mom,* Cassie thought.

Agatha's voice swooped in like a hawk to a baby bird that had fallen out of a tree. *Don't feel sorry for her, she should be the one worried about you.*

Cassie tapped three times on each side of her face with the first, second, and third fingers of each hand while she stood, frozen, next to the phone.

"Hey Cassie," Nana called from her chair, "your teacher called me this afternoon and said you talked to a lady after school today. She said you haven't been keeping up your grades."

Cassie continued tapping, her feet glued to the floor.

"Come in here, missy. I want to talk to you."

Cassie blinked and walked slowly into the living room while tickling the tip of her nose with the ends of her straight brown hair. Nana glanced up over her round glasses, continuing to loop each piece of powder-blue yarn around the shiny purple needle.

"Are you going to tell mom?" Cassie asked, whisking her hair back and forth across her nose. "I'm trying to study, I just can't."

"I'm not going to tell your mother a thing. I want to know

what happy-horse doodoo that lady said to you today." Nana's eyes returned to the television screen.

"What do you mean?" Cassie asked.

"What I mean is, no granddaughter of mine needs a shrink," Nana Helen said sternly. Bruce sneezed into the hem of Nana's green flannel nightgown.

"I can't go back and talk to Mrs. Beals?" Cassie asked, gnawing her lip.

"It's up to you what you do after school—talk to her, don't talk to her—I don't care. All's I'm saying is, you're fine. You're not going to turn out like your great grandmother or anyone else in the family, for that matter." Nana cleared her throat as she knitted.

"Like what great grandmother?" Cassie asked, leaning against the wall and looking over at the family photos, surrounding the cuckoo clock, on top of the radiator next to the TV. Her mother's high school photo was on the far left, followed by her parents' wedding photo, Nana and Grandpa's wedding photo, Cassie's baby picture taken at Sears, and her fifth grade photo with the black stand that had buckled behind it and now needed to rest against the wall. "I don't even know my great grandparents," Cassie realized.

"That's right, and it's a good thing they're up there," Nana flicked her gaze toward the sky. "You've got a long line of crazies behind ya, not on my side, of course, but on Grandpa's. I won't even put the picture out—stays in my bottom drawer. Bad omen if ya ask me." She shook her head, looping another piece of yielding yarn around the rigid needle.

"What picture?" Cassie asked, scratching her foot against the living room rug.

"Of Grandpa Jack's mother. A real nut case. Ended up in the funny farm. Best place for her, if ya ask me—used to talk to herself all the time. Oh, son of a . . . " Nana banged the needle on the arm of her chair as the Yankees scored three runs.

"Allllright," she sighed, tossing her supplies in a canvas bag by her chair. "Since your mother's not here to give me a hard time, we're going to do this my way." Nana hoisted her stocky body out of her armchair, which took a minute. "Gin rummy and a midnight snack?"

Nana loved her midnight snacks, which she defined as anything eaten past ten o'clock. She pulled the plastic container of rainbow sherbet from the freezer, while Cassie got the coffee-stained deck of playing cards from the drawer under the microwave.

"Why do you keep Grandpa's mother's picture in a drawer? Does Grandpa Jack know?"

"You mind your business, Lady Jane. It's my house and I said it's a bad omen." Nana scooped the sherbet into bowls and plunged a heaping tablespoon in her mouth before shoving the container back in the freezer. "Mmmm. *Mmmmm*." She said, smacking her lips.

Cassie wasn't going to object to staying up later than usual and having ice cream. Rainbow sherbet was her favorite. While she ate her sherbet at the table, she wondered if Grandpa knew Nana kept his mother's picture in a closed drawer. Maybe that was the reason they slept in separate bedrooms.

Nana included a midnight snack as part of her nightly routine after Grandpa left to go up the line. Every evening after supper, at promptly 6:15, Grandpa snagged his pale-yellow, scally cap from the coat rack in the front hallway and placed it on his sun-damaged scalp. Grandpa's light skin, combined with his nonexistent upper lip when he smiled, prompted Nana to refer to Grandpa Jack as "The Map of Ireland."

After Grandpa positioned the cap just right, he zipped up his tent-green canvas windbreaker, walked out onto the porch, down the three front steps onto Selwyn Street, and turned right at the corner onto Knoll. Three blocks up, at the end of Knoll, ran Belgrade Avenue, the location of Clancy's bar. Grandpa frequented Clancy's every night, even on holidays, and every single night he came home drunk.

Most of the time, she lay in bed and didn't see Grandpa Jack when he got home, but she always heard him.

Cassie and Nana Helen were enjoying their second bowls of rainbow sherbet with colored sprinkles and Cool Whip when the front door edged open. Cassie heard the scally cap tossed onto the coat rack. Then came the heavy, labored breathing as Grandpa pushed the door shut, over the hallway rug, locking them in for the night.

"Eh-lo," Nana Helen said with her mouth full, her eye on the gaudy, gold watch resting on her sun-spotted forearm. "Oy vey, I didn't know it was that late. You better get upstairs Cassie or your mother'll have my head."

Grandpa mumbled, then belched.

I wonder if he'd have the nerve to do that in church, Cassie thought.

The cellar door next to the kitchen opened and Grandpa plodded downstairs to the musty basement. *Ker-thunk, ker-thunk, ker-thunk.*

Next, Cassie heard four lighter thuds behind him. *That must be Grandpa's Entity, Chuck.*

"And there he goes," Nana muttered under her breath, scooping another tablespoon into her mouth.

The clanking of the cans began. Grandpa liked to organize things. He kept dozens of Narragansett beer cans lined up on wooden shelves he built next to the washer and dryer. He also arranged hundreds of little glass mason jars filled with hardware. The jars lined up on the shelves like soldiers, proudly displaying their uniform, typed white labels: nuts, bolts, and screws. Cassie heard clanking and then silence, as Grandpa rearranged the empty cans. She recalled the afternoon Nana folded laundry and hung her girdles from the basement pipes, spewing under her breath, "I'll tell ya who's screwy and nuts."

Tired and full, Cassie made her way upstairs. Grandpa would come up from the basement soon to take his contact lenses out at the kitchen table, his paraphernalia stored next to the puke-green, horizontally lined salt-and-pepper shakers and napkin holder, which looked like they hadn't been cleaned in years.

Cassie was relieved she went to bed when she did, because right after she burrowed under the covers, Grandpa started. He always did this. He became mean, yelling about politics, the city of Boston, religion, Nana, anything really. But tonight, he yelled about Cassie and her mother. She could only hear fragments of the conversation because Nana Helen kept hissing, "*Shhh!*" It was also hard to hear because Grandpa slurred his words and didn't make a whole lot of sense. Cassie heard enough though.

"Ungrateful little . . . don't they know nothing's going to change . . . he's a . . . they're fools to think . . . and the kid, too . . . a decent roof over their head . . . ungrateful little . . . "

Cassie's stomach ached. Sharp, knife-like pain seared into her sides, making it hard to breathe. *I didn't mean to be ungrateful. I'm trying to like it here. I just don't.* Not without her dad to scratch her head like a puppy when she felt sick or when she panicked after seeing the news. There was no one here to do that for her now. Her mom worked nights and was too tired.

I have nobody.

Tears filled Cassie's eyes as she lay watching the curtains move slightly from the autumn breeze coming in from the crack in the window. Squeezing her eyes shut, she pulled the covers around her head like a helmet to muffle Grandpa's anger, wriggling her way down to the middle of her bed. She always had to be right in the center, equal from both sides, and yet still able to see out the top of her covers. She started sleeping that way when her mom and dad used to have loud parties at the apartment.

Cassie remembered them vividly. The men drank beer and the ladies sipped mixed drinks and wine. Cassie sat with them while they played cards, laughing and dancing, until her mother ushered her off to bed. The later it got, the louder it got. Cassie used to lie awake, feeling afraid. If only she could tell her six-year-old self, *Did they really think you could sleep through all that?* That's when Cassie started hiding under the covers, to try to block the noise and to feel safe.

She curled herself into a tight ball as Grandpa's voice faded. She remembered the time one of the grown-ups opened her old bedroom door, turned the light on and announced, "Wake up, this is a great tune!" Cassie lay still, pretending to be asleep until someone came in and shut the light back off. She wished she knew who turned the light off and gently shut the door so she could thank them, now that she was older. A thought crossed her mind, like an airplane slicing through the sky, that it might have been her mother.

Unable to sleep, Cassie played the game she used to play when she lived in the old apartment. Buried in the middle of her mattress, she imagined herself deep in the ocean, surrounded by sharks she couldn't yet see. If she moved her sheets a little, there would be light, like the ocean's surface. She visualized frantically swimming toward the light when the sharks appeared so she'd be safe. She played with the covers, keeping the light out, just to scare herself. When the faces appeared in the darkness like they always did—one-eyed beasts, headless trolls, scaly creatures with massive teeth—she yanked the covers, exposing the light. Dark. Light. Dark. Light.

She controlled whether she would be torn apart by the sharks and destroyed by the beasts, or not. Moving the sheets gave her all the control. Finally drifting off to sleep, Cassie faintly remembered it was during her parents' parties that Agatha talked to her for the first time.

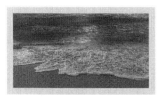

CHAPTER
SIXTEEN

Cassie's eyes opened with a start. She had been dreaming about her dad and Agatha driving together on the racetrack in the Midst at breakneck speed, recklessly rounding the corner as the crowd screamed in horror. The window shade flapped in the night wind, her alarm clock glowing 1:00 a.m. in blood-red light.

Be ready at dusk.

Creak. Bump. The closet door opened.

Cassie sat up in bed and rubbed her tired eyes.

"Told you I'd be here soon, and it's a good thing I bypassed the hallway, with all the activity in this house," said Agatha, stepping, in shadow form, out of the closet.

"Agatha!" Cassie said in a loud whisper, throwing off her covers. Her Entity smoothed her glittery, disheveled hair, gradually coming into solid form.

"Now, let's get back to business," Agatha said, closing Cassie's bedroom door tight. "I'm pleased to report your father's been taking his Have to Haves, restoring balance to our system. Therefore, as promised, I've come to take you back. Maybe you'll have some fun together in the Midst—before you bring him home, of course." Agatha plopped down on the corner of Cassie's downturned bed.

"I'm ready!" Cassie plunked her feet down on the floor and grabbed her Dad's old sweatshirt from the bottom dresser drawer. Pulling it on, she opened the closet door, preparing to Zipper when Bruce growled from Nana's bedroom.

"Huh?" Nana Helen said groggily, coming out of sleep. "What the . . . is all that racket? Don't make me come in there! The cold floor hurts my bunions!"

Cassie gulped.

Agatha raised her palm. *Leave this to me.*

"I just had to go to the bathroom, Nana. Go back to sleep," Agatha called out in Cassie's voice.

"Bathroom, my eye," Nana Helen said gruffly, repositioning herself in the creaky bed. "Keep talking to yourself like that and you'll end up in the funny farm, just like your great grandmother, Lola O'Brien. You hear me? I'll tell you what I'm going to do if I hear you talking to somebody in that closet again. I'll put my Singer machine back in there where it belongs. Then I'll get some peace and quiet!"

Zzzzz. Nana fell asleep.

Cassie exhaled, sitting down beside Agatha.

Suddenly, an image of Nana's clunky sewing machine popped into Cassie's head. *What if Nana puts that huge thing back in the closet? How would Agatha Zipper me to the Land of Blue?*

Agatha patted Cassie's hand. "There's no sewing machine going in there and interrupting our plans. Agatha here will make sure of that. Pay your Nana no mind, she's probably in a bad mood because she's married to that grandfather of yours."

Cassie managed a smile.

"Now, we can't leave until dusk. Always at dusk. Oh, and must we bring your friend this trip? Her Vibration isn't the type we ordinarily entertain on Blue. Perhaps it could be just you and me this time?"

Agatha's dark eyes gleamed in the light of the full moon radiating through the curtains.

I need Mariana. I don't like to be alone.

Agatha observed Cassie's expression, and moved a little closer on the bed, "You're not alone dear, you have me. And TJ."

Cassie bit her thumb.

"Well," Agatha said, sighing, "Mariana did have fun last Zipper, I suppose I can make another exception. After all, the more the merrier on Blue."

Cassie took her nail out of her mouth. "I like when Mariana's with me."

"You can all have some last-minute fun before you take your loved ones back from where they belong."

"You mean back *to* where they belong?" Cassie asked, her chin to her neck.

"Oh, and Cassie, when I return for you and Mariana, please wear your Potential badge."

"Okay," Cassie yawned, climbing back under her sheets.

Agatha rose and strolled over to the closet, her long, black cloak blending into the darkness. Cassie smiled as she drifted back to sleep, knowing her dad was feeling better. Now he could come home and they could be a family.

———

The next day, Cassie could barely keep her eyes open during science.

"Now class," Mrs. Doyle said, clasping her hands, "the parts of a hurricane, if you'll recall from last night's assignment, are the eye, eyewall, and feeder bands."

Cassie bent her elbow on the desk, resting her head in the crook of her arm, as if it were a soft pillow.

She spent the entire forty-five-minute period fighting to stay awake, and when the lunch bell finally rang, she felt relieved.

"Do you have a TV in your bedroom?" Riley Avery asked Cassie after the bell rang.

"No. Why?" Cassie gathered her binders, loose papers sticking out everywhere.

"Cause you have dark circles under your eyes. That's what happens to my brother when he stays up late watching TV." Riley walked next to Cassie down the hallway to the lockers, holding her books against her chest. "My uncle's a pediatrician and he says kids our age require nine hours of sleep a night, you know. It affects academic and athletic performance."

Cassie stopped in front of her locker, trying to concentrate on turning the dial of the combination lock to the right numbers. She stuffed her binders in her locker.

Riley Avery, you think you're so smart.

"I don't have a TV in my room, okay?" Cassie said, her eyes bugging out of her head, leaving Riley to watch Cassie walk away to meet Mariana in the lunchroom. Cassie felt only a little bit sorry she snapped at Riley. She didn't feel like being pestered by a girl who got straight A's every year, played on the elite softball team with all the popular kids, and didn't have any problems.

Slumping in her seat, the glare of the harsh lunchroom lighting overhead made Cassie wish she were wearing sunglasses. She took one of Mariana's brown rice cakes from the Whole Foods snack package.

I'm sure Grandpa's enjoying his salami on rye, while I forgot to make my own lunch. Cassie chewed on what tasted like cardboard.

"You look tired," Mariana crunched loudly. "I'm getting

worried about you."

"I know, okay? I wish I remembered to at least pack a drink," Cassie complained.

"My mother always tells me you can get dehydrated if you don't drink enough water." Mariana continued crunching.

Cassie bounced her leg up and down under the cafeteria table. *I don't drink any water. What if I get dehydrated? What if I get sick and I can't go back to Blue tonight?*

Mariana slid her carton of organic rice milk in front of Cassie. "Here, have half my milk, but just air sip it, cause that's gross, no offense."

"I'll just drink from the bubbler," Cassie said, sliding it back. Then she whispered to Mariana so the rest of the table couldn't hear. "Agatha visited me this morning. We're leaving tonight."

Mariana choked on her milk. "Tonight?" Renee Gangemi, Kathy Kostigen and Kira Slatnick looked over from their end of the lunch table, as if whatever Cassie and Mariana were talking about was stupid. "But my aunt Susan's coming over with my Ya-Ya for dinner! I'm supposed to help make the meatballs after I finish my homework. But I have to go with you. You get so nervous." Mariana glared back at the mean girls and said, "What are you looking at?"

Cassie pretended to pick up something off the floor. Kathy ignored Mariana, making conversation about her older sister, who recently got her hair highlighted.

"I'm going to do my hair in ninth grade. That's when my sister had it done," Kathy said, twirling her hair into a perfect bun.

Their mothers must do their hair every morning to make them look so perfect, Cassie thought.

"You give the popular girls way too much power," Mariana said, sipping her healthy milk.

"Huh?" Cassie asked.

"Anyway, I'm not sure how I can go with you this time."

"But what am I going to do now?" Cassie whispered loudly,

digging her nail into the table. "You're my best friend! You have to be there for me." Cassie felt like her feet weren't connected to the floor. "Besides, you told TJ you'd be there for him, too!"

"I know, don't make me feel guilty," Mariana said, biting the tip of her straw. "I want to go. Honest!" Mariana gulped the last sip of milk, proceeding to clean up her section of the table. "Let me see if I can sneak away after I help with supper. If I can, I'll call you. Okay?"

That afternoon, barely giving her English homework a glance, Cassie bit every fingernail down to the tip of each finger waiting for the phone to ring.

Gnawing at her cuticle as she sat cross-legged on her bed, thoughts attacked her brain like wasps. *I'm a baby. I don't want to make Mariana feel like she has to come with me. I just don't want to go alone.*

She slapped at her head while she stared out the window, the sun hanging low in the autumn sky.

Cassie's thoughts yo-yoed from one side of her brain to the other, making her feel tired. *No wonder I have dark circles under my eyes.*

The phone finally rang during their supper of flank steak and boiled potatoes, Mom opting again to stay in her room. Cassie knocked over her chair in her scramble to answer the phone in the front hallway.

"What the . . . kind of manners are those?" Grandpa Jack belted, picking his teeth with his pinky.

"Kids got no respect for their elders these days," Nana complained. "A good wooden spoon to the fanny would fix that."

Bruce stood on his hind legs under the table, licking remnants of steak from Nana's fingers.

"Can you?" Cassie asked immediately when she picked up the phone.

"Jeesh, don't you get in trouble when you answer like that?"

Mariana asked. Loud, festive voices floated out of the receiver from the Papadopoulis's kitchen.

"Can you?" Cassie repeated.

"I just finished the meatballs," Mariana said, breathlessly. "They weren't really round, more like crooked, because I made them so fast. Anyway, Aunt Susan hasn't stopped talking about her new boyfriend, so she won't even notice me leaving."

Cassie relaxed her grip on the telephone, while Nana Helen and Grandpa Jack bickered in the background.

"Thanks, Mari," Cassie sighed.

"That's what friends are for," Mariana said, laughter in her kitchen erupting in the background. "Besides, I know you think I'm the one who keeps you from being a nervous wreck."

At dusk, after Mariana came over to "do homework," Cassie and Mariana Zippered with Agatha, this time with ease. Even though Nana yelled, "What in the devil is going on up there?" Cassie just yelled back, "We're working on a science project about wind velocity!" Because Nana had just sat down with a bowl of Oreo cookies to watch the Bruins game, she let it go. There'd have to be a fire in the house before she'd get out of her armchair.

Arriving directly on *The Enticer*, in a discreet spot Agatha designated for them at the back of the ship, Cassie, Mariana, and Agatha shimmied into form. Across from them, a yawning pack of Mooshkoos huddled together on a bench.

"Look at them, " Mariana said, charmed by the cuteness. "I wish I could be their babysitter. Hey! Oip oip! Remember us?"

"We're back!" Cassie said, bending down and pressing her hands on her thighs to see the Mooshkoos at eye level. The Mooshkoos, however, merely glanced up, raised their rubbery paws mid-air, and dozed off.

"How come they don't remember us?" Cassie asked, biting the side of her thumbnail.

Agatha checked her Surveyor to be sure everything stayed on

schedule. "They do dear, they're just tired. Even Mooshkoos get tired, you know."

"That's not the Mooshkoos I remember," Mariana said, under her breath.

"I know," Cassie agreed. But once Cassie joined the card table, teaching a group of Mooshkoos how to beat their opponents at gin rummy (Nana Helen always cheated whenever they played), the Mooshkoos came around. They even gave Cassie and Mariana Bads from their stash hidden under the card table.

They played several games of gin rummy while Agatha tended to the business of making sure new Potentials were treated hospitably, and something about making sure there was enough "Feed" on board. Cassie felt important that she already knew what to do, even if the Mooshkoos hadn't fussed over her and Mariana like they did the first time on *The Enticer*.

"Have you noticed they're treating us like we're one of them?" Mariana asked, wiping down the floorboards after the Mooshkoos assigned them the task.

"That's a good sign, isn't it? They know us now," Cassie said, scrubbing a plank drenched with spilled Escape from one of the passengers who climbed a mast.

"I guess," Mariana shrugged, chewing a green Blob that made her face turn the color of a highway sign. She spit it out in her hand. "Gosh, those get gross after a while."

The Trespassers, back in full force, slithered over the side of the ship, taunting Cassie. *Think you're going to have fun? Think again. Your father doesn't want to go home.*

Just then a Mooshkoo came by carrying a helmet. He showed it to Cassie, and gesturing, made it clear that this helmet was designed to muffle the Trespassers' intruding messages. Holding the helmet up high, he dangled it in front of Cassie's face, as if offering it to her. But when she tried to take it, he pulled it back.

"Oip, oip, oip," he said, indicating the helmet wasn't a gift. He

THE LAND OF BLUE

wanted her to tell the new Potentials about the great time they'd have in the Midst since many of them were feeling a bit sick from the wild ride aboard *The Enticer*, and needed a morale boost. Without a second thought, Cassie shook hands with the navy-blue Mooshkoo.

"Oip," the Mooshkoo pressed his mouth on top of Cassie's pale hand, leaving a moist "O" mark.

Cassie fitted the dark-blue helmet snugly against her head, and dragged Mariana with her to visit the family of five sitting on the quarterdeck. She took a seat next to them and explained, "You can eat as many treats as you want on Blue. The Yum is the best, and Bad comes in flavors like . . . "

"Bad is amazing!" Mariana interrupted, spreading her hands wide. "I'm getting highlighter yellow when we dock. Except I already had one of the clown-nose-red flavors and my thoughts are racing. Can you hear it in my voice? I get a little hyper when I have dyes and sugar. No wonder my mother never lets me have that stuff. I don't know how you've already had three, Cassie."

"Are you kidding? I could have ten! And this time," Cassie continued talking to the family, "my dad gets to come home, so it's an extra-special trip."

Mpuck!

The Mooshkoo ripped the helmet off Cassie's head. "Oip, oip, oip, oip, oip," he scolded, ushering her and Mariana away from the family, back down to the main deck. Two little teeth protruded from its jaw like an angry bulldog.

"What did I do?" Cassie asked, taken aback.

The Mooshkoo scowled, and scurried back to the family, bombarding them with Bad and Blobs in tie-dye colors. At one point, he discreetly made a mean face at Cassie, then turned back to the family with a smile.

"That's a moody one, huh?" Mariana said, finding an empty seat on the main deck. "That's how Gina has been this week with college midterms."

"Hey," called a red-eyed Entity named Henry from the card table. "Don't take it to heart. Everyone's a little cranky. Word has it they might not have picked up enough Feed for everyone on Blue."

Henry reminds me of Grandpa Jack, Cassie thought.

"Whatever Feed is," Mariana replied, inching closer to Cassie on the bench. "You must be wicked excited to see your dad. Maybe we'll get to hang out with him in the Midst before we go home! I've never really seen your dad much, since you usually come to my house, and at your old apartment he was always sleeping."

Cassie stared at the cards scattered on the card table. She thought about all the times Dad stayed in bed, missing work at the moving company because of his backaches. Cassie usually found him resting on the couch, half asleep, when she got home from school. But when her mom and dad had parties or went to China Dragon, Dad was awake and happy. Cassie wondered if Dad liked the Midst as much as he liked China Dragon.

A Trespasser slithered all the way up to the hood of Cassie's sweatshirt as the Mooshkoo who reprimanded Cassie earlier threw the Trespasser a treat.

What if your father doesn't want to go home, and you came all this way for nothing?

Cassie hurried over to the masts, wishing she had the helmet. She didn't like it when people didn't like her—even Mooshkoos.

Music blared on *The Enticer.* Mariana hummed, moving her head to the beat of the music, ignoring the Trespasser attempting to hiss in her ear.

"Don't they bother you?" Cassie asked, as Mariana sat on the bench, oblivious.

"Who?"

"What do you mean who? Those Trespasser things Agatha told us about last time. Don't they get in your head?"

"They don't bother me. Watch this." Mariana stood up, turned around, and took an aggressive step toward the slimy Trespasser.

"Sssssssss!" she hissed. Within seconds, the creature retreated into the water.

Cassie stared at the empty railing and back at Mariana.

"What?" Mariana said, whipping her wind-blown hair over her shoulder. "They don't scare me."

"How'd you do that?" Cassie asked, her mouth open.

"It's a technique I learned from the Animal Channel, in case you ever get attacked by a dog. That Caesar guy knows everything. You just have to show 'em who's in control. Try it."

Cassie tiptoed over to the railing, her heart beating fast. Like clockwork, two yellow-green eyes appeared above the railing, the creatures ready to strike. Cassie felt adrenaline course through her veins, as the skinny, scaly beast slithered over the railing, lunging at Cassie's head.

Maybe you won't go home either.

Cassie felt her blood drain, like a toilet being flushed.

"Sssssss!" she hissed, using her fingers as claws for effect.

You are no match for us.

The Trespasser laughed as it threw back its head, slinking back down in the water, but its laugh lingered in Cassie's ears, long after it disappeared beneath the surface.

Mariana moved her leg to the pounding music. "Just keep trying."

Sometimes I wish I wasn't me.

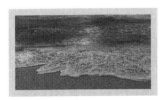

CHAPTER
SEVENTEEN

Cassie closed her eyes as she sat on the bench, her hair lashing against her face, just before *The Enticer* dropped down into Blue territory. With the mask on that Agatha provided, she began the deep-breathing exercise Mrs. Beals demonstrated during one of their appointments. Cassie didn't understand how breathing might help her feel better, but as they plummeted down the steep waterfall, her heart flying wildly into her throat, she figured this was as good a time to practice.

Breathe. Squeeze. Release . . . Breathe. Squeeze. Release . . . Breathe. Squeeze. Release . . . Suddenly, Cassie sensed an envelope fluttering into her mind's eye.

Hey, are you almost here? I heard Mind Mail works out of range if you're on the

> same frequency. I'll play a few Stimulators
> until you get here, okay? I kinda miss you
> guys.

Cassie abruptly opened her eyes as *The Enticer* leveled off, a smile spreading across her face.

Carlos was right, Mind Mail did work out of range.

Cassie squeezed her eyes shut again, excited to reply to TJ.

> We'll be there soon.

The atmosphere grew colder, Cassie's breathing becoming heavy and labored. The surrounding air thickened and the dark sky transformed to dusky gray. Pulling her sweatshirt tighter, the gold-rimmed glasses jingled in the pocket.

"We're almost on Blue!" Mariana shouted, jumping up and leaning over the wooden railing.

"Oip!" A do-ragged Mooshkoo stomped past, scowling at Mariana. He hoisted himself up one of the lower, thick wooden masts and blew a small trumpet-like instrument.

"I think I stole that Mooshkoo's thunder!" Mariana said, picking up a littered Blob wrapper sticking to the moist deck. She tossed it into a nearly full garbage can. "That 'oip,' meant 'back off,' didn't it? I swear I saw a row of teeth on that little thing."

At the front of the ship, an Entity bellowed, "Land of Blue Ho!"

The Mooshkoo shimmied down the sails, and stuck his tongue out at Mariana.

"Since when did they get so feisty?" Mariana asked Cassie, while the Entities and Mooshkoos celebrated noisily at the back of the ship. *The Enticer* steered into port, the girls turning to view the harbor across the water. They could see Robin waving sweet, sticky Yum in the air to the crowd, high atop his unicycle.

"How can he sit up there and perform *all* the time? He must get tired . . . " Mariana said, as Robin juggled tankards of Bad for a horde of Potentials.

Cassie stared at the Bads going around and around in the air. *Maybe I could ask Agatha now why my dad talked about going to the Settling.*

As they closed in on the pier, Mariana pointed to an overloaded trash can, "That's gross. Don't they have any pride?"

Bump. The ship docked.

Cassie and Mariana watched attentively from their places in the front of the line to see if anyone would be sent home for not having their energy Vibration in alignment with the Meter.

"Next," Kurt called from his chair. He sat with one of his little legs swung over one side, a grungy T-shirt exposed under his black shirt.

The girls stepped forward.

"Hey guys!" Mariana said, waving to Big and Small, who flanked Kurt. She drew a line with her finger back and forth between her and Cassie. "Remember us?"

"Let's go, we got a lotta Potentials, so keep the line moving," Big said, jerking his large chin.

"Okayyy," Mariana said, crossing the wooden platform to be measured.

Agatha coughed while Kurt observed the wavering arrow on the Meter screen of his Surveyor. He looked over at Agatha, with an eyebrow raised, as the arrow landed in the clear space above the black line at the top of the color range.

"Again, I assure you there's no threat with this one," Agatha stated. "Also, it's her last time here, so it won't be a problem."

Cassie rose up on her toes. *That's because we're bringing Dad home and won't need to come back!*

Stroking his chin in consideration, Kurt jerked his thumb for Mariana to move aside. "I'll take your word for it, Aggie. You're higher on the staff than I am on Blue."

Mariana mouthed to Cassie with her palms turned up in the

air, "Am I the only one who lands above the black line?"

Cassie shrugged as she waited for her turn while Agatha chatted with new Potentials in line, goggling at the diversions in the Midst just beyond the Welcoming Gate.

Agatha doesn't need to babysit me. She knows I already know what to do, Cassie thought as she approached the platform. Kurt sipped Escape as Small scanned the energy space around Cassie.

"Boss, we good?" Small asked, showing Kurt the Meter reading.

Cassie couldn't see the arrow from where she stood.

"Agatha," Kurt beckoned with his ring finger, "come have a look."

Cassie waited, confused. She looked over to Mariana, but Mariana wasn't paying attention, straining her neck toward the Midst, probably looking for TJ.

"Just want to make sure there ain't any funny business going on," Kurt whispered to Agatha, pointing back and forth between Cassie and Mariana.

Agatha assessed the screen for a few moments with her eyes narrowed. Tapping her chin with her finger, she appeared to be deep in thought. "Let me take care of things," she said to Kurt, then she raised her chin toward Cassie. "Proceed."

"If you say so," said Kurt gruffly, handing Cassie an updated Potential badge and throwing the old one in the trash. She didn't take the new badge though, instead standing at attention in front of Kurt, waiting for him to attach the badge to her sweatshirt.

"It's your second visit, kid. Do it yourself," Kurt said, dropping the badge onto the ground. Wriggling back into his chair he called, "Next!"

Agatha picked up the badge, put an arm around Cassie, and escorted her to the side of the pier. Pinning the badge on her sweatshirt, she asked in honey-dipped tones, "Are you still loyal to me, dear?"

"What do you mean?" Cassie asked.

"Your Vibration dear, while still low on the Meter as required to help bring your father back to your dimension, was slightly higher than usual. It would be like going from being a tremendous Potential to just merely a Potential."

There are different kinds of Potentials? Cassie wondered, noticing where the wooden planks of the pier changed to cobblestones on the Welcoming Road under the black iron gate. Several grassy weeds sprouted up from the cracks in the stones, causing her to want to pull them out. *Now I can't ask about the Settling.*

"Has anything changed?" Agatha asked, searching Cassie's eyes for answers. "Any new players in the game, shall we say?"

Cassie wrinkled her nose. "I don't understand."

"How about that guidance counselor you've been speaking with?" Agatha asked, glancing passively at her fingernails.

Cassie paused, wondering how Agatha knew about that. "Mrs. Beals just wanted to talk to me because my grades haven't been good. She taught me breathing techniques to try and relax and stuff like that."

Agatha tipped her head back and laughed out loud. "Cassie darling, do you honestly think breathing is going to help your situation? Who could possibly relax at a time like this? This Mrs. Beals doesn't understand what you're going through, with her cushy office job and her happy home life. These new-age do-gooders, trying to help, as if they know."

Agatha tilted Cassie's chin with her palm and looked directly into her eyes. "Hear me clearly, Cassie Connor. Only an Entity who feels your pain in its entirety, with all its tears and frustrations, its fears and its uncertainties, could possibly assist you in the appropriate manner."

Cassie stammered as Agatha's eyes bore into her. "I-I don't get how breathing can help either. It didn't make sense to me."

"Now that's what I want to hear!" Agatha said, placing one hand atop the black spindles of the Welcoming Gate. "I know what's best for you. After all, we're going to your father, just as soon as I take care of a few things. I dare say, I'm afraid it may be your shortest trip here . . ." She waved her other hand over Cassie's head like a magic wand. "Having said that, would you like to have some fun in the Midst with your friends before you travel home?"

Cassie squeezed her shoulders to her ears, the waft of Yum filling her senses, like a homemade bowl of chicken noodle soup when you're sick.

Agatha takes better care of me than anybody.

"I do want to try some Bad flavors I haven't had yet." Cassie threw her arms around her Entity, hugging her tight. When she pulled away, she said, "Thanks Agatha, for everything."

Agatha curtsied, and nodded to Big, who unlocked the heavy gate. "Perhaps I should let you lead the way this time. Come along, Mariana."

Fun-loving Entities, with their robust noses and oversized ears, accompanied their excited Potentials at the long vendor lines inside the frolicking Midst. Cassie and Mariana coughed as they navigated past vendor carts and the Vibration Meter still hovering in the gray-blue range on the Welcoming Road and turned into the Midst, the raw air settling into their lungs.

An Entity, with an elongated chin, careened hastily across the cobblestones in his black-soled shoes toward Agatha at the tip of the Midst. "Great Gatsby, we're almost out of Bad!" He complained in a hushed tone. "And the word in the Midst is we may be out of Have To Haves! Some of the Permanents are starting to quiver!"

"Yes, Fitz, I'm aware of the problem," said Agatha, waving to newcomers. "With the recent influx of Potentials, we're busier than ever."

"I hope they don't run out of Bad while we're here," Cassie said, biting the nail on her ring finger.

"Jeesh, you've already had three. Aren't you sugared out?" Mariana asked, moving closer to Cassie to allow a group of newcomers to pass by on their way to the racetrack.

"Three's not a lot," Cassie replied. "Do you think so?"

Agatha had moved with Fitz to the side of the street. "*The Enticer* just brought in the latest Feed. The Mooshkoos are unloading now. Let's put our game faces on, shall we? Remember, Fitz, high demand means greater numbers."

Agatha strolled back over to Mariana and Cassie and said, "I suppose helping the Mooshkoos unload the shipment wouldn't nearly be as much fun as hanging by yourselves. Go enjoy, while I tend to distribution management. We'll head out to the Fix-It in a pulse. Just a couple of hours, your dimension's time, should be enough for me to take care of business."

"Of course," Cassie said, feeling a bit more grown up.

Agatha always comes back for me.

"Yes," Agatha lifted her nose, sensing the smell of grease. "Sal is nearby. His Vibration is quite tangible in the field."

"What field?" Mariana asked, searching the brick buildings and shops inside the Midst. "There aren't any fields here."

"It's the Vibration field," an Entity said, twitching down the cobblestones like he had ants in his pants, while transporting a large white container into the Midst from the pier. "What do you think the Meter reads? Unless you're referring to the Praying Fields. Right, Aggie?"

"Carry on, Truman," Agatha said sternly, handing him a few Blobs, which he popped in his mouth upon walking away. Agatha rolled up her sleeves and said to Mariana, "The field I refer to is the field of energy. Your best friend here," she bowed her head toward Cassie, "is quite adept at picking up on other people's energy fields."

That's why I can pick up on TJ's thoughts, and some of the others in the Midst!

"Okay, but how would you know Sal's here if you can't even see him yet? I don't get it." Mariana said, checking for immediate signs of Sal. All she saw were balloons and Blobs, vendor carts and blue lights, and kids tripping over uneven cobblestones trying to keep up with their parents.

"Like this," Cassie closed her eyes in concentration as she stood in the frenzied Midst, sending a Mind Mail envelope down into the top of TJ's dark, gelled hair: We're here!

The reply came back immediately: I'm in the Cove!

Cassie opened her eyes. "TJ's in the Cove."

"How wonderful! You learned some of our tricks on your own," Agatha said, ruffling Cassie's already wind-blown hair.

"How do you guys *do* that?" Mariana asked, stomping her feet. "You have to teach me!"

"I don't know if it's something you can do," Cassie said, putting her hair in a ponytail.

"Yes, it's an innate talent, and would take too long to explain how one is able to feel another's Vibration so intensely. Now, why don't you two run along. Oh, and Cassie, once I'm through helping the Mooshkoos unload the Feed, would you want to take a field trip to the Settling to get your father's things? Remember, it takes special status to get into the Settling."

Cassie felt her belly flip-flop with excitement as hyped-up elves performed acrobatics on the grass.

I knew Agatha would come through. "Will TJ be able to go, too? Maybe Eric'll be there."

"That's a fantastic idea. I'm sure Sal would agree. I'm surprised I hadn't thought of it myself. See you in a pulse." Agatha returned to the pier while Cassie and Mariana headed to the Cove.

"Young Potentials, where ya going?" Robin shouted, his voice projecting like a megaphone as he pedaled wildly in mid-air.

"We'll be back with TJ!" Cassie and Mariana yelled, cupping the sides of their mouths. Robin saluted and continued his seven-tankard juggling act to entertain the growing crowd of Potentials fresh off *The Enticer*.

Cassie and Mariana wove through the crowd until the big,

blue canvas tent came into view.

TJ stood in line, waiting to play a Stimulator with the words: "Got Rage?" flashing across its small screen in blood-red letters. He stared at the boxing ring on the screen, where a Permanent went head to head with a troll.

Cassie tapped TJ on the shoulder.

He wheeled around, saw Cassie and Mariana and said, "Hey!" giving each of them a hug. He gently elbowed Cassie and said, "You got my Mind Mail, huh?"

"I have to learn how to do that," Mariana interjected. "Hey, what's this Stimulator all about?" The Permanent and the troll used clubs instead of fists.

"It's a Stim to get out your anger," TJ replied. "Sal said it'd be good for me."

Mariana cringed as the Permanent, clubbed in the back by the troll, fell to his knees. "Wow. That's intense. No wonder parents don't want their kids playing these games at home. Ouch! Wouldn't this just make you more angry?"

Maybe I should play the Stimulator too, and forget the breathing, Cassie thought.

"Well, I'm not up for bludgeoning anyone, so I guess I'll go get a few more Blobs before they run out. Okay, who's with me?" Mariana clapped once and turned to head back out into the packed slew of people and creatures in the street.

"Run out? What do you mean?" TJ's voice cracked. "Sal, what's going on?"

"Chill, my Potential," said Sal, shuffling over in his black shoes. "The Feed's being unloaded as we speak. Should be distributed before the next Glimmer." Sal dug his claw-like hands into TJ, massaging his upper back. "Sal always takes care of things. Haven't you learned that by now? I'm probably the best thing that's ever happened to you, huh?"

"We better go get Blobs now," Cassie said, "because we're

going to be visiting the Settling soon!" She grabbed TJ by the arm. "I have to get my dad's things before we go, and Agatha said you can come with us! Maybe you'll find Eric there."

TJ pounded one fist into the other and turned to Sal, who checked his Surveyor. "Did you hear that? I can go there this time?"

"Sure! Seems like the right time, eh?" Sal said, eyeing a crowd beginning to place Lures on whether the troll or the Permanent would win the round.

"Go, you troll you!" A man in a scally cap hollered.

"Get him!" a twig-like creature yelled, banging the side of the Stimulator.

"My Lures on the Permanent," Sal said before strutting over to join the crowd. "It says he hasn't had any Escape for two days!"

TJ laughed, shaking his head. "C'mon, we'll catch up with Sal later."

As TJ, Cassie, and Mariana started out of the Cove, they passed a red-haired boy holding a bottle of Bad in his hand, waiting to throw it at a Stimulator where a large, empty windowpane appeared on the screen. A harried-looking, middle-aged woman appeared in the window, waving her finger and warning, "Haven't I taught you not to throw things when you're angry?"

Smash! The glass bottle missed its target.

"Didn't that Stimulator have a monster in the windowpane the last time?" Cassie asked.

A female Entity behind the red-haired boy, with seven fingers on one hand, jeered, "C'mon, you were so close! If you want to get to level three, you've got to get her!"

Cassie couldn't tell whether the boy noticed his Entity or not because he never took his eyes off the screen, waiting for his second chance.

"Right for her forehead," the glossy Entity encouraged as the boy gripped the bottle tighter. "Focus on how she nags."

"Yikes," Mariana said. "I'd hate to see what level three

looks like."

A group of teenagers gathered around the Stimulator of the taunting, middle-aged woman behind the windowpane, lining up to play. Cassie felt sorry for the drained–looking woman, and the way the kids harassed her, even though she was just a character on the screen.

Mariana tugged Cassie's sweatshirt and they exited the grassy-floored Cove, pushing their way through the crowd as nicely as they could.

"Does anyone else notice the music is different?" Mariana asked.

Cassie tilted her head as they crossed the street, listening to the loud music. The bass line beat like a hypnotic chant. "I hadn't really noticed."

"It sounds different from last time," Mariana said, catching a Blob one of the vendors, perched atop a street lamp, threw down and handed it to TJ.

"I thought so, too, but I like it. Eric listened to music like this at home," TJ said, ripping open the Blob.

Mariana shrugged. "Maybe it's me."

Everything looked the same to Cassie as they headed to Robin's station. *Although maybe the music is a bit louder . . .*

"There you are, friends!" Robin gave Cassie, TJ, and Mariana each a forty-seven-fingered Bad as they joined his audience. "There may be another few fingers thrown in for good measure, but who's counting?"

Sipping their sweet, highlighter-yellow frosty Bads, baseball-sized bubbles floated out of their noses.

"Just a little something special I added. We gotta keep it interesting." Robin said to the applause of the crowd.

Cassie and TJ delighted in the more advanced Bad, but Mariana took a few sips and said it was too much. Hanging out by Robin's cart, they tossed balloons back and forth with some other kids while they waited for Agatha's return. Cassie felt like a half hour had passed, even though there weren't any clocks.

Who keeps track of the time? Cassie wondered.

I was thinking the same thing. Cassie turned to see a teenage girl dressed in all black wearing black lipstick standing beside her. The girl grinned as she sipped her forty-five-fingered Bad, adding, *That's so cool, I can hear your thoughts and you can hear mine. Everything about this place is amazing!*

Cassie playfully hit the balloon floating near her head back to its server. *I feel way more connected to the kids here than the ones at school.*

"You've returned, lads and lasses!" a booming voice reverberated above the noise. "In my panic, I perseverated that you had left our frenzy for good! Couldn't get enough though, could we?"

"Hi, Captain BP!" Cassie, Sal, and Mariana said in unison, eyeing his black trench coat.

"Yes, yes, you may select a few. But listen," he instantly lowered his voice, "save some for the other compulsive Potentials, as there's a bit of a shortage on Blue if you haven't heard. With the demand, I wouldn't want to disappoint."

"We can do that," Cassie said, preparing to dive into Captain BP's stock. *I'll give one of mine to Dad!*

"I can definitely do that," TJ said, as Captain BP opened his coat to reveal a vertical stash of organized Blobs.

They grabbed a few hard, root-beer-flavored, gun-shaped Blobs, a plastic Have to Have container filled with Blobs they could share, and a fist-sized wad of pink-neon Blobs that exploded with flavor every time you chewed.

"This is the best one yet," TJ said, chomping down on the pink Blob.

"I think half the fun is just looking at everything, you know, like window shopping," Mariana said, clapping her hands together.

Captain BP let out a long sigh and sat down on the curb on the side of the street, his neck hung low, drooping off his tall body.

"What's the matter, BP? Are you feeling all right?" Cassie scooted next to him.

"Suffering from melancholia. Practically catatonic," he answered.

"Huh?" TJ asked.

"Troubled, unsettled, sad," he explained.

"But why?" Cassie asked.

"It's the lack. The lack Captain BP experiences when the Feed gets low. On rare occasion, I take some. I can't help it. But I'm supposed to obey the rules strictly and make sure everyone else enjoys the Blobs. Quite alienating," he whined.

"My sister always sampled the ice cream at her summer job. She considered it part of the perks, even though technically she wasn't supposed to," Mariana said, standing above them.

"Who would mind if you had some? I mean, they're yours, right?" TJ raised his shoulders, biting into the root-beer-flavored, gun-shaped Blob.

Captain BP perked up, like he was hearing the rap music in the background for the first time. "You know, by Blue, I think you kids are on to something."

"You could have some of mine," Cassie offered, holding out her handful of Blobs.

"No, no, I couldn't," he muttered.

"Take them. You've been so nice to us," TJ said, holding open his palm with half his supply.

"Help me? In my anguish? You'd do that?"

"I don't see why not," Cassie said, standing up alongside TJ and Mariana.

"Well, I can't let them see me. You don't know what they'll do." Captain BP glanced nervously over both of his black-covered shoulders. "Perhaps if we merely journeyed down that alley there, and if you blocked me from view, well, then I could enjoy a few of my very own wares. I've not had a pick-me-up all day because of the shortage, and I dare say I've become quite fatigued." BP breathed heavily, as though on a respirator.

Cassie scanned past the green turf behind Captain BP, down to the pier. "I just wouldn't want to get in trouble with Agatha."

"Oh, child," Captain BP said, shaking his head. "Once Entities know they can trust you, the lure is fastened." His head slumped, like an actor who plays dead.

"I think this guy needs something quick," TJ said, with alarm.

"Maybe he has low blood sugar!" Mariana exclaimed, reaching in her pocket for a Blob. "You know how Brady Henderson in English gets like that sometimes before lunch?"

"Okay," Cassie agreed, chewing on her lower lip. When she made sure no one was watching, glancing down the alleyway to be sure it was empty, she said, "Let's go."

I just hope no one gets mad at me. Cassie bit into her lip until she tasted blood.

"C'mon Captain BP," TJ said, crouching down. "Just try to get up so you can make it over to the alley."

"Oh!" Captain BP moaned, dramatically lifting his head. "Thank you, lads and lasses!" He stood, clearing his throat as if preparing a speech, and winked at them. "Let's get some more Blobs for the extraordinary influx of Potentials arriving on Blue, shall we?" He darted across the street toward the alley, TJ, Cassie, and Mariana following behind like his shadow.

"He sure bounced back quick," TJ whispered to Cassie and Mariana. "Maybe he's just moody."

"Kind of like the Mooshkoo on *The Enticer* earlier. It's like everyone on Blue is moody today," Mariana said, nearing the alleyway.

"Not Robin," Cassie said, pointing back at the vendor happily entertaining Potentials on his unicycle.

Captain BP beckoned quietly to them at the top of Charcoal Alley. "Stay in character now, and toss this balloon around," he instructed, pulling a black balloon from his trench coat. "I need to pretend I'm going to get more wares for Potentials."

"Got it," TJ said, bouncing the balloon on his knee.

Captain BP nonchalantly sauntered his way between the buildings while TJ, Cassie, and Mariana did as they were told, tossing the balloon outside one of the Zebbies. Upon Captain BP's signal, one by one, they slipped down the gray brick alleyway, past the garbage cans lining the concrete walls.

"I owe you, my fine friends. It's debilitating when there's a shortage," he said, and clapped his hands together. "Hurry now, I'm weak. Stand in front of me, and I'll crouch down. Woooeeee, I can hardly wait!"

Turning to face the street, Cassie, TJ, and Mariana created a wall with no air between them as they stood next to each other, while Captain BP munched on the remainder of Blobs from his trench coat like it was his last supper.

"Here, for your risk." He inserted three black-colored Blobs between Cassie and TJ, shaped like shoes the Entities wore.

"Not my first choice, but whatever," Mariana raised her eyes at the dark Blob in her hand. TJ, Cassie, and Mariana ate their Blobs, each of them turning pitch black.

"I feel like my head's going to explode," Mariana said.

"Mmmm, mmmm, *mmmm*," Captain BP gorged. "You young 'uns are the best—the best, I tell you!"

"I bet you say that to all the kids on Blue," Mariana said, rubbing her forehead. "Seriously, I have a bad headache. Hey, was it the Bad? It's probably too many Blobs. Maybe this is why my mother tells me to have junk only on the weekends." Mariana grimaced. "That's all anyone does here is drink and eat until they're literally Blue in the face! Ugh. Maybe it's the music. It's so loud!"

"Maybe," TJ said, as a screened back door of one of the Pits flapped in the alley. "I could have a hundred of these, though."

"Me too," Cassie said, catching her reflection in the metal sign that read "Line Trash Here." Her face still hadn't returned to its regular color.

"Some can't stop. It's in the genes," Captain BP reflected, stuffing his face. "I should know, coming from several generations in the Settling."

"We're going to the Settling! I heard it's cool. A bunch of kids talked about it at the Cove," TJ said, keeping his part of the wall intact to hide Captain BP.

"New Potentials aren't supposed to be in the Settling unless accompanied by an Entity," Captain BP said, slurping his fingers until the last morsel was gone.

"Agatha is taking me," Cassie said proudly. "We're getting my father's things before he comes home. Besides, she said I was ready."

"Did she now?" he asked, his voice sounding more even-keeled as he laced up one of his black boots. "Clearly a lure no more. This one's been hooked."

"Huh?" TJ asked.

"Oh, drat and dread, the rumination and perseveration are setting in as I realize I've prioritized my own pleasure instead of following the rules. I'm not setting a good example," Captain BP moaned, hanging his head low.

"Do you feel okay? Do you need more Blobs?" TJ asked.

"Thank you m'boy, but I must go back and entertain the masses, with a newfound strength thanks to all of you. For now though, leave me be to sit in solitude." He leaned against the gray brick wall like it was a cozy mattress and closed his eyes.

"Are you sure you're all right?" Cassie bit a hangnail, torn between getting out of the alley or staying with Captain BP to be sure he was okay.

Captain BP silently waved his hand in the air. "I'll be fine, friends. You all go on ahead. The Feed will be distributed soon, I'll replenish my wares, and get back to business. Just be careful not to let Kurt or anyone else of that status know I'm out of stock, or catch you leaving here for that matter. Good Dusk."

"Right," TJ gulped. "I don't want to mess up our chances of going to the Settling."

"Not to worry, TJ, not a chance of that," Captain BP said, shaking his head before drifting into a carefree stupor. "Not a chance."

CHAPTER
EIGHTEEN

Cassie looked toward the top of Charcoal Alley, where a pack of older teenagers gathered in the dusk, comparing bags of Blobs they held in their hands.

"Just act like we're with them," TJ instructed, leading the way up the gray bricks.

"How do you know what to do?" Mariana asked, holding her nose by the garbage cans.

"I have an older brother, remember?"

A black-and-white, hand-painted sign they hadn't seen on the way in now faced them on the way out.

REMEMBER TO SMILE! YOU'RE ENTERING AN ON-STAGE AREA!

"What does that mean?" Cassie asked.

"No clue," Mariana said, following TJ into the rowdy group of teenagers. "Let's blend in, but please, no more Blobs. My stomach hurts."

"Check these Blobs out!" a girl with bangs exclaimed, as bubbles floated out of her armpits.

"I've never had any this good," said a boy in a jean jacket.

They wove through the pack of teenagers, seamlessly blending into the larger crowd in the street, until TJ bumped into Sal.

"Where'd ya go? I've been looking for you!" Sal said, clutching TJ's arm and pulling him in close. He opened his palm to reveal dozens of dazzling pewter coins. "Just scored fifty Lures! It's time to celebrate." Sal began to lead TJ toward one of the Pits.

Cassie impulsively positioned herself directly in front of them and said, "TJ and I are going to the Settling with Agatha. She said she'd be back in a pulse, is that soon?"

"Yeah. Okay, we'll celebrate later." Sal eyed a group of elves divvying containers to be delivered to the Fix-It and dashed off toward them.

Mariana whispered to TJ, "You always do whatever he says."

"No I don't," TJ scoffed.

"Yeah, you do. Sal almost talked you into going to the Pits to celebrate his winnings or whatever, when what you really wanted to do was go to the Settling." Mariana poked a finger into his shoulder. "You might want to work on that."

TJ's cheeks flushed scarlet.

"In my family we call that giving away your power," Mariana stated.

Cassie whispered to TJ as they headed toward the Settling, "Her family is totally different than ours."

"I kind of got that," TJ replied.

"Don't get mad, I'm just encouraging you to speak up for yourself," Mariana said while she gently pushed someone out of her way.

"Yeah, yeah, I got it," TJ said.

Approaching the Welcoming Road, a woman wearing a Permanent badge and an Entity with two enormous, fishbowl eyes rushed past. The Permanent pouted, "I just want to go to the Pits first before we help with the Feed. I think I deserve a few Bads and some rest after that Zipper."

The female Entity instantly inflated three sizes like a puffer fish, glaring down into the Permanent's terrified face. "How *dare* you try and tell me the order of things after I've been running the show for you all these years! I'll tell you when and what you're worthy of. Remember that."

"I-I, I'm sorry, Jean," the Permanent trembled. "I just had a different idea. It won't happen again."

"Carry on." Jean shrank back down to her normal height of three feet and accompanied the Permanent over to the group of elves on the turf grass behind the vendors.

"That's what I don't want to happen," TJ said, as he noticed Sal close by, talking with a group of Entities.

"I see your point. But still . . . " Mariana said.

"Sal's nice to me, but I'm afraid of getting on his bad side," TJ squinted, not looking at Cassie and Mariana.

I know just what you mean. "It's like we should do what they tell us to because they're there for us," Cassie said.

"Exactly," TJ nodded.

Except, you always have a choice.

Cassie stopped on the street and turned to TJ. "Did you just say that?" she asked.

"Say what?"

That voice again. Where did it come from? Cassie waited a moment, to see if it might say something else. When it didn't, she continued walking beside her friends toward the entrance to the Midst.

"Hold up," Sal skidded on his heels, while he checked out

the racetrack on the corner, one of the cars stealing his attention. Shoving his hand in his pocket, he retrieved a few Lures and held them high in the air. "Mine's on the red one!"

Like magnets, Entities flocked to him at the fence, thrusting Lures at Sal as they shouted, "Mine's on the red too!" and "I'll take the highway green!"

Sal grimaced at TJ. "I can't pass this up, eh? We gotta wait for Agatha anyway. Gimme a pulse."

They viewed the race from behind the fence as a teenager jumped behind the wheel of the yellow car. Mariana turned sharply to Cassie and asked, "Don't they know it's against the law not to wear a helmet?"

Cassie glanced behind her at the pier, where elves and Entities under Agatha's direction unloaded hundreds of containers off the underbelly of *The Enticer*. With a grandmotherly smile, Agatha waved a finger in the air to let Cassie know she'd be done soon.

The whizzing sound of the speeding cars pulled Cassie's attention back to the track.

"Sal told me last time we Zippered, after one too many Escapes, that Eric was living with another family in the Settling." TJ lightly banged the bottom of the fence, watching the cars fly by. "He gets to go to the Cove and drink Bad whenever he wants. Sal said the family had room for another kid if I wanted to stay too."

Cassie clutched the links on the fence while behind her Mariana complained to other spectators about the helmet issue. "Don't you think your parents would miss you, even if they're not around much?"

"I doubt it," TJ said, digging his sneaker into the bottom of the fence. "Besides, I'm figuring out how to take care of myself. Maybe I will stay here if I want, if Eric wants me to." TJ's voice wavered, then shaking his head rapidly, like he was coming out of a trance, he said, "I hope we find Eric in the Settling. I want to tell him he already has a family, and maybe we'll play one Stimulator, but then I'm having Sal Zipper us home. Unless he really wanted me to stay. I don't know, it's all messed up." TJ stepped a foot back from the fence, turning his attention to watch two teenage boys playing balloon volleyball.

"Did I just hear you wanted to stay here?" Mariana said, coming toe to toe with TJ. "Even though you might want to play Stimulators every day, wouldn't you get sick of them? If I hear one more bell or see one more flashing light, I'm gonna go nuts."

Cassie stared at the red car rounding the track at full speed, the driver holding on for dear life. *We could stay here if we wanted to?*

The roar of the spectators around the track and the *bang! bang!* of the large containers unloading onto the pier surprisingly didn't drown out the small sound coming from Cassie's pocket. *Jingle Jingle!*

The glasses! Cassie stepped back from the fence and reached in her pocket, squeezing the gold-rimmed frames.

Mariana noticed Cassie holding the glasses in her hand. "I thought you passed the school vision test."

"I did," Cassie said, placing them on the bridge of her nose. "But I found these and . . . "

". . . And you wanted to look sophisticated!" Mariana interrupted. "That's cool! They look good!"

Cassie blinked, adjusting her eyes to the new lens as she stared down at the cobblestones. They fit perfectly. *Why do I feel like I have to hide them?* Then she looked up.

Cloaked Entities in their dark shoes, their faces hidden under dark hoods, prowled about the Midst. Stout, ashen-faced trolls with irregular noses and lopsided ears, more eerie than adorable, conversed under street lamps lining the cobblestones. Slurping their long tongues over razor-sharp teeth, the trolls eyed Potentials like dessert. Cassie stared openly as slick-winged creatures paced the pier with long arms clasped behind their back, like they were guarding something. Kurt resembled a piranha, his teeth sharp as spears, as he shiftily kept watch over the elves unloading the ship.

Cassie shuddered. *Why does everyone look so scary?*

At the Welcoming Gate, horned Entities assessed Potentials entering the Midst, drooling out the sides of their mouths. Behind them, on the pier, wooden shingles hung off the sides of *The Enticer*, making it look less like an adventurous pirate ship and more like a dilapidated boat that had been through one too many storms.

Kurt snapped a whip in his hand every few seconds against a metal street lamp on the pier, ordering, "Supply and demand! Supply and demand!" Cassie gulped as the already sweaty elves worked faster, furiously loading smaller packages into the giant plastic containers.

That must be the Feed Agatha talked about. Cassie scanned the pier, but Agatha wasn't there. Cassie removed the glasses from her face. Entities jovially strolled about the Midst, once again looking like harmless little Hobbits. She checked the pier where *The Enticer*, with its bold colors and sturdy frame, returned to a fun pirate ship. *Everything is back to normal.*

"Cassie, dear," Agatha called from behind. Immediately, Cassie slipped the glasses back into her pocket and whirled around. "Where's Sal? I'm afraid he may have to accompany you to the Settling, at least initially, as I've been called to another area for an important matter."

"But I need my own Entity to take me to the Settling, right?" Cassie fretted.

"Don't get yourself in a tizzy. Sal will be sufficient. I'll meet you there when I'm done. I've never let you down, have I?" Agatha picked up an empty bottle of Bad off the street, closing one eye to be sure it's contents were completely empty, before tossing it in a nearby trash can.

"No," Cassie answered, relaxing her shoulders.

"All right, then. Oh, there he is, I should have known." Agatha observed Sal leaning three quarters of the way over the fence at the track shouting, "I better get my ten Lures back, you worthless . . . "

"Sal, Sal, it doesn't take you long, does it?" Agatha said, striding over and whispering something in his ear.

Sal looked back at TJ, Cassie, and Mariana. "Okay, we'll head out in a half a pulse. I swear just one more race."

"Those race cars really are fun," TJ said to Cassie and Mariana as a swarm of Mooshkoos lined up at the fence to have a turn. "Scary, but fun."

Agatha checked her Surveyor on her way back over to the kids. "I'll leave you with Sal and rejoin you in the Settling."

"You're a busy woman, Agatha," Mariana commented. "Do you run this place?"

Agatha patted Mariana on the head like a good dog before departing in the opposite direction, toward Strays.

While they waited for Sal, Cassie looked over at the pier and asked TJ and Mariana, "Do you see those Entities?"

"Which ones? There are hundreds of them," TJ replied.

"All of them. Do they look different to you?" Cassie probed.

"Different from us, you mean? Of course they look different from us, they look like freaks in a funhouse," Mariana said, moving out of the way of a group of Permanents playing a rowdy game of balloon toss.

"I know they look different from us, but I didn't know if you thought they looked, I dunno, scary," Cassie said, beginning to chew on her nail as several Mooshkoos loaded containers onto the backs of the elves' flying bicycles.

"I think they look the same as they ever did," Mariana scoffed. "Weird."

"They look the same to me too," said TJ.

It must be the glasses. Cassie reached in her pocket. "H-here, try these on and tell me what . . . "

"Listen up, Potentials," Sal interrupted, wiping beads of sweat from his greasy forehead. Cassie shoved the glasses back in her pocket. "I got this great game going, see, and well, it's just going to be hard for me to go right now . . . "

"But you promised!" Cassie cried. "We can't go without an Entity!"

"Hold your Constantines, will ya?" Sal scolded. "If ya let me finish, there's a way around everything. Just tell Big or Small on the Settling platform just up the road there that you're going to check out housing for your mother who's in the Pits. You'll get in, no problem."

"Just like that?" TJ asked, stepping back to let an elf fly by above the cobblestones.

"Just like that. When the kids are doing the job for the parents, that's a sign its time for the Settling." Sal wiped the end of his nose.

Cassie, TJ, and Mariana left Sal at the track and crossed the Welcoming Road, past the main Energy Vibration Meter holding steady on a pigeon-blue color near the bottom of the blue range. They walked toward the paved road leading away from the Midst, where a bright and shiny silver "Welcome to the Settling" sign stuck out of a small patch of fake grass on the corner.

A quarter of the way down the dim road, a lantern shone down on Big. Sitting on a small platform, he alternated between checking his Surveyor, tossing bright pink Blobs into his wide mouth, and swilling sips of Escape. He raised his head slightly when he heard their approaching footsteps. "Permission?" he asked, not bothering to look up from his Surveyor.

"Hello, sir. My mother . . . she's at the Pits," TJ said robotically as Big looked him up and down. "Sal Hawke sent us to check out housing."

"Mom's had one too many Escapes, huh?" Big chuckled and gulped some Escape. "These your siblings?"

"He doesn't even remember us," Mariana whispered to Cassie.

"We get kids like you all the time," Big chugged the entire mug, nearly falling out of his canvas chair. Steadying himself, he let out a burp, and said in a gravelly voice, "Lemme check your energy Vibration. Should be real easy since you're at this point."

He switched the Energy Vibration Meter to the Ready option on his Surveyor, the black arrow, on command, settling on the solid black line, ready to begin.

"Who's first?" Big asked, with half-mast eyes.

"I'll go," Cassie said, clenching her fists and stepping up to the Meter.

Big finished another bottle of Escape while he measured Cassie's energy space. The arrow landed on the same pigeon-blue color as the Meter for the Land, two notches above the gray hue at the bottom of the color range. "That works."

Cassie stepped aside.

"You're up, pretty boy," Big said, swaying side to side. First the arrow teetered on the gray color at the very bottom, and then rose one notch above, in the range of elephant-gray blue. "Thataboy, nice and low. Next." Big staggered, waiting to measure Mariana.

Oh no. Cassie scratched her leg. *How will Mariana get through without Agatha?*

"Ah, just so you know, I always land in the same place for some reason," Mariana said somewhat apologetically, her arms in position by her side.

"Huh? Wait, I gotta check my Surveyor, hold on. The boys are signaling fuh me at the Pits, or maybe they said the Cove. My shif ens soon," Big slurred.

"Sure," Mariana raised her eyebrows.

Big scanned Mariana while distractedly checking his Surveyor for his friends' whereabouts. The arrow settled swiftly on the clear space above the line. Under half-closed lids, Big looked confused, rotating the Surveyor upside down.

"Good enuf. They're waitin fu me at the Pitsh." The gray monkey yawned, revealing several silvery teeth in the back of his throat.

"Let's go," TJ whispered.

Big raised his empty bottle of Escape. "The Powa of Numbas."

"The Power of Numbers," TJ, Cassie, and Mariana repeated.

Once out of Big's earshot, Mariana asked, "What does that mean?"

"I dunno," TJ said, leading them away from the platform.

Cassie checked over her shoulder, wondering if Big would even make it to his friends as he stumbled over on the platform. Then she reminded herself to look forward.

I'm in the Settling and it takes special status to get here.

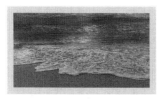

CHAPTER
NINETEEN

The bright lights and noise of the Midst diminished the farther they walked down the Settling road, which changed from paved to broken pieces of concrete once they passed the platform. Agitated wind howled through the twisted and gnarly bare trees lining the gloomy road. TJ moved closer to Cassie and Mariana, their shirts brushing against one other.

"How come you always measure above the black line?" TJ asked Mariana.

"I don't know. My Ya-Ya says I'm consistent. Maybe that's why."

"Well, I'm consistent. I measure near the bottom every time," TJ said.

"That's true. So does Cassie. I don't know. Maybe it's a measure of confidence."

"I'm confident," TJ said, scuffing down the road.

"You are? What are you confident about?" Mariana asked.

"I don't know. But I am," TJ said, tripping over a broken piece of pavement.

"I'm not so confident," Cassie said, avoiding the woods.

"I know. Remember that time in math when you totally had the right answer on your homework but didn't want to raise your hand in case you didn't? You pretended you were tying your shoe," Mariana laughed.

Cassie clenched her jaw, glad the darkness hid her red face.

"I do that sometimes," TJ said. "But it can't measure confidence because Sal's colors are low, and he's confident. He said he knew I'd easily follow him to Blue to find Eric and . . . here I am."

"Well, maybe not landing on ugly colors means I don't have family in the Land of Blue," Mariana suggested.

"Maybe," TJ said.

"That might be it," Cassie said, trying to ignore the spooky sounds of the creaking trees. "The only reason Agatha let you come here is because I didn't want to go without you."

"Well, I'm glad I'm here, even if it is really creepy on this road. That's what friends are for." Mariana put her arm around Cassie.

"Thanks," Cassie said.

"And you too TJ," Mariana said, putting her other arm around him.

"Yeah, thanks," TJ said, stuffing his hands in his pockets.

The line of tall, twisted trees cast creepy shadows on the dusty road.

"Is this even the right way?" Mariana asked. "There's nothing here."

Dry leaves rustled among the sparse shrubbery at the foot of the scraggly trees.

"It's like we're surrounded by shadow monsters," Cassie said, pulling her sweatshirt tighter.

"I know, look at that one, it looks like a devil with horns," Mariana pointed to the side of the road.

"Cut it out," Cassie said, pushing Mariana to the side so she almost fell over.

"Well, it does."

"Look," TJ said, pointing to a wooden gate fifty yards ahead spanning across the road, illuminated by a swaying street lamp. Wild creatures hooted from the haggard trees as a small, rundown wooden shack, stationed behind the gate, came into view.

"That sure doesn't look like Agatha's hospitality suite," Mariana grimaced.

"This can't be it," Cassie said. "Why is it so dark, and not lit up like the Midst?"

"There's only one way to find out," TJ said, walking ahead to the creaky gate. The shack displayed the words "The Settling" in white spray-paint on a rickety sign hanging unevenly over its threshold.

"Look at this place," Mariana said, stopping in her tracks. Cassie felt like when she was little and would stop in the Ferris wheel line with her grandparents, not sure she wanted to go through with it. Her heart sank when they reached the gate.

Three-story apartment houses with dirty laundry hanging out of the windows lined a cracked sidewalk that went all the way around, in a square formation, beyond the gate. Small patches of dirt and occasional blades of grass that didn't stand a chance from lack of sunlight lay pitifully in front of each bland apartment. In the middle of the dim square, a playground with rusted seesaws and swing sets lay scattered across the dirt. People congregated on stairs and porches in front of their urine-colored apartment buildings and spoke in hushed tones upon Cassie, TJ, and Mariana's arrival.

"This reminds me of our old apartment," Cassie said quietly, sliding her pinky finger in her mouth.

"Oh, yeah!" Mariana whispered loudly, outside the gate.

"Strays is definitely nicer, but at least people have a place to live, right?" TJ asked.

A woman with hair piled on her head like a bird's nest leaned out of her second-story apartment window to take in laundry. Noticing TJ, Mariana, and Cassie standing under the street lamp outside the shack, she grabbed her clothing, abruptly pulled down the flimsy shade, and retreated inside. Two mothers gathered on the sidewalk in front of their homes whispered nervously, pulling their unkempt children close to their waists.

"Why are they looking at us like that?" Mariana asked.

Just then, a man with hair the color of baby powder and ruddy, pockmarked skin, wearing a Permanent badge on his flannel shirt, poked his head out of the doorless threshold of the shack. A wart on his chin wobbled as he chewed on a weak brown blade of grass. "What do you want? You ain't got an Entity with ya."

"They're with me, Mickey," Agatha's voice rang out in the darkness behind them as she strode down the Settling road. Reaching the gate, she wore an unpleasant look on her harried face. "I heard Sal gave you kids the code to get past Big. I'll take care of that later. It's a good thing the Ruler has me to take care of things."

"Good Dusk," Mickey said, straightening his spine. "We got some newcomers, do we? It's always good to see kids learning the ropes at a young age." He saluted Agatha.

"No need for your opinion. We're actually here to retrieve Craig Connor's things. This is his daughter."

Does Mickey know my dad?

"Getting Craig's things?" Mickey scratched his powdery hair. "I thought he took his Have to Haves and now he's staying. This is news to me."

A large black crow-like Entity with a rather large forehead and a small, dark moustache flew out from the shack down onto Mickey's shoulder. Leaning in close to his ear, the Entity whispered, "When 'Landlords' turn the drunken Bee out of the foxglove's door—when Butterflies—renounce their 'drams,' I shall but drink the more!"

"Mickey, are you having too many Escapes on the job? Is it time for a replacement? Because, as we both know, I can make that happen." Agatha ushered the kids through the swinging gate and across the dirt road to the concrete sidewalk.

"I just had a couple, I didn't mean nothing by it. Go on, kids, get what you need," Mickey said, hanging his head while his Entity whispered once more before flying back to the roof of the shack. "Wine comes in at the mouth and love comes in at the eye; that's all we know for truth before we grow old and die."

"Good Dusk, everyone!" Agatha's voice echoed down the sidewalk. "Accommodations are fine, of course?"

"Of course," two women answered flatly from their broken-shingled porch, reminding Cassie of the orphans answering Miss Hannigan in *Annie*.

"How could they like these accommodations?" Mariana whispered, eyeing the bland apartments with flowerless pots sitting sadly on depressing doorsteps.

Agatha turned on her black soles. "Because some people are grateful for being cared for while they have access to . . . "

"Lighten up, everyone!" Sal said, scaling the gate and slapping Mickey on the shoulder. "They're all just looking at ya funny because they thought you might be with Them."

"My, my, isn't everyone chatty this Dusk," Agatha said, patting the head of a little boy riding by on a dented big wheel.

"Don't even mention it, Sal. I still think of the last time," Mickey shuddered.

"Who's 'Them'?" Cassie asked.

Before anyone could answer, a door to one of the apartments creaked open. A woman with dark hair the color of pond scum, appearing like she'd been in bed for months, peeked out from behind a damaged front door. Timidly, she looked left to right, like she wanted to go outside, but was afraid. Placing one foot down on the front porch, a roly-poly Entity instantly jumped out from one of the dry, thorny bushes outside her apartment. "Ahhh!!"

The woman bolted back inside as the Entity staggered down the steps, laughing hysterically.

"Why did he do that?" Cassie asked, her eyes on the now-closed front door. "That was mean."

"Oh, that's Penny's Entity. Penny's scared of her own shadow. Just let her be." Agatha waved a hand like she was swatting a fly in the twilight atmosphere, continuing down the crumbly sidewalk.

"Maintenance should fix these," Mariana said, avoiding the cracked pieces of concrete. Cassie checked to see if Penny might try to come out again while her Entity sat on the porch with his arms clasped behind his head.

Mind your own business, kid. It's not like I'm yours . . . unless you want me to be.

Startled, Cassie ran down the sidewalk to catch up with the others, careful to step over the cracks.

"No one's trying to take our housing, Agatha, are they?" a man with a deep bass voice in a black shirt, black jeans, and black cowboy boots called out from his porch as Agatha led the kids down the first block. "I heard we're at maximum capacity and the Feed is getting low. We've waited a long time to get our own place, and I don't exactly want to share."

The man's wife pulled at his arm.

"Now, Johnny," Agatha said, reassuringly. "Once you're Permanent, you're Permanent. No one's taking anything from anyone."

"I don't think they like us," TJ whispered, avoiding the strangers' suspicious faces.

"Are we safe here?" Mariana asked.

"Don't be frightened," Agatha said. "They just don't want you to take their accommodations. Permanents do whatever it takes to keep their housing, loving Blue the way they do."

"They like this?" Mariana mouthed to Cassie.

Well, at least they get to be with their families, Cassie thought, as a pretty teenage girl hung out with her father on the front steps of their apartment.

With closed lips, Cassie smiled at women standing on porches beside their husbands and children, in an attempt to be friendly. No one smiled back. Sal, like he was mayor, kept running up the stairs of each apartment, hugging Entities and Permanents he hadn't seen in ages.

"Maybe they'll like us better if you tell them we're just getting my dad's things so he can go home," Cassie suggested.

"Oh look," Agatha said, as they neared the second block. "It's the last apartment on the end, before the turn."

"Do you know where Eric's host family lives?" TJ quietly asked Sal and Agatha.

"Host family?" Mariana sneered. "I thought that's who you lived with when you traveled abroad in high school. If this is where host families live, I'm definitely not signing up for student exchange."

Agatha shot Mariana a disapproving glance. "Eric is staying with a lovely family that is currently training him elsewhere, in exchange for rooming. If you look across the way, you'll see a lemon-yellow apartment, which is the Jackson residence."

Cassie gazed across the square sidewalk, thinking the three-story more resembled the color of plaque. Beyond the building, they saw the massive stone wall standing erect behind the entire Land of Blue.

Sal clutched the back of TJ's neck like an eagle grabbing a snake. "The Jacksons are a great clan! I told ya we'd take care of your brother."

"We always take care of our own," Agatha remarked.

"I thought families were the ones who took care of their own," Mariana disputed.

"I wasn't speaking to you, "Agatha said, not bothering to turn around.

Mariana raised an eyebrow, turning her attention to a man and a woman playing cards for Lures on a lantern-lit porch, their two young children playing nearby in the dark. Approaching an apartment at the end of the second block, Mariana tapped Cassie on the shoulder.

A young girl, around the age of seven, sat on her front steps, pulling out pieces of her golden hair, one by one, like strands of straw, seemingly unaffected by the pain.

"What is she doing? Doesn't that hurt?" Mariana asked.

Several toddlers played nearby, dirty diapers hanging off their behinds. A toothless Entity sat next to the girl, mumbling in her ear. She seemed oblivious to the chattering Entity as she watched her younger brother play with a toy truck, alone on the patch of brown grass outside their apartment.

"That's her Entity, isn't it?" Mariana asked Cassie as they walked past.

"I guess so," Cassie answered, unable to take her eyes off the girl.

"Then why isn't he helping her?" Mariana asked. "Aren't Entities there to help you when things are tough? I mean, Sal and Agatha help you and TJ, right?"

Energy began to swirl inside Cassie, like it was desperately seeking to get out. *That was the same girl I saw leaving the Midst, looking for her father.*

I wonder if Daddy will be back soon . . . Cassie heard in her mind.

She froze. *We're on the same frequency.*

She wanted to tell the girl she understood how she felt. She also wanted to tell her to stop that bad habit of pulling her hair. Cassie bit her lip. *I'm no better. Why would she listen to me?* She tasted the warm blood, her heart speeding like a freight train.

Once a habit, always a habit. Bite three times, and I'll make you feel better.

Cassie bit three times, her heart rate returning to normal.

Or you could breathe and try something new.

Cassie stopped, as the others continued down the sidewalk. *There it is again, that other voice. Where is it coming from?*

"Anna and Michael," called a worn woman with tired skin from the front door of the apartment. "Time for supper." The mother caught sight of Cassie, and wiped her apron.

"Cassie, c'mon," Mariana called impatiently. "What are you doing?"

Cassie lazily tapped her foot on the broken concrete until the girl named Anna looked up.

I hope your dad comes home soon, Cassie said in her mind.

The green-eyed girl stared at Cassie, like she was somewhere else. Cassie met her stare for a moment, and then stepped over the cracks, rejoining the others.

"Here we are," Agatha said, somewhat breathless as she arrived at the end of the sidewalk. "Cassie, why don't you run in and gather your father's things? There shouldn't be much, since our competent workers have already tidied up." Just then, Agatha's Surveyor glowed. Glancing at it quickly, her mind clearly somewhere else, she said, "You can have a look about the place. I'm being called back to the Midst regarding the Feed so I need to go. Sal, bring them in. You know Cassie gets so nervous she can't do things independently." Agatha left in a hurry, like the white rabbit that was late for a very important date.

"Sure thing, Agatha. You can count on me," Sal said.

Her cheeks flushed, Cassie followed Sal over to the stairs leading to the rust-colored apartment. She skipped every other step until she reached the top of the porch, while neighbors spied behind smudged windows. The ripped screen door slammed shut as Cassie, TJ, and Mariana entered the moldy smelling apartment.

"How many people live here?" Mariana asked, counting the

endless coat hooks lining the walls. "I thought I had a big family."

Sal led them to the back of the house, where ripped shades and leaky ceilings framed the fluorescent-lit kitchen. Dirty dishes filled the sink, and a full ashtray on the table lay next to plates of half-eaten food.

"My dad doesn't smoke cigarettes anymore," Cassie said. "I don't think this is the right apartment."

"It's not just your dad who lived here," Sal informed her. "That'd be a waste of space." Sal checked out the contents of the refrigerator. "Dang, no Escape."

"Who would want to live here?" Mariana said, inching by the kitchen table to avoid touching anything.

"Folks like me," answered a quiet male voice from the adjacent room.

Cassie spun around and said, "Who's that?"

"I dunno," TJ said, coming to a halt.

"That's Andy," said Sal, shutting the refrigerator. "Sometimes they sleep on the job."

"I'm just taking a nap, er, cleaning up," the sleepy voice said, dreamily, "before I go to the Fix-It to get my Have to Haves."

Mariana tentatively stepped toward the room.

"You gonna let a girl go before ya?" Sal elbowed TJ.

TJ cleared his throat and moved in front of Cassie and Mariana. A man with his shirt opened halfway, lying on a ripped, white leather couch—that and a coffee table the only pieces of furniture in the room—saluted them in the dark with the whisk broom he held in his hand. His long, wavy hair drooped over half his face.

Sal pulled the man up to a sitting position and switched on the overhead light. "C'mon, Agatha'll have my head. We got visitors checking out housing here, see?" Sal spoke loudly in Andy's ear.

"I know, man. They wanna know why I live here, and I'm gonna tell them. If they're paying us Lures to eat and drink Escape as long as we do our jobs, why wouldn't I settle in at the Settling?" Andy chuckled.

"Guy's got a point," Sal said, picking up empty cans off the coffee table.

"Personally, I'd rather starve than live here," Mariana said, pursing her lips.

Sal glared at Mariana, who glared right back.

"Craig's stuff ready to go?" Sal said, ignoring Mariana. "Doesn't look like much is here."

Empty bottles of Escape littered the faded couch.

"I thought Craig was coming back," Andy said through closed eyes. "That's why the place looks like this. I let the other guys carry on last Dusk, in celebration that Craig was back on his Have to Haves. Since when did the orders change?"

"Since Agatha said so," Sal said, pulling Andy up by a tuft of hair.

"All right, man, I didn't know," Andy said, making an effort to stand.

"Why would the orders change?" Cassie asked, stepping back.

"She's full of questions, this one . . . " Sal said, moving a pack of cigarettes stuffed in between the couch cushions onto the glass table. "I wouldn't last a minute if she was my Potential. Any Escapes left?"

"In the other fridge. You know where we keep it," Andy nodded. "You haven't been gone that long, my friend."

"Right," Sal snickered. "I'll be right back."

Andy, who appeared to be about thirty years old, feebly whisked crumbs of food off the couch onto the floor, like he was ninety.

"What's your job?" TJ asked, noticing Andy's Working for Permanency badge hanging lopsided on the bottom of his opened shirt.

"Clean up after tenants, and, of course, offer new Potentials the latest Have to Haves. C'mon, kid, if you're ready for housing in the Settling, you gotta know what we do."

"We're not here for housing," Mariana scoffed.

Andy's brow furrowed as he asked Cassie, "Aren't you Craig's kid? I thought you were gonna stay here with your dad. There's even a hook for ya." He lazily tilted his bushel of hair in the direction of the front hallway.

"Huh?" Cassie grunted.

"Here, I'll show you," Andy sauntered into the entranceway and dragged his finger along the wall of gold-plated hooks, jackets and knapsacks dangling from some, while others were empty.

Cassie examined the organized rows. Family names engraved on larger hooks hung above individual hooks assigned to first names.

"Callahan, Chung, Coletta, you gotta be close . . . " Andy mumbled.

Cassie inspected the individual hooks, assigned to Jennifer and Stephen, under the hook labeled Chung.

"Here you are," Andy declared. "Connor."

Cassie stared at the metal hook. Underneath the family name, a navy Land of Blue sweatshirt hung from an individual hook labeled "Craig." Cassie reached out her hand to the cotton sweatshirt, slowly taking it off the wall. Pressing it to her face, she remembered the familiar smell of cologne and sweat whenever Dad came home from work. That was her favorite smell in the world.

Cassie read the names of the empty hooks above her father's, "Margaret" and "Joseph." Those were her dad's parents, the grandparents she never met because they died before Cassie was born. Staring at the gold hooks, she wondered what her grandparents were like, and why their names were on hooks in the Settling. Then Cassie found another hook, underneath her father's, with only the letter "C" engraved.

"Who's this one for?" Cassie asked Andy, while Mariana and TJ stood behind her.

"I told ya, we had one for you. I got the order to add the hook today, straight from Agatha's mouth, so I know I didn't mess that up." Andy crossed his arms over his chest.

There's a hook for me?

"Why are my grandparents names here?"

"Oh!" Andy said, pointing a finger in the air, "I can answer that. I just learned that in Working for Permanency training. Whenever someone stays in the Settling, they get a hook, because once they're here, they're usually here for good. We add hooks for family members after that, as we're told."

"But my dad and I are going home today. I'm not living here."

"That's too bad. You'll miss a good time," Andy leaned against the wall, his eyelids closing.

"I wonder if Eric has a hook where he's staying," TJ said, searching the names on the wall. "Do you know my brother Eric? He's living with the Jacksons."

"Eric, Eric," Andy said, in a sleepy voice. "Big kid? Obsessed with Stimulators?"

"Yeah! That's my brother!" TJ said, excitedly, turning to Cassie and Mariana.

Andy nodded. "Eric's been over here to play cards with Craig and the gang. Your dad's a great poker player."

Cassie rose up on her toes. Her dad's games went for days at the Knights club. *He's the best poker player.*

TJ elbowed Cassie and said, "They know each other!"

Cassie gathered her dad's sweatshirt under her chin as her heart leaped with excitement.

"Eric's going to be working with us soon, to support himself on Blue. He wants to go for Permanent status. Yeah, he's a fun one, that Eric," Andy said, shaking his head. "I heard he was even considering to Give It Away."

"What do you mean?" TJ asked, scratching the leg of his jeans.

"You know, ya give up your form and become an Entity, in exchange for a whole slew of Lures. I've considered it a couple of times, but I always lose my nerve. They said they'll get me eventually," he laughed.

Sal reentered the room, double-fisting two dark brown bottles of Escape. "All set?"

Cassie kept the sweatshirt close to her chest. "Yeah, I got what I came here for," she said, quietly. *Now I just need my dad.*

"Sure you don't want to see the cots upstairs in case you need a place to sleep?" Andy asked.

"We're good," Sal replied. "But we may have a need soon, right TJ? Nothing better than playing Stims all day and crashing here when you're done. Trying to get him to stay with us." Then he whispered to Andy, "Shouldn't be too hard of a sell. Kid loves Stimulators."

"Just like his brother," Andy said, nodding.

"Yup. That's what keeps us in business." Sal slapped Andy hard on the shoulder.

"The Power of Numbers," Andy said, rubbing his shoulder.

"Right," Sal said, like Andy had said too much.

"Don't take too long, kid, in figuring out if you want to stay; there's a waiting list for those cots," Andy said.

The front door opened, Mickey plodding into the dimly lit apartment in his heavy steel-toed work boots. Ducking his tall frame under the stained yellow hallway light, he brushed off bits of ceiling chalk that had fallen in his white hair when the door slammed shut. He looked around and said, "Decent job cleaning up."

Mariana's lip curled up in disgust and she mouthed to Cassie, "Seriously?"

"You can head down into the Midst," Mickey said to Andy. "Agatha sent me to tell you the Feed is ready to be distributed in the Settling."

Suddenly much more energetic, Andy bowed to the kids and sauntered his skinny frame out the unhinged front door.

"Wait up," Sal called after him. Quickly, he spun around as if he forgot something and said, "You kids know your way back, right?"

"I got 'em," Mickey said. "Go enjoy yourself. After all, the Feed's here! Just remember ole Mickey, huh?"

"You got it, my friend," Sal said, jumping from the porch to the sidewalk, hurrying to catch up to Andy.

"Jeesh," Mariana said, squinting through the ripped screen. "Are you getting a complex? Sal leaves you every chance he gets."

"That's all right. I'm used to it," TJ said, peering over Mariana's head.

"Don't feel bad," Cassie said, tying her Dad's sweatshirt around her waist. "Agatha leaves me to go to work, too, but I think it's because they know we know our way around."

Mickey clapped his mitt-sized hands and said, "All right! Let's head back to the Midst. I'm sure Sal already told ya, now that you're special status, the rules are: we don't let any new Potentials know what the Settling looks like, because well, you know, they think everything looks like the Midst when they arrive." Mickey smiled, exposing a rotten tooth in the back of his mouth, which sent a chill up Cassie's spine.

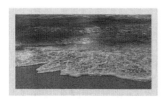

CHAPTER
TWENTY

Cassie, TJ, Mariana, and Mickey crossed the dusty, pebbled road under the dusky, night sky, leading from the housing sidewalk to the wooden shack by the front gate. Tenants turned up music they played on their porches, settling back into routine as they watched the kids leave the Settling.

"When we first got here," TJ asked Mickey, "why did people think we were with 'Them?' What does that mean?"

"Oh, 'Them'," Mickey began, in a solemn tone. "They're the creatures who showed up many pulses ago, going door-to-door in the Settling—they knew they didn't stand half a chance in the Midst—but when the Ruler found out, he didn't take to their offering kindly. Anyone caught opening their doors to 'them' lost their Lures for thirty pulses. A couple of the wives did speak to the creatures, admitting they might want something different. Ended up costing their family food and drink, nearly starving to death."

Mickey shook his head and continued, raising his voice so Cassie and Mariana could hear too. "Grim times. A whole lot of quivering going on, people afraid their Feed would be taken away next for what their wives, and some husbands too, had done, by entertaining the creatures. Grim times."

"It looks like it's always grim times here," Mariana said, turning back to see who had thrown an empty bottle of Escape that landed with a thud behind them on the dirt road.

"What did the creatures look like?" Cassie asked, tugging her dad's sweatshirt tighter around her waist.

"Not like us on Blue, causing enough of a stir in the Vibration to almost start a quake," Mickey answered, stopping in front of the shack. He raised an arm and the black crow-like Entity flew off the roof, landing just above one of the dark tattoos on Mickey's arm, where the words "Settling for Life" stretched across his bicep. The Entity recited, "'And so faintly you came tapping, tapping at my chamber door, that I scarce was sure I heard you—here I opened wide the door—Darkness there and nothing more.'"

Mickey stroked the Entity's head. "Yup. The Ruler made sure it won't happen again."

"How?" Cassie asked.

"Cause we got the Energy Vibration Meters now," Mickey said, looping his fingers through his belt loops. "Making sure the colors stay at the same low Vibration as they've always been on Blue. Only place we don't have one is on the Praying Grounds, cause if you're there, well heck," Mickey chuckled, "the Ruler knows you're committed. You don't need to be checked."

"What's the Praying Gr—?" Cassie started to ask.

"Hey! Is that Wisdom Glass?" Mariana interrupted, scurrying over to a rusty old gate, barely visible amid the mid-size gnarled trees and shrubs on the other corner of the road across from the shack.

Mariana crouched down and quickly picked up the piece of glass. "Ouch!" she said, flinching, "it's a broken piece of bottle." She sucked the dot of blood from her finger.

"Whoa, ho, ho, you can't go that way," Mickey reprimanded. "Exit's this way." He jogged over to the wooden gate spanning the concrete road where they originally entered. "No one goes that way except the Rec—I mean, the Entities in charge. I gotta tell them to be more careful with those bottles of Escape they bring back there. Anyway, back out the way you came. Agatha'll be waiting for you. Ought to slow down now as she's getting up in years, but don't tell her I said so. I don't know how much longer she can keep this pace up, running the place like she does."

Mickey opened the long, wooden gate with one hand, while the crow cawed loudly on his shoulder.

"I know, Eddie," Mickey swung the gate back and forth three times while the thin-nosed Entity flapped his wings. Mickey glanced sheepishly at the kids as he explained, "I gotta do it three times for good luck, or he gets mad." Then he opened the gate wide.

TJ, Cassie, and Mariana, still nursing her wounded finger, thanked Mickey as they left.

"Hope you got what you came here for," Mickey said to Cassie, who took one more peek back at the apartment house where the little girl lived. "Maybe we'll see ya again sometime, if you end up staying. C'mon, Eddie."

"Ah, for me, staying here would be a 'no'," said Mariana, straddling the broken concrete.

"Even though the Settling wasn't the fanciest place or anything, if Eric worked here, and if I stayed, at least we could be together . . . " TJ's voice trailed off as he shuffled a few paces behind Cassie and Mariana. He heard the cracking sound of a large tree branch in the eerie woods beside the road before the branch gave way and fell forcefully on the pine-needle floor. "Wait, what if he actually goes through with the Give It Away? What would happen to me?"

"Okay," Mariana said, turning around and placing her hands on her hips. "Who would transform themselves into an Entity, just for fun?"

"I dunno, Sal and Andy made it sound pretty fun," TJ said, stuffing his hands in his pockets.

"I'm just glad I got to see where my dad was staying all this time," Cassie reflected. "I wouldn't want to live here, even though it was nice they put a hook on the wall, in case I did. I bet that little girl, Anna, could use a good babysitter, though. Did you think any of the older kids looked responsible there?"

"There you go again," Mariana shook her head ruefully, "taking on everyone else's problems in addition to your own."

"Thanks for pointing out I have problems," Cassie said, chewing on her lip.

"I wasn't trying to point out your weaknesses, I was just saying. You have enough to worry about."

Cassie sighed resignedly. "By the way, did anyone else wonder where that rusty gate led to? I didn't see it the first time."

"Me neither," TJ said. "It reminded me of the field behind the high school where Eric and his friends used to hang on the weekends. You had to jump over the fence behind the school to get there. All kinds of stuff went on in that field."

"Like what?" Mariana asked.

"You know, teenage stuff," TJ said as the trees rustled in the woods.

"I want to know where the gate leads to," Cassie shuddered, thinking about the creepy woods, the gate, and Anna all at once, wishing she could have seen her one more time before she left, maybe just to say hello out loud.

"It must run behind the Midst because . . . there's nowhere else to go, right?" TJ reasoned.

Noise from the Midst came within earshot, flashing lights bouncing into view as they neared the platform at the entrance of the Settling road. The pine trees lining both sides of the road turned into manicured grass, where the back of the Welcoming to the Settling sign read: SMILE! YOU ARE ABOUT TO ENTER AN ON-STAGE AREA."

"There's that sign again," Cassie said.

"Who are they telling to smile?" Mariana asked, while a family of five with balloons in their hands danced with vendors along the Welcoming Road.

"Probably the people who work here," said TJ, "so they're all chipper and stuff, you know, kinda like when you see signs in bathrooms that say, 'Employees, don't forget to wash your hands before returning to work.' Cause I mean, who'd want to buy stuff from people who are in bad moods?"

"Good point," Mariana nodded.

Asleep on the platform, Big let out a loud snuffling snore. They quickly snuck by on the tips of their toes without a word so as not to wake him, and once again reentered the Midst, with its glaring lights from the race track, vendor carts, and blue-lit buildings.

"It's good to be back here," TJ said, crossing the Welcoming Road.

"You know what?" Mariana shouted over the blaring music, and long lines of boisterous Potentials waiting for Bads inside the Midst, "I'm not drinking anymore Bad. I'm kinda over them."

"Not me, I'm ready for another one, all right. Plus, I gotta go find that Give It Away line, in case Eric shows up there," TJ said, straining his neck over the crowd.

"Seriously, I hope your brother isn't going to do that. The Entities are oddly cute and everything, but bulging eyes and irregular-shaped noses just aren't stylish," Mariana said, gently toe-kicking a ball to return it to a group of teenage boys playing in the street.

"Yeah, but Entities are like bosses here," TJ reasoned, "and if I did stay, even though I don't know if I'm gonna, that would be pretty cool to have a brother with that kind of power."

"Okay, tell me you're not thinking about Giving It Away yourself, TJ. Did you ever hear the saying, 'If Timmy rode his bike off a cliff?'" Mariana asked, exasperated.

Cassie kept bumping into Entities and Potentials on the cobblestone street as they played kickball and waited in lines to get into the jammed Zebbies. As hard as she tried to put it out of her mind, she couldn't stop worrying about Anna.

I wonder if I'll see her again. I hope she's okay. I hope her dad comes back soon.

Agatha's voice stopped Cassie's thoughts like a blanket smothering a fire. *Your concern for others is an admirable trait. Perhaps staying on Blue, to offer your assistance to those like you, would be a noble response. However, you must help your father first.*

Cassie bit into the side of her thumb, avoiding the nail this time, but still experiencing the sensation. *Agatha's right. I'm not here for anyone else except my dad.*

But thoughts of the golden-haired girl returned to Cassie's mind, as if someone were dropping them like golden parachutes inside her head.

Just then, Agatha appeared in the middle of the street, holding a flailing Mooshkoo by the back of his rubbery blue neck.

"Good Dusk, you three!" she said, sweat beading down her forehead. "I'm looking forward to hearing about your experience in the Settling, but first I must tend to this annoying little matter!"

The rebellious Mooshkoo clamored the air, kicking his rubbery legs.

"What's the matter with him?" TJ asked, preoccupied as the vacant Give It Away area flashed out of the corner of his eye, the sign out front pulsing in blue light, "Closed. Won't Reopen until the Next Glimmer."

"Oh, there's always one bad Blob in the pack," Agatha scowled.

The Mooshkoo behaved like a wound-up toy, spinning himself around and around with no sign of stopping.

"Chill, buddy," TJ said, stepping back a few feet.

"I told you they were feisty," Mariana said, stepping back as well.

Agatha summoned Small from the pier and handed the Mooshkoo off.

"You shouldn't have to be dealing with this," Small said, taking the wriggling Mooshkoo by the neck with his thick forearms.

"Yes, well, unfortunately, without me most things don't get done the way they need to. Take care of him appropriately, won't you?" Agatha turned her nose up in disgust and brushed her hands together as if she was wiping crumbs from her palms.

Exhausted, Agatha faced TJ, Cassie, and Mariana. "I'm sure you have kids who act like this in your classrooms in middle school. Nothing we can't handle. Once they give him a few Have to Haves, he'll calm down. Now," Agatha said to Cassie as she straightened her wrinkled cloak, "Shall we?"

"You mean, get my dad?" Cassie asked, her lips parted.

"Why, of course," Agatha purred. "That's the reason you've come all this way, isn't it?"

Cassie squeezed the cuffs of her dad's sweatshirt as they moved through the Midst, coming upon an Entity, in his Sunday best, operating a small streetcar that hovered above the payment, handing out pamphlets in the street.

"Learn about Blue's Mission!" he called, in a long drawn-out voice.

Another Entity with a mustache staggered past, a wool coat buttoned to his neck. Holding a can of Bad directly beneath the bow-tied Entity's nose, he said with an Irish brogue, "Hey Tenny, want one?"

Tenny lifted his round glasses and eyed the Bad for a moment before replying, "Thank you, James, but I haven't had a Bad or a Blob in twenty Zippers!" He continued to preach. "Join us! Keep your colors low! Learn how!"

TJ scratched his cheek as he asked Agatha, "If you don't have

Bads and Blobs, why would you be here?"

"Creatures behave all kinds of ways to cause one's colors to vibrate on our frequency," Agatha explained, leading TJ to an outdoor Pits halfway through the Midst, where Sal entertained a group of Entities at a high-top table. "Blue's mission is to encourage them to continue those behaviors and therefore maintain that low frequency. The reward is that one receives our support, from an Entity attachment, for life."

Sal beckoned TJ toward an empty seat, dangling a handful of Blobs from his arm.

TJ turned to Cassie and gave her a small hug. "Good luck getting your dad," he said and ran over to Sal.

Agatha checked her Surveyor. "Visiting hours have started Cassie, and as promised, you've been given first status. Come along, Mariana."

"Oh, good. I was afraid I'd have to go to the Cove again," Mariana said, rubbing her forehead.

"I'm sorry to hear that. Perhaps there'll be some Have to Haves you can take at the Fix-It for that headache," Agatha said, shaking hands with Permanents in the Midst.

As they turned out of the Midst, past Strays and to the road leading to the Fix-It, elves pedaled with extra effort on their flying bicycles, whizzing by in their Land of Blue sweatshirts. They carried plastic containers labeled HAVE TO HAVES stacked ten feet high.

"That's a lot of packages!" Mariana exclaimed.

"Thrilling, isn't it?" Agatha said. "We've had a steady stream of Potentials, as I mentioned, and now that the Feed's been fully unloaded, everyone's looking to avoid the quiver. The Dusk Ruler is very pleased, and also pleased at your gallant efforts, Cassie. You helped your father feel better and, in turn, aided Blue's mission." Agatha patted Cassie firmly on the head.

"Will we see the Dusk Ruler this time?" Cassie asked, wondering if he looked like an Entity and if he heard Cassie's worried thoughts like Agatha did.

"Only delegated Entities such as myself may see the Ruler. We usually have meetings every third Zipper, but he can summon us at will," Agatha said, licking her finger and smoothing her penciled brows into place.

"Why? Is he mean?" Mariana asked.

"Only if he needs to be," Agatha answered, picking up a small vial that had fallen off the back of one of the elves' flying bicycles.

Cassie bent down to tie her shoe, sending Mind Mail to TJ.

Any sign of Eric?

She watched Agatha put the vial in her pocket for safekeeping while she thought about the Settling and wondered if this was the right time to ask Agatha about the hook that bore her name.

Maybe Agatha made it for me in case we didn't make it back before the next Zipper; then there would be a place ready for me and Dad. Cassie's body itched inside as if she swallowed a swarm of bees. Just then, an envelope from TJ appeared inside her mind.

Not yet. Sal introduced me to some other Potentials in the Cove, though, who are really cool. Sal said he knew Blue would grow on me.

Cassie bit her finger as she trailed behind Mariana and Agatha. *Mariana's right, TJ is easily talked into things. Why would Sal want him to stay on Blue instead of sending TJ and Eric home?*

The Fix-It seemed to glare down at Cassie as it spread its invasive fluorescent lights across the facility and all surrounding areas. Carlos busily picked up trash in the courtyard while a long line of creatures waited noisily in front of the main entrance. Cassie dashed past Agatha and Mariana.

"Carlos!"

"Hola chica," Carlos said, somewhat preoccupied as he

grabbed his broom and added under his breath, "buen trabajo on thee Mind Mail. Did chu keep up chur studies?"

"Sort of. Does my dad know I'm here and that we're going home?"

"Sí, he knows you're here," Carlos swept some brown leaves that had blown in from the gnarly trees behind the building. "I going to let Agatha do her thing. I don't want to step on anyone's toes, chu know what I saying? Enjoy visiting hours and we'll charla later. This chur amiga?"

Mariana joined Cassie at the fence.

"Yeah, this is my best friend, Mariana," Cassie said. She bent down and picked up a crushed paper cup outside the fence and handed it through to help Carlos.

"Chu's a good frend to come all this way," Carlos said, extending his hand through the fence to take the litter from Cassie.

"I know," Mariana said, listening to the rowdy creatures offering to give up some of their Have to Haves if they could cut the line.

"Come, girls," Agatha said breathlessly, waddling up behind them. She laid her hand on her chest and said to Carlos, "I can't keep up with them anymore, they're so excited to be here. Nice job in the courtyard, by the way. I'll put in a good word."

"Gracias. I take my trabajo seriously." He saluted.

"That's a good thing," Agatha said, returning the salute and escorting Cassie and Mariana past the long, boisterous line up the walkway, beside the Energy Vibration Meter that remained hovering in the pigeon-blue range, to the steel front door.

"That's not fair!" complained a tattooed woman in a tank top in the front of the line displaying a Permanent by Association badge.

"I ended up drinking the Escape we brought my brother cause we've been waiting so long," grumbled a man in sandals with a head of messy hair wearing a Permanent badge, who reminded Cassie of a college professor.

The slot in the cold door opened. Nurse Moody said to the tattooed woman, "Go on Debbie, refills are ready."

Nurse Moody saw Cassie and blew a big Pepto-pink bubble out of the opening. "Well, what do you know, it's the rule breaker."

Cassie's face turned tomato red as the woman rushed to open the little steel door, labeled Pick-Ups, retrieving a small vial.

"Relax, sister," Nurse Moody said. "Your dad is ready and waiting."

Cassie's body raced, feeling like she would lift right off the ground.

"Good Dusk, Agatha," Nurse Moody said, unlatching the door.

"Hey!" yelled the rest of the crowd, lunging at Cassie and Mariana.

Nurse Moody used her beefy arms to open the steel door just enough to allow Cassie and Agatha to slip through. Then, like a bank vault, it sealed shut.

CHAPTER
TWENTY-ONE

"Finally, peace and quiet," Mariana said, gazing at the sterile white walls inside the Fix-It.

Cassie followed Agatha past the nurses' station in the lobby as elves stocked small containers of Have to Haves in a row of white cabinets above the nurses' station. After, they unloaded wheeled carts loaded with hundreds of plastic containers filled to the brim with Have to Haves.

"That's a lot of stuff to put away," Mariana said, scratching her head as elves worked in assembly-line fashion, having their routine down.

Agatha turned right at the end of the lobby, behind Nurse Moody's oafish body as they all traveled down a long, wide corridor. The gray, tiled walls reminded Cassie of Nana and Grandpa's shower tiles; they looked clean from faraway until you actually got in the shower and saw the grime and mold stains up close. Cassie stepped over the cracks in the larger, white, tiled floor, wiping her sweaty palms on her jeans, when agitated voices erupted from behind closed off-white doors.

"Are the Have to Haves here yet??"

"I want to get back to the Midst!"

"Jeesh! What kind of a place is this?" Mariana said, standing as far back as she could from the doors in the corridor.

"Not to worry," Nurse Moody said back at the girls, as she waved one of her thick arms for them to keep going and ignore the voices behind the doors. This caused a few pieces of paper on a clipboard outside one of the rooms to lift in the breeze. "They'll all be taken care of soon, once the Feed's been distributed."

Agatha paused for a moment, releasing some hand sanitizer out of a dispenser on the wall, and turned to Cassie in the echoing corridor. "This is how your dad felt when he was in pain. It's an awful sound, isn't it?"

Cassie halted, almost landing on one of the cracks in the tiles. She had never seen her father in real pain because he always took his medicine every few hours.

Just then, a memory exploded in Cassie's mind like someone yelling, "Boo!" on Halloween. She remembered Grandpa Jack saying one Thanksgiving dinner that Dad took too much medicine. Dad responded, "Have you counted the beers in your basement fridge lately?" He stormed out before dinner ended, without so much as a good-bye. Cassie had watched through the sheer curtains as her father sped all the way down Selwyn Street, skidding left as he turned onto Colberg, until he was out of sight. She wanted to cry, but couldn't. It was as if the sadness had lodged a ball in her throat, and it got stuck. He didn't even come back for pecan pie, and that was his favorite.

Back in the corridor of the Fix-It, Cassie tried to block out the yelling and wailing from behind the doors, wondering, *It's a good thing Dad takes his Have to Haves, isn't it?*

Just then, Nurse Moody stomped her heavy clogs on the floor in the center of the corridor and hollered, "Shaddup, everyone! You're gonna scare the visitors!" She trudged forward in her off-white uniform, leading Cassie, Mariana, and Agatha to a door at the end of the long corridor, putting her hand up to hold them back when they reached the threshold.

"Dr. Fox is just finishing up," Agatha whispered to Cassie and Mariana, similar to the way the nice librarian at West Roxbury library asks you to wait patiently and quietly when you're in line for a turn at one of the computers. Meanwhile, Nurse Moody stepped to the right side of the threshold, where an adjacent, smaller hallway, with the same small tiled walls and larger tiled floors, led to more closed rooms.

The back of a tall, lean man with white hair and an off-white lab coat blocked the doorway. The man scribbled notes on a clipboard, as he spoke with someone inside the room.

Is that my dad he's talking to? Cassie stood on her tiptoes. She couldn't see past the tall doctor, who took out a handful of candy-corn-orange-colored circles from his lab coat pocket.

"Two, four, six, eight, ten, twelve, fourteen, sixteen, eighteen. There, that should do it. And we can always do more if you want." The doctor moved to the side, hung the clipboard back outside the room, and put the bright orange circles in a cup, along with a mug filled with golden Escape. He handed the mug to the person Cassie couldn't see inside the room.

"Now that's a lot of vitamins," Mariana observed, straining her neck. "My mother makes us take like eight supplements every morning, and I thought that was a lot!"

"Right after you take these like a good Cog, you can see your long-awaited visitor," said Dr. Fox. Cassie thought he sounded like he was talking to a five year old. *Are there kids in the Fix-It too?*

"There you go! See how easy they go down?"

Nurse Moody took the empty mug from the doctor and added it to a cart outside the door. Cassie heard muttering between the clanks of the mugs and containers. It was a man's voice, but so quiet Cassie couldn't understand what he was saying. She turned to Agatha. "Is that my dad?"

Agatha put up a finger for Cassie to wait. Cassie impulsively grabbed the back of Mariana's arm, squeezing it as hard as she could.

"Ow," Mariana gritted her teeth, but didn't say another word. Cassie used to do that to her in kindergarten whenever she got excited; Mariana was used to it. Cassie suddenly felt like she had to use the bathroom as she watched Nurse Moody move clear, plastic containers that resembled Tupperware around on the cart.

Finally, Dr. Fox turned his thin frame around and smiled at Cassie like she was five years old too. "Well, this is the one we hear so much about. Come in, come in, child," Dr. Fox spoke with a Southern drawl and beamed, his teeth so blinding they looked the same wattage as the outside Fix-It fluorescent lights. "Your fathuh's just takin' his first round of Have to Haves, and doing a great jawb, I might add. Raight, Craig?"

Cassie's knees wobbled. She locked them to catch herself and strained her neck forward to peer into the open room when Dr. Fox stepped aside. She could see only a cot in the middle of the room, with a thin blanket messily bunched on top, and a small trash can in the corner. A half-dozen empty Have to Have containers lay piled on the floor next to the trash, reminding Cassie of the time she ate so many freeze pops, she had to put the empty plastic sleeves on top of the white lid because she couldn't stuff any more in the garbage pail. A dark blue door on the back wall was closed, leading to the dumpster grounds outside at the back of the building. And on the far side of the room, in the very chair Agatha had shown Cassie in the palm of her hands on the front porch over a month ago, sat her father.

Dad!

"It's him, it's really him!" Cassie cried, rushing in the room.

Agatha rose up on her soft black shoes while Mariana watched Cassie from just outside the doorway, rising up and down on her toes like she wanted to go inside too, but wanted to respect Cassie's space. Craig Connor never took his focus from the floor beneath his bare feet.

How come you're not looking at me, Daddy?

Cassie turned to the Doctor.

"Craig," Dr. Fox spoke in a commanding tone. "Yuh daughtuh is heah to see yuh now."

Craig Connor slowly lifted his head of straight brown hair, beads of sweat forming around his hairline. His half-opened eyes met Cassie's, and then returned to the floor. After raising his head a second time, as if he recognized something but wasn't sure, he resignedly dropped his head.

Cassie placed her arms around her father's shoulders, his rough stubbly skin scraping the side of her cheek. Craig stayed slumped over in his white tank top and faded blue jeans, in the hard metal chair.

"W-what's wrong?" Cassie asked, trembling. She crouched down by the side of his chair. "Look, I brought your sweatshirt from the Settling, and I have your old Knights one on, do you want to see it?"

"Cassie," her father's voice trailed off as he hung his head. "I tried, I really tried."

"Tried what?" Cassie squinted back tears as she looked into his face.

Craig slowly placed the palm of his hand to his daughter's face. Holding his hand there a moment, his drowsy eyes searched for Cassie's, her brown eyes matching the shade of his own.

"The Settling is where I . . . " her dad mumbled incoherently, his bare feet letting go on the cold tiles.

"He just needs uh few minutes," Dr. Fox interrupted. "The Have tuh Haves ah kicking in naow. He'll be abul to uhscape thuh sufferin' pain from those dreadful headaches." The doctor recorded something into the Surveyor attached to his hip, half looking up when he spoke. "Naow that we have him on a reguluh schedule, he's goin' tuh do much bettuh. "Cause thuh system works, duhn't it, Craig?"

Twisting his toes slightly, Craig mumbled, "It sure does."

"What's happening?" Cassie asked Dr. Fox. "He was supposed to feel better so I could take him home."

Mariana put her hands in her pockets and stepped inside the room just before a male voice spoke at the doorway. "Excuse me," Carlos said, waddling inside and retrieving the empty containers in and around the trash can. His face downtrodden, he looked at Cassie while he knotted the white bag of trash.

Cassie crossed her legs on the floor, wrapping her arms around her father's calves as he began to fall asleep.

"Off to the othuhs." Dr. Fox flashed his blinding smile and checked off something on the clipboard Nurse Moody handed to him before he left the room. "Give it uh little time . . . Cassie, is it?"

Cassie realized instantly, without knowing how she knew, that she didn't like Dr. Fox.

Trust your feelings.

Cassie turned toward Agatha, who whispered with Dr. Fox in the doorway.

Why does that other voice keep speaking to me? Cassie leaned against her father's knee.

"Thank you, doctor, for helping Craig feel better," Agatha said, dropping a few Lures in his lab-coat pocket as he left the room.

Dr. Fox nodded, his voice as slow and thick as maple syrup, "It's uh nobul profession to help those who ah in paain." With that, he strode down the small, adjacent, dark hallway.

"What do we do now? Is he going to be able to Zipper back

with us?" Cassie asked, looking back and forth between Nurse Moody and Agatha, who stood in the doorway like guards. Mariana leaned her leg against the wall, a worried expression on her face.

"Clearly your father is in no condition to Zipper," Agatha said. "Perhaps he can be moved to the Settling until the Have to Haves have taken root and he is a bit stronger."

"But you said this time we'd be going home!" Cassie protested, jumping to her feet. Carlos flicked a new, plastic trash bag in the air to open it and place it in the trash bin.

"Now don't get yourself in a tizzy," Agatha said, placing her hands on Cassie's shoulders. "Your nervous system is fragile as it is."

Nurse Moody chomped her gum while Cassie's father nodded off in the chair. "Look at it this way," she said. "You gotta feel good your dad's pain is gone. Focus on that. Stop trying to fight the system." She flashed Cassie and Mariana a flamingo-pink Have to Have that looked like a Blob from Zebbies. "Care for a stress reliever?"

Carlos glanced over at Cassie as he hoisted a bag of trash on his shoulder. *No, thanks*, his voice spoke authoritatively in Cassie's mind.

"No, thanks," the words flowed out of Cassie's mouth before she even had a chance to think. Then Carlos left.

"Leave one up front for me," Agatha instructed, leading Cassie out of the room and shutting the door behind them. "I'm going to speak to the doctor for a moment."

"Do you need one, princess?" Nurse Moody asked Mariana as she gripped the handles of the cart outside the room.

"I think I'll pass, I have a bit of a stomachache," Mariana replied, pumping some hand sanitizer out of the wall dispenser.

"If ya need something to settle your stomach, I can help with that." Nurse Moody raised her eyebrows up and down as she opened a cabinet door on the large cart and waved her hand like Vanna White across the hundreds of containers of Have To Haves stacked up, down, and sideways.

"That's okay," Mariana said, turning away from the cart. "We take homeopathic remedies at my house. My mom's not a fan of pain relievers. Thanks, though!" Mariana said with a polite smile.

Nurse Moody scrunched up her fleshy face into a fake smile, making her look like a balloon about to burst. "All righty then!" she said like a bubbly cheerleader. "Your mom doesn't know what she's missing!" She slammed the door of the cart, the sound reverberating throughout the Fix-It.

Mariana walked down the corridor, her head held high, while Cassie stayed behind, next to Nurse Moody, who mumbled under her breath.

"Where's my red-Slurpee Have to Haves?" cried a young voice from behind one of the closed doors in the dimly lit corridor.

"Is that a kid in there?" Mariana asked, pointing to the room.

"I don't know," Cassie said, walking into the corridor to listen.

"It's not fair! You promised!" the voice cried.

Mariana sounded like she had had enough. "He sounded like he was nine! That would totally stink to have to be in here."

"Okay, everybody back to the nurses' station," Nurse Moody said, wheeling the cart in Mariana's direction. "Let's leave the patients in peace."

To her left, down the adjacent smaller hallway, Cassie saw Agatha and Dr. Fox speaking privately, under a low-wattage light bulb in front of another patient's room.

"Doctor," Cassie said as she ran over to him. Dr. Fox immediately reached behind him and closed the door, where inside a woman wailed for more Have To Haves. Cassie winced, wanting to ask if the lady would be okay, but realizing when she got nervous she had a tendency to forget what she really wanted to say. "When will my dad be ready to go?"

"Child," said Dr. Fox, clasping his hands in front of his waist. "Yuh fathuh needs to readjust, from havun spent so much time without his Have tuh Haves. Allow him thuh rest he needs from thuh awful pain, and then yuh can both be on yuh way."

Agatha's shoulders twitched a few times. "I have to get to the nurse's station, those Have to Haves are calling. Send Cassie back when you're done with your conversation."

"Yaes, enjoy. I mean, take good care uf yuhrself," Dr. Fox called out as Agatha made her way down the hall.

"My neighbor had back pain and had to take medicine," Mariana said, joining Cassie. "But my mom and dad said they didn't know if it actually helped him or not because he was always in bed. They said you're supposed to walk more to help back pain."

Nurse Moody wheeled her cart around and abruptly bumped the girls from behind. "Let the doc finish his rounds," she ordered.

Cassie resisted the urge to stomp her sneaker down on Nurse Moody's fat foot while Mariana, to calm her, placed a firm hand on her forearm.

"Thank yuh," the doctor said.

Nurse Moody winked and gently rolled the cart back in the direction of the main corridor. The doctor waited for Cassie and Mariana to follow Nurse Moody before opening the door to the patient's room and slipping inside.

"She's pushy, but you gotta practice impulse control. Remember that from wellness class in second grade?" Mariana noted, as Cassie reluctantly passed her dad's room and continued behind Nurse Moody in the direction of the nurses' Station.

Cassie slowed her pace in the middle of the echoing corridor, deep in thought. Carlos held several bags of trash over his shoulder and was about to take them out to the dumpster near the exit door leading to the back of the building, when Cassie stopped him.

"Could you get me back in to see my father? I know I can talk to him and get him to come home, even if he doesn't feel strong enough," she kept her voice low as Nurse Moody pushed the cart to the end of the corridor.

"I no have that kind of power, Cassie," Carlos replied in the same hushed tone as he adjusted the clanking bags, filled with empty Escape and Have to Have containers, on his back. "Why don't chu try sending chur papa Mind Mail if chu got someting to say? Chur familia, en that means you understand each other's frecuencia, even if chur're off a color or two."

Cassie eyed a spot on the long, windowless tiled wall. "I hadn't thought of that."

"Well, until chu think of theese things on your own, dat's what chu have me for. Just remember, when you're home, you gotta put it an envelope," Carlos directed, whistling as he hoisted the trash over his shoulder and left through the double exit doors.

Mariana covered her ears three quarters of the way down the corridor to shut out a groaning female voice behind one of the doors.

Well, I won't be leaving without my dad, Cassie thought, *So I won't need to use the envelope.* Cassie caught up with Mariana and rounded the corner to the nurses station. Agatha finished taking her Have to Have with a half mug of Bad and Nurse Moody dropped into a seat behind a window in the nurses' station like she was selling tickets at a movie theatre.

"Come you two, I'm wanted back in the Midst," Agatha said, leaving the empty mug on the nurses' desk and gesturing Cassie and Mariana into the pristinely clean lobby, where a huge glass jar of Pepto-pink Have to Haves rested on a wall shelf with a sign underneath that read, "Help Yourself!" Above the main entrance door hung a large, gold-framed caricature of Agatha, Dr. Fox, and Kurt, with a gold plate underneath engraved: "Generous Donors."

Cassie curled her toes in her shoes, panicked at the notion of leaving, as they stood in the lobby. "Agatha, could I have one minute to talk to my dad again?"

"We really need to . . . "

"Just one more minute. Please . . . " Cassie pleaded, wringing her clammy hands.

"Besides," Mariana said, with an ear to the steel door, "they sound angry out there."

Agatha strode to the door and peeked through the slot, the mob outside ranting and demanding to see their loved ones. Wiping her brow, Agatha signaled to the elves filling vials in the area behind the nurses' station. "Let's get on those refills." Then, turning to Cassie she said, "I know how important this is for you. Of course I'll give you one more visit. And I'll even go with you."

"Thank you," Cassie said, darting off to her dad's room like she was trying to win the fifty-yard dash on Track-and-Field Day at school.

"He's not going to hear you, anyway," Nurse Moody mumbled, getting up from her seat to help the elves fill the vials containers.

"Watch out for cracks in the floor," Agatha warned in the lobby. "We wouldn't want anything to interfere with our plans to bring your dad home . . . " but Cassie didn't hear her. She was too far ahead.

Agatha gestured for Mariana to stay put and rounded the corner after her Potential.

Cassie arrived at the room at the end of the corridor. She opened the door to find her dad fast asleep in the chair. Agatha's shoes pressed against the tiles, *slap, slap, slap,* as she grew nearer. Cassie rushed to crouch beside her father.

"I've come all this way. You have to get stronger, so I can bring you home. I'm going to send you Mind Mail later, okay? You'll be able to answer me, because we're family, and on the same frequency! Don't worry, it's my job to help you. Agatha told me. I'm going to save you, Daddy."

"Ready?" Agatha asked, coming into the room huffing and puffing. "I hear the crowd out front has calmed a bit."

Cassie quickly adjusted herself and stood up.

"Let your father sleep, his body needs the rest from all that fighting."

Cassie gripped her father's tank top at the shoulder and walked back down the long corridor beside her Entity, extra careful to step over every crack in the tile floor. She had to make sure what she told her dad was true.

CHAPTER
TWENTY-TWO

Cassie, Mariana, and Agatha squirmed their way through the mob outside the Fix-It as Nurse Moody yelled from the entrance slot, "Don't worry, sunshine, your dad's in good hands!" But even so, Cassie worried all the way to the Pits, where they met Sal and TJ for lunch, and she worried while waiting for the server to bring her favorite food. Even when the plate of greasy fries was set before her, she found it hard to eat.

Weren't the Have to Haves supposed to help? she wondered. *Is it supposed to take this long? Should I have signed that form? Maybe Mariana's right and Dad should try walking instead. I'll ask him in my Mind Mail.*

Cassie sipped her Bad, though she wasn't thirsty, while TJ slowly chewed his traffic-cone-orange cheese sandwich in silence,

Eric still nowhere to be found.

"Here kid, have another Bad," Sal said, sliding a golden tankard down the table. TJ drank a few sips, and after several minutes, perked up and began talking to everyone about the arrival of the latest Stimulator.

Mariana listened with her elbows on the dark wooden table, and then lifted them, saying, "Eww," rubbing them with her napkin because they felt sticky. "Any chance we can rest back at that nice hospitality suite? I haven't napped since kindergarten, but I feel like I need one." She slowly brushed hair off her face.

"Of course," Agatha said, raking the bill off the table. "Then you can get up and do it all over again, while we're waiting for Cassie's father's Have to Haves to kick in."

"Could I give them to my dad at home? Maybe he could try and get through the pain until we get there." She flicked her ankle back and forth. "Maybe he could try walking, like Mariana said, to see if that would help."

Agatha placed the bill back down and turned to Cassie in the seat next to her. "Since when did you replace Dr. Fox as the specialist? They're called Have to Haves for a reason. The doctor knows what he's doing. Our system hasn't failed you yet, has it?"

"No," Cassie said, jiggling her entire leg under the table, "but I thought he'd be better, and we'd be home by now . . . "

Agatha closed her eyes, like she was in pain. "My, my. We're not talking back to our elders, are we?" Opening them, she glared at Cassie. "I am your Entity. Leave things to me." Agatha stood up and sauntered over to the countertop, where she handed three Lures to the creature behind the counter as payment.

The glasses jingled in Cassie's pocket, fluttering like a little fairy. She watched Sal chug the rest of his Escape. *I wonder if Sal would look the same if I put on the glasses.*

Cassie's body began to vibrate, a fast and furious speed like one of the racecars on the track, causing her to wonder, *Does that mean I'm supposed to put them on here? No, I can't. What if I get in trouble? Agatha's already aggravated with me.*

The Vibration in her body ceased.

Cassie felt a sinking feeling in her stomach as she moped back with Mariana, Sal, and TJ to Strays. Even when Agatha offered her as many Bads from Robin as she wanted, as a way of apologizing for scolding her at the table, Cassie didn't want any. She agreed only because Agatha insisted.

When they arrived at Robin's station, they found a sign taped to the wheel of his unicycle reading, "Back In A Pulse!"

Mariana pointed. "Look, even Robin gets tired," she said.

Agatha whipped around to see.

"Uh, oh," Sal said under his breath.

Robin, his eyes drooped, sat in a patch of perfectly manicured grass behind the long row of vendor carts.

"Whatcha doing? Meditating?" Mariana asked, skipping over.

"Hey Potentials, or are you Permanents yet?" Robin chuckled, slowly twirling a blade of grass between his fingers as TJ and Cassie followed behind Mariana. "I'm just taking a break. The Feed's here, so I'm just waiting for my late afternoon pick-me-up."

"What do you need a pick-me-up for?" TJ scoffed, "You have the best job in the world!"

"Oh yeah? What job is that?" Robin asked, snatching fistfuls of grass and releasing them blade by blade to the ground.

"Eating, drinking, and making people laugh all day long . . . right?" TJ shot a look at Cassie as if to say, "How come I need to tell him he has the greatest job ever?"

"Yeah, right," Robin said. He saw Agatha coming and wobbled to his feet. "Look, I'm sorry you three, I'm just having a rough dusk that's all, don't pay any attention to good ol' Robin. I'll be back to my Blue self in no time at all, and certainly by the next thirty-second Glimmer." He saluted, which appeared more like he was flicking something off his nose.

"I should say so," Agatha said with a tilt of her head. "Unless you'd like the perks of your job to change significantly . . . ?"

"A-Agatha, I just took a rest since the Feed had to go to the Fix-It first, which of course you know I understand . . ."

"One would hope, since you are well versed on Blue's ways . . . or are you questioning the system?" Agatha's voice rose as she straightened the cuffs of her cloak.

"No," Robin said, avoiding the stares of the other vendors. "I'll get back to work. Please don't order any Withholds. I was just thinking is all."

"You're not here to think," Agatha said, her shadow looming over Robin under the street lamp.

"I . . . I know that. And I'm so happy to be on Blue . . . "

"That will be enough. I'll bring this up at the Meeting."

"Please don't mention Withholding. It was merely a slip, I swear . . . " Robin rubbed the back of his neck, teetering his black-soled shoes on the curb.

"Enough. You're in the presence of Potentials, yet another mark against you. Return to your duties." Agatha turned away from Robin, and instructed Cassie and Mariana to head directly to Strays.

"TJ, meet me at the Cove," Sal said with a nod.

"Talk about harsh," Mariana said to Cassie and TJ when they scurried forward, into the crowd and out of Agatha's earshot. "I mean, the guy took a break."

Cassie and TJ turned back, hearing the sound of clanking metal as Robin clambered atop his unicycle and began soliciting Potentials and other creatures to his station, just as a performer gets into character. Cassie tried to make eye contact with him as he pedaled in the air, but Robin never took his eyes off his growing audience.

A buzzing feeling erupted around Cassie's head as she wondered, *Why was Agatha mad at Robin? Is he okay? Is Dad ready to go yet? I wonder if Anna is okay, and if her dad is back yet.*

"Hey," TJ said, squeezing Cassie's shoulder outside the Cove. "Robin'll be all right, probably just a bad day at work. My parents had those all the time. All they used to talk about was their stress."

"Yeah, adults get stressed a lot," Mariana said, yawning and nodding her head vigorously.

Cassie tried to manage a smile before TJ ran inside to meet Sal. Meanwhile, Agatha whistled from the end of the walkway outside Strays and strolled over the bricks to hold the door open for Cassie and Mariana.

When they entered the cottage, the Mooshkoo took Agatha by the hand, bringing her over to the white leather couch in the foyer, a stone-blue chenille blanket nicely laid over one side, where three middle-aged women waited. Cassie noticed they each had saggy, mottled skin, probably from too much sun. Agatha, delighted, welcomed the women and turned to give the kerchief-wearing Mooshkoo a few Blobs and a list of instructions for the new Potentials.

The Mooshkoo slurped her lips and whirled down the hall to prepare another guest suite. On her way, she kicked open the girls' room and gestured for them to enter. Mariana trudged inside and threw herself down onto a beanbag, instantly closing her eyes. Agatha finished her pleasant conversation with the women and strode in behind Cassie, stopping to adjust a shelf on the wall holding one book, titled, *Dark Night of the Soul.* Moving it down an inch to the left, she closed one eye to be sure it leveled.

"Agatha, what's wrong with Robin?" Cassie asked, settling into another beanbag as her Entity closed the door.

"My turf, my questions," Agatha said, playfully, propping Cassie's white pillow. "Is that to your liking?"

Cassie nodded, molding her head into the cushion. Agatha retrieved a chair from the wall and positioned it next to Cassie's beanbag. "Now, do tell me what's on your mind. It's not like you, to speak to me the way you did at the Pits. Remember, Entities sense the worry thoughts, that's how we gain, I mean, that's how we help—by being right beside our Potentials whenever they're afraid."

Guilt spread through Cassie's body like a carton of milk spilling over the kitchen floor. *What if Agatha got upset with me like she did with Robin? What if she doesn't bring me back to my dad? Is that what Robin meant by "withholding"?*

Anxious feelings climbed the walls inside Cassie's body. "Why did you put my name on a hook in the Settling?" she asked. "And why were my grandparents' names there? And why isn't anybody helping that little girl, Anna? She has bad habits, too, like me."

Mariana, half asleep, stirred on the beanbag against the gray wall.

"Sweet, compassionate Cassie," Agatha said, stroking the side of Cassie's brown hair. "The more people visit Blue, the more they understand the need for the Settling. Family members like the Costas support their loved ones by living in our housing. They're sacrificing for the people they love most, who have given their lives to the Land of Blue. As for your grandparents, they were here before you were born. Naturally, your father followed in their footsteps. Therefore, I gave the orders for a hook to let you know you're welcome too. If your father wanted to return to the Settling, wouldn't you choose to stay, so you could be with him forever?"

Cassie thought about that for a moment, staring at a vat of multi-colored Blobs across the room. *I'd rather be with Dad here than be without him at home. But why would he want to stay, when he can come home to me and Mom?*

Agatha neatened a photograph on the table next to Cassie's beanbag of two Mooshkoos happily holding housemaid-training certificates. "Because you've spent time in our Land, you're coming to understand our ways, and to feel compassionately for our dwellers. That's The Land of Blue's mission—to have more people like you, who want to help and support our inhabitants. Just like the Fix-It staff who help those in need."

"But it seems like my dad's worse on all those Have to Haves. Dr. Fox gave him more than he takes at home." Cassie's voice grew soft. "He wasn't even ready to go with me."

"I understand your concern," Agatha said, fixing the collar of her cloak that hid her wrinkled neck, "but you must trust Blue's process. Only we know what a person needs in order to feel good."

"But he practically didn't know me, he was so sleepy. I just want things the way they were," Cassie answered, never taking her eyes off the Blobs.

"Yes, keeping things as they are is good," Agatha said, patting her hand twice. "That's why he must continue doing things the way he always has, on a low Vibration, in a low range of colors. Another one of Blue's jobs is to help keep one's colors low."

"What's your job?" Cassie asked, turning to look into Agatha's dark eyes.

"Helping people find their families in the Land of Blue?"

Agatha shifted in her seat. "I've dedicated my life to keeping Blue intact and increasing our population by entanglement, and I know a good one when I see one. I realized that about you before you knew I existed. The children in the Settling are your people, Cassie, TJ's people. Our people. That's why you feel so intensely about little Anna, and why your friend here can sleep the time away," Agatha chuckled, gesturing toward Mariana, snoring loudly in her beanbag.

Cassie bit her lip and said, "My family always tells me that I worry too much."

"You're a feeling person," Agatha said, leaning over. "And perhaps one day you might even follow in your Entity's footsteps, and help other children like you."

Agatha rose from her chair and retrieved a silver can of mist from the fancy bookshelf in the far corner that looked like it belonged in a spa. She began spraying the intensely fragrant mist around the room.

Instantly, Cassie's lids grew heavy. She imagined herself as Nurse Moody's replacement at the Fix-It, distributing Have to Haves to the ailing patients and getting them well so they could go home to their families.

Agatha tiptoed over and tucked Cassie in—better than Nana Helen ever had—under the white blanket. Softly, as if reading a bedtime story, she said, "As Entities, we guide children to their generational destiny—a very purposeful role in one's existence. Now, get some rest. I have a meeting to attend and will come back when it's finished. I may not be able to pick up any worry thoughts, though, as I'll be a bit out of range, but I don't think there are any fears right now, are there?"

Agatha got up and placed the spray back on the bookshelf, stopping by Cassie's beanbag to whisper, "Remember, always feel deeply for the children."

Suddenly, the glasses vibrated in her pocket.

Cassie!

Cassie heard her name being called, from somewhere inside her mind.

Put on the glasses!

Glasses? Cassie felt herself resist as she drifted in and out of sleep. *I don't wear glasses . . .*

Cassie! Put on the gold-rimmed glasses!

Agatha opened the door.

"Are you going to a meeting about your mission?" Cassie asked her Entity drowsily, as the voice that called her began to fade.

"Yes. Don't worry, I'll be back. Entities always stay close."

With that, Agatha left the suite. Cassie felt like a balloon floating in the sky, the wonderful fragrance of the mist filling her entire being, until thoughts of Anna, Dr. Fox, and her father filled her head.

Dad,

Carlos said I could Mind Mail you. Are
you better yet? Can you hear me? Are you
ready to come home?

Cassie waited for an answer.

Slouching deeper into the beanbag, she began to spiral into
a dream when she felt the Ripple. It moved beside her left arm—a
wavy, floating wall.

She tried to open her eyes, but they were too heavy. She heard
Mariana napping in front of her, but like a veil had been draped
over her face, she felt far away, in a different world.

The Ripple swelled. Cassie realized she didn't need to put her
arm out to feel it this time. It expanded, like a mighty wall. In her
mind, she opened her eyes to see through the veil and on the other
side there appeared a mysterious room.

What would happen if I pushed through?

The Ripple pulsed against her body with a gloriously soft
force—solid, yet transparent and flowing. The pulse intensified, like
billowy clouds on a warm spring day. Finally, like a gentle animal
waiting for attention, the Ripple nudged Cassie's shoulder.

Ready? the Ripple seemed to ask.

Yes.

Immediately, Cassie found herself slowly pulled in by a tractor
beam. It wasn't the same wild sensation as Zippering, it was more of
a merging, an allowing, and a letting go.

Cassie fell through to the other side.

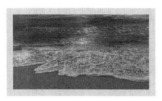

CHAPTER
TWENTY-THREE

Cassie felt as light as a sheer, gossamer scarf. Hundreds, possibly thousands of ripples floated in the field of space around her weightless body.

It's like they're dancing for me, she thought.

Then she heard, *We've been waiting for you!*

Cassie gasped in recognition. *It's that voice. It's here with me, but where am I?*

Taking a few weightless steps, she entered a divide of clouds, moist and cottony against her skin. Cassie pictured herself striding across the sky as the cotton-ball clouds began to stretch apart, spreading thinner as rays of light shone through the open spaces. The light grew brighter and brighter, like when the shades are pulled up on a late Sunday morning. The separating wispy strands parted and Cassie emerged in a pasture, witnessing a scene like nothing she could have ever imagined.

Golden rays of sunlight poured down from a pale, ocean-blue sky, creating a backdrop for a royal blue Palace at center stage, reminding Cassie of Cinderella's castle at the Magic Kingdom. Grassy fields the color of green apples stretched out around the glistening Palace, where ruby-red Gerber daisies, blue delphiniums, and butterscotch poppies sprouted like annuals in mid-July. Cassie recognized flowers from Nana Helen's small garden outside the unattached garage behind their house—yellow and purple tulips, lavender pansies, and mauve chrysanthemums. But they appeared brighter and bolder here, and in plentiful amounts beyond anything Cassie had ever observed in one space.

Who planted them all? she wondered.

Sturdy, snowcapped mountains in the distance projected harmonious, yet faceless voices, like carolers at Christmastime, singing from the mountaintops, prompting Cassie to look up. Library-brown and notebook-white bald eagles, with their enormous wings, soared through the center of the magnificent blue castle, the sun's rays illuminating its expansive marbled, open interior.

Large, dark-green leaves, in the shape of elephant ears, shook at the foot of a group of tall spruce trees. Cassie inhaled, smelling the fresh pine air. From the rustling leaves, she could hear children's voices, whispering excitedly, "She's here, she's here!"

It looks like an enchanted forest, she thought.

On Cassie's left, turquoise-blue pools shimmered in the dazzling sunlight. Tropical fish in hues of geranium red, sunshine yellow, and aqua blue swam rhythmically in the glistening water. A waterfall raining crystal-clear sheaths splashed into the pools, delighting the playful fish.

Cassie pressed her palms to her cheeks. This place, this glorious place, felt as refreshing as a spring morning and looked as breathtaking as an autumn afternoon. Freeing herself from her own sweatshirt in the seventy-degree air, she tied both hers and her dad's together around her waist, letting the warm sunlight bathe her lightly freckled arms in her short-sleeve white shirt that hadn't been washed in weeks. She was wriggling her toes in too-tight sneakers when a fancy, dawn-misted, paved pathway appeared at her feet. Big, gorgeous flowers blooms in deep shades of red, orange, and purple lined the path. Pressing her shoes against the flat pavers, Cassie stepped lightly toward the marbled Palace stairs.

"She's here! She's here!" the voices whispered a second time.

Delicate, paper-like butterflies in pastel pink and orange, translucent white spots on their wings, and dragonflies of deep maroon and royal blue, fluttered out from the shrubbery right by Cassie. Giggling erupted within the colossal, green cascade lining of the forest. Cassie paused on the pavers and peered toward the bushes, where brown, blue, and green eyes peeked through little spaces between the leaves.

"Won't you come out?" Cassie called, without a shred of fear.

In a flurry of activity, the children burst forth, joining the pastel-colored butterflies and dragonflies flitting in the warm, sunny air.

There must be hundreds of them! Cassie thought, observing the younger children running alongside the older eight year olds, their white knicker pants and clean white T-shirts looking like they had just been ironed. Cassie glanced down at the ketchup-stained rim of her shirt from lunch at the Pits.

The children ran barefoot upon the grassy, powder-blue meadow adorning the Palace when a woman with olive skin, wearing a light purple dress that wisped about her bare ankles, emerged between two swirled marble pillars atop the wide, swooping steps marking the Palace's entrance. Hawks cried out as they flew in from the thick, pine-green forest, announcing the radiant woman's appearance. Her tiny, dancing eyes rested upon Cassie on the pavers as Cassie twirled around, absorbed by the sights and sounds of the meadow.

Running with their arms spread wide, the children welcomed Cassie with a chant:

> Darkness threatens those we love,
> Hopes for this one yet remain
> Choice and selection
> One's own election
> Welcome to Bright Blue domain.

That's Agatha's chant, Cassie thought.

"Good Dawn," the shimmering, dark-haired woman called gracefully from the top of the steps. Cassie squinted up at the beautiful and now-familiar face.

"Tufa?" she asked, shielding her eyes from the sun.

"Welcome to the Land of Bright Blue," Tufa swept her arms out across the meadow, light radiating around her entire body "We've been waiting for you."

"I-I thought I'd never see you again," Cassie said, her heart beating at the sight of Tufa, the way it did the time she thought her mother forgot about her at afterschool pick-up, and a half hour later the Ford Escape drove into the parking lot.

Tufa smiled as if she understood. "Yet, I knew I would see you. Would you like a cup of Kamalu?"

Cassie craned her neck over Tufa's shoulder to view the Palace's open interior. A small table set for two sat against a white marbled wall, the sun's rays illuminating a mosaic circle in the center of the floor, like stained glass. Past the table, and several large paintings on the walls, Cassie admired a field of daisies out back, behind the massive structure, where the sun's rays rolled down like a carpet through the clouds, landing upon their petals.

It looks like I could walk all the way up into the sky, right up to meet the sun itself, she thought.

Staring up at the wide, tan-and-white winding stairs facing her, Cassie counted the seven ledges with her finger. Thoughts dropped like pellets of hail into her brain and she bit her lip.

Will I be able to skip over those steps? Does anyone else know about this place? What if I hadn't said yes to the Ripple?

Tufa placed an elegant hand on the white railing lining the stairs. "Fearful thoughts do not resonate on Bright Blue."

Cassie paused and huffed and puffed, straddling to climb every other step of the wide staircase.

"As you please," Tufa said, waiting for Cassie at the opening to the Palace.

Inside, Cassie passed a small, gleaming, honey-colored closed door to the right of the entrance. Paintings with deep red, orange, and yellow autumn tones hung on the inside walls, like a museum. Vases of freshly picked blooms perched proudly on small tables, next to plush red benches.

The freshly dried cappuccino color of one painting proved tempting to touch. Cassie reached her hand out, and then pulled it back, as if she touched a hot oven. She remembered how Nana Helen had scolded her in third grade, in front of the entire pew during Stations of the Cross, for touching a gold-rimmed painting of Jesus hanging on the wall next to one of the confessional booths. Cassie's heart rate sped up in her chest as she looked over at Tufa to see if she would be angry.

"There is no harm in your curiosity," Tufa said, standing in front of the newly completed painting. "After all, that is the reason for your visit, is it not? Curiosity is often an invitation to understanding."

"My Nana says I'm too curious for my own good," Cassie said, and bit her thumbnail.

Tufa observed her and said, sweet as a songbird, "That is up to you, you know."

"What?" Cassie asked, gnawing on the skin around her finger.

"Whether you do that or not." She pointed to the remnants of Cassie's fingernail.

"I can't stop. I'm a nail-biter," Cassie replied, putting her finger back in her mouth while she admired another painting on the wall of a view from a boat on the ocean, the waves the color of spearmint.

"If you say so."

"No, really I am. And my dad was too. That's what my mom says." Cassie tugged at the last piece of shredded skin protruding from her thumb.

"What precedes does not guarantee what proceeds," Tufa declared, crossing over to an azure vase of flowers and removing a brown stem, whose time had come to pass.

"Huh?" Cassie asked.

"Just because someone in your family behaves a certain way doesn't mean you have to follow in their footsteps."

"That's not what Agatha says," Cassie said, securing the sweatshirts around her waist.

Tufa snipped another brown flower in the vase as an elf, dressed in a lemon-yellow shirt and blue knicker pants with blue-and-white-spotted knee-high socks in black-buckle shoes entered the Palace, scurrying through with a stack of leather-bound books in his hand and heading toward a set of winding stairs next to the honey-colored door. "I know the Entity of whom you speak," he said at the mention of Agatha's name.

"Are you friends with her?" Cassie asked, as he climbed the winding stairs.

"We all were, once," Tufa answered, with her back turned.

A simple chalk drawing of blue and orange flowers in a ceramic vase on the wall, just past where Tufa stood, caught Cassie's attention. Her mother used to paint similar pictures in the art class she took with a friend, before Dad left. Cassie noticed how the colors of the flowers blended seamlessly with the cornflower-blue background, requiring real talent. Her mother had painted for a few months, hanging pictures throughout the apartment, but for some reason, she stopped. Cassie always wondered why. A bright-red cardinal distracted Cassie from her thoughts as it flew in from outside, gliding through the Palace and landing on Tufa's shoulder. A shred of a thought breezed through Cassie's mind at the same time, but she couldn't recall its content.

"How high up are we?" Cassie asked, looking through to the back of the Palace, where past the meadow of daisies she spied a long, rolling carpet of emerald-green hills.

"The highest elevation in the Land, unless you count where those stairs lead," Tufa said, sitting on a red bench, the red bird jutting its beak a few times, as she gestured toward the winding spiral staircase across from the mosaic-jeweled circle on the floor.

"Can I see?" Cassie asked, stepping closer to where the elf had gone.

"Of course," Tufa said, rising from the bench.

She led Cassie onto the smooth, circular stairs, with the cardinal flying up ahead, rounding the staircase that wound five or six times, growing narrower the higher they climbed.

When they reached the semi-enclosed rooftop, Tufa presented Cassie with a breathtaking view of the radiant, baby-blue sky. "Welcome to the Elevated View, the place where everyone can see clearly."

"Wow," Cassie said, stepping onto the marble rooftop, the puffy white clouds so close Cassie felt she could reach out and squeeze them, like cotton candy.

The cardinal perched atop an alabaster railing encircling the upper level, and then flew to a far corner with several white feeders and pink-and-orange birdhouses. As the cardinal pecked at a feeder, Cassie imagined he was providing for his family.

Cassie leaned over the white wall, pretending she was in an airplane. *I'm not even scared!* she thought.

"As I mentioned, fear is not a Vibration that resides on Bright

Blue," Tufa explained, as the bright-red cardinal flapped its wings and landed on her shoulder.

Cassie tried to scare herself, leaning farther over the side of the lookout.

Tufa patted the cardinal's head as she leaned against the wall. "Fear is a low Vibrational frequency, no match for the energy that abounds here."

"Do you check your colors here to make sure?" Cassie asked, continuing to lean way over, and then pulling herself back. "Where's the Vibration Meter?"

"You mean like on the Land of Blue?" Tufa asked, with her arms crossed.

Cassie stopped to listen.

"It is right there," Tufa said, indicating the base of rolling green hills at the foot of the daisy fields, far in the distance.

Cassie searched past the expanse of green, seeing only dots of gray. Squinting, she tried to get a better view.

"Have a closer look if you like." Tufa gestured to a long, silver telescope in the center of the rooftop.

Cassie's sneakers smacked across the white floor toward the telescope. She bent down and with one eye closed, saw past the field of daisies and down the rolling green hills to an enormous, ugly, gray stone wall. A thick, nearly impenetrable band of gray smoky matter, similar to smog, lay behind it.

"That's Blue?" Cassie asked, her brow furrowed. "It's so gray there, but it's so bright here and they're right next to each other, really. How come they don't know you're here?"

Tufa faced in the direction of the smog. "They know."

Cassie glimpsed back through the silver telescope. "Agatha is very important there. I don't think she'd want to keep this beautiful place from me. I bet the people in the Settling would love to come here."

"Perhaps they would. Our creatures would very much like

255

those on Blue to know we are here. We have tried, but they resist our efforts."

Cassie closed her other eye to try to see past the smog through the telescope. "Even though it's always like nighttime there, it's fun. You get to drink as much Bad as you want."

"Yes, I know," Tufa said, offering an oriole some seed out of her pocket.

"But then it gets noisy after a while, and you get kinda tired," Cassie said.

The glasses jingled in her pocket.

Should I?

Cassie stepped back from the telescope. "Can I show you something?" Reaching inside her pocket, she brought out the gold-rimmed glasses. "I found these. I didn't mean to take them; I guess I was curious. Everything looks different on Blue, though, when I put them on."

"Perhaps you'd like to try them on right now," Tufa suggested. She stroked the bright-orange bird with one finger before it flew back into the nearby forest.

Cassie placed the delicate rims on her face. Pausing for a moment, she scanned the entire open, upper level of the Palace and the surrounding landscape.

Everything looks the same, she thought. *It's beautiful.*

Confused, she removed the glasses and put them back on, to be sure.

"There is no illusion here," Tufa said, facing the front of the Palace. The children's shrieks and laughter echoed throughout the meadow as they splashed and played in the shimmering pools.

"What does that mean?" she asked, placing the glasses back in her pocket.

"There is nothing to hide." Tufa answered, as a stream of adult voices conversed below, like the commotion that occurs when a train opens the doors to release its passengers.

"The trash in the Fix-It dumpster turned to jewels the first time I wore the glasses. The colors of the jewels were like here," Cassie's eyes swept the panoramic scene from the Elevated View. "Did I imagine it? How can trash turn into something beautiful?"

"The difference between trash and treasure is wisdom," Tufa replied, as an owl hooted from inside the lush, green forest.

Cassie searched in the direction of the hooting sound, to no avail.

"Do not stress your mind any further," Tufa said, placing her hand on Cassie's back. "What is meant to be understood will be understood when the time is right. Let's return to the first floor, so we may enjoy some Kamalu."

Cassie followed Tufa back down the spiral staircase, jumping from the third step into the sparkling clean center of the Palace and over to a table set with a vase of flowers, a small silver pot, and two cups. A few bright-green leaves of lemon balm swirled in the pot of water.

"How is Blue treating you in your quest to save your father?" Tufa asked, sitting down and sipping from her cup.

Cassie's face turned down. "It's like the Have To Haves are making things worse, but Agatha told me Dad needs them to get better. I have to wait until he's ready. But I just want to bring him home." Cassie stared into her cup of Kamalu. She perked up. "Could I bring him here before we go home? He has to see this place! Maybe he could come here to get better!"

Tufa placed her cup down on the table. "I understand your desire to bring your father to Bright Blue. But it is up to an individual whether to go beyond the Ripple, as you did. The Ripple is one of the ways we try to reach those on Blue, to let them know we exist. However, it takes courage to surrender your fear and venture through to the other side."

"But if I could just tell him about it, I know he'd want to go. If only he wasn't so sleepy." Cassie's eyes followed a bluebird that had flown down from a higher branch in the trees and in through the open interior back wall. "When he gets stronger and we can go home, then I'll be happy."

"Although your father's preferences affect your course, they do not determine your fate. It is up to a person to decide that for himself or herself," Tufa said, raising her cup of Kamalu to her lips.

Cassie spotted her reflection in the silver pot on the table, revealing the strawberry birthmark on the top of her forehead, which always made her feel weird. "Carlos said it's up to my dad whether or not he takes the Have to Haves to get better."

"Carlos sounds wise," Tufa said, lifting her chin.

"He's nice. He takes out the trash and stuff at the Fix-It." Cassie kicked her legs back and forth under the table as she drank her Kamalu.

After finishing her cup, Tufa gently pressed her hands on the table and strode across the floor to a large, wooden-and-hammered-copper chest against the Palace's west wall, her lavender dress trailing behind. The massive chest resembled a sunken treasure chest one might find at the bottom of the ocean. Cassie got up and approached the closed, copper lid.

"Would you like to open it?" Tufa asked, crouching down and opening her hand to reveal a copper key.

Cassie knelt and twisted the key into the chest's keyhole. When the lock clicked, she waited a moment before slowly creaking open the lid.

Inside, an array of glass in jeweled hues of ruby red, emerald green, dark purple, yellow the color of burnt honey, autumn orange, and sapphire blue shone like pirate's treasure.

"Wisdom Glass!" Cassie said, scooping up handfuls and letting them filter through her fingers like sand. "There's so much! Where does all this come from?"

"Wisdom Glass is made from the rubbish on the Land of Blue."

"But how does it get here?"

"The rubbish is transported by our task workers and then each piece is transformed and assigned to a special creature responsible for delivering a message to one in need," Tufa explained, just as an elf in a purple kerchief barreled through the small, honey-colored door, yelled "Delivery!" and poured a hefty burlap sack full of Wisdom Glass into the chest.

"Does it always end up on Option's Port?" Cassie asked, as the elf curtsied to her in long, velvet green socks before zooming back into the meadows.

"There, and other places in the Universe where people require wisdom," Tufa answered. "The creatures bring insightful messages so one may come to know a different experience. Many who discover Wisdom Glass find that their journey alters course, often in a beautiful new direction they previously thought impossible. Whether one believes or doesn't believe in the power of the message, however, is their election."

An owl hooted in the forest.

"It is almost time for me to go," Tufa said gently, "but there will be a little girl, one of our brightest task workers, to take you on the rest of your journey on Bright Blue."

"But . . . are you going back to Option's Port? Is that far from here?" Cassie's voice grew high-pitched.

How come everyone always leaves?

"It is not far," Tufa responded. "Nor am I ever far from you, Cassie. To think otherwise is another illusion."

Cassie felt a pang in her heart. Rising to her feet, she followed Tufa to the back steps of the Palace as birds flew overhead, landing to visit their nests and care for their young. Cassie stood next to Tufa in silence, as close to her dress as she could, feeling the warmth of the sun. A hawk, with a scroll of parchment in its beak, glided down to the three half-circle marble steps.

Tufa unrolled the scroll, read its contents, and rolled it back into a tube. "It's time." She gazed toward the smoggy area of Blue, far down at the base of the fields and spoke. "I will return. Until then, listen for my voice, on the frequency of Bright Blue."

Cassie spotted the owl perched overhead in a yellow oak tree, illuminated by sunlight. With her lips parted, she turned back to Tufa. "You're the other voice I'm hearing?"

Tufa's kind eyes reflected the sun as she spoke. "Yes, and it is up to you which to give attention to."

Cassie considered all the thoughts and voices constantly bombarding her mind. "Are there good voices and bad voices?"

"That, too, is for you to decide. Yet know this: selection is crucial." Tufa placed the scroll back into the hawk's beak, and it flew away into the treetops. Cassie could see that the thinning smog on Blue had developed a slight hole in its center.

Without another word, Tufa stepped gracefully down the three stone steps, through the waist-high daisy field in the direction of the foggy cover of Blue. The daisies grew taller and taller as Tufa strode through, and then she disappeared.

"Cassie," an upbeat girl called from back inside the Palace as an elf with long blond braids tidied the table and disappeared down through the little door. "I'm Annelies. I will take you to meet the others in the meadow."

Cassie turned her attention back inside the Palace to a girl who looked to be about seven years old, with straight dark hair falling about her face, reminding Cassie of the top of a mop. The radiant girl reached out a delicate hand.

She looks so happy. I bet she's happy all the time living here.

Cassie accompanied the slender-framed girl over the mosaic tiles through the Palace and down the stairs to the paved path. The expansive blue meadow surrounding the pavers was an ideal paradise. Rows of yellow sunflowers the children ran behind seemed to exist for their games of hide and seek. Other creatures, not present when Cassie arrived, now chattered alongside the path running through the meadow to the open pasture.

A jolly, wrinkled woman wearing a white-and-blue-trimmed headdress greeted Cassie with a wave. "Come to Agnes's area, won't you?"

The old woman hummed while she worked, lining trays of golden baked treats next to one another and retrieving limes and lemons, raspberries, strawberries, and blueberries from a basket on a table. Placing the luscious fruit into a bowl, she spun it with merely her bare hands, transforming the freshly squeezed fruit into rainbow-colored juice. Agnes poured the finished product into tall glasses for Cassie and Annelies, topping them each with a straw.

"Mmmmmm," Cassie said, sipping the cool, refreshing drink. "This is even better than Bad!"

Annelies giggled, watching Cassie lick a layer of strawberry pulp off her upper lip.

"I use my hands to serve," Agnes said, pouring a drink for herself and raising her glass to Cassie's own.

Next, Annelies brought Cassie farther along the pavers to a stubby, pale-faced man, his strawberry-blond hair tied back in a ponytail, with his ear bent to a large rectangular cage draped with a white sheet. Listening, the man scratched copious notes onto a large pad of paper while loud buzzing, like that of bees, sounded from inside the cage. A radar screen positioned next to the box flashed intermittent pulses of white light as the incessant buzzing continued.

"What are you doing?" Cassie asked, stopping at the man's station on the cobblestones.

"Hello! I am Benjamin, keeper of bees," the man said, grasping the point of his long red beard while rising up on his toes.

"I don't like bees. They're scary," Cassie said, stepping back from the buzzing cage.

"Ah, this is a different kind of bee," Benjamin winked, gesturing Cassie to come closer.

Annelies grinned as Cassie reluctantly let go of her hand. Cautiously stepping forward, Cassie stood within two feet of the mysterious crisp white sheet, when Benjamin magically swiped it away. Cassie took another step closer. She didn't see any bees. The cage appeared empty, filled only with a buzzing, agitated sound.

Cassie shuddered, as if thousands of bees swarmed her body. "But it's only noise. What's the point of that? To drive someone crazy?"

Benjamin wagged a finger in the air. "There is always pertinent information contained in any disturbance one feels, my dear girl. When someone in the Universe requires assistance, Bright Blue dispatches the bees, or, more accurately, the energy of the bees."

"But who would want to feel bees around them?" Cassie asked, feeling itchy all over.

"I understand your perspective. However, a little buzzing discomfort, used to get someone out of their climate of comfort, well, that's a good thing! Once a person figures out what the disturbance is communicating, well, that's when the fun happens." Benjamin wiggled his eyebrows up and down.

"How do you send the bees, I mean the energy of the bees?" Cassie asked, peering inside the noisy box.

"I thought you'd never ask!" Benjamin clapped his hands together.

An easel instantly appeared next to the flashing screen, a roll of paper unfolding to reveal a formula written in black letters.

"See here," Benjamin began, like a science teacher. "When people are dissatisfied, yet continue to repeat their behavior, we call that a Vibration of *complacency*. Usually around the time of complacency, however, an *opportunity* presents for people to change their circumstances and to raise their Vibration. The bees are the secret ingredient, see? The energy of the bees is the tool Bright Blue uses to help one make the shift, albeit from a Vibration of *discomfort*. Discomfort is what often makes a creature move forward toward the highest Vibration of *achievement*. And, here's the really exciting part: when people raise their Vibration and consequently their individual colors, they, in turn, affect the color Vibration for the entire Universe!"

"How do you know when someone needs the energy of the bees?" Cassie asked.

Benjamin pointed to a red dot on the radar screen, radiating like Rudolph, in an area of the world Cassie couldn't identify.

"See here. Krystyna, Eastern Europe, age forty-four, currently working at a job she detests. Krystyna just got asked to work overtime, at minimum wage, again," Benjamin rolled his eyes. "A corporate slave, I tell you. Don't get me started. Now," Benjamin said, his eyes widening, "This is when I go to work."

Benjamin reached a wand into the "bee" cage and scooped a handful of buzzing, frenetic, invisible energy. He carefully pressed the wand to the screen, on top of the little red dot. The dot went haywire, moving around like a little kid trying not to scratch poison ivy.

Cassie cringed. "Does it really help when you send the bees? It seems mean to make someone that uncomfortable."

"It's a marvelous and trustworthy process, though admittedly not enjoyable for the individual experiencing the discomfort. What is certain, though, is that a person always knows, within themselves, during that time of discomfort, something is not quite right, and it is up to them, and only them, to alter their situation."

After several moments, the agitated dot grew still, as if it stopped fighting. Benjamin observed the screen, smiling when the dot simmered down, pulsing more rhythmically.

"Takes some longer than others," Benjamin said with compassion. "Care to put in a good word for anyone?"

Wow! TJ could use the energy of the bees, since he might not go back to his family. But I wouldn't want him to be uncomfortable.

Cassie's mind raced, her eyes darting back and forth. *I felt the energy of the bees in my bedroom doing homework, and on Blue, too.*

Cassie looked up. Benjamin grinned ear to ear, like a little leprechaun caught hiding under a mushroom.

Annelies tugged on Cassie's shirt.

"Yes, yes, advance to the Seeds, a very important lesson ahead," Benjamin said with a nod. "And Cassie, should you feel that someone requires assistance, by all means, send me Mind Mail." Benjamin reached into the pocket of his green velvet blazer and pulled out a pair of golden-rimmed glasses, placing them on his face.

The glasses!

"I have those glasses!" Cassie exclaimed. "Well, they're not really mine."

"Ah, so refreshing when one recognizes what is right in front of them; not everyone in the Universe does, unfortunately. Use the glasses wisely, for when you require a better view."

Cassie started to leave, but quickly turned around to ask Benjamin to send her dad the bees. To her surprise, however, Benjamin had disappeared. The cage, the easel with the formula, and the radar screen had vanished. Cassie looked side to side, the other creatures hard at work, unaware of Benjamin's disappearance.

Annelies pulled Cassie by the hand, farther along the path.

"We only materialize until you get what you need. After that, it's not necessary to remain in form," said a fast-speaking voice, like an auctioneer. The man in the meadows with windblown, rainbow-colored hair that stood on end, like he'd stuck his finger in an electrical socket, coughed, choking on his words and then bowed like a gentleman to Cassie. "I'm Simon, Sower of Seeds."

Gesturing his hand wildly for Cassie to follow him to a workstation set up like a mini-laboratory in the meadow, Simon plunked into a rollaway chair.

"Care to have a look? I'm putting the finishing touches on my latest experiment." Simon spit as he spoke, blowing his wild, pointy hair away from his intensely focused face.

Cassie peered over Simon's shoulder as he fiddled with a Bunsen burner, simultaneously moving dials and switches on another machine causing a display of colors, from muddy brown to a brilliant burst of Valentine red, to come into focus on the glass.

"Observe." Simon's voice grew quiet as he closed his eyes, the screen erasing to clear. Focusing, his eyes squinting while the corners of his mouth turned downward, Simon sprung open his eyes.

The color on the screen had changed from clear to a dark, dirty stain. He nodded, looking pleased. Again, Simon closed his eyes in concentration. This time, the corners of his mouth turned upward, his brow relaxing. His green eyes flew open like a cuckoo clock at noon, as he watched the color on the glass turn from the offensive brown to an explosion of pumpkin orange.

"Tremendous, tremendous," Simon muttered, feverishly writing notes on a piece of parchment with a fancy quill pen, his pointy hair waving back and forth. "The power of thought Vibration!"

"It's like the Vibration Meter," Cassie said, observing the pink screen. "But how did you get the colors to change?"

"Excellent question! Would you like me to show you?" Simon asked, handing Annelies a basket and switching a few gadgets to clear the screen.

"Sure," Cassie said.

"All right, then, stand beside the screen! Here we go! Ponder a word that makes you feel good," Simon instructed.

Cassie scratched her head, glancing sideways at the neutral-colored screen and back at Simon. Annelies giggled, twirling the basket in her hands.

Cassie closed her eyes, and after a moment, pictured the word "together," recalling a time her dad took her for ice cream at Brigham's.

"Very good!" Simon exclaimed, haphazardly adjusting dials on the machine.

Cassie opened her eyes, as a sunburst of orange mixed with soaring pink butterflies appeared on the screen.

"Wow," Cassie said, her mouth dropping. "So if you think

something good, you can change the colors?"

"When you think something good, you feel good! Therefore your colors change. Now, let's test for understanding, as we always need something to compare data to! This time, if you will, focus on a word that makes you feel sad." Simon fast and furiously moved dials on the large clunky machine, erasing the glass.

Annelies wore a concerned look on her face as Cassie closed her eyes a second time. The word "abandoned" popped into her mind, causing her jaw to clench, recalling the morning she woke up and her father was gone. Quickly she opened her eyes. The screen turned to dark gray, the color of old movies.

"Doesn't feel good, does it?" Simon asked, solemnly shaking his head, and pausing, as if he remembered something. "Comparably, if we think sad thoughts, otherwise known as low Vibration thoughts, our feelings, inevitably, will be sad."

Cassie stared at the screen before Simon erased the ugly color and said, "That is your first lesson in Thought Vibration Education, the most powerful education in the Universe."

Seeds fell from a shaft out of the side of the machine and Simon shepherded them into small container packets, handing one to Annelies.

"All I have to do is think good thoughts and my colors will be bright?" Cassie asked, as Annelies opened the packet of seeds and sprinkled them in the space around Cassie's body, though Cassie didn't see her do it. They vanished before touching the ground.

"Seems easy enough, doesn't it?" Simon asked, crossing his legs in his rollaway chair. "Knowledge is power, but wisdom is application." Picking up a glass from the side of his workstation, he took a sip of the bubbling, clear liquid, missed his mouth, and dribbled it down his chin.

Cassie eyed a messy stack of paper next to the machine. "But to go back to the Land of Blue, my colors have to match the Vibration Meter. I don't understand how . . . "

"How time flies!" Simon said, loudly banging the glass back on his workstation so hard it spilled over the side of the half-filled glass and onto the paper.

The rays of the sun shifted suddenly across the blue meadow, late afternoon setting in. Cassie listened as a breeze rippled through the grassy meadow, creating a whispering sound. And in that moment, Simon also disappeared, along with the other creatures who had been working along the path.

Hundreds of little creatures carrying Wisdom Glass on their backs scurried toward her, evaporating into thin air once they entered the pasture.

Children skipped in from the meadows, chanting, "It's a choice to listen to the voice." The fluttering of their footsteps grew louder, like a flock of birds beating their wings, about to take flight.

It's a choice to listen to the voice. But which one did they mean? I have to listen to Agatha, don't I? Who else will help me get Dad back home?

Annelies tugged on the ends of Cassie's sweatshirts. "For you," she said, handing Cassie a bouquet of red bee balm. "Your time has come to return to the Land of Blue." She looked past the Palace, making a clicking sound with her tongue.

A beautiful white horse galloped in from the fields, slowing to a trot when it got close to Annelies and Cassie, stopping dutifully at Annelies' feet.

Cassie gasped, stunned at the sight. The animal was the most beautiful creature she had ever seen, like a cloud shaped in the formation of a horse from Heaven.

Annelies stroked the horse's shiny mane before retreating with the other children into the enchanted woods.

Then Tufa appeared. "Now that you have met our task workers, tell me, do you have any questions before you leave?"

Cassie's heart skipped a beat as she brushed the horse's silken fur. "If Agatha's the only one who can help me get to my dad, shouldn't I listen to her? How else will I bring him home?"

"That is for you to determine," Tufa replied as the sun moved across the sky.

"I wish you could come with me to Blue," Cassie said, the rustling leaves in the woods growing more still.

"We have our own creatures there, for we will never give up trying to reach its inhabitants, even when the Dusk Ruler and his staff resist us."

"You have creatures there? Do I know them?" Cassie asked, feeding the horse some grass as the enchanted forest and the blue meadow fell silent.

"In time," Tufa responded. "But now you are needed back in the Land of Blue. It is time to apply what you have learned. Know this. You are never alone. Even on a rainy day, the sun still exists in the sky."

"Tufa," Cassie said, gazing into the empty pasture, uncertain if she should share her feelings. "Sometimes Agatha's voice makes me feel afraid."

An owl hooted in the distance, a third time.

"Why, then, are you listening?"

Cassie looked up, and Tufa was gone.

The white horse nuzzled Cassie's hand before bowing down so she could climb on its sturdy, saddleless back. The majestic horse slowly trotted through the meadow and though she had never ridden a horse before, it was as if Cassie knew what to do, as if the horse communicated that he would keep her safe. The tall green trees of the forest grew closer as the horse began to gallop toward the pasture. Faster and faster, the trees whipped by Cassie's peripheral vision until she rose off the needled ground, up into the magnificently azure sky.

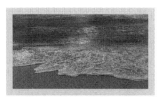

CHAPTER
TWENTY-FOUR

Cassie groggily opened her eyes back in the Strays suite. The flickering lights of the Stimulator screen cast shadows on the walls. Mariana and TJ spoke to one another excitedly as TJ chewed a handful of Blobs he grabbed out of a brown paper bag while playing *Bad Hero* on the Stimulator. The Mooshkoo housemaid nestled in between Mariana's cushy beanbag and TJ's leather-backed chair.

"Hi sleepyhead!" Mariana said, noticing Cassie's half-opened eyes. "Agatha will be psyched! She was upset when we couldn't wake you. I said it was like you were in another world, and she stormed out and slammed the door. I didn't think it was that big of a deal." Mariana shrugged. "You must have needed rest."

Cassie blinked, feeling somewhat disoriented, and tried to sit up.

"Look at this little Mooshkoo, she's so cute!" Mariana patted the housemaid's blue head while it purred "oip oip," puckering its wide lips into a kissy face while staring up at the bag in TJ's hand.

"Hey!" TJ said, his elbows on his thighs like he was about to tell Cassie something important, but first he fed the adoring Mooshkoo a square Blob that made you pass gas. "I found Eric! He was in the Cove like Sal said! He introduced me to a bunch of kids from the Settling and we played *ten* Stimulators before he had to go back to his new job. He helps hand out the Have to Haves to the Settling families." TJ chomped on a circular red Blob, tearing off a second piece for the Mooshkoo, who had quickly gobbled the square Blob and began laughing its rubbery head off while Mariana held her nose.

I have to let Dad know about Bright Blue! Cassie thought, rising up on her elbows to join the conversation, despite the heaviness of her eyelids. "Why is Eric staying with his host family? Isn't he going home with you?"

"Will you both please stop saying host family?" Mariana asked, throwing her hands in the air. "It sounds like we're in France!"

"I know you're going to try and talk me out of it, and I know the reason I came to Blue was to bring Eric home, but Sal keeps reminding me how my home life stinks! He said if I stay, I can work with Eric." TJ fed another Blob to the whining Mooshkoo with his other hand.

"But . . . " Cassie began.

"Ouch!" TJ exclaimed, looking down at the Mooshkoo, who now had two sharp teeth protruding from her mouth. "It bit me!"

"Oip Oip Oip!" she ranted, her face turning fire-hydrant red.

"Greedy little sucker, aren't you?" Mariana scowled, pursing her lips together.

"Oip! Oip! Oip!" the Mooshkoo demanded, coming within inches of TJ's face.

"That means she wants them now," Mariana said, narrowing

her eyes.

"Yeah, I get it," TJ said to the relentless Mooshkoo as he retracted the bag of Blobs high in the air. "Hold your Constantines, will ya?"

After TJ gave the Mooshkoo another Blob, she settled down next to his feet, sweetly purring, "Oip oip."

"Yeah, nice and polite until the special effects wears off," Mariana said, raising an eyebrow.

While the Mooshkoo eyed the bag in TJ's hands, Cassie felt like part of her was still in the Land of Bright Blue.

Without warning, Agatha burst through the suite. "While I understand you are excited to share the news of meeting up with your brother, TJ, unfortunately, you and Mariana must join Sal in the foyer once the elves arrive. There is a need for an urgent Vibration measure."

"Here?" Mariana said, crinkling her nose. "We've never been checked here before."

"That is because something on Blue has changed," Agatha said suspiciously, looking in Cassie's direction, "and the Ruler has ordered everyone to be scanned."

"What's going on?" TJ asked, gathering Blobs that had fallen out of a hole in the brown bag, torn at the bottom by the Mooshkoo's needle-sharp teeth.

"You may find out exactly what's going on by looking out that window," Agatha said crossly, striding over to the shutters and throwing them open. "We'll inform you when the elves arrive." Whirling back around, she departed the suite, slamming the door behind her.

TJ, Cassie, and Mariana scrambled to the window.

"Was it you?" they heard a middle-aged woman in a gypsy skirt ask Potentials in line waiting to be scanned.

"Have your colors gotten brighter?" a twitchy-shouldered man whispered to a group of teenagers.

Elves, stationed in the middle of the street, measured Potentials, Permanents, and Permanents by Association as children huddled in long lines with their families. Those Working for Permanency were scanned directly at their stations. Big, carrying a small axe, and Small, holding a large pair of scissors, flanked Kurt, keeping order on the cobblestones.

Cassie saw Anna and Michael beside Mrs. Costa, as she spoke to her husband outside one of the Pits. Mr. Costa held a forty-seven-fingered bottle of Escape in his hand while he tapped Anna on the head like a farm animal you're wary to touch at the petting zoo. The bottle brushing against her scalp, Anna clung to her father's thigh.

"Are you the one who's disrupted our system?" an elf asked Mrs. Costa in the Midst, as people nervously huddled with their loved ones in line.

"Her?" Mr. Costa thrust his head back in laughter. "We got a great set-up here, right darlin'?"

Mrs. Costa paused and whispered, "We're very grateful for our house in the Settling that keeps our family together."

Cassie thought Mrs. Costa didn't look very convincing as her scan landed on the color of steel, allowing her to pass, while the Mooshkoo played *Bad Hero* in the suite, banging on the controller when she lost.

A woman with flamboyant scarves draped over her body, who Cassie recognized from the Settling, stood next to Mrs. Costa with her arms crossed as an elf took out his Surveyor and began to question her.

"Where else am I gonna go? I hope they figure out who messed things up pretty soon, cause I wanna get back to the Pits!"

The elf scanned the woman, watching as the arrow on the individual Meter swiftly landed on the stormy gray. "All right, Janis, you're cleared," he said.

Cassie noticed Mrs. Costa's solemn gaze linger for a moment upon her neighbor, as if maybe she had been hoping Janis might say something different.

"Look," Mariana said, wiping fog from the window, their noses pressed so closely to the glass. Cassie's heart skipped a beat. Wisdom Glass, scattered like shiny pennies on the ground, lay beside Potentials' shoes.

"It's everywhere," Cassie whispered, her eyes landing on a spectacular green jewel by Janis's high-heeled sandal, while groups of Potentials and Permanents spoke among themselves.

"But no one notices," Mariana said.

"Notices what?" TJ asked, scratching his head.

"You don't see them?" Mariana asked, staring at the glittery gems strewn about the Midst.

TJ squinted as Entities and Permanents bickered, looking for someone to blame for the upset to their schedule. The golden glasses jingled in Cassie's pocket.

Benjamin said to use them wisely.

Cassie looked over her shoulder at the Mooshkoo, who was completely engrossed in the Stimulator game, and not watching them at all. Cassie plunged her hand into her pants pocket, fidgeting for the rims.

Outside, in the Midst, the noise grew louder.

"I hope it wasn't someone we know. Then we'll all get in trouble!" complained a bleach-blond to her neighbor.

"I know I'm loyal!" barked a sixty-year-old man in short trousers.

"How long before our next Escape?" asked a silk-turban-wearing woman, nervously rubbing her fingers together.

Cassie grasped the glasses, and placed the golden rims on her nose. Instantly, the landscape of the Midst changed. Entities, with long drawn eyes and ghost-like faces you see in a fun house, dug claws into their young Potentials' arms, shoving them back into the Pits and Zebbies once approved by the Meter.

Cassie blinked behind the golden frames. Potentials and

Permanents revealed tarnished gold hooks sticking out of their upper backs as they headed indoors, celebrating their clearance.

They're the same hooks on the wall in the Settling. Why are there hooks in people?

Cassie heard loud growls coming from outside the window. Creatures resembling male tigers prowled across the cobblestones, on leashes held by elves. The tigers sniffed the space around frightened Potentials and Permanents who hadn't yet been cleared.

"D-do you see those?" Cassie asked, gulping as she stood behind Mariana and TJ.

"What, everyone freaking out?" Mariana asked, leaning her elbows on the window as she observed the drama. "This looks like my house when my Papou finds out someone's too busy for Sunday dinner. I'm glad we're in here, where it's safe."

"Not the people," Cassie said, as one of the tiger beasts gnashed his spear-like teeth together on a piece of meat fed to him by an elf. "Those wild animals . . . I-I've never seen them before."

"Wild animals? You must have had some deep sleep, huh? I don't see any wild animals," Mariana said, squinting, "unless you count everyone out there acting like one."

"Look at that group of elves questioning Robin," TJ said, cracking his knuckles. Robin tottered on his unicycle answering the elves' questions. "I wonder what happened to make everyone so afraid."

Others, freed of any wrongdoing, swiftly returned to the Pits and Zebbies. Robin answered the interrogating elves, who let the leash out on the tiger beasts. "I-I'm not thinking of going anywhere. I swear." Robin dropped a handful of Bads, causing them to smash on the street.

Like looking through her own kaleidoscope, Cassie viewed Robin through the glasses, his face different, ashen-colored, like the hue at the bottom of the Meter. A group of Entities congregating on the cobblestones watched the drama unfold, bearing the same ashen look.

It almost looks like Robin's an Entity, too, or changing into one.

"Rumor has it you've been dissatisfied, Robin. Let's let Lewis determine if you're the one who raised the Vibration," an elf said with a sly grin. "Let's go."

Robin slowly abandoned his unicycle and stood still, so the tigers could smell the space around his gray-colored body.

Cassie's stomach did a somersault. *Is that what the Tigers are searching for? To see who changed the Vibration?*

"Someone had to have done something big," TJ said, standing on his tiptoes to try and see over the gathering crowd. "I hope this doesn't wreck my plans to see Eric. We were meeting at Zebbies after he finished work. He gets five Lures for Stims just for bringing the Feed to the Settling."

Cassie picked her forearm. *I didn't do anything by falling through the Ripple, did I?*

"Well, if you are going to stay here with your brother," Mariana said to TJ at the window, "your parents should know."

"Oip!" The Mooshkoo threw the controller against the wall in frustration, startling the kids.

"Easy, there," TJ said to the Mooshkoo, as she rolled off the beanbag and gave up on the game. Then he said, "My family doesn't sound like your family, Mariana. My parents called Eric a 'good for nothing'! and they'll probably give up on me too. I just wanna know who did it, cause that affects all our plans."

"Oip Oip!" the Mooshkoo chirped in agreement.

Cassie tried not to look down, keeping her hands steady by her sides as the Mooshkoo neared Cassie's hands, razor-sharp teeth sticking out of her mouth, ready to strike.

Suddenly, the tigers roared outside, and Cassie instinctively flinched, bringing her hands up to her cheeks. The elves handed the leashes over to tall, black-hooded figures who had come in from the pier. The hooded figures huddled around Robin, and led him to the walkway outside Strays where Kurt, Big, Small, and a group of Entities gathered.

"Duck so they don't see us!" TJ shrieked. "They might think we did something wrong!"

Cassie, Mariana, and TJ crouched down, listening from underneath the window.

"Get the Detectors back to the Ruler," Kurt commanded the hooded figures, "and get Robin a dose of what he needs to stay loyal to the system."

Cassie, Mariana, and TJ peeked up over the windowsill. Cassie spied the hooded figures grasping Robin's skinny arms, his head hung in defeat, leading him away from the Midst and in the direction of the Fix-It.

"Let that be a lesson to all of you!" Kurt yelled, pointing a finger before marching his little black boots off the brick walkway and back onto the cobblestone street.

Where are they going? Cassie gnawed on her lip as Robin was dragged down the road. The other Workers for Permanency quickly returned to their workstations and began soliciting passersby, order soon returning to the Midst.

Cassie yanked the glasses off her face, thrusting them in front of Mariana and TJ. "Put these on, you have to see . . . " when suddenly Kurt burst into the suite, nearly knocking over the Mooshkoo. "All right, you three, out to the foyer, although I think we already got our guy."

"Fine, let's get this over with," Mariana replied, leaving the window. "I know I didn't do anything."

"Me neither," TJ said, stuffing his hands in his pocket behind Mariana.

Cassie slid the glasses back into her jeans and turned to follow her friends.

"My colors never even change," Mariana whispered to TJ and Cassie. "Does Agatha have to explain that again?"

"I don't know," Cassie said.

Kurt put a hand up so Cassie couldn't go any farther. "Not you. Agatha wants a word first. Stay here until she's finished talking with the Ruler."

Kurt exited the room with TJ and Mariana, who both looked back at her over their shoulders.

Cassie stood in the center of the room, while the Mooshkoo paced back and forth like she was doing laps, because there weren't any Blobs left in the suite. Cassie was too afraid to put the glasses back on to see what the Mooshkoo looked like under the circumstances.

Her knees weakened, thinking about having her Vibration measured. *Did I do something wrong? Was it me?*

Cassie wondered if she ought to tell Agatha about the other voice she had been hearing and how she was a little confused. Maybe if she told Agatha she had gone to the other side of the Ripple and found Bright Blue, Agatha would understand. She knew how curious Cassie was. But a feeling inside her, like a stomachache after eating too much candy when you knew you shouldn't have, made her decide not to tell. Her forehead began to sweat.

But Agatha brought me here. Shouldn't I tell her the truth? Cassie closed her eyes, wishing the moment would go away, when she received Mind Mail.

> Hey Cassie,
>
> There's a chance chu might be delayed in getting back to the Fix-It to see chur papa. There's a Glimmer coming no one planned for. Don't chu worry though, I keep an eye on things, okay?

Cassie replied without hesitation.

> Another Glimmer? But we just had one! Agatha never told me. How will I get

back to my dad now? I have to tell him
something really important.

As quickly as Cassie responded, Carlos was quicker.

Nurse Moody's off duty and the doc's in
a big entrevista with the Ruler because of
the unexpected rise in Vibration. I'll stay
with chur Papa. But his next round of Have
to Haves are due soon, the other ones are
wearing off, so he might be uncomfortable,
espeshially in the cabeza. I'll do my best if
chu don't make it back in time.

A thought, like a raindrop, plopped down into Cassie's mind.
She gulped.

Could you hide my dad's Have to Haves
before he takes them?

There was a pause in Carlos's reply.

Dat's a tuff request, chica. I heard your
papa asking the doc for dem already. It's
too risky for me to do what chu are asking.

Cassie squeezed her fists until they were white, barely noticing
the Mooshkoo panting like a dog as it maniacally zipped back and
forth across the suite.

I know he might be uncomfortable and
maybe in pain, too, but when I get back
there, he might be so sleepy from the next
round of Have to Haves that he won't hear
what I want to say. Please, Carlos, won't
you help me?

And Carlos replied:

> Well, maybe I could take your papa por
> un paseo if things settle down here, since
> everybody's in a tizzy over the Meter.
> That's supposed to help back pain, chu
> know?

Cassie relaxed her shoulders a little, though she didn't want her father to be in any pain.

> If he could just hold off a little longer . . .
> He'll do that for me. I'm his daughter. I
> have to tell him something about . . . well,
> someplace I'd like him to see. A place that
> would really make him happy.

Carlos replied:

> It sounds bueno, this place. Lemme see
> what I can do. But chu understand chur
> dad has to make up his own mente.

Cassie thought about that. She didn't want Carlos to get in trouble, but she felt strongly she had to get her dad to stop taking those Have to Haves. Cassie wanted him to hear her when she told him all about Bright Blue, how beautiful it was, and how they could visit it together if he wanted to. She would teach him how to change colors and all about the energy of the bees. Oh! The bees! She remembered she wanted to ask Benjamin to help her father.

Would Dad be okay until then?

Cassie blinked her eyes three times on each side, to keep her father safe, in case a Glimmer really was on its way and she couldn't get back to him in time.

Just then, the door to the suite opened.

> Cassie, no reply. I send chu another Mind
> Mail soon. And try not to worry.

Cassie stayed still, with her eyes shut, not wanting to move a muscle.

Agatha held the door open with her black shoe for the Mooshkoo. "You won't need to be scanned, because you're a good little apprentice."

Upon leaving, the rubbery housemaid stuck her tongue out at Cassie.

Agatha let her foot go, the door closing with a bang as she strode across the room and placed two stiff hands atop Cassie's shoulders. "Perhaps you've heard. There's been foul play on Blue." Agatha's dark eyes searched Cassie's like they were foggy windows, hiding something Agatha desperately wanted to see.

"Did someone do something wrong?" Cassie asked, curling her toes in her sneakers.

"Someone has had . . . inspiring thoughts," Agatha said, releasing her hands from Cassie's shoulders and waltzing over to the window.

"Inspiring thoughts?" Cassie asked, in a high-pitched tone, as the Stimulator screen turned dark as it shut off.

"Yes, you know, of better lands and happy places," Agatha said, lifting her chin as she observed creatures in the Midst talking about the incident as they stood in lines at the vendor carts. "The effective Land Meter senses such things, and as a consequence, the Land Vibration has been raised two color notches." Agatha turned to face Cassie. "Very serious indeed, as one person's inspiration has affected our entire Blue system. Naughty. Naughty. Naughty. Therefore, you'll need to go home. As a result of the atmospheric change, another Glimmer is approaching. The poor creatures out there don't even know yet. It's the first time this has happened in many, many pulses. However, it will pass, as all things do, and once it does, and things settle down again, I'll plan for your return, but only, *only*, once I deem you ready. Understood?"

Cassie stepped forward. "B-but, when can I come back?"

"Perhaps you should think about that the next time you feel lazy and fall asleep," Agatha said, pulling at the sleeves of her cloak.

Cassie's underarms began to sweat. "I'd like to think I was refueling. I was so tired!"

Agatha stepped closer, her eyes boring into Cassie's. "I said lazy and lazy it is. It isn't enough I have to cover for your friend, explaining to my staff that she's merely a Lu . . . "

Suddenly, a warm breeze funneled in through the open shutters.

"Oh, my," Agatha whisked her head toward the window. "That was quicker than I calculated."

Outside, creatures began to cry.

"There's a Glimmer!"

"No one told us!"

"Run!"

Agatha marched over to the shutters.

"But the breeze feels so nice," Cassie whined. Why does every—"

"There will be no more questions!" Agatha scolded, slamming the shutters closed. "From the beginning, I told you we needed to take care of your father so he could get back to where he belongs. Perhaps you ought to have trusted in my voice—the one who has taken care of you all this time. Unfortunately, someone took too long of a nap, and now your plans are delayed."

Cassie hung her head in the center of the room.

"I'll spare myself the embarrassment of scanning your energy in front of my staff members, as my predictions are likely accurate. Let them think it was someone else. I'll gather Mariana and we'll Zipper you home." With that, Agatha turned on her heels and stormed out.

Cassie's heart felt like it had been dropped down an empty elevator shaft. She pressed her toes inside her sneakers until they hurt.

I shouldn't have fallen asleep. Maybe I am lazy. Maybe I did mess everything up by going to Bright Blue. I know Agatha is helping me, but why does she make me feel bad?

Hearing the frantic cries outside, Cassie waved her hand in the space beside her, but felt nothing.

Will the Ripple be there again? Nothing ever goes right for me.

Cassie hurried to the window, squinting to see the scene through the narrow space between the shutters. Creatures chaotically crammed into doorways of every shop as the dusky sky thinned overhead, stretching like taffy. Mrs. Costa stood at the back of a jammed line outside the Pits, trying to pry Anna from her father.

"I don't want to go in there, Daddy, let's go home!" Anna cried.

"Enough!" Mr. Costa barked. "We'll be able to get Bad here. There's none at home. C'mon, Michael!"

Michael clung to his mother's leg in the middle of the frenzied street as Mrs. Costa attempted to reason with her husband that going back to the Settling would be best for the children.

That's what mom used to do whenever Dad wanted to stay out late at the Knights club, Cassie thought. *She told him it was beyond my bedtime.*

Grabbing her hair in clumps and looking up at the sky, as Mr. Costa paid no attention, Mrs. Costa abruptly turned, as if she noticed Cassie at the window.

"We can make it home, Daddy, before the Glimmer if we hurry! No one's faster than you!" Anna pleaded.

Mr. Costa waved his catcher's-mitt-sized hand in the air toward his family as he crammed in line. "Well, you better run home quick, cause I'm staying."

Cassie's heart pounded in her chest. *They're not going to make it. They have to get indoors!*

Elves raced in, mid-air on bicycles, whisking people up and thrusting them into thresholds of buildings as the sky gradually lightened. Cassie felt her face grow hot as Mrs. Costa stood on the cobblestones with her children, as if she was frozen.

"Please! You can carry us so we make it!" Anna yelled, her father pushing his way inside the crowded Pits.

What will happen to them if they get caught in the Glimmer? Cassie panicked.

The Midst emptied as Potentials, Permanents, and Permanents by Association, caught by surprise, ran for cover. Creatures Working for Permanency ditched their carts and darted into the alleyways to hide in dumpsters.

Cassie ripped off a fingernail in one fell swoop as Mrs. Costa continued to stand in the street with her children, as if she was waiting, tempting something to happen.

Why isn't Mrs. Costa keeping her kids safe?

Cassie felt the impulse to run outside and bring them to hide in Strays, when an angry elf grabbed Anna and Mrs. Costa by the arms, little Michael still grasping his mother's leg. Reprimanding, "You know better! It's too early for him to go home!" the elf shoved them inside another Pits next door.

Cassie gripped the windowsill. *Anna wanted to go back to the Settling. Was TJ right? Maybe it wasn't that bad. Maybe Agatha's right, too. Mrs. Costa is supporting her husband so they can all live together.*

Cassie realized she hadn't known her family's apartment wasn't that nice until she went to Mariana's brick house with the two-car garage on West Roxbury parkway. Cassie didn't care, though, because her family was together, even if they couldn't afford a house like Mariana's. *Is that how Mrs. Costa feels?*

Staring into the now-empty street, her heart racing as light began to appear through the dusky sky, Cassie heard muffled voices from the foyer.

Is Agatha coming back for me? I wonder if the energy of the bees would help Mrs. Costa. Maybe Benjamin could help.

Cassie closed her eyes, sending Benjamin Mind Mail.

Immediately, she received his reply.

Hello Cassie!
Receipt Confirmed!

Your friend,
Benjamin,
Keeper of the Bees

Cassie felt like she grew three inches. Even though Benjamin didn't say he would help Mrs. Costa, Cassie knew he would. She felt tempted to ask him to help her dad too, but she didn't want to annoy him with another request so soon. Observing how the rising light caused the Wisdom Glass to glisten on the cobblestones, Cassie jumped as the door to the suite opened abruptly.

"I'm staying during the Glimmer!" TJ announced, diving onto a beanbag while Cassie grabbed the top of a high-backed chair for support, exhaling in relief.

Mariana pulled her thick hair back upon entering the suite, and collapsed into another beanbag. "Kurt thought I might be causing a problem because my colors are always above the line, but Agatha spoke privately to him and he let me go. Phew, right? My parents always tell me how powerful I am, but to singlehandedly raise the Vibration of a Land? I mean, that'd be pushing it! I think they'd need more than one person to do that. Besides, I'm ready to get out of here. I'm craving my Ya-Ya's Moussaka."

Agatha entered the suite and slammed the door. Cassie gripped the back of the chair and asked, "Can I stay during the Glimmer too?"

"Not this time," Agatha declared. "Not until I'm sure your Vibration is in alignment with Blue, as your friend TJ's has remained. Perhaps this time, before you're able to return, you'll need to prove yourself."

Cassie's cheeks flushed. "But how?"

Agatha tapped her chin. "Mmm, I'll let you know."

"Wow," Mariana said quietly, sinking deeper into the beanbag.

"Sorry, Cassie," TJ mouthed, clasping his hands between his legs.

It's not your fault, Cassie thought.

Outside, the Glimmer grew brighter and brighter. Agatha ordered Mariana to stand and huddled her and Cassie together after yanking them by their elbows. Light meekly filtered through the shutters, causing the dim room to brighten, and Agatha set a Zipper in motion.

How did Agatha know the Glimmer would happen? Where does it even come from?

Cassie felt the warm air coming through the walls, breezy and comforting like it had been on Bright Blue.

Cassie kept her eyes on the carpet. *Is that where the Glimmer comes from? Bright Blue?*

Cassie continued to wonder as the warm air gave way to the howling raw winds of the Zipper, causing the perfect tornado.

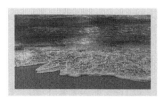

CHAPTER
TWENTY-FIVE

The dry, brown leaves whirled around the dark parking lot in the chilly November air. Cassie followed them from the back seat of Nana and Grandpa's Chevy Impala, her mom staring out the window on the other side of the car, squeezing the seat belt when she thought about how jarring the last Zipper had been. She arrived back in her bedroom that morning right before dawn. Now, after four o'clock Mass, she watched the whorl of leaves while Nana and Grandpa bickered in the front seat.

"How about that Eleanor O'Donnell, praying so long after communion she didn't bother to sit back in the pew to let us go by?" Nana Helen scoffed while Grandpa Jack rigidly held the steering wheel with both of his raw, cracked hands. He inched out of the parking lot behind the line of cars attempting to merge onto busy

Center Street.

"She thinks she's more pious than us, Helen," he bellowed, his neck practically invisible under his green parka when he looked left and right.

"Pious, my eye," Nana Helen hissed, digging in her pocketbook for Chap Stick. "I could give you an earful on her and I just might when Cassie's out of the car. Pious . . . " Nana flared her nose as she retrieved a hairbrush with stale Cheez-Its stuck in it from the bottom of her purse. "She's no closer to God than you and me, despite that black lace handkerchief she wears on her head." Nana turned and tried to glance over her shoulder in her stiff red wool coat from the passenger seat to ask, "Do you want fish and chips from the Corrib?"

Mom stared blankly out the back right window while Cassie stared out the left, both of them watching the red taillights of the cars in the lot, transporting their families home for the evening.

"Well for God's sake, if you don't answer me, I'm gonna go ahead and order it," Nana barked, pulling her cream-colored knit hat more snugly over her ears.

"Sure," Ann Marie Connor answered on autopilot, twirling her long red hair around one of her unpolished fingernails.

Cassie's mother stopped painting her nails and wearing makeup ever since she started going to those Al-A-something meetings at the church. The other day, when Nana Helen cut back hydrangeas in the yard, Cassie heard Nana tell Barbara Heimer that the meetings were Mom's "new social life."

Cassie figured Mom felt sad because she had seen her old friend, Paula Paolini, and her husband at Mass. She didn't want to answer questions about why Dad wasn't with them. Not that he ever attended church . . .

"Oh for crying out loud, Helen. Imagine this! Old Maid Lambert's taking her sweet time getting outta here, like we have all day." Grandpa Jack breathed heavily through his nose, waiting for

Ms. Lambert's Cadillac to exit the parking lot. "The Corrib better not be out of tartar sauce by the time we get there."

"She's probably driving like she's ninety on purpose cause Father Bill just came out of the rectory. Trying to show him she doesn't drive like a maniac. Wouldn't he like to know how many times she's gotten pulled over on her way to bingo," Nana said, her chin rolling over the collar of her coat.

"Hypocrites," Mom muttered under her breath, continuing to twirl her hair as she gazed out the icy window.

———

That night, Cassie found it hard to sleep. Agatha's voice kept waking her up.

Did you straighten your bureau? Did you shut the door all the way . . . not even a crack?

"Get back into bed!" Nana yelled each time Cassie got up to heed Agatha's instructions in the middle of the night.

Cassie ignored her grandmother, checking her closet to prove to Agatha she was listening. She also secretly hoped to find her Entity in there, ready to take her back to Blue. *I'll do whatever she tells me so I can be with my dad,* Cassie thought. But the closet remained empty, every time.

The clock flashed 2:00 a.m.

That's when the gray, transparent faces, like they had put Nana's nylons over them, appeared. They floated in the dark around Cassie's bed, like they used to when she was small. Some looked familiar this time, their distorted faces like Entities she saw in the Midst when she wore the glasses. Cassie's heart pounded in her ears as she stretched the covers over her head.

In Carlos's last Mind Mail, he reported her dad had demanded his Have to Haves. Carlos had tried to stall him, though, like Cassie requested. Worried, curled up in her bed, she replied.

Carlos,

As soon as Agatha knows for sure I'm on her side, I know she'll take me right back to Blue. Please try to keep the Have to Haves away from my dad so he can be awake when I get there, but I don't want you to lose your job or anything.

Carlos's response came back quickly.

Chu need to do what is best for chu, Chica, which probably means right now to go to sleep. Chur papa has to figure things out for heemself. If a person is forced to do sumthing, he no going to do it por Sí mismo, so it will not . . . how you say? It no have power. One other thing, what other side would chu be on?

Lying under her covers, Cassie's stomach ached, as if braided ropes pulled her sides tighter and tighter, making it hard to breathe.

What if Dad doesn't want to come home? What if I don't get to tell him about Bright Blue?

Cassie's head hurt now, too. The gray faces bobbed up and down, moving closer in the dark bedroom as she lay nestled down in the middle of her sheets.

Dad didn't understand that Cassie's job was to help him. He didn't know she had seen the Land of Bright Blue either and planned to take him there so he could learn new things and be happy.

No one else was doing anything to bring him home. *Did they give up on him? Mom never even mentions him, although she still waits for the mail every day. Nana and Grandpa never mention him either, but they never mentioned him before.*

I signed those documents to get Dad better. Did something go wrong?

Cassie's heavy, overloaded brain began to topple toward sleep when another Mind Mail envelope floated down with her name on it.

Cassie,

> Sorry it's taken a while. I played a Stimulator that lasted three pulses! Anyway, after the Glimmer, which was longer than usual, things settled down. But now that the Meter for the Land is on that navy-blue color, the checkpoints are tighter than ever. Sal's giving me a lot of freedom, though. He says he can count on me. And Eric and I can share a room if I stay! Sal went to my house to get some of my things and he said my parents don't even know I'm gone. I told you no one would miss me.
>
> Hope to see you and Mariana soon,
>
> TJ

Cassie felt a pang in her chest. *That's so sad TJ's parents don't miss him. No wonder he wants to stay with his brother.*

Biting her lip, she wondered if anyone would miss her. Mom worked most nights and on the other nights, she attended those meetings. Nana always seemed so aggravated with Cassie too. "You're always underfoot!" she'd say whenever she stomped in the pantry to get dessert.

Cassie didn't feel up to responding to TJ. She wanted to see him in person. *But when?* She did everything Agatha asked. Even when Cassie curiously reached her hand out at home a few times, to see if the Ripple would be there, she pulled her hand back because she knew it messed things up the last time.

Cassie tossed and turned in her bed, wondering if the faces were still there, and if they would ever leave her alone.

CHAPTER
TWENTY-SIX

The next morning at school, Cassie caught up with Mariana at her locker.

"You look really tired," Mariana said, hanging her plaid cardigan on the hook inside her locker. "Are you getting enough sleep?" She examined Cassie's drawn, pale face. "Is your grandfather waking you up again after he gets in from Clancy's? You know, if I tell my mom, she's going to make you stay at our house."

"I think TJ is going to live on Blue," Cassie said, hoisting her heavy backpack higher on her shoulder. "Sal told him his parents didn't even miss him."

"Seriously?" Mariana asked, turning to Cassie as she reached up on her tiptoes to put her math textbook on the top shelf. "Wait, isn't Sal supposed to be helping to bring Eric home, like Agatha is trying to help your dad? That's what your Entities promised, isn't it? I think what TJ needs is a better home life. Maybe he can come stay with me—he looks Greek, right?" She put on her backpack. "Besides," she said with a shudder like she had the willies, "who would want to sleep in the Settling?"

"But if he gets to be with his brother, he probably doesn't care where he sleeps," Cassie replied, leaning against the locker next to Mariana's, eyes half-closed.

"I'd care," Mariana said, reaching for her gym sneakers on the locker floor. "We need to talk some sense into that kid, to give him some better options. I mean, the Land of Blue's fun and everything, but last time I had wicked indigestion. I'm going to take probiotics next time, before we leave. When are we going, anyway? Your dad has to be better by now."

"I can't go until Agatha says I'm ready," Cassie said. "She got upset last time, you know, when I got lazy and fell asleep."

"Lazy?" Mariana asked Cassie in disbelief as she tugged her fancy brown boots off her feet. "You're exhausted! You know how you practically drool when you're in a deep sleep? Well, that's totally how you were. No offense to Agatha, but . . . couldn't we just go to Blue without her? Maybe we could try that chant. We know it by heart."

"No way," Cassie said, shaking her head. "Agatha would be mad. Besides, once we got there, how would we get past the gate?"

Mariana put on her new pink-and-green Nike sneakers. "I know you're a loyal person Cass, and that's great. I'm just saying, Agatha keeps promising she'll bring you to get your father and well, it doesn't happen. It's like she's delaying it on purpose."

Cassie hesitated and rubbed her eyes. "It was my fault. I took a nap and . . . " The second-period bell rang, interrupting her train of thought.

"Not everything is your fault, you know," Mariana said as they headed to class. "My mom says it's important for people to talk nicely to themselves, otherwise they'll develop a complex."

Cassie ruminated as she walked down the hall with her best friend. *She doesn't get it.*

———

"Hello Cassie, how are things at home?" Mrs. Beals asked after school, wheeling her rollaway chair closer to her desk, where she picked up a pen and yellow lined pad of paper.

"You mean at my Nana and Grandpa's house? We're only staying there for a little while, until my . . . " Cassie scuffed her grimy red sneakers. She didn't want to tell Mrs. Beals where Dad was. That was between her and Agatha.

"Yes, your Nana and Grandpa's house," Mrs. Beals said, politely folding her hands around the pen. Cassie liked the antique wedding band on her finger. It was shaped in a figure eight, with a pearl in one end and a diamond shaped like a flower inside the other loop. A little line of diamonds swung to either side under both the pearl and the bigger diamond, like lollipop stems.

"It's okay. I think I get on my Nana's nerves, though," Cassie laughed nervously, sitting on her hands.

"It can be hard for elders to have children in their home after they haven't had any for a long time," Mrs. Beals said reassuringly.

"Yeah, that must be it," Cassie said, as a creepy insect with lots of legs crawled across the braided rug.

Let's not go thinking warm and fuzzy thoughts about Nana Helen. Tap each of your feet three times on the floor to show you're heeding my voice. If you want to get back to your father, I am your only way.

Cassie quickly tapped her left foot and then her right while Mrs. Beals scribbled notes on the yellow pad.

"So, is there anything you'd like to discuss today?" Mrs. Beals asked gently. "You look awfully tired."

Would everyone stop saying that to me! Cassie yelled inside her head.

She wanted to tell Mrs. Beals she was tired because she was up all night proving herself to Agatha, and that she hated when her Grandpa came home drunk, and that Mom spent all her time going to that dumb church group and praying alone in her room. She also wanted to tell Mrs. Beals that she had gone to the most beautiful place but that she was kind of afraid to think about it again, because she didn't want to cause a problem on Blue or for Agatha to be mad.

Cassie wanted to say all these things that burst inside of her, because well, Mrs. Beals seemed like a really nice lady. But she couldn't. She couldn't tell her Agatha's voice spoke to her all the time, and her head felt heavy, and now she'd been hearing a new voice and felt even more confused. How could Mrs. Beals possibly help her with all of her weird problems? *She'd probably think I was crazy.*

"No, there's nothing else," Cassie mumbled, so quietly that Mrs. Beals strained to hear. Cassie began chewing her lip.

"Okay," Mrs. Beals said, nodding as if she understood. Then she perked up and asked, "Want to play a game?" Cassie noticed how straight and white her teeth were—the color of cream.

Cassie shrugged. "Sure."

"Great." Mrs. Beals got up from her chair and retrieved a blue cardboard box from a pile of games she kept stacked on the bookshelf. The game had little green cards with lots of questions, like: "When was the last time you felt proud?" And, "Have you ever felt disappointed? Why?"

Setting the game up on her desk and selecting a card from the middle of the deck, Mrs. Beals asked in a playful tone as she leaned over, "What's the worst thing someone could say to you?" to which Cassie replied sheepishly, "I'm not coming back?"

Next, Mrs. Beals turned over a blank white card with no question on it. She explained this meant she could create a new question all on her own. "If you could ask your grandparents to stop doing one thing, what would it be?"

Cassie answered without hesitation: "Please stop leaving used tissues in a pile in front of the microwave."

Mrs. Beals picked up a green card and asked, "What's the worst thing you've ever said to yourself?"

Cassie searched for the insect, but she couldn't find it, so she rested her eyes on the dust bunnies collecting in the corner of the windowsill.

Maybe the right answer was that Cassie told herself she was "bad" when she stepped on the cracks by accident. Or maybe it was that she called herself "awkward" when she tried to have conversations with other girls at school about things she didn't know a lot about, like hair and makeup.

Her mind wandered. Since Mom wasn't wearing makeup anymore, Cassie probably wouldn't be able to wear it until she was grown up herself and could make her own decisions. But then who would teach her?

Sometimes I feel like a loser.

Mrs. Beals sat quietly across the desk, the game board positioned between them and said, "You're thinking hard about how to answer that question."

Cassie touched the yellow token on the board. Mrs. Beals picked the purple color because her birthday was in February, the day before Valentine's Day, which meant her birthstone was amethyst.

"Sometimes," Mrs. Beals began, neatening the deck of cards, "when we have gremlins running around in our heads, there are so many awful thoughts in our minds, it's hard to pick just one, isn't it?"

Cassie looked up. "What did you say?"

"You know," Mrs. Beals said, her stiff brown hair brushing against the tiny pearl earrings hanging from her earlobes, "the little voices in our head that cause a lot of ruckus."

Cassie pinched the skin on her hand. "How do you know about that?"

"About gremlins?" Mrs. Beals asked, raising an eyebrow. "Everyone has gremlins, honey."

Cassie pinched her skin until it turned white. For a moment, she forgot she was in Mrs. Beals' office. "Are they bad? The voices?"

"The ones that make you feel bad are. That's why I use the term 'gremlins'. And everyone's got 'em. But everyone has good voices, too. Sometimes we just need to practice listening."

"But how are you supposed to stop listening to the gremlins?" Cassie's shook her leg up and down like a bowl full of Jell-O.

"It's how you talk back to them that matters most," Mrs. Beals said, leaning closer. "And it's a lot easier to talk back to the gremlins when you've had a good night's sleep or when you haven't had a lot of sugar or other unhealthy foods in your body. That's one way to do it. But there are other ways, too. I'm impressed with you, because asking for help is a sign of strength."

Cassie just stared at Mrs. Beals' face, her skin the nice medium kind that tans easily.

"Would you like to learn how to talk back to the gremlins the next time we meet?" she asked, cheerfully folding her hands in her lap.

Cassie nodded silently.

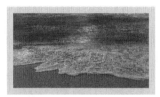

CHAPTER
TWENTY-SEVEN

At Mrs. Beals' request, Cassie did her homework at the kitchen table after supper, instead of alone in her room. She tried to concentrate on her vocabulary words like "melancholy," "antagonistic," and "belligerent," while Nana Helen, bent over in her green polyester pants, made clanking noises storing the leftover fish in the bottom refrigerator drawer.

Then the front door opened. Cassie had just finished writing the definition of the word "resentful" when she lifted her head and discovered her mother sporting a new, blunt haircut, making her look exactly like one of the nuns at Holy Name.

"Oh, for heaven's sake!" Nana cried out, like a complete stranger had entered her house. "Now you just need the habit!"

Ann Marie ignored her mother, walking directly to the

microwave to heat her Dunkin' Donuts coffee. Cassie eyed the straight line of hair across the back of her mother's neck. When her mother turned around, Cassie quickly looked back down at her homework. Her mother, pale-faced, avoided Nana Helen as she slowly sipped from the reusable cup.

Should I say something? Cassie wondered, scribbling in the blank space on her vocabulary worksheet.

I feel bad. Mom doesn't see her friends anymore, she looks different, and she has that weird bumper sticker on her car that reads, "Honk if You Love Jesus." I mean, I love Jesus too, but . . .

Cassie kicked the rung of her chair.

Then Grandpa Jack marched into the kitchen, passing by Nana Helen, who chuckled under her breath as she left the room.

"What in the hell did you do to your hair?" he barked, yanking his chair out from the kitchen table. Without even waiting for an answer, he sat down and started to take out his contact lens.

Cassie's mother ignored him, too, and moved into the pantry. She started humming songs Cassie recognized from Mass. Pressing her pencil harder as she tried to concentrate on her homework, she accidentally tore the flimsy worksheet.

Grandpa opened the jar of lens cleaner lined up next to the napkin holder. "Ah, c'mon," he said, while poking his finger in his eye as he fished around for the contact lens sliding around his eyeball.

Cassie refused to watch.

"Uh, Cassie," Grandpa said, his dry, cracked lips open wide as he held one eye open with his finger. "I meant to tell ya, ya gotta put a little more mustard on the bread when you make my lunch. Spread it all the way to the crust, otherwise the sandwich is dry. Got it?"

"Okay," she answered through clenched teeth, her mother's singing growing louder from the pantry.

"And another thing—damn you contact lens, you—who was the last person to drink the OJ?"

Suddenly, Cassie couldn't move, feeling as if she was a criminal on trial. "I-I don't know," she answered.

"Well, the cap wasn't on tight. If it's not tight, it's not right. You know that. I've told ya a hundred times." Grandpa blinked, searching for the evasive lens.

Mom banged some cabinets in the pantry.

Please come get me, Agatha. I can't take it anymore. My father will want to come home just so he can get me out of here. I know he will.

"Gotcha, you son of a gun!" Grandpa exclaimed, banging the kitchen table in victory.

Mom scurried to the front hall. "I'm heading to my meeting," she said. "Cassie, get your homework done and get to bed on time, okay?"

Cassie didn't answer, reading the word "resignation" on her unfinished worksheet.

"Who goes to those ridiculous Al-Anon meetings anyway?" Nana growled from her armchair, as Mom threw on her coat.

Placing her hand on the front doorknob, Mom hesitated a moment and then blurted, before scampering out the door, "Maybe you should come and find out."

"Hmmph," Grandpa said, hearing Ann Marie as he put on his dark-rimmed, coke-bottle glasses, making his eyes look distorted—ten times their normal size. "I'll tell you who goes to those meetings. Kooks."

That night, Cassie wrestled with sleep, her second night home from Blue.

Did I prove myself yet? Why is it taking so long?

Fearful that Nurse Moody might get to her dad before she did, she started her Mind Mail.

Dad,

I hope you aren't mad at me because I
asked Carlos not to give you your Have to

Haves. I don't want you to be in pain, but I
want you to be able to hear me. I need you
to come home, more than you need to take
your Have to Haves I think. I don't like
it here without you, and as soon as I get
back to Blue, I want you to be ready to go.

Please try your hardest to walk off the
pain. I promise I'll take good care of you
and I'll make sure you take whatever you
need to feel better when you get back, but
we need to leave Blue right away. I want
you to be here, with me, and Mom, too. I
love you.

Cassie

The plastered swirls on the ceiling morphed into pictures of
snakes. The fierce pounding of Cassie's heart kept her awake while
she waited for a reply. Car brakes screeched outside in the distance.
Cassie wondered if Grandpa was on his way back from Clancy's and
if he would be thoughtful and come in quietly, or loud and mean
like the angry giant in *Jack and the Beanstalk*. The not knowing was
the hardest part.

Suddenly, an envelope appeared.

Cassie, my girl

Thanks for the Mind Mail. I always hoped
you'd figure that out since I'm not a big
talker.

Carlos tried to take me for walks. Don't get
mad at him, but I gotta take those Have to
Haves. I appreciate you trying to help, by
signing that paper when I was trying to go
my own way, but the doc's right. The Land
of Blue is what I know, just like my family

before me.

But this place isn't for you, Cassie, and I don't want you to come here any more. Stay where you are and do things differently than I did. I know you love me and how much you want me to come home. I love you too, and I don't want to disappoint you, but sometimes a person has to accept where they came from. It's just too hard for a guy like me. When you're in all kinds of pain, well, sometimes it can be too much to handle. I hope you never have to understand.

Tell Mom I love her, too.

Dad

Cassie sat up in bed, gasping for air in short, noisy gulps. She tried to make sense of her dad's Mind Mail, experiencing stabbing pains in her chest. The darkness closed in. The floating, gray, scary faces appeared, drifting around her bed like jellyfish.

Suddenly, in the corner of the room, the little circle of light broke through the darkness. Slightly bigger this time, the size of a donut, it contrasted with the gray faces floating around her bed like creatures at the aquarium. A sunny yellow tang swimming among the creepy, murky fish.

Cassie swore she saw a face inside the glowing circle, but it was still so small she couldn't be sure. She had a funny feeling, though, that all she had to do was concentrate on the little light, and it would expand. She fixated on it, trying to hear its call.

You're never alone.

"Tufa?" Cassie whispered in the darkness.

Immediately, Agatha's voice seared through.

If you want to see your father, listen to me.

Cassie's head swayed. She wanted to fall asleep and never wake up.

Why wouldn't Dad want to leave Blue? What's wrong with me?

"I'm sorry if I caused you problems, Agatha," Cassie said aloud. "Please don't leave me."

Instantly, the closet door opened with a bang as it hit the wall beside it.

"Look who you can count on when you're in need. I don't see anyone else offering to help your father, do you?" Agatha asked with her arms crossed as the glowing light in the corner of the room extinguished. "It feels so good to be rescued, doesn't it? You're so cute when you're upset. Now, go get your uniform, er, rather your dad's old sweatshirt, or his Land of Blue one if you prefer, and make sure the badge is affixed. Thankfully, your colors are right where they need to be in order to return," she said, tapping the Surveyor in her cloak. "FYI, without your friend. She doesn't fit in with our people. Let's not have anything interfere with getting to your father this time, shall we?" She clasped her hands under her chin.

Cassie pushed her covers back without a word. Holding Agatha's hand, she stepped carefully around the floating gray faces that had grown in number, got the Land of Blue sweatshirt out of her dresser drawer, and followed Agatha inside the closet.

Once she closed the door, in a tone never more determined, Agatha began her chant.

Darkness threatens those we love,
Hopes for this one yet remain
Choice and selection
Once an election
Now we enter Blue Domain

From her bedroom, Nana yelled, "That's it! My Singer machine is going back in that closet today!"

But Cassie was too tired to worry about Nana Helen and her clunky sewing machine as the Zipper thrust her forward. Besides, Agatha would take care of everything.

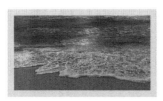

CHAPTER
TWENTY-EIGHT

Cassie ran through the Welcoming Gate into the Midst, like a person in jeopardy of missing an airline flight, while Agatha stopped to talk to newcomers on the lit-up Welcoming Road. Cassie didn't bother to look for Robin, or even to get a Bad or Blob. She ran straight for the Fix-It, until she collided with TJ standing outside the Cove, unaware of the presence of a sapphire piece of Wisdom Glass lying several inches from his high-top sneaker.

"Where ya going so fast? It's only been a few days and I missed you!" TJ leaned to one side of the tent in his Land of Blue sweatshirt, as he held up a forty-seven-fingered Bad. Sal and a group of boys waited for TJ inside the Cove while they played the latest Stimulator.

Cassie stopped short, aware of TJ's slicked-back hair and cool demeanor.

He's beginning to look like Sal.

"Come play a Stim with me! Hey, where's Mariana?"

"She's, well, Agatha wouldn't let her come with me because of the Vibration risk. And I can't play any Stimulators. I have to go see my dad."

"Maybe later?" TJ held up his mug in a toast gesture. "By the way, cool sweatshirt."

"Thanks. Yeah, sure," Cassie answered, checking out the group of unfamiliar faces in the Cove.

Sal strutted over and put his arm, bent like a boomerang, around TJ's neck. "C'mon. There's lots of other Potentials willing to play."

TJ, seeming uncertain at first, high-fived Sal as if he didn't want to disappoint him.

Agatha breathed heavily when she caught up to Cassie, Sal, and TJ. "I've got to keep this one on a leash! She's so excited to be here, I can barely keep up the older I get."

"This one doesn't need a leash," Sal said, digging his knuckle into TJ's head before TJ raced back under the tent to join the group of boys crowded around the latest Stimulator. "The boy's stayin'. He knows a good thing when he sees it. I'm good, huh Agatha?"

Agatha patted Sal on the head. "Yes, you're good." Then she whispered in his ear, "But it wasn't much of a challenge, now was it?"

Sal's face sunk like a little kid who shows up late to a birthday party.

"Can we go now?" Cassie asked her Entity, straining her neck around the corner of the Cove toward the road leading to the Fix-It.

"Yes, yes," Agatha said, winking at Sal. "I've got to get her to her father, Craig Connor, who should be ready after all this time."

"Ready for the Settling, you mean. I heard he . . . "

"We'll be on our way, Sal," Agatha interrupted, flicking her hand in the air. "Run along and enjoy yourself in the Cove. I'll see you this dusk at the meeting."

"Sure, Agatha, whatever you say." Sal lowered his head and scuffed back inside the Cove.

Cassie sprinted most of the way up the dimly lit road, passing a few stragglers on their way back to the Midst. Since no one waited in line on the walkway, she ran right to the main entrance and banged incessantly on the steel door. Nurse Moody finally opened the slat.

"Refills? Oh, it's you," she said, smacking and chewing her gum. "It's not visiting hours you know, don't you see there's no one else here? You're the only one who doesn't follow the rules."

"I need to see my dad," Cassie said breathlessly.

"Where's Agatha?" Nurse Moody snapped.

"Back there," Cassie said, barely looking back at her Entity, who hobbled up the road.

Nurse Moody closed one eye and spied down the hill. "All right. C'mon in."

Cassie bolted under Nurse Moody's arm, past the jar of pink Have to Haves across from the nurse's station, and down the long gray-and-white-tiled corridor, ignoring the howls of patients behind the closed doors. At the end of the corridor, where the nail for the clipboard hung empty on the wall outside her father's room, she halted. The door was slightly ajar.

Cassie took a deep breath and stepped forward, toward the open off-white door. Peeking around it, she saw the trash can filled halfway with Have to Haves, the unmade bed, and a man with brown hair sitting uncommunicative, alone in the hard chair. Except it wasn't her dad.

Robin.

His eyes glossy and unresponsive, Robin slouched in the chair, a strange look across his face, like he was frozen in time.

"Robin?" Cassie asked, in disbelief.

No answer.

"What happened to you?" Cassie asked, entering the room,

the bland bed cover wrapped around Robin's body.

"Oh, I forgot to tell ya," Nurse Moody said, barging through the doorway, "this is Robin's room now. Hiiiii Robin." Nurse Moody waved and tilted her head, speaking to Robin like he was a child. "You're doing great! You just needed a little more Have to Haves than usual to get you back in line. Isn't this much better? Now you're not in trouble anymore! Meanwhile, we've found a replacement for you, who's doing a great job with the new Potentials!" Nurse Moody picked up the trash, thought better of it, and put it back down on the floor with a thump.

"Where's my dad?" Cassie asked, standing beside Robin, who kept nodding off.

"They moved him since he's back to normal. Woohoo!" Nurse Moody said, pumping a fist in the air as she prepared to leave.

"So he's ready to go with me?" Cassie asked, standing before Nurse Moody in the doorway.

"Look at you, making it all about you," Nurse Moody shook her head in disgust. "You didn't even ask if his pain was gone."

Cassie's cheeks flushed. "I-is his pain gone?"

"For a pulse or two," Nurse Moody said, traipsing over to the loaded cart outside the room, where she filled a syringe with a pink solution.

"Then how is he all better?" Cassie asked, unable to take her eyes off the scary-looking syringe dripping pink droplets onto the floor.

"Because according to the system, he's 'better' and that's all you need to know." Nurse Moody set the syringe on top of the cart and rolled it over to a closed door in the corridor. "I'm sure Agatha will further explain. Stay put."

Bang. Carlos came in from the double exit doors on the right side of the corridor, carrying an empty metal trash bin. Placing it in the corner, he saluted Nurse Moody before she opened one of the rooms, ignoring him.

Cassie ran to him and whispered, "My dad isn't in his room. Do you know where he is? You were supposed to help."

"Oye chica, listen," Carlos said. He checked something off on a clipboard that hung beside the doors and faced Cassie.

"No, Carlos, I won't listen," Cassie said, her voice cracking as she stepped backward. "Did you hide his Have to Haves?"

Carlos scratched the top of his curly brown hair. "Chur papa, he asked for dem. I tried, but dey gave him what he wanted. After, well, dat's when he told the doc he wanted to stay on Blue. I real sorry, chica."

He left you. He left you for good.

Cassie clawed at her neck, making red marks on her pale skin.

She lifted her chin and said, "Take me to Dr. Fox's office. Where is it?"

Carlos rubbed his forehead and pointed down the corridor, in the direction of the smaller hallway, checking over his shoulder to be sure no one else heard him say, "It's over dere. But chu have to understand, chica, this isn't chur responsibilidad…"

But Cassie had already started back down the corridor, past her dad's old room, turning right into the adjacent hallway. She passed a few closed doors, crossed under the low-wattage light, until she got to the last door, open just a crack. A black-and-white sign hung next to the door that read, "Dr. Fox, Have to Haves Headquarters."

She spied through the opening with one eye as the doctor counted Have to Haves on a small bookcase next to his desk and spoke through a receiver to a person on the other end, whom Cassie couldn't hear. "Yayes, should be stocked 'til the next Feed. And about tha other thing—nice jawb leaving that pest behind. We don't need huh anymore. As fah as yuh Potential, lawd, don't fret, it's easiuh when they'a young to win 'em ovuh. Now that Craig came tuh his senses, she'll settle in no time. They ahways do. The powa of numbuhs. Keep grooming 'um, as good recruitas do." Dr.

Fox let out an evil-sounding laugh that reminded Cassie of Vincent Price in *Thriller*.

Feeling light-headed, Cassie held her breath as she backed away from the door. She turned and awkwardly headed down the hallway, past several closed doors, stopping outside her father's old room, where Robin now sat like a vegetable. Steadying herself against the wall, she slumped down to her knees, thoughts entangled in her mind like spider webs.

Dad isn't coming home. He wants to stay on Blue, without me. He must not love me as much as I love him.

"Agatha, why aren't you here yet?" Cassie cried out, her words echoing in the empty corridor. Hazily, as if in a dream, Carlos approached her with a concerned look on his face.

"Why isn't anyone helping me?" Cassie asked, staring at the tiles.

Carlos crouched down next to her and whispered, "I tried, chica. Chur a good kid and I wanted to help chu but my job is valuable here. I can't jeopardize . . . " Carlos drifted in and out of Cassie's sight, her helplessness rising inside her like a thermometer during a heatwave.

Mr. Papadopoulis wouldn't do that to Mariana. My dad doesn't love me like her dad loves her.

Suddenly her body felt lighter and lighter, as if someone had lifted her out of her sneakers. Cassie sensed she was no longer in the Fix-It. Darkness surrounded her, until a line of woods appeared next to a sidewalk with a street lamp on the corner. Children were playing, even though it looked like it was 10:00 at night, creating hiding spaces in the dark. They called to her when they felt her presence, asking her to join them in their hideouts. A sudden longing to go with them into the dark bushes surged through Cassie, when she heard Tufa's voice.

Cassie.

"Where am I?" she asked.

You have catapulted to the Portal of Fuchsia, Tufa's voice explained. *It is a place where children go during times of intense pain. I cannot vibrate on this plane, so you will only hear my voice. It is safe here. However, you must stay tethered in order to remain where you belong. Your suffering due to your father's decisions has not gone unnoticed by the Land of Bright Blue. Though you are fearful, we are with you, just as the sun is present even when it rains.*

The children gestured to her from the cozy hideaways they created in the woods.

If they're sad like me, maybe I should stay here too, Cassie thought somnolently.

Tufa's voice became faint as Cassie rose and floated up to the sky, higher and higher like a balloon that had been let go.

Stay tethered, child. For there is more work to be done.

As if a bucket of cold water had been dumped on her head, Cassie, by some silent force, sprung her eyes open. She found herself outside of her father's old room in the Fix-It, with Carlos and Agatha standing over her.

"Poor dear, you must have fainted from the news," Agatha said, wiping Cassie's forehead with her sleeve. "I'm sorry I wasn't here to help. I think I'm slowing down in my old age. Or perhaps I'm coming down with something."

"Agatha," Cassie said, rubbing her forehead, her thoughts slowly drifting away from the hiding place. "Why did you bring me back to Blue if you knew my dad didn't want to come home?"

"Dear, I . . . "

"I only wanted him to stop taking the Have to Haves for a while, and to go for walks to try and get better," Cassie said, her eyes on a white tile that held an insect plastered in its grout.

"Walks? For a backache? Who put that foolishness in your head? Let's get you a bed to lie down." Agatha scanned the main corridor for Nurse Moody, finally spotting her large rear end sticking out of a doorway.

310

"Did someone call?" Nurse Moody's voice echoed, wheeling her loaded cart out of one of the Cog's rooms.

Cassie squeezed her fists between her legs. "I don't want to lie down. I want to see my father."

"Of course you do, dear," Agatha said, patting her shoulder. "Phew. I feared you might ask me to take you home. Thank Duskiness, because if you went home, you'd likely lose connection with your father forever. That's not a future you'd like to see."

Cassie kept her head hung low, wondering if the insect in the grout ever had a chance.

If I did stay here with Dad, the only one I'd really miss at home is Mariana . . . well, maybe Mom and Nana a little.

Agatha's Surveyor glowed blue. "I'm now running late for the meeting in the Pr . . . . Regardless, your father has been moved to the Transition Room prior to his official release as a Permanent. There are no visitors allowed in the Transition Room. You might consider having a few Bads in the Midst with TJ while I attend my meeting. Robin won't be there to serve you, at least not until we decide his fate, but once your father is released, you'll be able to join him in the Land of Blue wherever and whenever you like."

"But you promised you'd help me bring him home," Cassie said, scrambling to stand, her stomach tied in knots. "I-I'm the only one who can save him, remember?"

Nurse Moody ordered Carlos to transport a load of empty containers to the outside dumpster as she wheeled by with her cart in the direction of Dr. Fox's office.

"Cassie, dear," Agatha said, pausing as she first looked over at the wall and then back at Cassie, "you did save him. Your father tried to fight the system and you helped him get back on track. He realized it wasn't worth the fight. Don't you also think it's time for you to give up the fight? How about the hook we already have in place for you at the Settling? It's not like you'll be missed at home." Agatha reached over and dispensed some hand sanitizer from the wall outside Robin's room, briskly rubbing her palms together before Nurse Moody called her over to speak with Dr. Fox in private.

Maybe I will stay in the Settling, like TJ, Cassie thought as Agatha sauntered quietly in her soft-soled shoes down the dim hall. She reviewed the possibilities in her mind. *If I could only get in the Transition Room. I promised Dad I'd save him. What do I do now? Tufa said there was more work to be done. But what else can I do?* Cassie clenched her fists and held them tightly to her forehead. *What more could I possibly, possibly do?*

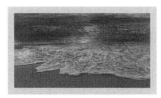

CHAPTER
TWENTY-NINE

Cassie scuffed down the Fix-It corridor alone, exited through the main entrance and trudged past the accumulating line of Permanents on the front walkway as visiting hours approached. The Vibration Meter at her back now glowed a midnight-blue color. She barely lifted her head as she proceeded down the walkway, but saw Carlos waddling down the back lane toward the dumpster, clutching a wrench in his hand.

Maybe if Carlos had helped, Dad would want to come home. Did all those Have to Haves change his mind and make him want to stay on Blue?

Kicking a few pebbles on her way back to the Midst, she wondered if Agatha and Dr. Fox were planning to get that hook in her back after their meeting, like the others she saw in the Midst when she wore the glasses.

Rounding the corner at the end of the road, Cassie found TJ inside the Cove, playing the Stimulator game that required players to throw objects at the nagging mother in order to advance to the next level.

Cassie gently pushed past two Permanents lounging in the aisle and stood beside TJ. "I need your help."

TJ shot a quick glance toward Cassie. "But I haven't finished the game," he whined.

"Please. I . . . " Cassie said, putting her thumbnail in her mouth.

"Okay," TJ said, reluctantly letting go of the controller and stepping away from the game to let someone else take over. "What do you need?"

"Go with me to the Settling," Cassie said, searching TJ's face for his reaction.

"Are you staying?" he asked, his eyes widening.

"I don't know. I guess I just want to see it one more time," Cassie said, squinting like she had a migraine as the flashing lights bounced off the walls.

"Okay, I'm in," TJ said, clapping his hands together as he led the way out of the Cove.

Cassie and TJ swiftly made it past inspection at the Settling platform, Cassie's color vibrating at the same midnight-blue color as the Land, and TJ's landing one below in the navy-blue range that matched the skin tone of the Mooshkoos.

Small high-fived them both after they were measured and opened his arm wide so they could continue on down to the Settling, the gesture reminding Cassie of Willie Wonka opening the gate to the Chocolate Factory.

Cassie stayed silent most of the way, sensitive to every squeak, creak, and rustle coming from the brush on either side of the rubbled road. Halfway there, she asked TJ, "Do you know what a Recruiter is?"

"I don't know what they do, but Eric told me there's a lot of them on Blue. He said he might want to be one someday too, now that he's not going to Give it Away." TJ rolled his eyes in relief. "That's what happened with Sal, you know, but he said it was worth the transformation."

"But do you know who any of the Recruiters are?" Cassie asked.

A scampering sound in the woods, like a creature in search of his burrow, reminded Cassie of the children hiding in the Portal of Fuchsia.

"No. I think it's top secret. Why?" TJ stumbled over a rock, swore, and tossed the softball-sized boulder into the woods.

"Just curious," Cassie said, stepping over a broken piece of tar. "So, my dad is staying here now. I need to get to him and try and talk him out of it."

"But why?" TJ said, throwing up his hands. "That'd be so great if you stayed here with him, we could hang out all the time. We're a lot alike, you and me, and it's kind of nice having a girl friend. I mean, not a girlfriend, a girl . . . friend. Er, you know what I mean."

"Yeah, I know what you mean," Cassie replied, tucking her hair behind her ear. "But my dad said it's not the place for me."

"Oh, Eric tried that one on me, too, but Sal totally overruled him. He wouldn't even let me go home to get my stuff, said he'd take care of everything. I guess I have to stay here now anyway, since Sal said my parents don't want me back." TJ kicked a rock and a few pebbles grouped together in the road.

"And you believed him when he said that?"

"Why wouldn't I? He's my Entity. Don't you believe everything Agatha tells you?" TJ looked at Cassie.

"I did," Cassie said, stuffing her hands in the pocket of her dad's sweatshirt. "It's just that there are two voices in my head these days. Sometimes I get confused by what I hear."

"I can't imagine having two Entities in my head," TJ said, the shadowy pine trees creaking as they leaned all the way left and then all the way right, like the scarecrow in *The Wizard of Oz.*

The glasses jingled in her pants pocket. Pulling them out and placing them on her face, Cassie didn't know what she needed to see since there was only TJ, herself, and the trees.

TJ tripped again, this time on a piece of broken concrete. He cursed, and stooped down to pick it up. "You could hurt yourself on these!" he said, whipping the jagged piece into the woods. That's when Cassie saw it. A tarnished gold-plated hook protruded out of TJ's upper back, like a baited fish.

TJ doesn't know the hook is there. Should I tell him?

"Hey, you look nice in those," TJ said, gesturing to the glasses. "At least you'll be able to see if there's any more obstacles in our way."

Cassie's stomach hurt as they continued on in silence, nearing the Settling. When they crossed through the gate, onto the dirt road before the sidewalk, no sign existed of Mickey or Eddie, the crow-like Entity.

Mrs. Costa stood on the porch of her dilapidated home, wiping her hands on her blue-and-white-checkered apron as she watched Anna and Michael playing a few doors down with other kids from the Settling under the dusky night sky.

I wonder if Benjamin ever sent the bees to Mrs. Costa? Cassie wondered, staring at Mrs. Costa's face from her spot on the mangled sidewalk. Mrs. Costa stood under a stained yellow porch light, and stared back. Suddenly Cassie felt something race inside her, a feeling she couldn't let go.

"Could you give me a minute?" Cassie asked TJ while she bit her pinky finger.

"Sure, I'll go to the Jacksons' and see what's for supper. I'll meet you back here in a pulse."

Cassie waited as TJ jogged down the long sidewalk, the hook in his back reflecting off the porch lights as he dodged the broken slabs of concrete. Wiping her clammy hands on her jeans, Cassie stepped over the cracks in the concrete, arriving at the bottom of

Mrs. Costa's porch stairs.

"Hi, I'm Cassie," she called up in the dusk.

Mrs. Costa picked at her mauve-painted fingernails. "I seen you here before, and in the Midst, too. You with them Bright workers? Everyone thinks you're one of 'em, you know."

"Huh? I'm not with anybody," Cassie replied, pulling at the collar of her sweatshirt. "Could I talk with you, in private, if that's okay?"

Mrs. Costa's next-door neighbor with the crazy hair pushed open her ripped, screened front door, and pointed a finger at Mrs. Costa. "You better be careful, Judy," she warned. Abruptly turning and going back inside her apartment, the same tarnished hook protruded from the woman's upper back.

Mrs. Costa closed her eyes as if she might reconsider and quickly opened them, swatting the air beside her head as if there were a flying bug. Sighing, she invited Cassie up to the porch.

Cassie lunged up the crumbling brick stairs, resembling chipped teeth, careful to step only on the odd-numbered ones.

Mrs. Costa wiped her hands on her apron, nervously looking left and right. "Come on in," she murmured. "Not for long, though."

Cassie followed Mrs. Costa inside the tidy but sparse apartment. Tan patches sewn onto a brown wraparound velour couch sat in the family room off the hallway, reminding Cassie of how her mother used to sew patches on their old couch.

"Tell me why you're here," Mrs. Costa said, as Cassie followed her into the earwax-yellow kitchen at the back of the triple-decker. She motioned to one of the four seats around the circular table for Cassie to sit. "Cause I could get in trouble."

A drawing Anna had made of her family, hung on the wall next to the fridge squeezed behind the kitchen table, caught Cassie's attention. Mr. Costa, drawn in dark blue marker, loomed larger than the rest of the family. Cassie pulled out one of the wooden chairs and sat down. When Mrs. Costa reached into the oak cupboard for two cups, Cassie saw a faded gold hook in her back, too.

"I'm here because my father is almost a Permanent," Cassie said. "I'm going to talk him into coming home, but I was wondering. Do you like being a Permanent? Do your kids like it?"

Mrs. Costa placed a rusted teakettle on a heated burner on the old, cream-colored stove. "It don't matter what I like or don't like anymore," she snickered, sitting down at the table. "Trust me, you won't get your dad to come home. Permanents never leave. Oh, it seems great in the beginning, but then . . . " Mrs. Costa's voice trailed off, a picture of her family engaged in a water-balloon fight on the refrigerator behind her. "Of course, they want you to see it that way, all the fun, that's how the Recruiters bait . . . " She stopped, as if she had caught herself saying too much and began wiping down the already-tidied table. "I have no idea why I'm yapping away like this." Mrs. Costa swatted beside her head again, like being pestered by a fly.

"I don't know any Recruiters," Cassie said, as the teakettle began whistling on the stove. "All I know is that my Entity told me the Have to Haves would help my dad so he could come home. But now he's going to stay here in the Settling."

Mrs. Costa rose to pour water into the two cups. "Helping the Blue's cause is what the Have to Haves do," she said, slapping her head of auburn hair. "It's like I got swarms of mosquitos around me! Driving me crazy! I can't even sit still these days." She returned to the table, sprinkled a little salt in the two cups, and placed one in front of Cassie, avoiding her gaze. "Sorry, I ain't got no Bad to spare, my husband'd fly off the handle if I did."

Cassie politely accepted the cup of salted hot water and then, as if a hurricane flew in from somewhere inside her, she blurted out, "There's another land right behind Blue, you know. I've seen it. I'm going to tell my dad about it before he's released into the Midst. Maybe that would change his mind."

Mrs. Costa slid into her seat. "You seen it, girl? Did you go through the Ripple? Or did you hear 'em call?"

"How do you know about the Ripple?" Cassie asked, gripping the eggshell-colored cup.

"That's what them Bright workers spoke about when they showed up all those pulses ago. They said there's three ways they tried to reach us on Blue. I'll show ya cause I kept the pamphlet they handed out." Mrs. Costa scampered like a field mouse over to a cabinet above the counter on the far wall. Reaching her hand all the way to the back, behind an array of canned goods, she lowered her voice and said over her shoulder, "Mr. Costa don't know about this."

Retrieving an old, crumpled piece of paper, she smoothed it out as best she could and handed the faded manila parchment to Cassie. It read:

> *The Land of Bright Blue is accessible in three ways:*
> *1. The Ripple you feel when you are quiet.*
> *2. The Whisper you hear that speaks of hope.*
> *3. The Glimmer you see that brings light.*
> *We will wait for you.*

Cassie stared at the paper.

The Glimmer. Bright Blue causes the Glimmer.

"I feel it sometimes, you know," Mrs. Costa said, sitting down and leaning forward with her hands clasped together on the table.

Cassie looked up. "You felt the Ripple?"

Mrs. Costa hesitated. "Uh huh. A couple times. I even thought about staying outside during a Glimmer once," she said, almost with pride, "just to see if it did stay brighter for longer. That's what them workers told me would happen if we stood up to the Dusk Ruler—that the Glimmer would end up brightening the whole dusky sky."

"Why didn't you fall through the Ripple when you felt it?" Cassie asked, biting her nail. "Or why didn't you stay outside during a Glimmer? Maybe then others would too!"

"Girl, don't you think them Bright workers sparked our interest when they came around?" Mrs. Costa got up and paced the small kitchen. "The Ruler got word. Threatened everything. All the papers were burned, 'cept this one. I stuffed it in my shoe, I was so scared. It's too risky! If my Vibration changes, like them Bright workers said it would, well, then everything changes!"

Mrs. Costa stopped at the refrigerator and gripped the black handle. "I could lose my family. My husband's in line to be a Recruiter—the status no one is supposed to know about—for the extra Lures. My job—all our jobs in the Settling, as the wives—is to keep our colors low. We need to do as we're told, so our husbands can earn more Lures, and so we do our part to keep order for the system. Besides, the Ruler created the Meter after them Bright workers were here, so it'd know if I ever thought anything stupid." She tapped the bottom of the refrigerator with her red-heeled shoe.

Cassie listened as Mrs. Costa continued talking, imagining she hadn't spoken this freely in a long time.

"It's not so hard to do as you're told," Mrs. Costa said, smiling shyly over at Cassie. "We earn more Lures that way. And my husband spends most of his time at the Pits, so he needs 'em. Anna misses her daddy, though. She's . . . too young to understand." The flesh under Mrs. Costa's eyes sagged, the veins visible, her skin reflecting a hard life.

"But you could take your children through the Ripple, and go on your own," Cassie suggested, resting her sneakers on the wooden bar of the chair.

"How can I afford to go on my own?" she asked, picking up her cup and a tarnished spoon, slowly rotating it in the center. "I ain't got no skills. Those Lures pay for our food. Look, I'm just trying to raise my kids and do the best I can. And I love my husband, despite where we ended up. I just always thought we'd do better than this."

"Do you love your husband more than you love yourself?"

Cassie asked, feeling the words come from somewhere else.

Mrs. Costa shooed away something invisible around her bobby-pinned hair. "There's no time for that." She beckoned for Cassie to follow her through the kitchen to a den. Two walls showcasing rows of gold-plated hooks were engraved with dozens of first names underneath each hook, just like the ones Cassie saw for her own family. "Generations of both our families have settled here. Hard to change that." Mrs. Costa folded her arms across her chest.

Two gold-plated hooks, engraved with only the letter "A" and the letter "M," hung under Mr. and Mrs. Costa's hooks.

"I don't want this for my children, but how can it be different? They're smart, them Recruiters. Permanents by Association always follow our tribe. That's how we end up here, living like this." Mrs. Costa sounded angry as she looked over at a child-size chair covered in patchwork. She immediately scratched her back, in the area of the hook.

"But don't you hope your children do better?" Cassie asked, turning away from the hooks to face Mrs. Costa.

"Hope?" Mrs. Costa asked, pulling up her nylons falling loose around her ankles. "Words like that don't work here. You're going to hurt us all by that way of thinking, girl. Any rise in Vibration shows in your colors. Remember that." She stopped, narrowing her eyes. "Girl," she whispered, "are you the one who raised the colors?"

"I-I don't know, I don't know how I could, I mean by myself, anyway," Cassie said, digging her sneaker into the orange shag rug.

"You better be careful," Mrs. Costa said, biting her pinky nail. "Look at Penny. That woman had a dream of some happy colorful place and simply tried to speak of it to the others and the Ruler assigned her the worst kind of Entity. Can't even go out her own front door."

"What does the Dusk Ruler look like?" Cassie asked, noticing the torn, manila shades in the window. "Have you ever seen him?"

Mrs. Costa self-consciously pulled up the shade, a tarnished wedding band on her ring finger. "No one's seen the Ruler, except the Recruiters when they go to them special meetings in the Praying Fields."

"The Praying Fields? Where are they?" Cassie asked, the open window revealing a section of woods outside where a carved-out path exposed a pack of Permanents drinking Escape and laughing loudly with their neighbors.

"Listen, you seem like a nice girl," Mrs. Costa said, ushering Cassie to the front door, "and I hope you can get ya Dad to go home, but you're gonna get me in trouble the more questions you keep askin'. They'll know. They always know! They're like predators." Mrs. Costa wrung her hands in front of a quilt hanging on the wall behind the door, containing the stitched words, "Home Sweet Home."

Cassie imagined Mrs. Costa stitching the quilt daily, trying to create a nice space for her family, just like her own mother did.

"I'll show ya one more thing," Mrs. Costa stepped over to a little wooden table against the wall. "Anna found this in the Midst," she brought out a brilliant piece of yellow Wisdom Glass hidden in the drawer.

The message read: "The Sun is always in the sky."

Cassie felt the hair on the back of her neck rise.

"She asked me what the Sun was," Mrs. Costa said, tears spilling down her cheeks. "How do I explain to my only daughter there's never any sun in the Land of Blue?"

But there could be, Cassie thought.

"Mrs. Costa," Cassie said after standing quietly for a moment. "Could you tell me where the Praying Fields are?"

Mrs. Costa blotted her eyes with a tissue she pulled out of her apron pocket and said, "It's across from the main gate in the Settling, just down the hidden path. It occupies the entire area behind the Midst."

As Cassie opened the screen door to leave, putting her glasses back in her pocket, Mrs. Costa whispered, "They say the Praying Fields is where it all begins."

CHAPTER
THIRTY

Cassie and TJ passed by the empty Settling playground, stepped off the mangled sidewalk, and approached the empty shack. She wondered if the rails of the partially exposed rusty gate, hidden behind the uneven brush, could cause tetanus even though she had had her shot. Gripping TJ's arm, she said, "Let's go."

TJ looked to his left, where a heap of bicycle tires and old mattresses lay piled behind the shack, and right, toward the uninteresting line of scrubby pines that went all the way back to the other side of the Settling. "Go where?" he asked.

"Behind that gate Mickey didn't want us to see. That's where the Recruiters hold their meetings," Cassie said quietly, not wanting to get Mrs. Costa in any trouble. Grabbing at the side of her hand she said, "It's called the Praying Fields."

TJ considered the hidden gate as the sound of blaring rap music started from behind the row of houses on Mrs. Costa's side of the Settling. Turning, he asked, "How do you know that?"

"Someone told me," Cassie said, quickly glancing over at the unoccupied shack. "Mickey's not here. Now's our chance."

Acting like they were tying their shoes when one of Mrs. Costa's neighbors came outside to sweep off her porch stairs, they tiptoed into the patch of woods as soon as the hunched woman with the long silver braid went back inside, agreeing to communicate through Mind Mail at the risk of being caught.

They felt along each rusty bar concealed under branches and pine needles until they found the latch. Opening the gate, they pushed through, over mounds of dead leaves, making sure they closed it tight. Brushing back thorny branches and ragged weeds, Cassie and TJ discovered a flat, windy, dirt path. Following the path around many twists and turns, they reached a clearing the size of a football field. In her mind, Cassie pictured the route they had taken, realizing Mrs. Costa had been right. The clearing spread behind the Midst, halfway between the Settling and the Fix-It.

A fire burned brightly, like a bonfire on a beach, in the center of the clearing. A group of shadowy bodies, difficult to identify in the dark, huddled around the flames, chanting like witches circled around a cauldron. Behind them, on the border of the clearing, the ominous stone wall stretched up toward the dusky blue sky.

What are they saying? TJ asked Cassie through Mind Mail, tugging on a branch to see through the brush. *It doesn't sound like they're praying.*

Cassie reached for her glasses.

"The Power of Numbers," the dark figures chanted, like a cult. Then, louder, "The Power of Numbers."

That's what Big said the first time at the Settling platform, remember? TJ asked, cracking his knuckles.

And what Dr. Fox said, Cassie thought, placing the glasses on the bridge of her nose.

It was then that she saw the black-and-white images above the fire, like scenes from old movies, of children tossing and turning at home in their beds. The images floated away like bubbles, and instantly grim, gray faces, as if they were covered in nylon masks, roared out of the flames in pursuit of the children, like sharks to minnows.

The fire blazed, the voices continuing to chant, "The Power of Numbers. The Power of Numbers."

Too stunned to speak, movement at the left end of the clearing caught Cassie's attention. A dark, wispy figure rose into the sky. When it reached a certain point in the dusky atmosphere, it disappeared, as if slipping into another dimension. Looking back toward the circle, Cassie identified Kurt's small frame, and his piranha-like teeth, sitting among the others. Dr. Fox knelt beside him, tall and square-shouldered, his eyes glowing as yellow as a snake's.

Cassie blinked several times before discovering Sal, unmistakable with his nose the shape of a hawk's beak, turning to speak to Kurt. Next to him, Agatha's back faced Cassie. She'd recognize that coarse red hair and broad, cloaked back anywhere.

Suddenly, the shadow of a very long and thick creature, like a giant crocodile, emerged from the right side of the clearing, its body the size of three torpedoes placed end to end. Stomping toward the fire, the enormous creature circled the group, the chanting growing louder and even ecstatic—as if this was the moment they'd all been waiting for. Cassie yelped, grabbing TJ by the arm.

What happened? You look like you saw a ghost, he said in his mind.

Cassie ripped the glasses off her face, handing them to TJ. *Here.*

But I don't need glasses.

Neither do I, she replied, as the shadows stood, clapping and cheering for the beast.

TJ awkwardly put the glasses on and pushed a branch out the

way. With his mouth open, he held the branch as floating faces shot forth from the fire, now simply shadows to Cassie, as she stood next to him on the hidden path.

"Those f-faces in the air," TJ stammered out loud. "I-I see those at night when I close my eyes. They've scared me since I was little."

"Me too," Cassie said, quietly.

TJ put both hands up to his face, holding the ends of the gold rims with his fingers. "Where are they going? The faces are floating in the air. And there's a line of Entities over there on a dock. They're evaporating in the air, too, like they're on a mission."

Cassie's stomach felt queasy. "They are. They're going to find children."

TJ turned to his left. "What do you mean?"

Cassie scraped her lip with her teeth and said, "Agatha told me the Entities leave that dock when the children call."

TJ looked back to see the black-and-white images of children floating skyward as the shadows sat back down and entered notes in their Surveyors, as if getting to work now that the lizard beast had arrived. "Those kids in their beds? They call out for Entities?"

"Sort of, without realizing it," Cassie said, biting her lip. "Just like we did."

TJ locked eyes with Cassie. The Entities and other figures in the clearing began a different chant.

Darkness threatens those we love,
Hopes for this one yet remain
Choice and selection
Once an election
Now we enter Blue Domain.

"That's what Sal says before we Zipper," TJ said, leveling his gaze through the gaps in the scrubby pines. "There he is! There's Sal, and Agatha too! I can see the backs of them. Are they praying for us? Is that why they call this the Praying Fields?"

Cassie gasped, putting her hand over her mouth. Slowly, she slid it down her chin. "You can also spell praying p-r-e-y-i-n-g."

TJ yanked the glasses off his face. "Are Sal and Agatha Recruiters?"

Cassie picked at her chin. "They must be; they're the ones who make the most Lures."

TJ handed the glasses to Cassie and crouched down, grabbing at the sides of his hair. "Have they been trying to keep us here? Do you think they ever meant to bring Eric and your dad home?"

Cassie swallowed. "I don't know. But we can't say a word of this to anyone until we figure out what to do. There's no one we can trust except each other."

TJ pushed the hair off his forehead. "Right, okay, what about Mariana?"

"She's on our side, but she can't come back. It's just you and me now. It's up to us to bring our families back from Blue. You do want to go back, right, TJ?"

TJ kicked at the dirt, releasing a cloud of dust. "I don't know. I mean, there's nothing there for me. And even if I did, how will we do that now? Sal wouldn't even take me back the last time to get my stuff."

Cassie put a thumbnail in her mouth. "I think I know who can help us, if we ask. There's somewhere I need to take you . . . if you want to go."

TJ steadied himself with one hand on the ground, rubbing the other one over his face.

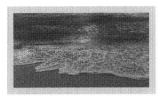

CHAPTER
THIRTY-ONE

A small hollow in the shrubbery lining the hidden path allowed Cassie and TJ a secluded place to prepare. Cassie sat cross-legged beside TJ and locked arms with him. Closing her eyes and waiting for but a moment, she sensed the Ripple.

It knew, she thought.

Cassie first felt the encouraging pull, and then the suction, as she and TJ slipped through the veil together. Floating through the rippling waves, she let go of TJ's arm so he could enjoy the weightless sensation. After a few moments, the sudsy clouds parted, revealing the Land of Bright Blue.

Landing softly in the open pasture, TJ's mouth dropped as he beheld the magnificent scene. The joyous children, in their colorful garb, ran directly to Cassie from the lush, green forest, chanting.

Darkness threatens those we love,
Hopes for this one yet remain
Choice and selection
One's own election
Welcome to Bright Blue Domain.

"Wow! Look at this place! It's so different than Blue, but they use the same chant," TJ exclaimed, scrambling to his feet. Droves of high-spirited children in red knickers and pressed, navy-blue shirts gathered around them at the tip of the pasture leading down into the meadows. The children showered Cassie and TJ with gifts of royal-blue dragonflies.

"The dragonflies help you run faster if you smooth their wings between your fingers," said Annelies, stepping forth from the group. This time she held the hand of a five-year-old boy with two front teeth missing. They began to walk toward the meadow, Cassie and TJ understanding that they were to follow.

Annelies and the boy led them through the waist-high grass, over to the pavered path, where dozens of elves tended fastidiously to their duties, like tidying work stations and transporting stacks of notes back and forth between several creatures, whistling while they worked.

They stopped first at Agnes's workstation, where she cheerfully transformed bowls of fruit into delicious smoothies, occasionally wiping her hands on pale-yellow towels. Handing one to TJ, she topped the tall, fruity drink with a straw.

"I've never seen someone look so happy when doing a job," TJ whispered to Cassie. Slurping the drink, he belted out, "This actually tastes good!"

"Feels not like a job at all, when one is fulfilling her purpose," Agnes said, winking at TJ.

Up ahead, a man's fast-talking voice called above the chatter, "Care to check your colors?" Cassie craned her neck as Simon gestured to them, his rainbow hair towering over the others.

Cassie and TJ thanked Agnes, passing a group of Elders she hadn't seen previously, with long white beards and white robes, hunched over a worktable in the meadow, engrossed in deep conversation. When they arrived at Simon's messy, paper-stacked station, he asked, "It's been quite a day, hasn't it?" observing Cassie while he rapped his quill pen on the table.

Cassie nodded, solemnly. "I'd like to check my colors, please."

TJ stayed back a few feet in the grass, holding both smoothies and staring with interest.

"Let's establish our set point!" Simon instructed, pointing for Cassie to stand next to the machine, papers flying into the meadow from the breeze of his hand. Simon reminded her of the hyper street performer hired by the Boys and Girls Club one summer who cranked out hundreds of balloon animals, encouraging Cassie to take one—*C'mon kid, have some guts*—when she was afraid some of the other kids might make fun of her.

Cassie took a deep breath, relaxing her shoulders while Simon fiddled with a few knobs on the clunky machine.

Dark colors instantly collided on the glass template as Cassie thought about the floating gray faces she had seen in her room all her life and how she had discovered that Agatha was a Recruiter. The murky colors on the machine looked like a mud puddle and dead leaves mixed together on a city street corner.

"Oof," TJ flinched.

"Look at that!" Cassie cried, opening her eyes and viewing the 3D screen. "My colors are terrible!"

"Be gentle with yourself!" Simon said, clearing the screen and tucking the pen behind his ear. "It's natural to display dark colors when one's been disappointed. Now!" he said, as Cassie straightened her spine, as if she were being measured for height at the doctor's office. "Focus on the word *opportunity* and see how it makes you feel!"

Cassie closed her eyes and visualized lemonade being made out of lemons, something Mrs. Papadopoulis said to her and Mariana once when it rained on their plans to have a lemonade stand. They ended up indoors, baking "healthy chocolate chip cookies," as Mrs. Papadopoulis called them, because they used applesauce instead of butter. She recalled how surprisingly delicious they tasted, just like Agnes's smoothies.

Cassie opened her eyes, the brownish colors on the screen giving way to a pale rainbow swirl.

"Nicely done!" Simon exclaimed, slapping his hand down on the metal workstation.

"That's so cool," TJ said under his breath, as a handful of elves pitter-pattered behind him in excited chatter—"It's going to happen! It's what we've worked for!"—and picked up a few strewn papers and placed them back on Simon's workstation on their way to the Palace.

"Now!" Simon said, clapping and rubbing his hands together as though warming them by a fire, "Let's take your Thought Vibration Education one step further. Tell me! What are the words you often think in your mind to describe yourself?"

Cassie touched a tall blade of grass. The word *nosy*, how her mother and Nana Helen described her, plopped into her mind like bird droppings on a windshield. Instantly, the pale colors on the glass formed into a dark gray funnel, like a fast-approaching tornado.

Cassie's shoulders drooped, like she had done something wrong. An elf, racing to keep up with the others on the way to the Palace, swiped their empty drinks off the workstation.

"Hmmm, *nosy*," Simon said loudly, tapping a long wizard-like finger to his chin. "What about considering its Elevated Companion: *curious*." Simon switched one of the knobs as Cassie held the word in her mind, and instantly the gray funnel transformed into a lavender hydrangea bloom.

Ripping out the blade of grass in excitement, Cassie whittled it between her fingers.

Simon sat back in his chair and crossed his legs. "Care to measure another thought?"

Cassie recalled all the times that Nana Helen and Grandpa Jack had termed her a nervous wreck, telling her she was destined for a heart attack by the time she reached thirty. Clenching her fists, Cassie said, "*Worried.*"

Examining the screen, she recoiled at the brownish-yellow, German-mustard color.

Simon stroked his chin. "Ah, *worried* implies such fragility." Raising a finger in the air, he said, "Try pondering *concerned for others!*"

Instantaneously, the German mustard morphed into a sunny splash of lemonade.

"I didn't even know we could have colors like that!" TJ said, never taking his eyes off the screen. "Every color on the Energy Vibration Meter looks pretty dull."

At the flick of Simon's wrist, the colors on the screen dissipated. "The colors under the black line *are* dull, my boy," he said.

"You know about the Meter?" TJ asked.

"Of course!" Simon answered, adjusting his swivel chair to face them. "The colors above the black line are where the Vibration of Bright Blue begins."

TJ and Cassie glanced at each other.

"Does Blue know that?" TJ asked.

"Certainly!" Simon replied with an edge, swiveling back to enter data with a few keystrokes in the machine. "They don't want you to know what's on the other side of that black line, for fear of curiosity. That would spoil everything! How are you feeling now, Cassie?"

"I don't know," Cassie said, envisioning the space above the black line on the Meter. Her insides raced, like a roller coaster barreling through her body. Then, as suddenly as it started, it stopped.

Simon observed Cassie's confused expression. "Ah, your face says it all. Been there myself!" he said. "A power surge occurs whenever there is a rise in one's knowledge! Step aside and take a moment. It's time for lesson three of your Thought Vibration Education! Would you like a try, boy?"

TJ shrugged and changed places with Cassie. He hadn't even stood for a moment beside the screen when a goopy, black, tar color dripped onto the screen.

"Ah, yes," Simon muttered to himself as he rebuttoned the bottom of his crisp white lab coat. Slapping the workstation, papers falling off the side, he said, "If you think consistently in terms of *failure*, this is the color your Vibration will emit, which is poison, my boy! Yet, if you think in terms of success . . . Go on! Feel the change as you concentrate on the word *success*! Visualize what it would feel like to achieve a goal!"

TJ's face grew intense, like he was trying to figure out how to reach the next level of a video game.

Simon's rainbow hair whipped in the air while the screen took a moment and then burst into a rich, purple eggplant. "Well then! You've successfully learned the concept of how to catapult yourself into the realm of achievement!"

"Woah!" TJ cried. "I feel kinda different, too. Like, good. Wait, is that because of me or you?"

Simon chuckled. "That was all your energy, dear boy, and the positive effect of Thought Vibration Education! I simply measure the data."

Cassie listened to the hum of a creature working in the meadow. "I wish I could teach my Dad this, but I think he's given up hope. Is there a way to change my father's color Vibration from here?"

The Elders, who had been brainstorming at the table, strolled along the pavers behind Cassie and TJ, pens and papers in their aged hands as they spoke thoughtfully to one another, in brief sentences, in the direction of the Palace.

Simon rested an elbow on his slightly exposed knee and said, "When a man gives up hope, that is the darkest color Vibration of all. Unfortunately, we cannot change people's Vibrations without their permission."

TJ tugged on a buttercup flower and handed it to Cassie. "Maybe your father will come here and learn how to do it for himself. Maybe we could bring Eric here too. He always said stuff at home like he was ugly and stupid in school. I bet if I told him about this place, he'd learn how to talk nicer to himself and maybe then he wouldn't want to live in the Settling. Wait, do you guys have Stimulators?"

Sounds of delight erupted from the turquoise pools on the other side of the meadow as children splashed and swam alongside radiant, racing fish. A freckled boy waved to TJ, inviting him to join the fun.

TJ waved back to the red-haired elementary school kid, whispering to Cassie, "This is the happiest place I've ever seen in my life. I hope I'm not dreaming."

"Go on! Enjoy yourself!" Simon said, scampering forward in his chair, knocking over his drink on the table. "You deserve to be a kid and have fun."

TJ stopped, wanting to tell Simon that no one had ever said that to him before, but just as he turned to speak, Simon and his entire workstation had disappeared.

"Woah!" TJ said, spinning around. "Where did he go?"

"His work is done for the moment," Tufa said, suddenly appearing behind them in the meadow, golden light radiating from her head and shoulders. "How brave of you, TJ, to trust your friend and venture to the other side."

TJ nudged Cassie on the arm and silently he ran, flinging off his sweatshirt and T-shirt and joining the boys in the pool.

Cassie took out the glasses, putting them on to see the gold-plated hook jutting out from TJ's back as he dove into the pool.

"He doesn't know about the hook. I don't have one, do I?" she asked Tufa, trying to look behind her.

Tufa touched the petal of the buttercup Cassie held in her hand while the other creatures continued working behind them. "A hook is only secured when one succumbs to the Blue way of life. At present, there is no hook in your field."

Cassie relaxed her shoulders, carefully putting the glasses back in her pocket, hearing the high-pitched squeaks of the eagles flying overhead. "We saw the Preying Fields. Agatha and Sal were there. That means they're Recruiters. What exactly does a Recruiter do?"

Tufa clasped both hands behind her back and tapped the ground with her feet, causing a small, stone labyrinth to appear. Entering the opening, she waited for Cassie to accompany her. "A Recruiter's job is to seek out vulnerable children in order to multiply their inhabitants on Blue. Recruiters also work to keep higher Vibrations out of the Land, in order to maintain a low level of consciousness. When children have no one to show them a different way, it is easy for Recruiters to add to the many generations of hooks in the Settling."

Cassie heard the scurries of elves going back and forth between the meadow and the Palace, working on something important, as she rounded the meticulously laid stones. "Is that why Agatha wouldn't let Mariana come with me this time? Because Mariana is different than TJ and me?"

"Your friend is different in that her base Vibration rests above the black line. She is a strong girl and has a loving, supportive family foundation. But having a strong family is not the only way to display bright colors in one's field," Tufa explained, as TJ slapped a large ball around the pool with the other kids. "You are a strong girl, also."

Cassie shook her head. "I'm not strong. That's why I like Mariana with me."

"Perhaps being without your friend during this part of your

journey will help you prove to yourself you are stronger than you think. You simply have yet to align with your true essence. Your election to come here, and learn a different way of thinking, naturally raises your Vibration. Whenever one spends time on Bright Blue, their colors automatically brighten."

Cassie shielded her eyes from the Sun's rays. "But what about the voices? Even though I know Agatha's a Recruiter now, I'm still confused. How do I get my father home if I don't listen to what she has to say?"

"The decision to leave the Land of Blue . . . is your father's," Tufa said, waving her hand over a stone birdbath a foot away, instantly filling it with water. "Just like living in the Settling is really up to you and to TJ. This is what Agatha would not have you know."

Cassie felt water droplets on her arm as a yellow bird swooped down, fluttering its wings in the cool, clear water. "But what if that's the only way to be with my dad?"

Tufa raised an eyebrow. "Is that your perception? Because if it is, be careful, for your perception becomes your reality."

Cassie listened to the merry chatter of the elves helping the other creatures at their workstations finish up, jotting notes on pieces of paper, and entering data into their shoe-boxed-sized machines. Reaching the halfway point in the labyrinth, she heard TJ burst out laughing when a waterfall cascaded onto his head in the oasis-styled pool.

I'm never one of those kids who has fun like that, she thought, her face expressionless.

After a moment, she asked Tufa, "The Bright workers that Mrs. Costa talked about, they're the creatures here, like Simon and Benjamin, and the elves, aren't they? You sent them a long time ago to help the people in the Settling."

The several creatures remaining in the meadow wiped their brows, beginning to line up at Agnes' station, while she hummed, handing out drink after fruity drink. Tufa signaled to a roly-poly elf in wooden clogs assisting Agnes at the front of the line. He brought over another healthy, berry-filled drink for Cassie in the middle of the labyrinth.

"Yes, these are some of our Bright workers who visited the Settling," Tufa replied.

The curly-nosed elf bowed before rejoining the others.

"The Sun sent our creatures long ago to deliver a message of freedom and election. It is different there now. The Ruler constructed the Meter to instill fear in its occupants for even considering our call. We have devoted our entire existence to letting them know we are here to help, but we will never use force. Our tool is the Power of Election. The Land of Blue robs its inhabitants of that power, tricking them into thinking there is no other option, and no other way to live."

"Election," Cassie said, spinning the buttercup in one hand and holding the drink with the other. "That's in the chant Agatha uses to Zipper. And the one you use here. Why do you both have the same chant?"

Tufa snapped a flower bud off a black-eyed susan, tucking it behind Cassie's ear. "Is it?"

Cassie tilted her head. "It sounds the same to me. Anyway, my dad thinks he belongs on Blue. I have to figure out how to save him."

"I understand your desire to save your father," Tufa said, as the sun cast strands of pink in the late afternoon sky, "but perhaps you might consider there may be something even more important for you to do."

Cassie let the buttercup she had been holding fall between the stones. "What could be more important than getting my dad home?"

"The Land of Bright Blue gives each of us tasks to carry out for the betterment of all. Consider Agnes, who creates wonderful food and drink for others to enjoy, and Simon, whose love of language and passion for education inspires others to new heights, and all the other creatures here, happily tending to their assigned duties in order to serve. That is the purpose of the unique gifts we are given when we are born."

Cassie rounded three quarters of the way around the stones as Agnes put a hand on her hip, tossed a hand towel over her shoulder, and raised a glass of fruit smoothie to Tufa once the last creature had been served.

"Do I have gifts?" Cassie asked, catching her balance as she stayed within the stones at the end of the design.

Tufa laughed. "Everyone comes into the atmosphere with gifts. It is up to a person, however, to discover those gifts and how they may be shared."

A whistle sounded, interrupting their conversation. At the edge of the meadow, Benjamin stood on a white chair, whistling and waving frantically to Cassie and Tufa. As they came upon the exit in the stones, they traipsed through the grass to Benjamin's station. Jumping down from his chair with a thud, he hurried to meet them in the grass. "Tell me," he asked, "how is Mrs. Costa? Has she sensed the bees? Dialogue has begun, yes?" He glanced down behind the Palace as if he was adhering to a schedule.

Cassie's lips slowly parted. "It was you. That's why she spoke to me. Thank you, Benjamin. She asked me to put in a good word for her and her children."

Benjamin raised a stubby arm in the air, his green velvet blazer coming just short of his wrist. "Yes, yes, the bees have done it again!" He leaned over. "I tried to go easy on her, just enough to get her out of the Vibration of *complacency* and into the higher frequency of *opportunity*."

Cassie looked left toward the bustling Palace and down at the soft, grassy meadow that felt like long, feathery eyelashes against her skin. "I wish Mrs. Costa could see it here."

At Tufa's request, two elves in blue-and-yellow suspenders and green velvet knickers pitter-pattered over to the pool carrying mounds of fluffy white towels for the children to dry off. "Mrs.

Costa is welcome any time to go beyond the Ripple. Bright Blue's mission is for everyone in the universe to see what we see, every moment of the day."

Benjamin rose up on his toes. "We have a better chance of that occurring now that she has begun having a dialogue with the other inhabitants."

Tufa softly pressed her finger on Cassie's forehead. "Since Bright workers are no longer allowed on the Land of Blue, it will take a new way to reach the others, and a very strong Vibration of courage. Someday soon, we hope to achieve our mission."

A glow instantly warmed Cassie's entire being, a feeling similar to staying under the covers on a cold wintery morning.

Tufa exchanged glances with Benjamin as an assembly line of diminutive creatures, carrying treasure chests full of brilliant Wisdom Glass, began marching in succession down the Palace steps toward the pasture.

Cassie stood mesmerized by the shining pieces while the children, obeying the elves, dried off beside the pool. "I saw Wisdom Glass in the Midst," Cassie said. "But strangely, I don't think anyone else did."

Benjamin chuckled, shaking his square-shaped head. "Not everyone is ready for wisdom, even when it stares them in the face."

Just then, something behind the Palace captured Cassie's attention: the silhouette of a woman with a blunt haircut wandering alone in the field of daisies.

"Mom?" Cassie whispered as she stepped closer on the pavers.

Tufa laid a gentle hand on Cassie's shoulder. "Your mother cannot hear you. Only the essence of her is here."

Cassie chewed the inside of her mouth. "But what is she looking for? She looks lost."

"She is lost because she is searching for something outside of herself," Tufa said softly, "to escape the pain since your father left."

Cassie touched the flower in her ear as her mother's silhouette

THE LAND OF BLUE

meandered in the field. "But aren't those meetings at church helping? She's out every night, even when she doesn't have to work."

"The meetings may help," Tufa explained, "however, some people replace one preoccupation with another in order to distract themselves from the true work that needs to be done. Though it may appear someone is behaving differently, energetically it's quite the same. Going outside to escape the pain still vibrates from a place of dependence."

Benjamin briskly stroked his chin. "Well said. True transformation in a person comes not from pain avoidance, but from consciously embracing pain."

"Huh?" Cassie asked.

Benjamin scratched his forehead. "You don't get an 'A' in academics without the necessary rigors of nightly homework, right?"

"Well, no, I guess not," Cassie said.

"It's the same theory! Now then, shall we call in the energy of the bees?"

Cassie clutched her hands together. "Can we send the bees to my dad, too?"

Tufa raised a palm to Benjamin as Ann Marie Connor's shadowy silhouette faded in the distance. "Not yet," Tufa cautioned. "Remember, one must desire change for change to occur. Otherwise, you are employing the same forced weaponry as Blue."

Benjamin folded his hands over his round belly. "Hmmm, true."

Cassie thought about that. She couldn't force her dad to come home. Just like Carlos said, a person needs to figure it out for themselves.

Carlos!

Cassie had to tell him she wasn't mad at him anymore. It wasn't his fault. She knew that now. Dad didn't know there were other options.

I'll be the one to tell him! she thought.

A rumbling sound erupted at the foot of the rolling fields

behind the Land of Bright Blue, sounding like a storm nearing, even though the Sun shone like the dome on the Massachusetts State House.

Tufa raised her chin. "It is time for you to return. As I said to you on separate occasion, there is more work to be done."

TJ, touching the wings of a red-netted dragonfly, raced the children to the pavers, towels clutched around them. His teeth straight and white, he smiled wide, reaching the stones first. Cassie wondered, as he high-fived the others, if TJ looked like that as a little boy. Free. Happy.

Have I ever felt that way? she asked herself. Her throat burned.

"That was a blast!" TJ said, pushing back his damp hair. He pulled his T-shirt and sweatshirt back over his head, his pants drying instantly in the heat of the sun. "I bet my colors are really bright now!"

Cassie pinched her hand. "If my colors get brighter when I come here, how will I get back through the Meter?"

Tufa tousled one of the children's hair. "It is true, both your colors are brighter. Wearing a Bubble, though, will aid your return."

TJ snickered as he scuffed the ground with his sneaker. "A bubble? Aren't bubbles for little kids?"

The children laughed.

"Bubbles are for everyone, TJ," Tufa smiled. "And this type of Bubble is special."

Cassie and TJ moved close to each other.

"Simply imagine your favorite color surrounding you in a Bubble, for protection upon entering a negatively charged environment. Like this," Tufa raised her finger like a wand and pointed it at Cassie and TJ. A shell instantly appeared around them, just like a clear bubble. Cassie felt safe, as though she were inside an egg. "Now you may create your colors," Tufa said.

TJ and Cassie closed their eyes in intense concentration. Cassie visualized an aquamarine space, with a little flap for her face to peek out. TJ visualized Kansas City Chiefs' red.

"Well done," Tufa said, her hands on her hips. "These Bubbles will keep your new and brighter Vibrations intact. To pass through the Meters on Blue, simply use your new knowledge of Thought Vibration Education to lower your Vibration."

"Wow," TJ said, "it's crazy we can do that."

The rumbling sound grew in the distance.

"It is time to apply what you have learned." Tufa signaled and the strong, white horse appeared in the meadows, trotting over to Tufa, Cassie, and TJ. The few Bright workers that had been sweeping the pavers to end the day's work disappeared one by one. The children waved and then evaporated once they retreated inside the enchanted forest.

As the pink-orange ball of sun descended behind the trees, Cassie and TJ climbed on the horse's sturdy back, TJ first, with Cassie behind him.

Tufa patted the white horse. "Though no one can see your Bubbles, trust that they are there. A Bubble only ceases to be when you allow fear to invade your personal space. Do not be afraid. Return now, and move through the Meter with ease. "

Tufa waved her hand around Cassie and TJ, as if she sprinkled confetti.

"Is there a reason to be afraid?" Cassie asked, holding a little tighter to TJ's waist. But before she received an answer, Tufa vanished.

The horse kicked its heels and trotted toward the pasture.

TJ glanced back at Cassie and said, "My Bubble must be working, because I don't feel afraid." He added, "You can hold on tight to me. I would never have come here if it weren't for you. Thanks."

Cassie cheeks flushed as the horse began to gallop, faster and faster, the flower Tufa gave her falling from behind her ear, until they lifted off the ground and flew across the serene azure sky.

CHAPTER
THIRTY-TWO

The Preying Fields were empty when Cassie and TJ found themselves back in the scrub pines, the ground covered with pine needles, on the path just beyond the hidden gate.

"We better get to the Midst," TJ said, rising and brushing off his pants. "I bet Agatha and Sal are looking for us."

Cassie scrambled to her feet, and they quietly followed the winding path back to the entrance, their Bubbles, invisible to others, bouncing off each other like astronaut suits.

TJ's mouth dropped as he looked down and around himself. "They really are there! Man, these would make great gut wars with Eric. I can totally picture us smashing stomachs to see who's left standing. If I could only tell him."

Cassie dodged branches jutting out on the path. "We have to

keep this between us, at least until we talk Eric and my father into getting out of this place."

Once they spied the rust-covered gate, they crouched down and low-crawled the rest of the way. Wearing a black T-shirt that had a picture of a frosty mug of Escape across the front and his faded jeans, Mickey whistled inside the shack across the dirt road while Eddie squawked atop his broad shoulder.

"Let's wait here," Cassie whispered. "Something tells me he'll get called away. Then we can weave through the woods and come in through the regular way, because I have to see Mrs. Costa one more time."

"Okay," TJ said. "I'm following you from now on."

Loud, rowdy voices shouted from the direction of the Settling gate as music blared from porches. A moment later, a flock of Permanents kicked the wooden gate open and stampeded through, dangling flasks of Escape in front of Mickey's face as he whistled from the threshold of the shack. One of the Permanents, wearing a pair of overalls, waved the flask under Mickey's nose so he could smell it. "You in?"

Mickey glanced around cautiously to see if anyone in authority was watching. Then with a wink he said, "You bet. Breakin' for a few won't hurt anybody. It's not like we ain't done it before."

Eddie flapped his wings in excitement and swilled from the flask of an older, gray-haired Permanent.

"Eddie taught me to never say, 'No'," Mickey said, with a salute from the tip of his nose. Accepting a swig from the same flask, he started to walk away with the group, then stopped to consider the half-open gate. With a wave of his hand, he said, "Heck, people can let themselves in."

TJ and Cassie waited until Mickey and Eddie were halfway down the sidewalk with the Permanents, then they zig-zagged through the thorny brush beside the gate. Cassie prayed silently that the branches wouldn't pop their Bubbles. Finally, they reached the border of the woods lining the Settling road and turned to go through the wooden entrance as though they were arriving for the first time.

Entering through the open gate, Cassie saw Mrs. Costa standing on one side of her porch, speaking with a neighbor who had tattoos all over her arms and neck. The neighbor leaned out of the bottom window of the apartment building next door. Several children played in the brown, sunless patches of dirt next to the sidewalk while the older kids monopolized the bumpy see-saw in the dark playground, preventing the younger kids from playing.

Mrs. Costa ended her conversation with her neighbor, saying she had to go lie down due to a headache, as Cassie and TJ approached her apartment block.

"That's some truck," TJ commented to Michael, as he played with a miniature toy car out front with a toothless friend, when he and Cassie passed by them.

Anna rose from the section of dirt where she played with half-dressed doll figures, her wavy hair covering most of her face as she whispered up to the porch, "Mommy, she's here." Cassie smiled at the little girl, who moved closer to her brother and the younger boy.

Mrs. Costa rearranged two empty flowerpots on the porch. "Yes. The girl filled with hope is back."

"May I come up?" Cassie asked at the foot of the stairs. TJ knelt beside the kids and asked to join their game. They happily agreed.

Mrs. Costa fiddled with her small hoop earring and said softly, as if she was trying to figure something out, "The strangest thing happened after you came to see me. I thought about painting again. I used to paint pictures when I was a girl."

Cassie lunged over each odd step to join Mrs. Costa on the porch. "But that's a good thing, right?"

Mrs. Costa wrung her hands. "Something's happening," she said, her voice trembling. "The Ripple, it calls to me, more than I said. But I can't. I just can't."

Cassie looked down at TJ, who pleaded to Mrs. Costa over the music, "But you have to go. Cassie showed me, she brought me through. Others have to see it."

Cassie followed Mrs. Costa to the side of the porch, sensing a neighbor peeking out at them through a curtain. "I know you're scared, but . . ." Ideas flowed through her head like water in a creek. "Maybe you could talk to your neighbors. Maybe they'll want to go too, and you could all help each other."

Mrs. Costa lightly banged her fist on the top of the porch rail. "I don't know what's gotten into me, lately. I was just fine before you showed up."

Cassie heard a loud hiccup and an ear-splitting squawk. Mickey staggered back along the broken sidewalk with Eddie perched atop his shoulder, talking with tenants on the sidewalk listening to loud, competing genres of music.

Mrs. Costa wiped her hands on the apron tied around her waist. "You better go now. The last time I went through the Settling Meter I went up a color notch. And Anna went up two, just from hearing me talk about painting. She encouraged me to hang them up in the house." She shook her head like someone coming to after losing consciousness. "But you don't understand. If our individual colors are rising, that causes the Vibration in the whole Land to rise. Our thoughts affect everyone else. I can't risk it. You don't know what my husband, let alone the Ruler, would do if he knew I had ideas in my head. Now go."

Cassie felt sorry for the flowerpots as she trudged down over the odd-numbered steps, checking on Mickey, who was now dancing with tenants at the far end of the block.

Mrs. Costa gestured for Anna and Michael to come inside for supper and sent the other boy home.

Anna looked back curiously at Cassie with her deep, green eyes as Mrs. Costa ushered them inside the apartment.

Anna wants me to help her mother and her family. But what else can I do?

Just then, a bleach-blond neighbor with scarlet-red lipstick stuck her head out of the second-floor window next door. "Psst," she called to Cassie and TJ as they started down the sidewalk. "My name's Norma. I-I might be interested in what you two have to say. I hear the whispers, though the others tell me it's my imagination. Maybe I can talk to Judy. I'd like to think there's something more for me, and my kids too, and for all of us in the Settling."

The window below in the first-floor apartment smacked open and the tattooed neighbor stuck her neck out.

"Don't go stirring up trouble, you two," the woman warned Cassie and TJ. Pointing her scrawny finger, heavy metal earrings swung furiously from her earlobes. "I hear you tawking to Judy Costa, givin' her false hope about some other place. The Recruiters will be on to you before ya know it, and they'll blame us."

Norma wore a sorry expression on her face before slowly pulling the shade.

"They gotta get their heads out of the clouds, cause this is the only life we'll ever know." With that, the tattooed woman slammed her window for the night.

Cassie and TJ didn't say a word to each other as they left the Settling, their heads hung low. When they reached the platform, they passed through the Meter with ease, thanks to the protection of their Bubbles. Cassie thought about making Grandpa's lunch, her Vibration landing on the Meter's fifth rung from the bottom, on the hue of a bruise. TJ pictured his parents working another long night at the store while he sat home alone watching hours and hours of television, his color Vibration landing four from the bottom in the range of steel.

Crossing onto the nicely paved Welcoming road, a bottleneck occurred where it merged with the Midst, since a stream of Potentials had just disembarked from *The Enticer.* Cassie searched over the heads of creatures and Potentials to find Agatha, who was typically at the Welcoming Gate greeting new guests, but she was nowhere to be found. Cassie and TJ moved with the crowd, the Energy Vibration Meter for the Land pointing its arrow to the black-and-blue, bruise-color notch, fifth from the bottom.

Once they entered the Midst, TJ pushed his way with Cassie to the racetrack, gripping the top of the chain link fence as the neon lights zoomed around the track. Tapping the bottom of the fence with his foot, TJ asked Cassie, "Do you think there's someone for me on Bright Blue? Like you have Tufa?"

Cassie watched a boy even younger than TJ at the wheel of a yellow racecar, his father egging him on outside the striped door. Waiting a moment she replied, "I don't know."

TJ paused and turned toward the pier to look for Sal. "If there was, that'd be cool." Lazily kicking a balloon that had floated near his feet, he said, "You'd think our Entities, if they cared, would be looking for us by now."

Cassie shrugged as Big and Small escorted new Potentials through the Welcoming Gate. "Maybe it's like what Captain BP told us—once they know we're loyal, we're free to do what we want."

They left the noisy track, shuffled shoulder-to-shoulder amid the crowd of creatures congregating outside the Pits and the Zebbies, and past Captain BP, who waved theatrically to Cassie and TJ in the crowd, like the main headline at a venue, as he distributed Blobs to a group of new Potentials in an alleyway. Rock music blared through the street, bothering Cassie's ears. On the other side of the street, Cassie caught sight of the new Working for Permanency who replaced Robin, his chin bobbing up and down as he awkwardly tried to gain balance atop the unicycle.

What happened to Robin?

TJ stopped in front of a bearded vendor in a pirate's bandana, just past Robin's station, and contemplated ordering a Bad while Cassie checked out Robin's burly, blond-haired replacement fall off the unicycle time after time. Suddenly, several Permanents in line for Bad began to murmur and point toward the Meter by the Welcoming Gate.

"What's going on?" a woman with a CARPE DIEM tattoo asked her bare-chested companion.

"The arrow's never landed there," said another woman in high-top basketball sneakers.

"If we need to know something, we'll find out from Big," said a guy wearing cargo shorts, his eyelids half-closed. "C'mon let's head to Zebbies before its standing room only."

Cassie turned toward the Welcoming Road. The arrow had risen to the range of midnight blue, only six colors below the black line.

Unaware, TJ tied his shoe in the Bad line. "Maybe you're right, maybe Agatha and Sal aren't trying to find us, because we gave them no reason to doubt us. We've done everything they told us to."

"Until now," Cassie said, grabbing TJ's hand. "I have to see my dad in the Transition Room now that we know the Meter is rising."

"Huh?" TJ asked, rising to see the Meter for himself as Cassie dragged him through the Midst.

"Besides," she said as they passed a group of teenagers who called TJ's name from the Cove, "it just might keep you out of trouble."

They rounded the corner to exit the Midst, strode past Strays, and down the flat road that would bring them to the Fix-It. When they passed the small road on their right leading to the dock in the Preying Fields, they did so without a word.

Approaching the Fix-It, TJ shielded his eyes from the glare of the artificial lights, where a long line of Permanents and Permanents by Association argued about who needed their Have to Haves first. The Meter, looming above their heads in the patch of brown dirt outside the entrance, measured slightly above midnight blue now, in the color range of hospital scrubs.

It's already risen? Cassie fretted from the end of the walkway near the courtyard. *Was Mrs. Costa right? It can't be me. I'm not that powerful.*

Carlos waddled across the courtyard, carrying a rake, as Cassie ran to the fence, grasping the chain links.

"Chur back," Carlos said coolly, raking dozens of littered Escape bottles thrown over from the Permanents waiting in line.

"Carlos," Cassie said breathlessly, pressing her face against the metal circles. "I know you tried to help my dad. I hope you didn't get in trouble because of me. I just thought if you hid his Have to Haves, maybe he'd change his mind and want to come home. I'm sorry."

Carlos strode over to the fence, his voice low. "I going to try to get chu in the Transition Room after my duties, but chugot to truss me, okay chica?"

Cassie swallowed hard. "Okay. One more thing. Agatha isn't what I thought she was."

Carlos held the rake in one hand and said, "Oye, listen to me. Agatha's gonna be giving chu lots of freedom now, it's a way to lu—"

"Hey, this place is even louder than the Midst," TJ interrupted, banging his foot against the fence as he caught up with Cassie, creating a clinking sound barely heard above the crowd of people screaming for their Have to Haves. "This is where your dad is?" he asked, cringing at the sight of the creepy brick building.

"Yeah," Cassie said, biting her lip. "He stayed here so he could get better. Well, that's what they said."

"Chu Sal's Potential?" Carlos asked, with a jerk of his chin. "I seen chu in the Cove one time when Sal n I shared some Escape."

TJ eyed Carlos suspiciously. "I remember you. You and Sal talked about how you Gave It Away. You said it was worth the transformation, too."

"Sí, dat's correcto. And it was," Carlos said, raking another section of litter and dropping it into a new trash bag, two bags beside it already full.

Cassie examined Carlos from the top of his thick brown hair down to his beige work pants covering his troll-shaped body and black-soled shoes.

"It must be confusing to be half-Entity and half . . . er, normal," TJ said.

"Yo se who I am," Carlos answered, adding more trash to the bag.

TJ lightly elbowed Cassie as the shouts on the walkway intensified. "At least he's upbeat about it."

Carlos chuckled, hoisting the full bag of trash over his stocky body. "No, I wasn't always this upbeat. No, no señor. It's a skill I lerned many pulses ago. Here, grab a bag."

Carlos opened the gate with one of the keys on his belt hook. "Chur just on time to help me load the dumpster. We got so many Cogs coming off *The Enticer*, there's more basura than usual."

"He even seems upbeat about the trash," TJ winced, grabbing one of the dark garbage bags. "Hey, I sound like Mariana."

Cassie managed a smile as she slung a medium-sized bag over her shoulder. She had to trust Carlos would take her to her dad in the Transition Room. It was the only way. They followed Carlos through the courtyard, and out another gate, leading to the lane behind the Fix-It, and away from the glare.

"What's that for?" TJ asked, staring way, way up at the wall looming several yards away, that appeared even higher the closer they got to the dumpster.

Cassie felt a Vibration, invisible waves moving in rhythm, like tentacles, extending out from the wall.

"Do you feel that?" Cassie asked, in front of the already-filled dumpster.

"I feel something," TJ said, shuddering as he stared up at the gloomy wall. "It feels like the wall is . . . alive."

The golden glasses vibrated in Cassie's pocket. *Maybe they're reminding me of how I first found them here,* she thought. *Maybe I'm supposed to return them.*

A stone the size of a fist crumbled down from the wall and landed with a thud right in front of TJ and Cassie's feet.

TJ kicked the rock into the woods. "That'd be one mess if that thing fell apart."

"It'd take some real weight to bring dat *muro* down," Carlos said, making room in the dumpster for the incoming trash. "Dat wall's been here as far back as anyone on Blue can remember."

The ominous, scraggly line of trees creaked behind dumpster, causing Cassie and TJ to look past the side of the large steel trash bin, and toward a section of matted-down dirt running behind the Fix-It in the direction of the Settling.

"Where does that go?" TJ asked, quietly.

"I don't know," Cassie replied, placing her bag of trash in the dumpster's open mouth and wiping her hand on her jeans. "Do you think it goes to the Preying Fields?"

TJ dropped his bag next. "It's headed that way."

Cassie's eyes traveled the path into the thicker forest. "Maybe that's how the important Entities from the Fix-It get there."

TJ hissed, "You mean the Recruiters."

Carlos rearranged trash bags in the dumpster with his back to Cassie and TJ, but tilted his head just enough over his shoulder so they could hear him say, "Those woods go to where the Recruiters hold der meetings. Dat's where they plan how to increase the power of da Ruler."

TJ's posture stiffened and he sent a Mind Mail to Cassie. *Does that mean he's one of them?*

Squeezing TJ's arm, Cassie asked, "How do you know that, Carlos? Have you been to the meetings? Have you seen the Dusk Ruler?"

Stepping farther back from the dumpster, TJ sent another Mind Mail. *How do you know we can we trust him? Remember his conversation with Sal? I heard it myself! He Gave it Away!*

Cassie felt TJ's Bubble deflate.

Carlos picked up a few empty bottles that had fallen from one of the overstuffed bags. "Sí, I seen the Ruler. I'm one of the lucky few."

TJ cracked his knuckles. *I think he's a Recruiter—he wears those same shoes that all the Entities do!*

Cassie's heart drummed inside her chest as she moved toward Carlos. "A-Are you a Recruiter?"

Just then, rustling came from deeper in the woods, the sounds of trampling brush heading toward them.

"Git down," Carlos quietly but firmly commanded, corralling Cassie and TJ behind the dumpster.

Sticks and twigs crunched and snapped as the footsteps came closer. Cassie tried not to breathe too heavily, crouched down beside Carlos and TJ. Then she heard voices.

"The Power of Numbers," several creatures chanted in unison.

Someone, a man, halted in his tracks and spoke. "Thuh Rulah will be pleased with ouwa dedication and with thuh influx uf Potentials tuh try tuh combat thuh mysterious rise in thuh Meter."

"The Power of Numbers," the voices answered. Resuming their march, they pressed their soft, black shoes on the pine-needle floor, like hunters stalking Bambi and his mother.

"Waait," the southern, slow voice spoke again, stopping, and then crunching toward the location where Cassie, TJ, and Carlos hid behind the dumpster. "Do yuh sense that?"

Carlos, his arms wrapped around Cassie and TJ, covered their mouths shut with both of his thick hands. Cassie, trembling with fear, felt her Bubble begin to deflate. *What if TJ's right? Is Carlos helping us or can we trust him?*

The sly voice continued. "Shhhh . . . I feel sumthin . . . There's more uf them who ah hopeful, who think there ah alternative ways." He sniffed the air. "They ah congregating among us, attempting tuh destroy what we have worked so hawd tuh build."

Cassie looked down at her faded red sneakers, concentrating on the voice.

That sounds like Dr. Fox, she thought.

"We will never be outnumbered," another male responded in a chirpy tone. "We're too good as Recruiters."

Cassie closed her eyes.

That sounds like Kurt.

"You ain't kiddin," another male voice chimed in. "We each know who we're responsible for, eh? It's in the bag."

"That's Sal!" TJ said in a high-pitched voice. He rose, wanting to see for himself, but Carlos yanked him back down. "Do as I say muchacho. Chu're en peligro."

TJ looked like a scared rabbit, sending Cassie his thoughts. *We have to go back to Bright Blue. Now. We have to let them know we're in trouble.*

"Shhhh," Carlos said, shifting his body weight, holding the kids tighter.

"It's tiime tuh let thuh Rulah know there ah more of them," Dr. Fox replied, closer to the dumpster as the group neared the back of the Fix-It. "We need tuh prove tuh him that everyone heaah is on board with his mission."

"The Power of Numbers," the voices rose louder, marching in army fashion toward the building.

Cassie hung her head between her legs, her body shivering. If they were in danger, where would her father be when they returned? She put her thumbnail in her mouth.

What do I do? Someone please help me.

Immediately, she felt the presence of the Ripple.

Cassie squeezed her eyes tight. Linking arms with TJ, she leaned into the flowing, comforting waves of the Ripple's energy, leaving Carlos behind.

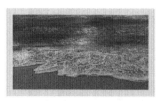

CHAPTER
THIRTY-THREE

The Land of Bright Blue was bustling with activity when Cassie and TJ landed softly in the pasture. Hurrying down the hill, Cassie thought it looked as if the Bright workers were getting ready for some big event. Simon and Benjamin barely looked up as they compared notes and tested experiments at their adjacent workstations in the meadow just off the blue pathway. Up ahead, Tufa was in deep discussion with both little elves and white-bearded Elders in the open center of the Palace. Every creature seemed focused on an important job, saying hello to Cassie and TJ good-naturedly and quickly returning to their duties. Even the children carried full glasses of Agnes's fruit drinks and trays of fresh baked goods, delivering the treats to those hard at work in the meadow. When she was younger, Cassie imagined the North Pole to look like this at Christmastime.

Tufa ended her conversation and strode down the Palace steps to greet Cassie and TJ. "Hello," she said. "I see much has happened on Blue since you returned. The rising of the color Vibration brings us much joy, though the Ruler is not pleased."

TJ cracked his knuckles as he stood on the end of the pavers. "Are we in danger, Tufa?"

"How will I get my father home now?" Cassie asked, squeezing her bottom lip with her thumb and forefinger.

Tufa placed loving hands on top of their heads. A current passed through Cassie, and on a scale of one to ten, she felt her worries release from a ten to a seven. "I know there is reason to be afraid, but you must trust Bright Blue. Remember, we are with you, especially during times of stress and fear. Come inside, as it is further guidance you seek."

Reaching the top of the stairs, Cassie lagging behind as she lunged over the odd ones, one of the white-bearded Elders hobbled with a cane to the top of the expansive staircase. He called to the children in the meadow as Cassie and TJ watched the children scramble to get in line. The Elder stared into each child's eyes individually, and held their faces with both of his hands, silently offering them direction as if they had graduated school and were ready to take on greater responsibilities.

The children bowed when they received their formal, private guidance, and skipped back down the stairs and into the meadow.

I wonder what they were told, Cassie thought. *I wonder what I'd be told if it was me.*

"That reminds me of kids completing basic training, ready for war," TJ said, following Tufa inside the Palace, looking back at the kids in line. He asked Tufa, "Are you Cassie's guardian angel or something? Do I have one?"

Tufa led them past the small door in the wall where elves scurried in and out, and over to a bench under a massive oil painting of a pink-and-orange sunrise. Making a space for them beside her on the bench, she said, "Everyone in the Universe has a Guide assigned to them from the Land of Bright Blue. When you need yours, TJ, he'll be there."

The Sun's rays shimmered off the top of TJ's dark hair. "Like Entities?"

"Yes," Tufa considered, "although at an opposing frequency."

TJ sat on his hands. "How do you know which one is right? The Entity or the Guide?"

"Well," Tufa said, thoughtfully, "if you think in terms of friends, there are those who support you, making you feel good, and there are those you realize you need to separate from. It's not easy, but embracing this truth allows you to align yourself with those who have your best interests at heart. Sometimes they are individuals you have yet to meet. Simply put, you have the power to decide who your friends are. And it is a great power, one to be used with care, one that makes all the difference in the Universe. For the frequency of your friends defines your frequency."

The mosaic jeweled tiles sparkled in the floor. "So, like picking friends, we can decide which voice we listen to?" Cassie asked.

"Precisely," Tufa replied, as the elves continued scurrying in and out. "One is of a darker Vibration, whose sole job is to keep you on a lower frequency. The other offers an alternative, lighter Vibration, and whose job is to guide one's essence higher. The rest is up to you."

TJ scrunched his face. "But does everyone know they have that option?"

"Though they may think they do not, they most certainly do. That discovery, ultimately, leads to one's freedom."

Cassie and TJ quietly processed Tufa's words.

"You are learning much," Tufa said, turning to the little door where an elf gave her a nod. "Let us proceed. You are ready for the next part of your journey."

Tufa stood and walked over to the spiral staircase in the Palace's center, leading to the Elevated View.

As they made their ascent, Cassie's mouth dropped. A second level appeared this time, midway through.

Where did this floor come from? Cassie thought.

Tufa led them onto the second floor to an expansive room filled floor to ceiling with brown, burgundy, and tan leather-bound books.

"Woah," TJ said, entering the library.

"Look at all these books!" Cassie exclaimed, tiptoeing down the dark wooden, narrow pined floor. There were books upon books, and books hidden behind books in countless rows of shelves that seemed to go on forever.

"That's a lot of reading," TJ said, with a look of disdain.

Cassie explored, eventually coming upon an area where light streamed in through the windows, shining directly on the gold-embossed titles on the spines of the books on dark wooden shelves. She spun around to face Tufa, who trailed behind them. "But who are these all for?"

"This is the Library of Wisdom, where every person in the Universe has their own book, and may write it, chapter by chapter, however they wish."

TJ stopped, causing the floor to creak. "How?"

The red cardinal flew in, landing on Tufa's shoulder. "Care to find yours? They're alphabetical."

Wide-eyed, Cassie and TJ slid their fingers along the bindings, searching for their personal books.

"Hey look, it's Mariana's!" TJ cried, carefully inching a brown leather book from one of the shelves and bringing it over to one of the gleaming mahogany tables spread throughout the Library. Cassie leaned over his shoulder as he opened it.

Fun, festive pictures and upbeat captions of happy family memories filled each page. Chapter by chapter, Mariana's large and boisterous family smiled radiantly at weddings, birthday parties, and Christmas dinners. Merriment sprung off the pages as TJ turned each piece of parchment. Cassie's throat burned.

The last chapter, located in the middle of the book, contained a three-dimensional image of what appeared to be Mariana's future wedding. Seen from behind, she stood in a long, ornate gown next to a sharply dressed groom. An enormous group of people attended the celebration.

"It's like a hologram of Mariana in the future," TJ said, captivated by the picture.

It looks so real, Cassie thought.

"The images on the last completed pages, only halfway because of your ages, hold the possibilities of the future," Tufa informed.

Cassie sensed something—movement—walking, not on the floor, but above it, light and airy. Raising her head she beheld the transparent beings—kind, old spirits coming into the Library through the cherry-finished walls. They drifted through the shelves and the books, a peaceful energy radiating throughout the Library.

TJ continued reading Mariana's book, unaware of the visitors. "How come we can't see who the groom is?"

"Future pages never reveal exact details, for there is always the variable of free will," Tufa explained, acknowledging several beings floating around the table that greeted her by grazing wispy hands atop her shoulder.

An elder Native American apparition, wearing an elaborately decorated headdress, paused solemnly behind TJ before drifting farther into the Library.

TJ remained focused on the book. "I hope Mariana invites me, cause that wedding is gonna be fun!"

"Why wouldn't it be, with a family like that?" Cassie asked, crossing her arms and checking out another section of books.

The elder Native American, his bare, tanned back strong and wide, floated next to Cassie. Reaching high above Cassie's head, he selected a burgundy leather-bound book with gold pages, the size of a middle-reader novel, and placed it in her hands.

Cassie met his kind, moss-colored eyes before reading the cover. "TJ, it's your book!"

"Lemme see!" TJ put Mariana's book back on the shelf and rushed over to Cassie, as the Native American moved to another area of the Library. Retrieving the book and putting it down on another mahogany table to read, TJ flipped through the soft pages, silently reviewing events and memories occurring up until he turned twelve.

The book contained a picture of TJ picking out a Christmas tree with his family at age three, and one of him sitting on his mother's lap, reading books.

"That was when I used to like reading," he said. Other pictures of him at the age of seven showed him playing soccer in an open field with other little boys in red T-shirts, and fishing with his brother, Eric, on a bridge across a bay. Memory after memory, TJ turned the pages of time.

"That was before my parents owned the store," TJ said flatly, pointing to a picture of his family grilling burgers on a porch. Reading a detailed journal entry of how he loved to ride dirt bikes with his brother, he added, "That was before Eric started hanging out with his new friends." When TJ reached the final page in the middle of the book, two moving images appeared, like movie trailers.

The one on the left showed TJ, a little taller than he was now, getting shoved around by other boys at school. He held a slouched posture, his hair flopping in his confused, sad face.

The page on the right depicted a different movie. TJ played soccer with younger boys at a Boys Club building, teaching them the rules, guiding them to be the best they could be. TJ emerged as a leader on the right page, one boy's parents thanking him for their son's progress.

"Why are there two movies?" TJ asked.

The Native American apparition appeared by TJ's side and

said in a strong voice, "Each image is a future possibility. There are always two roads to travel. Whichever road you select will transport you to the appropriate destination."

TJ listened intently to the being, studying both images again while Cassie stepped back to give TJ space.

Moving to the other side of the Library in search of her own book, Cassie reached a section containing all the names starting with C, noticing one on a high shelf, glowing with golden light. The name "Cassie Connor" appeared in gold thread on the spine. Reaching up on her toes, she brought the book over to an unoccupied table.

Cassie carefully turned the pages of her story. There were pictures of birthday parties her father didn't attend, images of her watching TV next to her father while he slept, missing all the funny parts. On each page Cassie came face to face with her loneliness. She read diary entry after diary entry, written during hours spent alone in her parents' apartment, trapped in worry. She even witnessed the image of the very first time she bit one of her nails, every picture thereafter of Cassie with her fingers in her mouth.

On another page, she recognized the picture Carlos brought out for her, of her father holding her on the Shetland pony. It was one of the few times Cassie and her parents had done something as a family, and why she cherished the photograph so deeply. After a few moments, she reluctantly turned the page, observing images of herself as an infant being bathed in the kitchen sink by her mother, her mom feeding her at 3 a.m., taking her by bus to the library, and trying to paint her nails as Cassie made a mess in the background, her mother in each image trying to be the best mom she could, yet wearing a faraway look on her face.

She recalled the image of her in the Minnie Mouse costume that her artistic mother made, when her father didn't show up to the kindergarten costume competition. Another image pictured her mother waking her up to watch TV when her dad stayed out late, and yet another of Cassie in bed during one of her parents' parties in the apartment.

Cassie felt top-heavy, and steadied herself in the chair at the table.

"It's not how I thought it was," she said, gripping the sides of the book. "Sometimes he really was the best dad in the whole world, but the rest of the time . . . " Her voice trailed off, tears forming in her eyes.

Tufa sat down in the chair next to her, the cardinal flying to one of the top shelves.

"Why did I think it was different?" Cassie asked, not taking her eyes from the pages as she revisited the memories. "Why did I think he was the best father?"

"Because it's what you wanted him to be," Tufa responded with compassion. "And at times, he was. The essence of a person is always good. Sometimes, though, when one falls prey to darkness, that good can be eclipsed."

Cassie listened. With a trembling hand, she flipped the page. An image faced her of the day of her First Communion, the sun shining bright as her mother and grandparents stood beside her on the steps of Holy Name. Her grandparents had been arguing right before the picture was taken, but when the photo was snapped, they smiled wide, cheesy smiles for the camera. It made Cassie chuckle now, because even though it wasn't perfect, like Mariana's family, they were there. They were always there.

Cassie stared at a dark design on the wooden table. It was Grandpa who taught Cassie that a watched pot never boils and to not give up finding the answers to crossword puzzles even when she grew frustrated. He even used to grab her knee in church to make her laugh during the boring parts. And it was Nana Helen who taught her how to play Scrabble and gin rummy, and to weed the flower garden weekly to keep it nice. Turning back to her book, Cassie viewed Nana Helen in her ugly, mint-green bathing cap, teaching Cassie how to do a dead-man's float at Carson Beach in

South Boston.

Cassie wiped a tear and turned to the next page, an image of her and Mariana in kindergarten and every year after that in school together, their friendship something she could count on. Her heart ached, like a kick in the shins, when she realized how envious she had been of her best friend.

Tufa placed a gentle hand on top of Cassie's. "We each have the family that is perfect for us and for the development of our unique gifts, even when it feels unfair. We are always given exactly what we need, that truth becoming clearer as we grow."

Cassie heard the owl hoot from somewhere inside the Library.

On one of the last pages of the half-filled book, an image of Cassie wearing the golden glasses appeared, her face suddenly glazing over with insight. "The glasses. They were meant for me to find."

Tufa leaned on her elbow. "You will always find what is meant for you."

Cassie asked, "Like I found you?"

"I have been assigned to you since the day you entered the Universe, my purpose to guide you to your personal power."

Cassie sat with that for a moment. "What about Agatha, though? She said she's been with me a long time too."

Tufa joined her hands on the table. "Agatha came to you during a time when your dominant thoughts were of sadness and fear. That frequency emitted a signal that Agatha was attracted to energetically. An Entity's mission is to keep you on that Vibration pattern by attaching to you and eventually putting a hook in your field. Many people succumb to that lower Vibration, because they don't realize that it is *their* space and *they* get to decide who is in it. They allow the hook to remain, as if they have no other option. That is how the Dusk Ruler remains in power and why the Vibration Meter is so important to him. As long as the colors for the population remain low, he remains in control. The more people the

Ruler puts hooks into, by taking away their power of election, the more powerful the Ruler becomes."

"But what if it's too late?" Cassie asked.

"There is always the opportunity to right ourselves whenever we fall out of alignment. That is why every election counts, for it serves either the Land of Blue or the Land of Bright Blue. Bright Blue's mission is to make people aware of this knowledge and of their ability to reclaim what is rightfully theirs."

Cassie drew her sneakers back under her chair. "Is that why Agatha didn't allow Mariana to come with me this time? Because her colors raised the Vibration and messed up the Meter?"

Tufa sat back in her chair. "Do not be fooled. One must desire change for themselves and their situation in order for the colors on Blue to change. Mariana's detachment from that desire would not affect the rise in Vibration. Mariana was allowed to accompany you because that is what helped Agatha to lure you to Blue. Agatha knew you would not have come otherwise."

Cassie ran her finger along the top of the table. "I trusted Agatha when she said Mariana couldn't go."

"And do you still?"

Cassie didn't respond, focusing her attention on the last completed page of her book. In the image on the left, Cassie stood alone in the middle of a busy college campus, swarms of students around her bustling about their business in a gray, colorless setting. Cassie absorbed the image, feeling numb. Crossing her legs under the chair, she observed the page on the right, viewing herself standing on the side of a mountain with her arms spread wide, surrounded by a bold landscape of radiant foliage, as people cheered for her in the background.

Cassie's eyes darted back and forth between the images. "Is it possible for me to end up in the Settling?"

"Just as possible as it is to stand on that mountain and feel joy after an arduous climb," Tufa replied. "Focus on what you want—

not on what you don't. For your perception becomes your reality."

Cassie's eyes filled with tears. "I just want to be okay, but what if my dad never comes home? How can I be okay then?"

"The ultimate decision to be okay will be yours. That decision must occur independently of anyone else's actions."

Cassie sighed, closing the book and examining her name, Cassie Anne Connor, etched in stately gold font. Then, as if she remembered, she gasped, "What is the Ruler going to do now that the Vibration is changing? The arrow was only four colors below the black line when we left."

Tufa replied, "The Ruler and his Recruiters are currently attempting to bring the colors back down with an influx of new Potentials, desperate to keep the wall intact."

Cassie held the book in her hands. "That huge wall that runs across the land?"

"The Dusk Ruler created that wall when he left Bright Blue in order to rule a land of his own. The wall is a symbol of his opposition, for it blocks the light."

"The Ruler was here?" Cassie asked, jiggling her left leg against her right.

"Everyone's essence begins from Bright Blue. Whether a creature stays aligned with the light or seeks out darkness is their election. The Creator granted the Ruler his freedom as he requested, under two conditions. The first being that a thirty-second Glimmer would be held every third pulse, to give the occupants the experience of the light. If the occupants elected to stay outdoors during the Glimmer, the light would grow. The Ruler, however, threatened access to the Feed if anyone dared remain outside."

Cassie's gripped her book. "He keeps them all afraid."

"Yes. The Ruler built a system based on fear. He will not let go of that control easily. However, this is something we have anticipated." Tufa raised her brow as Cassie remembered all the creatures in the meadow, tending to their assigned tasks.

"Why would the Ruler want to leave here?" Cassie asked.

Tufa crossed her legs in her chair. "Some desire a different kind of pleasure. You should know that Agatha was here once too."

"Agatha?" Cassie asked, doubtfully. "Why would she leave if she lived here?"

Tufa lifted her chin. "She chose to follow a different Ruler."

Just then, Cassie heard the familiar chant, sounding throughout the Library.

> Darkness threatens those we love,
> Hopes for this one yet remain
> Choice and selection
> One's own election
> Always in Bright Blue Domain

"That's Agatha's chant," Cassie noted, searching to identify the source.

"That chant originated here," Tufa said, taking Cassie's book and standing to place it back on the shelf.

Cassie leaned forward. "Did Agatha steal the chant from you when she left?"

Tufa explained, "She altered it slightly, though significantly, before making it her own. Our chant is 'Choice and selection, one's own election.' But Agatha's says, 'Choice and selection, once an election.' Agatha would have you believe that once you enter Blue territory, you cannot change your mind."

Cassie blinked. She had never focused on the words of the chant. "We have a choice on Bright Blue."

Tufa leaned over, placing her hands on her thighs. "You always have a choice."

Cassie's face brightened like the Sun in a dawning sky, recalling the message inscribed on the Wisdom Glass when they stopped at Option's Port.

We always have a choice.

Cassie scooted forward on her chair. "What's the second condition the Creator gave the Ruler?"

"That he take the Key of Selection with him upon his departure, a key meant to be used only once, in the chosen door of the key holder. The Ruler has guarded it since so no one would be able to use it for the way Bright Blue intended. The Ruler entrusts the key only to his most loyal servants. It would take a brave and compassionate creature to obtain the Key and use it for its original intention."

"Could you find out who is guarding the key?" Cassie asked.

"We have a Bright worker there, disguised among the Blue staff, who has given much in order to support our mission," Tufa said, leaning against the wall of books.

Cassie kept her head low, considering the many creatures in the Midst. She pictured the Entities she had met, those Working for Permanency, Nurse Moody at the Fix-It, and Carlos and his half-Entity physique.

Cassie raised her head as she put things together in her mind. "Carlos? Carlos Gave It Away. TJ heard him say it was worth the transformation. B-but he's not on Blue's side, he's on yours!"

Tufa's eyes sparkled. "Carlos made a worthy sacrifice."

Cassie pushed her chair back, and began pacing the shiny floor. "So if Carlos helped me find the key, I could save my father by unlocking him from the Transition Room before he becomes a Permanent?"

Tufa pressed a book back that stuck out among the others in the shelf. "You could, yes."

Cassie stopped pacing. "Tufa, can I speak to the Creator?"

Tufa laughed, her olive skin slightly creasing near her mouth. "Do you not feel Him all around you? Not only here, but everywhere?"

Cassie shifted her weight to her right leg. "But I want to see Him."

Tufa's face grew solemn as she placed a graceful hand on Cassie's shoulder. "It is just as the Sun is always with you, even when it is raining. The hour has come for you to take what you have learned and find your way. Remember, I have been with you since the beginning, and I will always be with you, as my task is to guide the blossoming of your essence."

As Cassie stood beside Tufa for a moment by the polished table and TJ spoke privately with the bare-chested Native American in the far corner of the room, Cassie became aware of many more translucent spirits walking about the Library of Wisdom. Multiple beings floated through shelving and rows of books, reappearing in other aisles. A dark-skinned woman with a cream shawl about her head skimmed through the aisles taking inventory, and an old Indian man relaxed in a corner of the room, closing his eyes in reflection as the cardinal flew down from the top shelf, perching upon his shoulder.

Go forth. Be brave. Do not be afraid to change what has come before. Use your gifts. Cassie felt the messages flow through her like currents of energy. Unspoken, yet received.

After a few moments of bathing in the messages from the wise, guiding spirits, Tufa led Cassie and TJ back down the spiral staircase.

"I met my guide!" TJ whispered behind her. "Now I have another voice to listen to instead of Sal's! He showed me how to imagine turning the volume down, like a radio, on Sal's voice, and turning the volume up on his voice so I can hear him, even when Sal is shouting at me."

Cassie skipped the odd stairs with a spring in her step. Reaching the bottom, she discovered that hundreds of translucent beings, elves, Elders, and children filled the center of the Palace, in intense conversation, as if something important was about to happen.

Where did they all come from?

Cassie noticed the empty treasure chest across the room, the Wisdom Glass creatures scampering across the floor, receiving pieces of the colorful treasure from a handful of elves in charge of handouts. Proudly joining their peers in assembly-line fashion, the creatures crawled down the Palace steps, heading for the pasture.

"What are those?" TJ asked, eyeing the dazzling jewels.

"It's Wisdom Glass," Cassie explained. "The creatures carry them to Blue for those who need wisdom."

Just then, Cassie deliberately stepped down on the first, odd stair . . . with both feet, as TJ raised both eyebrows. Cassie swallowed, waiting a moment.

An elf bidding the creatures good-bye returned up the steps and remarked, "A fine and noble job."

Cassie wasn't sure if he referred to the creatures leaving for Blue, or of her landing deliberately on an odd-numbered step for the first time since she started this habit.

Tufa beckoned to Cassie and TJ from the pavers to follow her to the pasture. The Bright workers in the meadows continued their lively, steady hum of tasks.

"This is what makes me tick, I tell you!" Benjamin exclaimed, beads of sweat dripping down his forehead. Scooping the kinetic, royal-blue Energy of the Bees from the covered box, he carefully matched it up to the frenzied red dots on his "Those Requiring the Energy of the Bees" machine. "Sorry I can't engage in dialogue with you now," he said to Cassie, his vest rising high above his thick waist, as he reached to the top of the map, "but I'm attempting to send as much productive energy as we can while there's still time!"

Some of the Bright workers occasionally glanced over at the base of the rolling hills where Bright Blue ended and Blue began, picking up the pace at their stations.

Simon chimed in, speaking rapidly at the adjacent station while he stood, hunched over as he analyzed data. "The colors are brightening on Blue as we speak, the Land experiencing great turmoil! We here on Bright Blue are counting on your return to their land! Using your Bubbles will be most important, you two, but might I also add assistance in the area of Word Vibration?"

Cassie nervously looked to TJ. "I could probably use some courage."

"Yeah," TJ said, checking out the thickening fog at the base of the hills, resembling heavy pollution. "Entities are pretty intimidating."

"No time to waste!" Simon gestured with his wrist for Cassie to take her place beside the screen. "Now then! *Courage.* Appropriate selection of verbiage! We can help you there! And with regard to our beloved chant, I see, Cassie, that you have come to understand the power of what a difference a few choice words can make!"

Simon joyfully pressed a few keys, like he was selecting candy in a candy store, bringing the words *courage*, *bravery*, and *strength* into view on the machine. Cassie instantly felt her body jolt as she stood with her arms pressed to her sides, the power of the words taking root in her energy field.

Simon rose up on his toes, with his hands clasped behind his back. "There now!"

Cassie marveled at the brilliant shades of blue, green, and red that appeared on the screen. "Those are mine?"

Simon lunged forward, sending his rollaway chair spiraling down the pavers, as he placed a packet of seeds he retrieved from his workstation into the palm of her hand and said in a low, determined tone. "You already have what you need. These packets are to be scattered in the most fertile and deserving fields when you return to Blue! Use them wisely, as there are only three. They hold the seeds of *strength, opportunity, and faith.*"

Before Cassie could ask questions, Tufa signaled from the path, gathering every creature, large and small, together in the Meadow. Next, she invited Cassie and TJ into the middle of the group. "Please wish our guests well on their journey back to the

Land of Blue," she said. "It has become evident that the Ruler's power has been severely threatened, by the rising of the colors on the Meter. Please share your light reserves, and your colors, with our friends."

Elves, Elders, children, and Bright workers congregated around Cassie and TJ, closing their eyes and holding their palms up, streaming rays of gorgeous, bold, multi-colored light from their hands.

Cassie felt a warm pulse radiate throughout her body, from her head to her feet.

After a few moments, Tufa released her palms, checking on the burgeoning wall overlooking the gray smog. "All right, get your Bubbles intact. We will miss you both and look forward to one day meeting again."

The circle of creatures slowly stepped back, giving them additional space. Cassie imagined a Bubble of alternating blue and green columns, like the color of the ocean, surrounding her body. TJ envisioned colors of red-and-white stripes from his soccer uniform, with black porcupine needles built inside, ready to dart out in case they were needed.

When they opened their eyes, the white horse appeared, lowering its back to transport them both back to Blue. Bravely climbing aboard, Cassie and TJ galloped away at full speed, in search of the Key, ready to face the darkness.

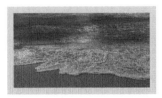

CHAPTER
THIRTY-FOUR

"**N**ever in greater numbers!" Captain BP's voice rang throughout the Midst as new Potentials disembarked from *The Enticer*. Cassie and TJ watched as he called out, "The Ruler will be pleased at the influx! Never needed it more! Here! Have another one as a courtesy!" His hat nearly fell off his head as he manically handed out Blobs. Every minute or so, he'd glance surreptitiously at the Meter behind him.

Meanwhile, Kurt, Big, and Small spoke secretly just beyond the Welcoming Gate at the pier, also keeping their eyes on the Meter. The black arrow was going haywire. The energy Vibration for the whole land wavered in a deep sea-blue color range—the kind of color where you expect to see sharks—only three rungs from the space above the black line.

"Check it out!" TJ said, leaning closer to Cassie as they skirted past the vendors. "There's Wisdom Glass everywhere!"

Cassie's lips parted at the shiny treasures lying visible in the street. At first, no one seemed to notice the pieces of glass lying by the garbage cans and protruding out of cobblestone cracks, until Cassie recognized the bleach-blond woman from the apartment next to Mrs. Costa, along with her teenage son, picking up some of the pieces and discreetly tucking them in their pockets.

Mrs. Costa exited from one of the Zebbies, Michael and Anna scuffing behind, holding fistfuls of Blobs in each hand. Anna caught sight of the sparkling glass, allowing a few Blobs to fall from her fingers in order to pick up an emerald-green nugget, exactly the same color as her eyes.

Mrs. Costa saw Cassie and grabbed at her long jean skirt, hurrying over to speak to her in the street. "Girl, the colors are rising. I don't know what'll happen to my kids if the Ruler finds out we spoke with you about that other place. The Land of Blue is all we know."

"Your children don't belong here," Cassie said in a voice that didn't feel quite like her own. "You and your husband chose to be here, but you can choose something different if you want."

TJ lightly kicked the back of Cassie's sneaker.

"Well, well," Agatha's voice cackled from behind. "I can see relationships developing as I had hoped they would for my young Potential, hopefully soon to be Permanent, if she wants to see her father. In the meantime, Mrs. Costa, and TJ, would you mind running along to support Ray? He's Robin's new replacement and he's fabulous." Cupping a hand to the side of her mouth, she added, "I hear Ray makes the Bads bigger than ever."

Mrs. Costa nodded several times, taking Anna and Michael by their shirtsleeves to the new unicyclist. TJ trailed behind, turning often to glance back at Cassie.

Agatha stroked her chin, tic-like. "Cassie, dear, would you

consider yourself helping or hindering the occupants on Blue?"

Cassie noticed the red hair around Agatha's temples had faded to a grayish white. "I'm trying to hel—"

"You should know Mr. Costa is a fine, upstanding Permanent. He does much to aid the Ruler and doesn't need a child interfering in matters that do not concern her. If I need something from you for those in the Settling, you will receive instructions from me. Have I made myself clear?"

Cassie swallowed a wad of fear and then spoke. "I'm sure Mr. Costa is a really nice person deep down, but Mrs. Costa and her children . . ."

Agatha moved closer, three gray whiskers visible in her chin as she came within inches of Cassie's face. "While your compassion is admirable, our occupants have an Entity they listen to, and don't need another voice to mess things up. Now," she said, standing up straight, "the Ruler has called a mandatory staff meeting. As you are no doubt well aware, the Vibration in the Land has been poisoned. There will be interrogations. I've always defended you, Cassie, but the time has come to attach the cord. I've worked too hard to have you go astray."

Agatha flicked her sagging, wrinkled wrist, materializing a long flimsy leash of magnetic energy glowing midnight blue that she instantly attached, tightly, to Cassie's belt loop.

"But, I don't understand. I haven't done anything wrong, I'm just . . ."

"Don't fret," Agatha interrupted, holding her palm up. "You're free to go about where you need to, but now I'll know where you are at all times, our bond stronger than ever. For I'm in charge of your thoughts, Cassie Connor, and don't forget it. As a consequence for your actions, head back to Strays with your friend until I get the word from the Ruler on what needs to happen next. Or else."

Agatha limped away like she had a bad hip, in the direction of the alley, the leash elongating with every step.

When she was halfway down Charcoal Alley, TJ returned, with a half-drunk Bad in his hand, his shoulder twitching.

Cassie sighed heavily as TJ clutched the Bad to his chest and said sheepishly, "I couldn't help it, Agatha told me to!"

Cassie felt the tug of the cord of light as Agatha limped down the long alley. She gnawed on her lip and said, "I still don't like disappointing her. It makes me feel like I'm doing something wrong and that I'm a bad person."

"Yeah, except that you're not," TJ said, swirling the remaining Bad in the mug in his hand, and then tossing it in the garbage. He wrapped his arm around Cassie's shoulder and said, "C'mon, let's go to Strays."

Ducking past Sal, who was engaged in a heated Stimulator game inside the Cove, they pushed open the front door of Strays, where a Mooshkoo went about like a whirling dervish, gobbling up every Blob in the cottage.

"Oip!! Oip!" it ranted in anticipation of the Ruler's wrath. Cassie, her head hung low, headed down the carpeted hall and entered the guest suite. She sank immediately into the billowy beanbag chair, desperate for a restful place to stop and think.

TJ nestled in his dark-blue beanbag, fighting the temptation to switch on the Stimulator. "I'll watch out for you, in case Agatha comes back. It's hard to wind down anyway after half a Bad."

Cassie sunk lower into the chair, her eyelids growing heavy. In that state between sleep and wake, a familiar voice called to her from somewhere far away.

Cassie,

Where are you? I think I figured out Mind Mail! Can you hear me? I'm worried about you!

Mariana

Cassie half-smiled, drifting in and out of sleep. Somewhere deep inside of her, she knew she needed to reply to her best friend.

I have to do this without you, Mari. Don't worry about me, okay?

Slowly, she fell into a dream. Her father was locked in a small room with one door. Through a black-framed window, he could see only gray clouds clogging the seemingly sunless sky. Hopeless and brooding, he stared out, as a wild animal growled and licked its lips outside Dad's room.

Cassie abruptly opened her eyes back in the Suite, her heart drumming in her chest. Instantly, a wave of understanding crashed over her, as if someone was trying to tell her something right at that very moment.

Dad's negative thoughts are what caused him to end up on Blue.

That's why Simon had taught her about the power of her thoughts, so she didn't end up a Permanent, too.

It didn't matter that the Sun shone behind the clouds in the dream. Dad only saw the gray. Cassie rubbed her forehead.

If I can get to my dad, and teach him to think good thoughts, maybe there's still a chance to save him.

"I'm not waiting for Agatha," Cassie stated to TJ as she scrambled to her feet. "We have to go to the Fix-It."

TJ, who had been twiddling his thumbs trying not to eat any Blobs that filled the jar on the table next to his beanbag, said, "But what if Agatha, or Sal—"

"She'll already know where I am," Cassie said, pointing to the cord. "Besides, Carlos will be there to help us. He's on Bright Blue's side."

CHAPTER
THIRTY-FIVE

The line for Have to Haves was longer and louder than ever on the walkway outside the Fix-It. Permanents pushed and shoved to get to the front, fearful the supply might run out since the arrow on the Energy Vibration Meter was moving up steadily from the deep-sea-blue color into the range of teal.

"Carlos!" Cassie said, trying to keep her voice to a whisper as she ran ahead of TJ over to the fence. "I know who you are!"

Carlos waddled across the courtyard, squeegee in hand, toward the chain link fence.

"Oye, my man," Carlos put up his hand to fist-bump TJ, who arrived at the fence. "We good? Chu and I could have some nasty gut wars wit our Bubbles. Mine's Pittsburgh Steeler yellow. Juss saying."

TJ returned the fist-bump.

"I told you he was on our side," Cassie said proudly.

"Listen," Carlos explained, as individuals in line cursed and threw empty Escape bottles at the brick building. "There isn't much time. It's because of chu dat the colors are brightening. Chu know dat, right chica?"

Cassie tucked her hair behind her ear.

"It was chur courage to listen to the other voice that created hope for some in the Settling," Carlos said.

Cassie stuffed her hands in the pocket of her sweatshirt. "I'm worried for Mrs. Costa and her children. I don't want anybody to get in trouble because of me. All I ever wanted was to bring my dad home."

"Yo se, chica, but what chu've done for some of the people in the Settling is a good thing. We've been waiting for chu for a long time." Carlos unfastened the opening in the fence as he looked up at the walkway and quickly locked it behind him. Bringing Cassie and TJ through the courtyard, he unlocked another opening at the other end, leading them out to the end of the building where the stone wall loomed a few yards back, behind a locked maintenance shed and the dumpster on the right that sat at the end of the dirt lane.

When they stepped out of the far end of the courtyard, Cassie stopped, recognizing a dark-blue back door at the end of the building. "This is like the dream I had. My father was in a room with one door. Does this open inside to the Transition Room?" She impulsively tried to turn the silver metal doorknob from the outside, but it was locked.

"Sí. Chur father is being held in there while Dr. Fox prepares the Permanent papers. Only one key will grant chu access from outside."

"But you have the keys! I've seen you go in and out when you come out to take the trash," Cassie reasoned.

Carlos shook his head as he waddled over to the dumpster,

the area behind the building a tad quieter than out front. "No, no, I have the keys for the courtyard and the shed."

Cassie kept her hand on the doorknob. "But what about the special key? Where is that?"

"Dr. Fox holds dat key, too, cause once dat key's been used, it turns into dust. Puro polva."

Carlos opened the mouth of the dumpster with one arm, its contents nearly empty, and asked, "Did chu see all the Wisdom Glass in the Midst?"

"Is that why the dumpster is almost empty?" Cassie asked, letting go of the doorknob and standing on her toes to peer inside.

Carlos pointed at her like she scored the right answer.

TJ scrunched his face, "That's where Wisdom Glass comes from? The dumpster?"

Carlos jerked his head toward the remaining few empty bottles inside. "One of da best parts of my job, amigo, is transporting dis to be turned into sumthing good."

"Carlos," Cassie asked. "Why did you want to stay here and help Bright Blue?"

"Once da Bright workers showed up many pulses ago, I decided to see past the Ripple for myself. Once chu go, once chu know, tings aren't da same. Chu learn every person in the Universe has a special task. Well my task is to be a helper for Bright Blue."

Boom. A loud noise, like the firing of a cannon, sounded from behind the Fix-It.

Carlos spoke sternly to Cassie and TJ. "The Ruler's meeting is done. He's going to search for those who betrayed him. I going to bring chu into the back double doors of the Fix-It now. Hopefully chu'll find a way into the Transition Room to see chur dad." Carlos gestured to the cord of magnetic energy dangling from Cassie's belt loop. "Andale. Agatha will be here soon."

Quickly, Carlos ushered Cassie and TJ around the building to the pair of steel double doors.

Boom.

Another cannon-like sound rattled the Land, causing a wave of panic that could be heard from the line in front of the Fix-It. Permanents in the back of the line charged forward, assaulting those who received their supply of Have to Haves, afraid they'd lose their chance.

Carlos issued instructions to Cassie outside the double doors. "Chu'll see chur dad's old room, where Robin is now, on chur left, at the end of the corridor. Two doors down the smaller hallway is the Transition Room, across from the supply closet. Chu have to go alone, chica. My job will be in jeopardy if I am wit chu. I'm going to take TJ back to Sal, so there'll be no suspicions."

Boom.

Boom.

"Will she be all right?" TJ asked, his voice cracking as he looked back at the woods behind the dumpster.

"Cassie is muy inteligente and knows what she needs to do," Carlos said calmly, his hand on the outside of the door. "Now go."

Carlos opened the doors, and Cassie peeked around the metal frame, surveying the empty corridor. Cogs yelled from behind closed doors, as they too heard the cannon fire, demanding Have to Haves before it was too late. Cassie looked left to right, hearing Nurse Moody yell down the corridor, still at the entrance slot handing out refills. Cassie stepped inside, identified Dad's old room, and quietly tiptoed down the corridor. Stopping outside the door, her compassionate nature getting the better of her, she checked inside. Robin sat immobilized in the lone chair.

"Robin," Cassie whispered, her hands gripping the side of the door.

The pale Working for Permanency slowly lifted his unshaven, stubbly face. "Hey, young Potential," he slurred. "Did you come to bring me my Have to Haves? My Entity said he'd make sure they were sent right away. Always gotta listen to them, you know." Then he dropped his head with the weight of a bowling ball.

Cassie knew she needed to get to her dad before Agatha showed up, but she felt sad for Robin. She told her feet to go but somehow her heart wanted them to remain in place. Suddenly, the glasses jingled in her pocket. She reached in to take them out, and instead felt a packet of seeds.

Use them wisely, in the most fertile and deserving fields, Simon had instructed.

Cassie took one out, checking over her shoulder as she opened the packet containing seeds of *strength*. She entered the room and sprinkled them into Robin's energy field as he sat oblivious in the cold, hard chair. Immediately he stirred, his body making a jerking motion.

Cassie bent down and whispered into his ear, "It's a choice to listen to the voice."

Robin snapped his head up as he tried to resist sleep, but then dropped his chin. "How come the simplest things are the hardest to do?" he said, just before drifting into sleep.

Cassie snuck back into the hall, closing Robin's door. The wailing sounds of the Cogs filled the long corridor, causing her to shudder.

"Hold on!" Nurse Moody yelled from someone's room. "I'm getting to all of ya! We'll get those colors back down. Don't anybody worry. For the love of Have to Haves, we better."

Cassie felt a tug on her waist and looked down. The cord was shortening.

She hurried down the short hallway, two doors past Robin's room. On the other side of the hall, the supply closet was positioned in the tiled wall. Cassie paused just shy of the slightly opened door of the Transition Room as horrible sounds of taunting, from a muffled, creepy male voice, came from inside the room. She stepped back, listening, and bit her thumbnail, reminding herself that she was curious versus nosy.

Is that dad's Entity talking to him like that?

Cassie plunged her hand in her pocket and steadied the glasses on her face, creeping a few steps forward, curious to see her father's Entity. She strained her neck just past the cracked open door where her father sat on the cold tiles gripping the sides of his short brown hair, wrestling in agony.

A tall, heavy, hooded figure in a dark gray robe with a shadowy face spouted at her father. "Think of the things you've done! Missing your child's birthday parties and school events all those years to sit in barrooms! You're despicable and hopeless! And what about the time . . . " The figure lowered his voice, mercilessly whispering something in her father's ear as he hunched forward, his head between his knees. "What kind of a husband and father are you? There's no other place for you than the Land of Blue."

Her dad rocked back and forth. "I've made so many mistakes. You're right. I can never go back. It was foolish of me to even consider it before my release."

The Entity spat, preparing to leave as Cassie pulled herself back from the door. "Now you're making sense." Then the Entity stopped. "Creatures like us, Craig, have no hope, because we never change."

Cassie dashed across the dimly lit hallway, cramming herself into the supply closet with the syringes and bottles. Her body shook as she waited, pressed against a dry mop, until she heard the long-cloaked Entity strut down the short hallway and turn left into the main corridor.

Cassie took a deep breath, attempting to regain her composure. Removing the glasses, she opened the door of the closet and snuck across to the Transition Room. A sink with a large cabinet underneath to the right was the only piece of furniture in the room. Her father sat catatonically on the floor. In the back of the room, a dark-blue door faced her, exactly like the one she saw in the dream.

Her legs wobbling, Cassie stood beside her father. "Dad, I

need to talk to you."

Craig briefly looked up, a lightweight blue robe like a Roger covering his dirty tank top and faded jeans. "I tried to tell you in my Mind Mail, I belong on Blue. Y-you don't know all the things I've done." Her father kicked at the tiled floor in his new black-soled soles, his heart laden with guilt.

"Those things don't matter anymore," Cassie said, crouching down to rub his back.

Her dad covered his face with his hands. "It would be too hard for me to go back."

"I know it's hard for you." Cassie's voice cracked, holding back a gushing flood of emotion in her throat. "But I believe in you, Daddy. You can still try to fight them. Fight the darkness."

Craig stayed hunched over, refusing to look up, as he put his hand on top of his head. "I'm a failure. I'm a failure, just like my family before me."

Cassie banged the ground with her fist and said, "No, Dad! That's what the Entities want you to think!"

"Oh, Craig . . . " Craig's Entity sneered from the hall.

Her father grasped the sides of her face. "Cassie, you have to leave! They'll blame you. You have to get out of here so the Ruler won't think it's you!"

Cassie's eyes darted about the room, landing on the large cabinet under the sink. She quickly hid her little frame inside, pulling her knees into her chest. The packets of *opportunity* and *faith* crunched in her pants pocket.

Will I get out of here to be able to use the other packets?

The black-hooded Entity entered the Transition Room, closing the door behind him. Cassie closed one eye, looking through the crack between the two cabinet doors. The Entity shoved neon-colored Have to Haves in front of her dad's face.

Cassie could see her father grow weary, rubbing both hands over his eyes.

There was a knock on the door.

The Entity snarled, "Go ahead. I'm just about done."

Cassie held her breath as Carlos bent down and opened the cabinet door. Before she knew what was happening, she was surrounded by a pink Bubble, reduced to the size of a grapefruit and tucked snugly in the front of Carlos hooded jacket while he grabbed the bag of trash.

Once they were out in the hallway, with the door closed behind them, Carlos took the pink Bubble out of his jacket, his hand trembling. Within seconds, Cassie found herself back to full size, Carlos quietly standing beside her in silence.

"And there she is, as I knew she would be," Agatha spoke from between wheezes as she limped around the corner of the corridor. "Trying to talk her father into coming home again I suppose. When are you going to give it a rest?" She clenched her jaw in anger.

"I found her here, Agatha," Carlos said, clearing his throat. "She didn't get inside, no te preocupes."

"Gracias," Agatha said, placing her hand on her hip to catch her breath. "I see at least your allegiance is with the Dusk Ruler. And you, leaving after I gave you orders to remain at Strays. Tsk, tsk. You are becoming quite the rule breaker indeed. You could be using your gifts of compassion to help us here, to help the children learn to appreciate this life. And all the while staying with your father, caring for him, like the other good family members do." She snickered in disgust. "What a waste."

Cassie's entire face flushed red. Suddenly, sirens wailed outside the Fix-It.

Agatha gasped, stopping underneath the yellow lighting that grew dimmer as the Fix-it began to lose power. "I never thought I'd see the pulse. The sirens indicate there is to be an emergency evacuation of all new Potentials! The arrow must be dangerously close to the black line." Agatha put a hand to her heart as though she was experiencing chest pain. "Blue is in jeopardy of going over to the other side. And for those who may have had a hand in the brightening of the colors, the order is that immediately upon inspection, they be destroyed." Agatha stepped within an inch of Cassie's face. "This means you. Get into the supply closet so we can Zipper home. Now."

"You're saving me?" Cassie asked in disbelief, as the light flickered above her head, the voice of her father's Entity growing angrier behind the closed Transition Room door.

Agatha weakly hobbled several feet away to pull the cord taut as Carlos grabbed a chair and attempted to try to fix the light fixture. "I'm saving my own hide. My mission is not going to be jeopardized by the likes of one rebellious Potential. Good thing ol' Agatha thought of the cord. "

"But what about my dad? What will happen to him? You can't take me home!" Cassie panicked.

Nothing will happen while the evacuation is going on, chica. Get out while chu can and try to stay calm. I will let chu know when it is safe to return. Bright Blue has a mission, too.

Cassie squished her toes in her sneakers, afraid to send her thoughts to Carlos with Agatha in such close range.

She can't hear chu anymore, chica. Chur energy Vibration has changed.

Cassie glanced up at Carlos, the voices muffled behind the Transition Room door, while Agatha fiddled with the cord. *Keep my dad thinking. I'm going to come back. You'll see!*

Agatha grabbed Cassie by the elbow as the Entity slammed cabinet doors inside the Transition Room, the cord reducing in size as she thrust her into the supply closet. "You think I can't take you home? You should have thought of that sooner. Now you can enjoy life for good without your father, for he is locked in that room now with his Entity, with only one way out and that is as a Permanent. Let's head back to your cozy grandparents' house, shall we?" Agatha scoffed, pulling the door shut behind them. "After all I've done for you."

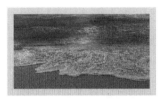

CHAPTER
THIRTY-SIX

F ast and furious, Cassie completed her social studies homework in the kitchen after supper. The cord of energy, which no one else could see, dangled from the hem of her shirt all the way to the hem of Agatha's cloak. Agatha held watch in Cassie's bedroom, keeping tabs on her at all times now that she felt Cassie couldn't be trusted.

Cassie stuffed the map worksheet into her binder, remembering she needed to make Grandpa's lunch. Pushing her chair back, she hastily got up to get out the rye bread, wax paper, salami, and German mustard. After she made the sandwich, carefully spreading the German mustard to the ends of the bread, she slid the foil-wrapped sandwich into the brown paper bag, realizing she hadn't bitten so much as one fingernail. Cassie didn't have time for that.

The phone rang as Ann Marie sauntered down the stairs, about to head to work for the night. At the foot of the stairs, she retrieved the ringing phone, responding with polite one-word answers, "Um, sure. Okay. Yes, tomorrow is fine. Okay. Uh, huh."

When she hung up, she ran into the living room and went back to using her regular voice.

"Mother! That was the school adjustment counselor, Mrs. Something or other." Ann Marie whined, "You know I can't handle those things. It's so humiliating! And the questions! I just can't. I'm trying to change my life, you know. It isn't easy, everything I'm going through!"

Cassie crumpled over the top of Grandpa's brown lunch bag in slow motion and heard Nana sigh loudly from her green armchair. "Oh shaddup, Ann Marie. I'll deal with the school shrink. You and your helpless generation, with all your complaining. In my day, you just pulled yourself up by the bootstraps and went with it."

The following afternoon, at the end of the school day, Cassie blazed by Riley Avery in the hall outside science class on her way to Mrs. Beals' office.

"Slow down!" Riley warned, clutching her shimmery hot-pink book bag against her skinny jeans. "You're going to hurt someone!"

Cassie ignored her classmate, continuing down the hall. She was glad Mariana was out of school getting braces, otherwise Cassie knew she would have heard it from her, too. She didn't want to explain that she felt like a bundle of nerves all day because she knew she had the meeting with Nana and Mrs. Beals after school.

When Cassie reached the guidance office, Nana was sitting with her hands over her large purse in the corner, the farthest place from Mrs. Beals. Cassie slid uneasily in the chair she always sat in, across from the desk, softly placing her book bag by her feet.

Greeting them both, Mrs. Beals chose a different chair today—one positioned in the middle of the room, between Nana and Cassie—and began jotting a few notes on her yellow pad of paper. Nana Helen, in her frumpy winter coat and two-sizes-too-small knitted red hat, glanced suspiciously up at Mrs. Beals's framed licensure certificate from Boston University hanging on the wall.

Mrs. Beals crossed her legs and began the conversation. "I'm concerned that your granddaughter has an excessive amount of anxiety right now, and that perhaps the situation at home may be a contributing factor."

"Who has anxiety?" Nana Helen barked.

Mrs. Beals uncrossed her legs, explaining. "Anxiety isn't such a bad thing, Mrs. Riley. Anxiety often helps us by sending our bodies a message to do something differently with our lives."

"Oh, ya, ya," Nana Helen nodded in her hat, as if she understood, her blue eyes landing on everything around the room except Mrs. Beals.

Mrs. Beals crossed her legs the other way and continued, "It's when we have a less productive kind of anxiety—the kind that causes us to look and feel tired and our grades to fall from where they were last year—that there might be a problem. I am hoping you might consider family therapy, perhaps weekly, while Cassie is going through this difficult time."

Nana Helen yanked off her shrunken hat, "Look. My only concern is that my granddaughter doesn't end up like the rest of them."

"The rest of them?" Mrs. Beals asked.

"She's been talking in the closet for months now. I don't know who it is she's chatting with, but I smell the funny farm coming to town, you know what I mean? Her great grandmother spent most of her residence there after she went through the change, and I'll be damn— sorry—darned, if that's going to happen to this one." Nana crossed her arms over her chest, settling farther into the rigid seat.

Cassie stared at a deck of feelings cards, the one on the top showing a boy with steam coming out his ears, on the bookshelf next to the stack of games.

"I see," Mrs. Beals said, tapping her pen to her chin, a thought coming to her. "Mrs. Riley, have you ever wrestled with gremlins?"

"Heh?" Nana asked, her face screwing up on one side.

"You know," Mrs. Beals said casually, adjusting the position in her chair, "the little wretched voices in your head that say nasty things. We all have them, Mrs. Riley, I assure you."

Nana vigorously began nodding her wig-like, coarse gray hair. "Ohhh, you mean like Saul and Paul. Oh, ya, ya, they've been with me for years."

Cassie slowly turned her head toward Nana.

That's who Agatha has been bumping into all this time outside Nana's room!

Mrs. Beals clasped her hands across her lap, her lips pursed. "Yes. Saul and Paul. That's perfect."

Nana raised both shoulders up by her ears and grimaced over at Cassie, like a kid caught with her hand in the cookie jar.

After Mrs. Beals and Nana discussed how Saul always spoke nicely to Nana Helen and how Paul was a "real son of a —," (and how Nana always ate more ice cream and cookies when she listened to Paul), the session ended. Nana Helen briskly stood the way she did when the priest ended Mass, grabbed her hat off the seat, the gold charms on her bracelet dangling from her fleshy wrist, and made for the door.

"C'mon kiddo," Nana said. She muttered "thank you" to Mrs. Beals as she approached the door to leave.

"Helen, perhaps I could make a referral for you," Mrs. Beals offered as she shuffled behind her desk, "to learn some strategies of your own to deal with all that is going on."

Nana Helen pulled her wool hat down snugly around her head. "Nah. No more psychobabble for me. And don't even think about suggesting her grandfather come in. The world would turn purple before my husband ever set foot in this office. No offense."

Mrs. Beals closed her eyes. "No offense taken."

Cassie rose and held the door open for Nana Helen as she exited the office, glancing back silently at Mrs. Beals before leaving. She noticed a piece of paper sticking out of the side of the corkboard hanging on the wall beside her desk with the words, "Radical Trust" printed in a large, black font.

"You're a strong girl," said Mrs. Beals, closing her manila folder.

Cassie chewed on her lip and left the office.

On the ride home, Nana Helen took Cassie to McDonald's for a treat, even though they didn't talk about Saul and Paul, or anything else for that matter, during the entire ten-minute drive back to Selwyn Street.

I'm glad Nana Helen met Mrs. Beals today. Cassie thought, slurping her thick, vanilla milkshake. "Thanks for going today."

"You're welcome," Nana said gruffly, pulling into the tarred driveway in front of the garage on Knoll Street. "Glad I could help."

That night Cassie put herself to bed, trying desperately to sleep as Agatha tapped her yellowed fingernail over and over on the top of the wooden desk.

"I told you I'd take harsher measures now that you are most certainly untrustworthy," Agatha said, coughing and hacking like a cigarette smoker, as she lay on the floor next to Cassie's bed. "Though I'm sure, now that we have the cord between us, I shouldn't worry so much. I suppose a little lie-down wouldn't hurt."

Cassie thought Agatha looked weak and sickly, her face sallow, her chest heaving up and down as she lay on the floor. She didn't want to worry about her Entity so she turned over in bed, waiting, trusting that Carlos would send her a signal of how she was going to get back to Blue, like he said he would.

Her breathing labored and heavy, Agatha finally fell asleep. Cassie also began to close her eyes when an envelope dropped down in her mind's eye.

Cassie,

There is a way. It's time, chica.

Carlos

She sat up.

A way? How? She thought for a moment and glanced down onto the floor. The cord wavered as Agatha snored, the Surveyor lying by her side. Cassie gingerly pushed the covers back and leaned over to retrieve a glowing blue device. A tab displaying the word, "Mission," highlighted on the screen. Cassie hesitated for a moment, before pressing the black tab.

Said Entity Agatha's mission: to keep Cassie Connor and her father, like generations before, where they belong. Long live the Dusk Ruler. Long live the Land of Blue.

Cassie felt a chill run down her spine.

Pressing her feet onto the floor, she tiptoed over to the closet, careful not to wake her sleeping Entity. When she opened the closet door, Cassie clutched the black doorknob.

Nana's clunky Singer sewing machine sat square in the middle of the closet, taking up the entire space.

A little yellow Post-It note stuck to the wooden table underneath the machine, written in Nana's handwriting, read, "Sorry kid, I'm only trying to help you once and for all."

How could she?

Cassie clamped her mouth shut to keep from yelling, when she noticed the yellow light forming in the high corner of her bedroom. Effortlessly this time, it evolved into a radiant ball of light, its energy pulsing in waves. Cassie felt the shape speak to her, without words.

Be not afraid. All that has come before you has led to this. It's up to you now, to speak to the false voice, and to face the darkness.

Cassie's energy merged with the yellow ball of light, its feeling so familiar. She felt her shoulders melt, a release of internal energy she hadn't realized she was holding.

Bright Blue. It's been trying to reach me at home. It's been with me the whole time.

Cassie's lips parted as she felt the warmth of the light and then remembered Agatha sleeping on her floor. She turned toward her Entity and then back at the yellow light.

But what do I do now? I've never gone to Blue without Agatha.

The light pulsed. *What you need is not outside yourself, but inside.*

Cassie knew then, without thinking twice, that she needed to return to Blue on her own. Immediately, she sent Mind Mail to TJ.

I'm going back to Blue. Wherever you are,
stay safe, and away from me, out of danger.
I'm glad we became friends.

Cassie

Agatha stirred. Grabbing her jeans and hooded sweatshirt from the bottom drawer of her bureau, Cassie felt the glasses vibrate inside the pocket. Quickly placing them on her nose, she felt guided to turn around and look at her sleeping Entity.

Cassie stiffened. Agatha's once-red hair now appeared gray and witch-like, stiffly covering most of her face. Her skin was a dark pine-tree blue, covered in warts, and wrinkled, like a repulsive lizard. Agatha no longer looked like an old, loving grandmother but a warped, distorted-looking creature. Turning her face to get the image out of her head, Cassie focused on the yellow ball of light. Thoughts of Anna and the other children in the Settling, of Mrs. Costa, the influx of new Potentials who didn't have a clue, and of her father in the Transition Room rushed through Cassie's mind.

She blinked, grounding herself. Then, standing in front of her dresser, she stared intently at a random spot on the wooden floor. Rapidly, dust collected near her feet and wind-like energy swirled about her ankles as the cord of magnetic energy detached from her Entity.

Darkness threatens those we love,
Hopes for this one yet remain
Choice and Selection
My own election
Always in Bright Blue Domain

Cassie's body lifted off the floor, her fear swelling, when she heard Tufa's voice.

You are never alone.

Lifting higher, energy catapulting her into the void, she heard Agatha, who realized her Potential was gone. Agatha's voice was sinister. *Pay your homage to me, you ungrateful child. How dare you leave me after all I've done for you. You will pay dearly for this!*

Cassie, propelling through the darkness, answered, "I trusted you, Agatha, because you came to me when I was lonely and afraid. But you don't want the best for me. You only want to add me to your list, and to doom me to a life like my dad's."

Agatha's voice melted into a sly tone. *I never meant to hurt you, child. I was protecting you.*

Hurling through the tunnel-like void, Cassie raised her voice and called, "You told me when we met that it's better to know the truth."

When we are ready for it, yes.

"I'm ready," Cassie declared.

Instantly, light appeared at the end of the dark void. Cassie landed in an open field, where the white horse was waiting. Galloping faster than it ever had, the horse brought Cassie through miles of lavender fields and raced up through the clouds, until they were above the blue sky.

Suddenly, as they merged into the midnight-blue air, highways, exits, and detour signs swirled haphazardly in front of Cassie, as though she was in the middle of a hurricane.

Confused, Cassie felt herself lean too far over to one side of the white horse. Then she heard Simon's voice.

Seize the reins! Stay the course in higher-thought Vibration!

Grabbing hold of the reins, Cassie centered herself, immediately sending Mind Mail to Carlos, asking for help. She told him she felt sure her father would want to return, knowing Blue was coming undone.

Instantly, Carlos replied.

> Agatha has sent word that chu are responsible for raising the Vibration. The Ruler will be looking for chu. I will meet chu by the courtyard like always. Andale, and cuidado.

Agatha's voice laughed condescendingly, calling to Cassie in her mind. *You are no match for the power of numbers. There are too many of us to overcome.*

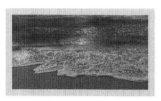

CHAPTER
THIRTY-SEVEN

Chaos erupted when Cassie returned to Blue. The white horse lowered itself down and released Cassie onto the pier, then quickly galloped away. Swarms of Entities and Permanents pushed and shoved each other on the pier, scrounging for any leftover Feed they could find. Kurt, Big, and Small argued on the platform over who was more loyal to the Ruler. None of them noticed Cassie slip through the Welcoming Gate.

Riots broke out in the Midst as the Meter gradually moved from the periwinkle-blue range to a dusty-blue, sidewalk-chalk color at the top of the color chart, and into the area of the thick black line. Inch by inch, it rose toward the feared blank space. Permanents barricaded themselves in the Pits and Zebbies, swearing they'd never leave, chugging Bads and Escapes and popping Blobs, attempting to avoid the Ruler's wrath.

Cassie pushed through the crowds, seeing Mrs. Costa's neighbor, Janis, desperately looking for a place to hide herself and her children. Janis climbed atop one of the vendor carts that had been tipped over and shouted, "They need to find the girl Judy Costa's been speaking to! Then the Ruler will spare the rest of us!"

Cassie's knees buckled. She drew her hooded sweatshirt over her head, as Sal ushered Eric and a group of boys into an alley. She wove through the crammed cobblestone street until Mrs. Costa spotted her.

Frantically charging out from a Zebbies doorway, her children by her side, Mrs. Costa grabbed hold of Cassie's arm. "The Ruler has a strict watch on the land. He's looking for you! Some of my neighbors told the Recruiters you were the one who brought hope. I'm sorry! Please, if there's anything I can do until the other side comes to help you."

Michael clung to his mother's leg while Anna tugged on Cassie's sleeve. "Please save us. My mom says you can." Anna looked torn, as she simultaneously held Cassie's sleeve and watched her father arguing with other Permanents nearby that he "was staying, with or without his family."

"I'm sorry," Cassie started to tell Mrs. Costa and her children, "But no one is coming to save—"

"Hey!" yelled a middle-aged man with a mullet, approaching Cassie from a line outside of one of the Pits. He held hands with his four small children and pleaded, "We're neighbors of Judy Costa! Help us, too!"

A small crowd had gathered around Cassie, mostly Judy's neighbors. Cassie looked helplessly at their desperate faces, wanting to help, but also wanting to leave them behind so she could get to her dad.

Mrs. Costa searched Cassie's face, worry lines encasing her hazel eyes. "Go on with your mission to save your father before it's too late. After all, that's the reason you're here."

"But if she's seen the other side, she can save our children, and maybe us, too," Norma pleaded.

Cassie scanned their faces from under her hood before reaching into her pocket. Retrieving the seeds of *opportunity*, she sprinkled the seeds around Mrs. Costa's neighbors and then turned and ran. She ran past cart after overturned cart, past creatures fist-fighting in the Cove to get last-minute Stims in, past Strays and its shattered windows as creatures broke inside, and down the heavily trafficked road to the Fix-It. Peeking out from under her hood, she blazed past dozens of Permanents ticking and quivering in the long line outside the front entrance of the Fix-It. When Cassie neared the courtyard, she saw Nurse Moody wildly administering syringes and brightly colored circles through the entrance slot, promising everyone things would return to normal.

Carlos, waiting for Cassie on the blacktop, acted hard at work picking up loads of litter.

Cassie was out of breath when she stopped short of the fence. "Is my dad still waiting to become a Permanent?"

Carlos elbowed the door open in the fence. "Sí. Da Ruler is sniffing out every Vibration in the Settling, looking for the source who betrayed him. I'm afraid he'll be here soon." Carlos whisked Cassie down the dirt lane behind the courtyard, toward the dumpster.

Thud.

The sound of the Ruler's steps, similar to a dinosaur's hunt, reverberated from the wooded area in front of the foreboding wall.

Cassie shuddered and said to Carlos, "I need to get that special Key."

Carlos led Cassie to the back door, across from the dumpster at the end of the facility—the door that opened directly into the Transition Room. "Sí, I know the one. Once chu made chur decision, señorita, I made mine."

There, on the ground outside the blue door, Dr. Fox lay face down, out cold. Cassie stood over Fox's still body and looked up at Carlos with a look of alarm.

Carlos shrugged. "I gave him some of his own Have to Haves."

Cassie managed a smile, and saw a shiny delicate silver Key, next to a few other copper keys, dangling from Dr. Fox's wrist.

Thud.

"He should be numb for a pulse. After dat, the Ruler will know what I did. Chu got to act now, señorita, and chu got to act on chur own." Carlos squeezed Cassie's shoulder and waddled swiftly behind the dumpster.

"Dad?" Cassie banged on the cold blue door.

"Cass! I knew you'd come back for me!" her father said in a funny voice on the other side of the door. "We can live here together now, where dusk is best, and where we can always escape the pain."

Cassie clutched the doorknob, realizing he was once again under Blue's spell. "There's a better way. You'll see! The sky is brightening. I can teach you what I learned!"

Dad's voice turned flat. "Glimmers don't last. You mustn't listen to the ones who speak of hope. The sooner in life you realize that, the less disappointed you'll be. Now let me out of here, so we can go to the Midst and prove to the Ruler we're Permanents for life!"

Cassie dropped her head. *It's too late. I failed.*

She longed to fall down and sleep forever, when a large stone fell in the distance from behind the Preying Fields.

"Senorita!" Carlos yelled, watching half-hidden behind the dumpster. "The Wall is in jeopardy now that los colores have risen too high. Chu must get the Key!"

Cassie looked down at the Key on Dr. Fox's limp wrist.

Thud. Thud. Thud.

He's coming for me.

A wave of fear crashed over Cassie. She could feel his thoughts pounding into her head.

How dare you interrupt all I have created! How dare you bring hope to my inhabitants. You will pay. Your loved ones will pay.

Cassie's legs shook like Jell-O as she crouched down and slipped the dazzling Key off Dr. Fox's hand.

"Let me out!" her father cried, banging on the other side of the locked door.

Cassie clutched the Key in her white-knuckled hand.

Thud.

A crocodile beast, fifty times the size of a regular crocodile, rounded the corner from the Preying Fields. Cassie came face to face with the Ruler. He crushed the gnarly trees standing in his way along the wooded path. Snarling, his hot breath like smog as he approached the area behind the Fix-It, he closed in on Cassie. His yellow eyes, the color of pus and the size of three baseball bats, seared into her.

She reached for the doorknob, the Key trembling between her fingers. The crocodile beast was bigger and scarier than anything she had ever seen hovering over her bed.

"Cassie, what's going on out there?" her father asked in the funny voice, jiggling the doorknob from inside the room. "Lemme out so we can have some fun!"

Cassie froze.

"WHO DO YOU THINK YOU ARE?" the Ruler bellowed.

Cassie answered in a shaky voice. "I-I just wanted to bring my father home."

"YOU FOOL. YOU PATHETIC, WOUNDED FOOL." The Ruler breathed a stream of fire, forcing Cassie to leap to the side to avoid it.

She fell into the door, still grasping the Key, her body huddled in the threshold.

Cassie suddenly heard Benjamin's gentle voice inside her clouded mind. *For when you need a better view.*

Reaching for the glasses in her pocket, carefully holding the

Key tight, she fumbled the gold rims in her hands.

The Ruler roared, nearing her face, his long teeth razor sharp. "WHERE DID YOU GET THOSE?"

"Cuidado!" Carlos yelled.

Cassie jumped back from the door as the Ruler swiped at her, almost causing her to drop the glasses. The Ruler swiftly turned, sniffing behind the dumpster.

Cassie jammed the glasses on her face, a golden doorknob appearing, shining between the gray stones.

A doorknob!

Her dad kicked the bottom of the door. "Come on Cassie, you know your dad needs his Have to Haves. Lemme out!"

Cassie looked first at the metal knob in the door of the Transition Room, and then at the golden doorknob in the wall.

But the Key can only be used once! What do I do now?

"Don't let me down!" her father demanded.

The Ruler snorted and laughed coldly in front of the dumpster. "WHAT IS YOUR MISSION NOW?"

More stones, boulder sized, tumbled down from the Wall behind the Settling as people screamed, running for cover. Cassie shook from head to toe, steadying the glasses on her face.

If I open that door, would it lead to Bright Blue? Would that save the people in the Settling?

The Ruler released fiery breath like a dragon, and roared, "YOU WOULD NEVER LEAVE YOUR FATHER, YOU NAÏVE CHILD. RELEASE HIM TO ME!"

"There she is!" Cassie heard someone whisper from halfway down the lane. "She'll help us before the Wall crumbles!"

The Ruler whipped his massive head and roared, sending its fiery breath up the dirt lane as people scattered into the woods.

The Key felt cool against Cassie's wrist as the golden doorknob pulsated in the wall, the line of Cogs screaming from the front of the Fix-It, "The Wall's coming down! What are we gonna do?"

From behind the dumpster, Carlos raised a finger to his lips.

"GIVE ME MY KEY!" the Ruler lunged at Cassie a second time.

Just then, Carlos dove out from behind the dumpster and stabbed the Ruler in his arm with the top of a broken bottle of Bad. When the Ruler flung his massive head toward Carlos, he sprayed a burning, chemical solvent in the Ruler's yellow eyes as shrieks burst from the lane. The Ruler staggered, attempting to strike Carlos with its spear-like teeth and missed. Enraged, the Ruler sideswiped the dumpster with its massive snout, hurling the dumpster into the woods.

"I don't know what to do!" Cassie said, as Carlos grabbed her hands by the Transition Room door.

"Cassie," he said, wiping his brow. "The Wall is going to crumble. When dat happens, there will only be destruction—not a Ripple for people to fall through or a Glimmer to be seen. That door is an opportunity for many to be saved. Chu hold the Key. If chu open that door, some will go through, and some will be left behind. Others may even destroy themselves without the Land to enable them. But many will build a better vida, and be saved."

"Honey, let me out so I can get what I need before it's all gone!" her father begged, banging on the door.

The Ruler laughed viciously, using its snout to search for Cassie beside the building.

"Carlos, tell me what to do," she begged, flattening herself against the wall.

Dr. Fox stirred on the ground and rubbed his head.

Carlos looked into Cassie's eyes. "It's not my task. It's churs. It's always been churs, since chu entered the Universe. The Land of Blue has been waiting for chu."

Rocks fell in pallet sizes onto the ground from the Wall at the other end of the Fix-It, crashing into sections of the brick building.

"Cassie, save us! We want to do better for our children!" Frightened voices of the Settling neighbors grew in number, moving closer to the edge of the woods bordering the lane. Cassie thought she heard Mrs. Costa in the swelling crowd as Dr. Fox began to look around, realizing where he was, growling at the sight of Carlos.

"YOU WILL PAY FOR YOUR DISLOYALTY," the Ruler roared in Carlos' direction, "AFTER I TAKE CARE OF HER!"

Cassie held her breath in front of the door as rocks streamed down on the far left and right of the Wall, like torrents of rain.

The golden doorknob pulsated as the Settling neighbors huddled at the edge of the woods in fear.

Cassie trembled and turned toward the Transition Room door, shouting above the heaving rocks as the Ruler sniffed along the side of the building. "I used to think it was my job to make you happy, Daddy. But it's not. You have to find your own way through your own pain. I can't save you after all. You have to choose to save yourself!"

The Ruler roared in anger, chomping his massive teeth down, missing Cassie by a hair.

Key in hand, Cassie slid away from the Transition Room door, inches away from the Ruler's snout, and toward the rock Wall, the burning solution wearing off just in time for the Ruler to see Cassie insert the silver Key into the golden doorknob.

The Ruler roared, "NO!!!!!!!"

Cassie turned the Key, sunlight slowly streaming through the gaps in the stones, shimmering like dawn on a spring morning. Turning to stare back into the eyes of the Ruler, she said, "You don't have the power to decide my future. That's up to me."

The Ruler charged forward, widening its mouth as the Key turned to dust and the door in the Wall slowly opened. Sunlight poured through like a waterfall. Permanents, those Working for Permanency, and Permanents by Association who peeked out from the woods, gathering to watch the commotion, gasped at the flood of pure white light.

Suddenly the Ruler began to shrink.

Dr. Fox, his face red and purple, stammered helplessly on the ground, "R-Ruler! We can rebuild! Ev-everything I've done to get you to where you are, t-there's plenty of them who will remain with us in the darkness! Won't you all?"

The now-enormous crowd watched in disbelief as the Ruler diminished to the size of a rat.

Permanents began to scream as the arrow on the Meter in the front of the Fix-It swung solidly into the clear space above the black line. The glass protecting the Meter cracked, and the heavy arrow sprung loose. A Permanent in a bandana pointed and cried, "The Wall! Someone saw it coming down entirely in the Preying Fields. It's going to destroy the whole Land!"

Cassie heard the deafening sound of the Wall tumbling down in the Preying Fields, the boulders shooting, like cannonballs, toward the Settling.

Just then, Tufa appeared barefoot in the doorway of the Wall, an array of Bright workers, barefoot, by her side. "There isn't much time," she called to the people on the lane. "We are here to help you."

"It's our chance!" a man with pockmarks on his face emerged from the woods, squinting at the light. "A real chance!"

"Vamos, everyone, vamos!" Carlos called, immediately removing his black shoes and tossing them in the woods. In his bare feet he escorted the crowd, who shielded their eyes as they tentatively made their way in a line toward the Bright workers in the lit doorway.

Nurse Moody appeared next to a slew of Entities hurrying down the lane. "What the—? D-did we plan for this?"

Captain BP shook his hands nervously as he stood nearby. "What to do? What to do?"

Some Entities and Permanents ran back up the lane, trampling past Nurse Moody, to take refuge in the Zebbies and the Pits.

Dr. Fox crawled backward, gasping, "Someone needs to guard

the Facility! The Feed!"

"I'm trying!" Nurse Moody yelled, pushed to the ground as creatures stampeded over her to get inside the now-open Fix-It. "I could use some help here!"

Cogs ran wildly from the front entrance of the Fix-It, arms of vials in hand, as Permanents on the lane followed, darting back to the walkway to obtain loosely guarded Have to Haves.

Mr. Costa, who had come to find his family, ran with the pack, away from the streaming light. Grabbing other Permanents by their shirts, he shoved them back inside the Fix-It. "It's a hoax! Don't trust 'em! Let's get some Feed and head for the woods! We'll be safe there!"

A man with missing teeth followed Mr. Costa, heading for the woods, "He's right! It's too good to be true!"

"Come now," Agnes said at the doorway, extending her hand to a gaunt woman who looked back at the man heading in the other direction.

"I don't think I can do it without my Have to Haves," the woman said, shielding her eyes from the light. "I don't think I'm strong enough."

"That makes two of us, Alice," said a man, biting on his nails. "We better stay here where we know what to expect. Once the destruction is over, we'll find a way." The man and woman left the line and ran the other way, joining the others who chose to stay.

"Ah, hello! Anyone?" Nurse Moody yelled, her body continually stomped upon by creatures running to hide in the dark of the woods.

Captain BP loomed above Nurse Moody and tipped his hat to her. "I'm sorry m'lady. I dare say, it's been a wild ride, but even old Recruits like me can learn new things." He jumped in line, removing his black-soled shoes at the Bright workers request.

Sal, who had been standing with Eric in the lane, grabbed Eric by the elbow and stepped over Nurse Moody, getting in line behind the others at the doorway. "What the heck, eh?" He took off his dark shoes and threw them up the lane.

Carlos helped individuals through the door, watching Cassie as she stared back at the locked Transition Room door. He stepped away from the others for a brief moment. "Chu done bueno, señorita. Come help us get the others through. Everything's going to be okay."

Suddenly, TJ and Mariana ran down the lane, pushing past the hordes of creatures running in the other direction.

TJ threw his arms around Cassie and held her tight.

"Mariana, you didn't have to come here," Cassie said, hugging her best friend. "They're my people, not yours."

"You're my people," Mariana said. "Besides, it was my decision. TJ sent me Mind Mail, since I know how to do that now."

"Hurry, everyone!" Benjamin yelled from the doorway. Boulders fell, barely missing a mother holding a baby.

"C'mon, they need our help to get through!" Mariana grabbed TJ's hand, running toward the bottleneck of people at Bright Blue's door. Briefly making eye contact with TJ from the line, Eric looked back at his friends who were waving Have to Haves they found inside the Settling in the air from the lane. Eric abandoned his place in line beside Sal and ran back to join his friends.

The color drained from TJ's face as he watched his brother disappear into the dark woods.

"Why isn't your brother going through?" Mariana asked, incredulously, hoisting a little girl up into Benjamin's arms. "He can be saved! Why are he and his friends staying?"

"Because it's what they know," Cassie replied.

TJ stopped for a moment and attempted to help kids from the Settling through the door in the wall, handing them over to the Bright workers.

"Don't forget the two images in your book," Cassie reminded TJ, as they quickened their pace. "Whichever road you take is up to you."

TJ solemnly continued moving kids through the Wall. "Yeah, I gotta try to remember that. I hope I do."

With his back turned, Cassie retrieved the last packet from her pocket and sprinkled the seeds of *faith* into TJ's energy field. Immediately, TJ's posture strengthened, his movements becoming stronger, more trusting, as he raised kids up and put them into the arms of the Bright workers.

Just then, a loud crack erupted in the Wall above their heads.

Simon called through the door, his hair standing on end, "There's only time for a few more!"

Mrs. Costa and her children stood in line, outside the overcrowded door, behind dozens more families waiting to get through to the other side.

"The Costa's have to get through!" Cassie called to Carlos over the roar of the falling rock. "And you!"

"Don't chu worry 'bout me," Carlos said, pushing other Settling families through the door. He got out of the way so others could go through, and took cover by the maintenance shed behind the Facility.

In a flash, the doors of the shed flew open, where a large, powder-blue car was parked inside, big enough to fit hundreds of occupants. Carlos waved the Costas over.

Mrs. Costa quickly handed Michael to Carlos, who put him in the enormous car, which hovered a few feet off the ground.

Mrs. Costa positioned Anna to go next and quickly turned to Cassie and took her hands. "Thank you, for all you've done for us. Thank you for caring."

Cassie hugged Mrs. Costa and watched her scamper into the car. Cassie removed her glasses and tucked them inside Anna's back pocket, as Carlos lifted her behind her mother into the back seat. Straining her neck, Anna searched in vain for her father on the opposite side of the woods.

She's leaving her father behind, too.

Jumping over the car with one hand, Carlos turned to TJ on the ground. "What's it going to be, muchacho? Dat Wall's going to break soon. Chur good with the kids, we could use someone like you back on Bright Blue, for those adjusting."

TJ cracked his knuckles, staring up at the half Wall. He looked back toward the woods, and then back at Carlos.

"Just because Eric opted to leave, mi amigo, doesn't mean there isn't someone else who has chur back," Carlos said, gripping both hands on the side of the car.

TJ exhaled and scaled over the side of the sky-blue car.

"Don't forget about me! I gotta see this place!" Mariana said, waving her arms for Carlos to take her, too.

Cassie dodged a falling boulder that split the entire courtyard in two, when suddenly she saw a shadow moving behind the Fix-It.

Robin dragged himself slowly but steadily toward Carlos' car. "You got room for me?"

"Robin!" Cassie cried.

"You look awful!" Mariana said bluntly from inside the car.

An elf from Bright Blue shuffled beside Robin, winking at Carlos before evaporating through the unsteady Wall.

"Plenty of room, my man," Carlos said, helping Robin's weak body over the side of the car and into the back seat. Untying his black shoes, he tossed them over the side.

"What's with the shoes?" Mariana asked.

Carlos replied, "There are no dark soles allowed on Bright Blue."

Cassie ran to the car, tilting her head. "But how did you . . . ?"

Robin mouthed to Cassie. "I somehow found my strength. Thanks."

Cassie paused. "Robin, do you think my dad . . . "

That's when the Wall began to sway. Cassie gripped the side of the car. "Carlos, is there any chance for the ones left behind?"

"Once the Wall crumbles, there's no more door, señorita.

Darkness always finds a way to rebuild itself. That will make it harder for creatures to hear the whisper or to go through the Ripple later on. People have to take the opportunity when it presents itself, chu know? C'mon, we gotta get this show on the road."

"Yeah, let's get out of here or we won't make it either," TJ said. "Besides, you gotta see your book in the Library, Mariana. Your whole life is one big party."

Carlos got behind the wheel and steered the large car up into the air like an airplane, Cassie watching as her friends waved good-bye.

No key in hand, Cassie stared at the Transition Door one last time until she heard a frantic neighing sound and turned as the white horse rode wildly toward her.

The shaky Wall exploded, coming down like an avalanche.

"Cassie, go!" Carlos yelled, taking flight over the crashing Wall.

Cassie immediately jumped aboard the white horse, the toppling Wall missing her by inches. Gripping the reins tightly, Cassie steered the horse high into the sky, over the chaos of the Fix-It and those desperately seeking darkness, over the Preying Fields covered in gray rock, over the Settling now covered in rubble, and over the ghost town that was the Midst.

Reaching even greater heights, the sun shone brightly in the sky, brighter than she had ever recalled. Holding the reins with one hand, she took off her hooded sweatshirt with the affixed Potential badge and let them drop from her hands. They fell below to the Trespasser-filled ocean past the pier, while she galloped home to where she belonged.

CHAPTER
THIRTY-EIGHT

Cassie arrived back in her bedroom to find an entirely white-haired Agatha slumped over on her bedroom floor. No longer in Entity form, Agatha resembled a fragile, fading woman.

She's dying, Cassie realized, dropping to her knees.

"Agatha?" Cassie whispered, the dawning sky lightening the window shade.

"Yes, though barely," Agatha said.

"Why are you dying?" Cassie began to cry. "Is it my fault? I didn't mean to make you die. I'll do anything, I'll listen again, I'll . . . " Cassie choked on her tears, the weight of her journey a thousand pounds.

"My dear child," Agatha spoke in the most peaceful tone Cassie had ever heard from her. "All the choices I made throughout my journey led to my status as a Recruiter. How fast it goes. Yet, fret not at the illusion. As an Entity, I served to block your path, to test the essence of who you are. In your choices, in finding your strength, you destroyed my power as an Entity, thus forcing me to also reconnect with the essence of who I really am."

Cassie sobbed, slumping down next to her dying Entity, overwhelmed by loss. "But I didn't mean to cause you harm. Oh, Agatha. My dad. I couldn't save him . . . I didn't." She choked on tears. "And now I'm losing you, too."

"Do you not remember? There is no despair in a life that has fulfilled its purpose."

Cassie slowly lifted her head. Instantly, spirits she recognized from the Library of Wisdom appeared in her bedroom, Tufa in the center of the circle. Suddenly, Agatha's gossamer cloak disintegrated into the hardwood floor, her dark-soled shoes disappearing from her feet. Light streamed through her body like fuel, her hair glowing strawberry red, her lips turned upward as she rose from the floor. Standing brilliantly before Cassie, Agatha appeared like a thirty-year-old woman with pearly, luminous skin.

"You're beautiful," Cassie said in astonishment.

Agatha bowed. "The darkness in me desired you to repeat what generations before you had done. But the light in you, caused by your hope, freed you from that pattern and therefore freed me from my role in that darkness."

Cassie turned to see the ball of light radiate in the upper corner of her bedroom. In its center there appeared a face, a kind face, like the grandfather bunny in her favorite Easter story, *The Country Bunny and The Little Gold Shoes.*

"This is the Creator of Bright Blue," Tufa introduced.

The Creator spoke in a firm and powerful voice. "We thank you for your curiosity, your compassion, and your choice to lead many to a new Vibration of existence."

Cassie stared down at her hands. "But I didn't save them all."

"Bright Blue acknowledges not all would be saved, but many were, because of your decision. It is no small feat, freeing generations of innocents from the patterns of repetition."

Cassie watched the early sun's rays creep in from behind her curtains as Agatha sat next to her on one side and Tufa sat on the other.

"Rest now child," Tufa said. "All is well."

• • •

"Good morning, sunshine," Mom said, lifting up the shades, letting in the warm light of the late December morning. "It's a special day, today. Let's grab smoothies on our way."

In the car, Mom pulled back her hair that had grown long enough to gather into a ponytail, mumbling as the stack of letters from Dad sat on the leather cushion between them in the front seat. "It's time you know. I've been thinking about it; if you want to read them, you can. You really are old enough. I'm learning that parents need to communicate more with their children. I mean, this is our life. There's no sense hiding it any more, right?"

Cassie looked out the frosted window, her heart light. Christmas wreaths on windows and doors with bright red ribbons whizzed by, inflatable Santa Clauses waving from people's front lawns as they passed. Cassie tucked her long, caramel-colored hair behind her ear, listening to Mom ramble. "So, it's been a while . . . rehab . . . addiction's a tough thing, like when I used to smoke, remember?" On and on she went. Cassie smiled at Mom every so often, appreciating her efforts, but she didn't need to read the letters. She knew everything she needed to already, really.

Turning the old car into the parking lot, the red-lettered sign on the old brick building read: Dedham Detox Rehabilitation Center.

Pushing down on the metal door handle to go inside, a short, stocky man greeted them in the hall. A Christmas wreath hung above the sign, "Visitors," in the front area.

The short man with the curly brown hair smiled and said, "Chur here for Craig?"

"Yes, we are," Cassie's mother beamed, grabbing hold of Cassie's hand.

"Bueno. Just un minuto. Great Christmas present, sí?"

Mom nodded, her leg jiggling under the long, cream-colored wool coat she got on sale at Macy's. The door to the side of the check-in area opened. Cassie's dad walked out, dressed in a green waffle sweater and faded jeans. His complexion looked healthy, his brown eyes clear. Teary, he walked over to Cassie's mom and hugged her for what felt like forever. Then, dropping to one knee, he embraced Cassie. Tears streamed down her face. Cassie didn't want to let go.

Her dad whispered in her ear. "I had to get better on my own. It's not anybody else's job to make me better. You know that, right?"

Cassie kept her face buried in his sweater, dampening his exposed, warm neck.

After thanking the attendant, Craig, Ann Marie, and Cassie Connor headed outside into the fresh, crisp December air.

"Is China Dragon open yet?" Cassie asked, stuffing her hands inside her puffy winter coat.

"I was actually thinking of trying that new sushi place that opened up in Jamaica Plain," Mom said, sliding her purse up her arm.

"Sushi sounds good," Dad said, draping his arm around Cassie's shoulder. "Let's give it a try. It's time to make some new memories."

Cassie and her parents drove to Tsang's restaurant in JP, listening to Boston's "Don't Look Back" on the car radio. The clock displayed 11:45 a.m. on the dashboard. Choosing a booth next to the brightly decorated Christmas tree, they enjoyed an early, healthy lunch, and three Shirley Temples topped with bright blue umbrellas.

ACKNOWLEDGMENTS

Thank you God, for hearing my many prayers and for breathing life into my myriad of intentions.

My editor Rebecca McCarthy – your brilliant intellect, thought provoking questions, and consistent support and encouragement of my manuscript helped shape and form *The Land of Blue* into what it has become. Our time collaborating on this project was one of the greatest experiences of my life.

My husband Carl – for all you do on a daily basis to make our family's lives easier and to support our goals and dreams. You are always there. I love and appreciate you.

My son Kyle – for your contributions to this story, and for your love, support, and never-ending belief in me and in my writing. I love you.

My daughter Michelle (my little in-house editor and the only one who knew about this book for a long, long time) – thank you for your intuitive feedback, your support of my writing time, and your countless, witty contributions to this story. I love you.

My English Bulldog Zack – my loving, loyal, writing companion— we live for rainy days!

Laurie – I consistently talk with my clients about how all you need in life are one or two true friends—the ones who really get you, who are always there to support you and who help you see yourself more clearly. From the deepest conversations to the most hysterical and ridiculous, you are my person. I treasure you.

Jody Amato, copy editor – your feedback motivated me to keep moving forward.

Ben Benitez – for your assistance in creating Carlos's speak—you brought him to life when you rehearsed it out loud in my kitchen—and for your family's homemade treats for Zack.☺

Janica Smith at www.PublishingSmith.com – for your guidance in the publication process, and Yvonne Parks at www.PearCreative.ca, for interior layout and creating a powerful cover.

Lastly, and most especially, to my clients – I am honored you share your stories and your time with me. You are my people.

Photography by Tracy Colucci

JILL SYLVESTER

Jill Sylvester is a licensed mental health therapist who works with adults and children in private practice. She's based in the suburbs outside Boston, Massachusetts where she lives with her husband Carl, children Kyle and Michelle, and a fantastic bulldog named Zack. *The Land of Blue* is her first book.

To contact Jill, visit her website at www.jillsylvester.com.

Made in the USA
Middletown, DE
14 August 2017